Courage Requires

A Pride and Prejudice Continuation

MELANIE RACHEL

Courage Requires: A Pride and Prejudice Continuation

Copyright © 2017 by Melanie Rachel

ISBN: 9781521252253

First printing 2017

"I am afraid," Darcy said haltingly, "I have made a rather specific promise to tell Elizabeth everything. Particularly if the Hawkes are to visit Pemberley with the earl for the festive season."

"I had expected that. No further, though. Not even Mrs. Bingley or Georgiana, if you please. The fewer who know, the better chance of this all fading away in time."

"Agreed." Darcy took a drink and looked down at the dark liquid in his glass. He tipped it back and forth before saying in a low voice, "I am sorry we left you to handle the carriage ride alone."

Richard held up his hand, palm out, from his own seat near the fire. "You could hardly have acted other than you did. In any case, I am pleased you were not there."

"That seems to be a common refrain," Darcy replied sardonically, but with a hint of complaint in his tone. "Elizabeth was pleased I was not here to keep her from having her way, and you are pleased I was not with you to assist. Am I truly so useless to have near?"

Richard chuckled. "There was no point. More heads, more targets. All I did was ride inside a box, if you can call being tossed about riding. I never got a shot off."

Chapter One

AN OPENED BOTTLE of fine brandy sat on the table in Fitzwilliam Darcy's Pemberley study, the amber liquor sparkling in the candlelight.

"That is quite a story, Richard," Darcy said thoughtfully. He handed his cousin a second drink and sat on a leather chair near the fire, stretching his long legs before him. "Almost worth the length of time you have made me wait to hear it."

Richard shrugged. "We were each of us occupied, and it is not the sort of thing one should commit to paper." He paused and ducked his head. "I must admit that I was waiting for the Bingleys to remove to town. For everyone concerned, this truly ought to remain between us."

"Did Captain Hawke?" They laughed lightly together, trying to ease the tension of the conversation while Richard shook his head.

"No, and that is one reason I cannot fault myself. If even the Captain could not discharge a weapon, what hope had I?" His face turned suddenly serious, and he stood to grope for something in the pocket of his greatcoat, which he had draped unceremoniously over a high-backed chair. James and then Wilkins had both been rather disconcerted to be waved off when he arrived. Richard felt the fabric and clenched his fist around it for a moment before withdrawing it. He tossed it in his cousin's lap.

"Miss Hawke asked me to get rid of it when we arrived at Matlock. Her sister was upset by it but would not stop taking it out to have a look. I am finding myself in much the same predicament."

Darcy set down his drink to pick up the crumpled remains of a bonnet. It showed deep creases from being carried in such a way, but he could distinctly make out two round holes at the crown.

"Good God, Richard," he whispered. He cleared his throat and spoke with more volume. "You told me, but seeing it. . ."

"You understand my dilemma. The story alone does not carry the same impact. I had thought to toss it in the fire, as it makes me ill to see it." Richard grimaced. "But it is also evidence, of a sort, that exonerates Miss Hawke from accusations of collaboration."

Richard closed his eyes and remembered Sophia Hawke's resignation as she comforted her sister on the carriage floor, the stunningly emotional welcome the earl had proffered when she made her unexpected appearance, and her strangely cool response to that display. It was as though she did not believe it genuine. Richard had no doubt it had been real, yet within days, Lord Matlock was again scheming and planning. Lady Matlock, on the other hand, had been thrilled to have two young women in the house to spoil. Miss Evelyn had quite taken to it, but he thought his mother might have forged a stronger bond with Miss Hawke, who seemed rather overwhelmed by the attention. He felt a kind of kinship with her on that score alone, though there were of course other reasons as well. His cousin's voice drew him back to the matter at hand.

"Circumstantial at best, Richard. Should someone be determined to doubt, there would be no way to prove that she was wearing it when the damage was done, or even that it was hers at all. No way to prove it was her uncle who hired the man to ambush you. Most would deny that Hawke would even take such a risk, particularly knowing that you were all under the earl's protection."

Richard closed his eyes. "I am aware, William. Still, with my testimony and that of the men riding with us, it might mean *something*. Hobson saw it at the same time as I." He ran a hand through his hair and sighed. "I cannot take the risk of burning the damn thing."

"Well," Darcy said stretching out his hand to return the article to his cousin, "put it away before my wife enters and inquires why we are looking at a woman's bonnet in my study."

Richard grinned. "Does Elizabeth often come to your study at this time of night, cousin? Are the sweet first moments of your marriage over so quickly that she must seek you here to induce you to retire?"

Darcy shook his head and stood, setting his half-full glass on a side table. "And with that, Richard, I shall leave you to it. When do you head back to London?"

"End of the week." He smiled tightly and added, "Thank you for hosting me. I am unlikely to leave London again until I return to Pemberley at the end of the year, presuming I am still invited."

"You have decided irrevocably, then?"

Richard heard the pain in Darcy's voice and tried to assuage the blow. "I have. I went to the general to discuss selling my commission, and he was rather cantankerous about it. He argued vociferously that there were offices I might perform from London to assist in our efforts. There is some worth in my old carcass yet, evidently, even if it is only to train recruits and write reports that go unread." He reached for Darcy's unfinished drink. "The general has assured me that I will not be sent abroad. I told him I would not lead men into battle. Not feeling as I do now."

Richard might have insisted on relinquishing his commission. He had no taste for battle now and knew he could not lead. The fire, the sense of usefulness, of mission and purpose that had supported his actions for over a decade had faded entirely away. What he still had was a desire to find the man who had ordered the attack on Miss Hawke and her sister. The offer with the War Office would provide him with the resources to track Archibald Hawke. As Richard finished Darcy's brandy, he stood. He did not look at his cousin.

"You are always welcome at Pemberley, Richard," was Darcy's quiet reply.

While Darcy was relieved to hear that Richard would not return to the Continent, he was certain that should he be requested to return to battle, his cousin would not shirk what he saw as his duty. *He has to sell his commission*, Darcy thought unhappily. The only way to keep him truly safe would be for him to resign everything and move into the life of a gentleman, a life Richard could have for the asking, if only he would set aside his pride and make the request. Between Richard's own investments and the support both he and the earl had promised, they would situate Richard well. Richard had argued that the money was Phillip's, but while his older brother could be thoroughly pompous when playing the role of a viscount, he loved Richard enough that he would offer no protest against the expense.

Darcy grimaced. He was in no position to argue about unnecessary pride and they both knew it. He turned to the door after wishing his cousin a good night, exhausted from his constant worrying. First it had been over Georgiana, he was still anxious about Elizabeth, and now he was again concerned for Richard, just when he had thought he could put that fear to rest. As he stepped into the hall and made his way to the stairs, Darcy felt an icy lump settle in his stomach. He was not certain how much more worry he could stand.

Chapter Two

ELIZABETH DARCY STARED at the ceiling in her chambers and tried not to move. She had finally found a position that did not make her stomach clench and roll, and if she remained perfectly still, there was a chance she might not be ill this morning. Next to her, lying on his stomach with his face turned towards her was her husband, whose relaxed features and soft snores made her smile. He had grown more anxious about her every day, more so now because she was long past the time Mr. Waters had suggested would mark the end of this constant nausea. The local midwife simply harrumphed at such pronouncements. Mr. Waters was a man, after all, nothing more than an apothecary, and should not have presumed to make such a statement. She would not hear that he had only offered Mrs. Darcy some general assurances but had indeed been wise enough not to make promises.

"The worse ya feel," the heavy woman had said with an unsympathetic cluck and a toss of her head, "the healthier the child." Elizabeth could have wept at that breezy dismissal of her misery, but she had decided to be angry instead. She wanted to eat, truly she did, but even when she could manage to force something down, it did not stay down for long. She was nearly desperate to eat something other than broth, but nobody seemed to be able to help. The ginger biscuits Mrs. Cronk sent up from the kitchen had no effect; the peppermint tea was useless. Fitzwilliam, in his deepening unease, had dismissed the midwife altogether in favor of seeking out an accoucheur, who had little of help to offer other than going through the menus for foods that might trigger Elizabeth's illness. As she was not eating much, it seemed a useless exercise. She closed her eyes and tried to think of something other than how very sick she felt, how sore her stomach and back muscles were, how the ceiling swirled relentlessly after every attack. One morning feeling well. One walk in the garden without dizziness or concern about casting up her accounts. Was it so much to ask? *This had best be the healthiest child in the kingdom*, she thought with irritation, holding her limbs rigidly in place.

As she lay unmoving on the bed, Elizabeth could hear the vague sounds of the house coming to life. The soft footfalls in the hallway, the gentle murmuring of voices, the slow opening of the chamber door as a servant entered to tend the fire. After a wet summer, the harvest months had been mercifully dry and mild, but the days had begun to grow cooler at last. The day before, sitting on the bench overlooking the garden, she had noted the men coming in from the orchards and walking the path across the meadow. They carried large sacks of what she knew must be the last of the apples, and she had thought how delicious apple cider might taste. Later, she realized she would not be able to abide it, but she was still thinking about the harvest at Longbourn and what a wonderful time of year this was. She only wished she could enjoy it more if for no other reason that she would like her sweet, doting, aggravating husband to worry a little less about her.

Cautiously, she breathed in and then out. She still felt fine. Slowly, she established a calm rhythm and opened her eyes. There was gentle pressure on her hand, and she turned her head very carefully to see Fitzwilliam watching her.

"Are you well, Elizabeth?" he asked, his fingers lacing with hers as he leaned just a little closer.

"As long as I do not move, William," she replied stiffly. The anticipation faded, and while very few people would have said that he looked any different, Elizabeth could see his face fall. Every morning he woke hoping she would feel herself, and every morning he was disappointed. It was an added burden, his anxiety, but it was impossible to disguise her suffering.

"It is temporary, love," she said, forcing the words to sound encouraging. "It will pass."

"You need not reassure me, my dear. Just inform me if there is anything I can do to help." Fitzwilliam shifted, leaning over her to brush a soft kiss on her cheek. As he pulled away, Elizabeth felt the bile begin to rise again. She rolled away from her husband with a moan, grabbed the pail sitting on the floor next to the bed, and was ill.

Darcy placed a hand lightly on his wife's back as she bent over the side of the bed retching. When she was finished, he helped her settle back onto her pillows. In a practice that had become routine, he made her comfortable before rising to walk around the bed and remove the bucket. He placed it out in the hall. Then he picked up the one that had been placed near the door, clean and empty, to set in its place. He moved away to wash his hands, though the water in the basin was cold. Finally, he poured his wife a glass of water from a pitcher on a side table and sat next to her. He brought the drink to her lips carefully, tipping it a little to help her sip.

He had been away when his sister was ill in the summer, arriving home just in time for his wife to begin showing indications that she was with child. Four months along now, nearly five, and she was still ill, more so now even than the earlier months. Mr. Waters had little of help to offer, and the midwife had made Elizabeth even more wretched than she had been before the visit. The babe seemed to be progressing well—Elizabeth's abdomen was clearly rounded and growing—but she had not gained any weight. Instead, all the weight that had settled on her abdomen seemed to come from somewhere else on her body. Her face was thinner than he had ever seen it, and she was unsteady when she walked. The intense relief he had felt upon arriving home to learn that she and Georgiana were both well had slowly given way to a paralyzing panic. Elizabeth might not be strong enough to survive the birth if she could not eat. He could barely stand to be away from her, but she insisted he tend to the estate, and because his loving concern and incessant hovering were all he had to offer, he reluctantly did as she asked. When she rose from her bed late each morning, she allowed a footman to assist her on the stairs and sat in the drawing or music rooms for a few hours just for a change of scene. She rarely appeared at the dinner table and had not walked in ages. Her easy agreement to being attended by a footman wherever she went alarmed him nearly as much as any of her other symptoms.

"You will feel improved soon, my love. I am sure of it," he said reassuringly, stroking her hair.

"William," she said in a breathy voice, exhausted.

"Yes, love?" Fitzwilliam asked, kissing her hand.

"If we ever want another child," she said faintly, though her eyes sparkled just a bit, "I must insist we find a ward to adopt."

Chapter Three

FITZWILLIAM DARCY SETTLED into the heavy leather chair behind the desk in his study to go over the quarterly accounts. The harvest had been surprisingly good, considering the unseasonably heavy rains over the summer—not as profitable as the previous one, but it might have been a good deal worse. He knew he was very fortunate, that many families had finished the year in debt. He was thankful that his father had long ago disregarded the fashionable dictates of society by keeping the family's wealth in various investments as well as in the land. In years like this, those investments made up the shortfall, helping him meet his obligations without appreciably drawing down the estate's accounts.

It had taken two years after inheriting, but once Darcy had felt more experienced handling the finances of the estate, he had been confident enough to evaluate and invest in a few opportunities brought to him by the earl. While he had been a highly conservative investor at the beginning he was now better able to understand when some level of risk might be worth the reward. He smiled at that, thinking of what he had once considered a risky marital alliance.

Darcy was certain his uncle gained political favors for convincing his nephew to part with his money, but so long as the investment was honest and sound and he was making money for Pemberley and his family, he did not mind helping his uncle. In the past year, after much discussion with his new uncle Gardiner about the increasing speed of changes in trade and industry, he had invested as a silent partner in Gardiner's import/export business. With Darcy's additional capital and Gardiner's contacts and supply lines, they had seen a reasonable return within six months and he had hopes that it would remain a steady source of income, particularly after the war with Bonaparte finally concluded. He would need those additional funds to offset the drop in agricultural prices he expected would follow the war's end, and Gardiner had recommended procuring practical items rather than luxuries for the same reason. *In times of uncertainty*, he had said, leaning back in his chair in the study at Gracechurch Street, *people will have neither the funds nor the stomach for fripperies.* Darcy shook his head recalling the conversation. *Not so long ago I thought relatives in trade would be a disadvantage*, he thought, reprimanding himself. *Another gift from my wife.*

Despite Elizabeth's recent difficulties and her teasing this morning, Darcy believed she harbored hope for more children, and he was determined to provide for them all. It would not be many years before Georgiana wed and her substantial dowry would have to be paid. He anticipated that by then he would have enough to completely replace it, careful as he had been in the years since his father's death. His wife, fortunately, was not one who required funds beyond those already set aside for her use. In fact, she had spent some of it on tenant matters until he explained that there was already a fund set aside for such things. She left much of it in her own account unspent, and she had already begun to accumulate a tidy sum.

His thoughts wandered back to some of the women of the *ton* who had demonstrated an interest in becoming his wife over the years. He chuckled quietly as he considered whether any of them would have money remaining in their account at the end of the quarter. More likely they would have spent everything and simply continued to spend, using his name for additional credit, particularly with the London merchants. Miss Caroline Bingley came to mind, with her fashionable gowns and turbans, her ostrich feathers, the silk slippers he had overheard her gleefully relate to her sister that she had worn but once before discarding them, and again congratulated himself that he and his bride were so well matched.

In one of the many little shops they had entered on their wedding tour, Elizabeth had tried to provoke him by picking up a fan of egret feathers and making a pretense of fawning admiration. Unfortunately, the jest was doomed to failure, as the feathers almost immediately caused her to sneeze several times over. It had been the first time he heard her sneeze, and he was still fascinated by the tiny little whistling noise she made as she fought valiantly for control. Truly, it could hardly be termed a sneeze at all. Richard always sneezed as though he was releasing a violent tempest, and even Georgiana's sneezes were far heartier than Elizabeth's. His wife was no fragile creature, thank the Lord, but her sneezes were incongruously dainty. He recalled her embarrassment as she had returned the fan to its place with an upraised eyebrow and he had struggled not to laugh.

"No," she had said, with an exaggerated shake of her head, "That will not do. I cannot attempt to tease you and make sport for you instead." Her dark eyes were shining as she said it, though, and she had stood on her toes and tilted her face up to his for a kiss, despite their location in the back of a public shop. He had been happy to comply.

Both before the wedding and following their return from the tour, he had insisted upon purchasing her a large number of new dresses. Ball gowns for the season in town, certainly, but also heavier clothing for the cold, windy winter months in the north and stout walking boots for the rougher terrain. Far from being pleased with him, Elizabeth had scolded him for spending so extravagantly. *Scandalous*, she had declared, stating quite firmly she should never be able to wear them all, and what did he mean by forcing her to stand still for so many fittings and alterations all at once? Despite having to bear the weight of her annoyance, he was glad he had insisted. She could certainly not stand for any length of time now, and even if she did not venture outside often in the cold, the house itself was difficult to keep entirely warm. The dressmaker in Lambton had promised she could simply let some of the gowns out now that Mrs. Darcy was increasing, and she would not even need to be present for a fitting.

Darcy tapped his fingers on the desk, thinking that as ill she was, there might yet be room in her gowns despite the growing evidence of her condition. The babe might be nourished and growing, but he was very worried about his wife. He ignored the account books as he thought about sending to London for a different accoucheur, perhaps even to Guy's Hospital in Southwark or the medical college in Edinburgh. Surely someone there must have had experience with a case like Elizabeth's. She could not stay well if she could not eat. The only explanation Elizabeth could offer was that she could smell absolutely everything, and it had become entirely overpowering. The staff had been warned not to wear scents. He had informed his valet not to use the sandalwood in his daily ablutions and Elizabeth had stopped using the jasmine he loved, but apparently, it was not enough.

I should at least write letters asking for help, he thought. *The worst they can say is that they cannot offer any new ideas.* He reached for paper and ink and had two letters prepared before the half hour was up, outlining the problem and everything that had already been attempted. He sanded them, folded the pages, and sealed them, pressing his signet ring firmly into the wax before walking them to the footman and ordering that they be sent express. *I wish there was more to be done, but I know we must simply wait.* He placed his palms on the desk and pushed himself to a standing position with a grunt. *Elizabeth would say I should speak with Mr. Redding on Sunday next. I believe patience is my least favorite virtue.*

Chapter Four

THE WEATHER HAD been unseasonably mild, but the harvest was completed, the cold had finally set in, and by the first week of November, Sophia Hawke had to admit that nothing more would be accomplished until the spring thaw. She turned to her correspondence, one letter in particular, written in an elegant feminine hand. Mrs. Darcy had invited the Hawke sisters to spend the holidays with them and stay afterward for a proper visit. Their hostess was all but confined to the house due to her *condition*, though the precise word was never used, and she felt a great desire for companionship. Sophia felt uneasy about the invitation. She was grateful for the courtesy, but was concerned that the invitation had been issued primarily out of pity, as the Darcys were aware that the Hawke sisters were living in the dowager's cottage while planning the new manor house.

Sophia grinned to herself. The dowager cottage felt quite spacious, even lavish to her, inured as she was to rented rooms and camp conditions. While Matlock had been rather a shock in its luxuries, and she had spent several weeks secretly sleeping on the floor before she could accustom herself to the mattress, she now adored her own soft bed in a reasonably sized bedroom, the fine clean sheets, the roaring fires that kept everything warm. She was nearly overset by the extravagance of well-cooked meals appearing in her dining room each night and a small but tidy chapel to visit each morning out on the grounds. Most importantly, it was all hers—the house, the outbuildings, the animals, the land, the decisions.

On the other hand, her younger sister Evelyn was accustomed to living in grander spaces and was feeling somewhat restricted, despite the small but well-stocked library and expensive pianoforte. While at first her younger sister had been pleased to be at Darlington and away from their uncle, Sophia knew that the adjustment had been more difficult for Evie as time wore on. Just the other day, she had delivered a few irritable comments about the length of time it took to build a proper manor house, as though the process was being purposefully extended to aggravate her. The day before, Sophia had even been forced to have a private conversation with her sister about topics to avoid when the staff were nearby. She trusted the servants, and there were not many of them yet, but Evie was far too unguarded. It was then she learned that "Uncle Archibald" had encouraged his youngest niece to speak without discretion, as he delighted in her intelligence and wit. More likely, thought Sophia sourly, it made his position quite easy, in that the staff would report everything back to him directly. She sighed at the thought of how changed her sister was from the chirrupy child of twelve she had last known, then chastised herself for mourning the loss.

Were she honest with herself, Sophia would have to admit that some sense of unseemly pride had always been at least a small part of her sister's character. Her father and Oliver had been able to laugh Evie out of any moments of improper display, but her mother had adored her youngest child, the only member of the family who resembled her, and had quite spoilt her. Still, her sister was full grown now. Teasing her out of her sense of entitlement seemed unlikely to succeed. Uncle Archibald had cultivated the worst parts of her sister's character, and it would be a difficult task to correct her now. Were they prepared to be guests?

Sophia wanted to accept. She believed she could learn a great deal about running an estate from the Darcys, and she did feel an obligation to Mr. Darcy in particular for his part in their surprisingly seamless extraction from her uncle's custody the previous summer. She would also require his help with negotiating contracts for the materials she would need next spring. Indeed, his influence had already saved her a great deal of money. During his visit almost six weeks ago, Colonel Fitzwilliam had read part of a letter from Elizabeth Darcy that praised the Lambton apothecary for his help during the influenza epidemic, the one that Mr. Darcy and Mr. Bingley had rushed away to confront. Judging by the way Evie's entire face had lit up, it was clear she would appreciate discussing her work in the still room with the man. Mr. Hobson and Jack were more than able to tend to things in her absence and could always send for her should her presence truly be required.

The next thing to consider would be the Fitzwilliams' attendance. Would the earl want her there? Had Mr. Darcy already conferred with him? Lady Matlock's delighted attentions had been an unexpected pleasure, but her very stolid husband might not wish to see her again so soon.

Over the years Sophia had been allied with the Earl of Matlock, she had been of great use to him. When her uncle had been at the height of his power, with wealthy supporters and dangerous connections, Sophia was able to predict her uncle's movements with an intimate knowledge of his habits and vices. She possessed a canny ability to draw Archibald Hawke out when the earl could not. *Cub hunting*, the earl had called it approvingly, and he had continued to find her skills helpful even after one of Archibald Hawke's off-handed remarks about certain royal proclivities made its way back to the Prince Regent and the man fell from favor. He had powerful friends yet, though, and could wield influence among both MPs and the House of Lords when he chose. Hawke's increasing need for funds, however, had at last induced him to resign from the Home Office last summer in a final attempt to access the fortune of his nieces.

The earl's assistance had been met with a deep and abiding gratitude, but Henry Fitzwilliam's material support had never extended to real friendship, despite his uncharacteristically emotional welcome when Sophia arrived at Matlock with the colonel. Evelyn had been surprised that the earl had not visited Darlington after such a display of affection, but her older sister understood too well that he would not. The connection was still a political liability. She had understood that even as a girl of sixteen, though that young woman, desperately in need of a father, had long hoped it might change. Hosting the Hawkes for a month had been a concession on the earl's part to ensure their physical safety, and she was of course thankful. *Why should he care?* she admonished herself. *You were simply an advantage for him.* That his cold politeness continued to ache in the way of old wounds she knew was due only to her own weakness.

She sighed. Meeting at Pemberley would be awkward but not untenable. Though her uncle's absence was noted, the resignation meant that Archibald Hawke's presumed disgrace was not publicly known, and the earl could have no control over the Darcys' guest list, after all. At Pemberley, the Hawkes were merely old neighbors recently returned to their ancestral lands.

She wondered idly whether the colonel would be in attendance. He was one of the few people who had the experience to understand what her life had been like the past three years. Corporal Jack Hobson and Colonel Richard Fitzwilliam. *A shockingly short list,* she thought.

The colonel was now in London. He had taken on new duties with the War Office after confessing to her that he had considered resigning his commission. His general had apparently not taken kindly to the idea. In truth, he admitted to Sophia that he himself did not feel comfortable leaving His Majesty's service before Bonaparte was defeated. Sophia had felt a pang of disappointment thinking that he might have a very long wait. Even if all he was doing was training recruits and filling out reports, he told her, he was freeing up another man to fight.

"Once Boney is captured," he had said with a determined nod, "I will resign from the Regulars and allow my father and cousin to make a gentleman out of me." His voice had lacked conviction, but Sophia was not certain whether it was the self-imposed deadline or the thought of being a gentleman that was causing him grief. Evelyn had listened to them carefully for a time, then faded away as she often did, smiling faintly in the right places, but not truly following. Sophia blushed a little for her sister's rudeness, but had offered the colonel the best smile she could muster, and had wished him well.

She was happy to hear that the colonel would not return to the Continent and quite pleased that he had come in person to make his farewell. After the warnings the earl had given her about her position in society, she had been rather surprised to see him and found herself in rather low spirits for a good week after his departure. Even Jack had inquired whether she was well, requiring Sophia to square her shoulders and shake off her melancholy. *Do not hope, Sophia*, she lectured herself. *He is not for you.* She did hope the colonel would continue to visit whenever he was able. She knew that she would not be invited again to Matlock until the issue of her uncle was resolved in a way that cleared the Hawke name.

Of course, Sophia had more than enough business to occupy her at Darlington. Learning to run the estate had proven quite difficult, and working with the architect exhausting. The sketches she drew for the man showed as much as she recalled about the old manor house, but he had pointed out that both architecture and construction had made a good many advances and recommended several changes. He was pleased to hear that she had read about Alexander Cumming's design for a water closet and wished to install one. They had worked together and she had incorporated many of his ideas into her sketches. He nodded, happy with the level of detail, and took the sketches with him to work up his own plans.

The tenants were anxious that the rebuilding would mean higher rents for them. The result of such rumors meant more disputes and a list of demands for improvements. She had no idea how Mr. Hobson had managed all these years, particularly the last three, when Jack was away helping keep her safe. She would never forget it. Nor would she forget Jack's assistance both in getting her home when she was hurt or later in slowing down her uncle's carriage. Jack had never admitted to having committed the act, but she was certain as soon as she had seen the damage as he always carried a small hand axe on his belt. Even in uniform, he had carried it, and she had often teased him about needing it when his shots went wild. Sophia was the better shot by far—in fact, she was one of the best in the regiment—but Jack could throw a hatchet with surprising accuracy and his use of the sword was clearly superior, so he took her mocking in stride and they had helped each other survive. She helped him improve his long-range accuracy, and he helped her learn to wield the knife she had always kept in her boot. She kept one still, but it was by necessity smaller, used more now as a tool than a weapon.

Sophia guessed that Jack had employed his hatchet rather indiscriminately not only to slow their travel, but to send a message to her uncle: *You are not alone. You are being watched.* Although she knew her uncle had been rattled, Matlock's men had still been a day behind. She was confident that she would have been able to escape her uncle. She had done it many times. She was less certain that even with Jack's help she would have could also safely extract her sister. Had Jack not written the letter at Vitoria and made sure it reached the colonel, and had the colonel, Mr. Darcy, and Mr. Bingley not taken the letter as seriously as they had and arrived at just the right moment, the situation might have ended quite differently. Even after that rescue, had the colonel not been riding with them as their carriage sped to Matlock, they might both have been killed.

Such a fine line between life and death, she thought, and tried to calm the flush of thoughts that followed. Sophia was used to anticipating her own demise, as much as it still sent her heart racing, but she could not stomach the thought of anything happening to her sister. As perplexing and exasperating as she often found Evie, her sister was her responsibility. More than that, Evie was the only immediate family she had left.

The younger Hawke sister looked like her late mother, and she was stunning; there was no denying that fact. Her black hair reached the middle of her back before it was pinned up to frame a face nearly perfect in its symmetry. Long, dark lashes contrasted with pale skin as smooth as glass. Her deep blue eyes completed a vision that was nothing short of arresting. However, where Sophia's gaze was intense and insightful, Evelyn's was unfocused, dreamy. Sophia was also convinced that unlike anyone else in her family, Evie might actually be something of a genius. She admired her sister's intellect and supported her need for books and still room supplies, but was concerned that an obsession with her studies often left Evie appearing distracted, even rude.

Evelyn had absorbed an incredible amount of information, particularly about medicine, in the years she had spent sequestered in her uncle's house. Apparently she had spent nearly all of her time in the extensive library. Sophia had been only too happy to purchase any books her sister requested for their library at Darlington, and the younger Hawke spent hours in a small converted servant's bedroom experimenting with combinations of herbs, constructing poultices, brewing teas, all based on her reading. Sophia supposed that had Evelyn been a man, she might have sent her to Edinburgh for a more formal education. Despite her keen mind, though, the young woman had a limited understanding of people and the world around her that was concerning to her older sister.

Evie had struggled to reconcile her uncle's recent behavior with the man she had known as almost a father since she was a little girl and was having difficulty sorting out whether her long-held opinions on nearly every issue were due to her own decided judgments or his. She did not, indeed could not, deny what he had done, and she was guilt-stricken for the mistakes she had made that had put her sister and herself in danger. Sophia had accepted her pleas for forgiveness and knew them to be sincere. Still, there were moments when something Evelyn had been taught about her parents or her older siblings would be stated as fact, and Sophia would patiently go about the business of acquainting Evie with the truth without revealing the kind of pain these derogatory statements caused. Having been isolated by her uncle for so much of her life, meeting the requirements of her social position, even here in remote Staffordshire, was challenging for Evie. A visit among those who would be patient with her and perhaps help coax her into a better understanding of her position and herself was a blessing Sophia desperately wished to accept on her sister's behalf.

Sophia tapped the edge of the invitation against her free hand. Did the Darcys know her story? Would they have issued the invitation if they did? Would they be offended by a refusal? She sighed. She longed to meet Mrs. Darcy who was, by all accounts, a witty woman with a good heart and just a little older than Evelyn. Then there was Miss Darcy, who was younger than Evelyn by several years but who the colonel had said was a gentle soul and might also be good company for her sister. She had hopes that they could all be friends. She smiled to herself. She had never had a female friend. She pursed her lips and gave in. The colonel would have filled in Mr. Darcy, and that must be enough. She would accept the invitation and pretend she had no qualms. *Pretend*, she smiled to herself. *At least in that art I am quite accomplished.*

Chapter Five

WILLIAM, THEY WILL COME," called Elizabeth happily from the doorway of the study. She stepped carefully inside where her husband was tending to his letters clutching one of her own. He looked up to see her smile, and it made him smile in return.

"Who will come, my dear?" he asked, setting his work aside. He wanted to jump up and guide her to the settee, but he was sure Elizabeth would only slap his hand away again. He forced himself to sit still.

"The Hawkes," Elizabeth said excitedly, holding up the letter. "Miss Hawke has accepted for herself and Miss Evelyn." One foot tapped the floor lightly in excited anticipation. "Oh, I am so pleased. I have longed to meet them." She turned as if to depart. "There are so many preparations to make."

Darcy called out to stay her departure. "Elizabeth, I do not want you overexerting yourself. Mrs. Reynolds can handle any preparations, and if need be, Georgiana can assist."

Elizabeth returned to the chair by his desk and sat carefully. "I will allow Mrs. Reynolds to assist, William, but I wish to be involved. They must be such interesting women! Miss Hawke in particular." Her eyes were shining with curiosity and eagerness. He hated to temper any pleasure she was taking in the anticipation of the visit, but she needed her rest.

"Elizabeth," Darcy said firmly, "you are not yourself. I do not wish to have you tire yourself for visitors when there are others who can do that work."

In a move he should have predicted but inexplicably had not, he watched his wife's chin come up just a fraction and her eyes narrow. *Oh Lord, now I am in for it.* He quickly changed his tone to one a bit more diplomatic, a skill his marriage had required him to practice assiduously, particularly in the last few months.

"Elizabeth," he said again, carefully but quickly. "I only meant to suggest that you reserve your energies for actually hosting the Hawkes rather than preparing for their arrival." He held his breath while she considered his statement. She looked him over from head to toe and let out a sigh so very sad and resigned that he almost regretted winning the point.

"I know you are only humoring me, William," she said, "and though I am loath to admit it, that does make some degree of sense." Darcy rose and escorted her to the settee, closer to the fire. She perched gingerly on the cushions. "I am not much good for anything of late, I am afraid."

Darcy seated himself beside his wife. He took her hand in his own and traced a pattern along the inside of her wrist. She closed her eyes and the tiny smile that appeared on her face set his heart racing. "You are doing the most difficult work there is, my dear," he said softly, "and our child is not making it easy for you. You should not be so impatient with yourself."

Elizabeth pursed her lips and leaned into his side, laying her head gently on his shoulder. "Hypocrite," she said fondly.

"I beg your pardon?" Darcy was startled but also amused.

"Truly, love, who are you speak to me of patience? I know you too well. I have never met a less patient man when there is something you desire."

Darcy closed his eyes, trying not to think about how much he desired a certain impertinent woman and exactly how much patience her illness had required of him—indeed, was requiring of him at this very moment. Still, if he wished to avoid an emotional scene, he could not mention this to her. It was patently unfair that he could not even defend himself. As he was ruminating, he heard a soft little rumbling laugh, and she hugged his arm.

"You are such a *man*," she said lightly. She hugged his arm again, placed a little kiss upon his cheek, and was gone. It was some time before Elizabeth Darcy's husband could return to his desk.

***

Sophia Hawke looked through her sorted letters of business and picked up the pile she had set aside.

"Ah, Mr. Hobson, please come in," she said to the man standing in her small study. He was a tall man, nearly as tall as his son and still possessed of a powerful frame despite his advancing years. His hair retained streaks of red amidst the silver, and while his clothing was in step with his position, it was well made, pressed, and clean.

"Miss Hawke, I understand I am to correspond with you at Pemberley should anything essential arise?" he asked quietly.

"I would appreciate that, Mr. Hobson," replied Sophia as she glanced around the study, certain she was leaving something important behind. "I shall take some additional monies for any post you might send and leave it with the housekeeper, a Mrs. Reynolds, I believe. She will see to it. If it is urgent, send one of the Clauson boys direct."

After a moment of silence, he spoke again. "Will that be all, Miss Hawke?"

Sophia tilted her head at him, distracted for a moment by how much Jack resembled his father. She had tried to get him to call her Sophia, but to no avail. She was the daughter of Mr. and Mrs. Hawke and the mistress of the house, such as it was, and he would brook no such informality with her. He was insistent that Jack address her likewise, and that had bothered Sophia a great deal more than she thought it ought.

"Please sit down, Mr. Hobson," she said calmly but firmly. The man seemed to hesitate, and she indicated one of two wingchairs crowded together by the fire. "Please," she repeated.

Her steward lumbered over to the wingchair and eased himself into it. Although he hid it well, it was a simple thing for Sophia to note that his back was stiff and painful. Though it was not the only reason for the conversation she was about to have, it made her decision even more important. She had to make this offer to him in a way that would not offend his pride.

Once he was settled, Mr. Hobson waited for her to begin. His two large weathered hands lay clasped in his lap, his thumbs rubbing anxiously against one another. Sophia cleared her throat. She was just as nervous, but seeing the man so uneasy in her presence, she squared her shoulders and began.

"Mr. Hobson," she said, rather a bit too loudly. He looked to her and she modulated her voice. "How old is Jack now?"

Stupid, she thought. *You know exactly how old he is.*

Mr. Hobson stumbled over his words briefly before saying, "Seven and twenty, ma'am."

"I see. And you hope for him to take over for you when you are ready to retire?"

"It is my hope, ma'am, to leave you in a few years with a man we can both trust in my office."

She gazed at Mr. Hobson's lined, craggy face with true affection. *How fortunate we have been to have such a man to watch over Darlington. We owe him everything.* She shook herself out of the reverie. *Pay attention, Sophia.*

"As you know," Sophia said, setting her lips in a line so as to appear she was deep in thought rather than stifling a smile, "there will be a great deal of work on the house this spring, and we plan to be in it before next year's harvest."

Mr. Hobson nodded once.

"I was rather hoping you might consider overseeing all that work and allowing Jack to take over both the home and tenant farms."

Mr. Hobson worried his hands a bit more. "Has my work been poor, Miss Hawke?"

She was ready for this. "Mr. Hobson," she said in an imperious, chiding tone. "False modesty does not become you."

"Miss Hawke?" Mr. Hobson looked confused.

"You know very well that your work is excellent. I should not have to say as much. Were it not, you would not be employed here. Is that not the case?"

"Of course not, Miss Hawke." She saw he was stifling a small smile.

"The work on the house is complicated. It will require constant management and there will often be multiple projects occurring at the same time." *And it will not require miles on horseback every day.* "I need someone with a great deal of experience, who can manage the men and make certain the project is completed enough for us to move into before the winter." She paused and said clearly, "I do not think Jack is yet ready for such a task."

Mr. Hobson grunted.

Sophia knew that Jack was learning quickly, that he would be able to take over the farms by the spring. Managing groups of men, however, when he could not simply issue a military order, well, that came with experience. Were she to make the attempt, the men would either ignore or attempt to cheat her. She would be fortunate to have a single wall constructed by Michaelmas.

She took a breath to finish. "That is not a great deal of time, I know, and work should be completed on the wings in the subsequent year, but the main house must be finished. I will not have my sister in the dowager's cottage any longer. She needs a music room, a proper library, and a still room. I want you to supervise this project, Mr. Hobson."

Mr. Hobson was quiet for a moment. "What about. . ." his voice trailed off.

"After?" Sophia finished the question for him. He nodded.

"If you are willing, I would very much like to keep you in the house to help me with contracts, correspondence—to act as my secretary." She saw his look of surprise, though he knew the accounts and finances better than anyone alive and had in fact recently helped her transfer her funds into new accounts completely under her control. "Mr. Hobson, you know Darlington. I need you here to advise Jack, and you would assist me with the business of running Darlington as a proper estate again."

From the look of stupefaction on his face, Mr. Hobson had clearly thought he was to be replaced by his son. Sophia was aware that eventually he would retire, but in the meantime, two men working for full wages would be a tremendous boon. They would be able to put something away for Jack's future family. She nearly rolled her eyes at the thought of requiring Mr. Hobson to leave his post before he was ready. She would pay him to be the steward for the rest of his life if he wanted.

"I need your expertise here, sir, at the manor house. It seems appropriate that as you were the steward when the house was lost that you should oversee its rebirth." Here she leaned forward to pick up her cup though the tea had long gone cold.

Mr. Hobson startled at the word "rebirth," just as Sophia knew he would. On this point, he was ridiculously easy to read. He nodded and finally spoke. "I suppose it would allow Jack to marry Miss Townson sooner than they thought."

Sophia squelched a smile. *He took the bait.* "That is true," she said as though the thought had only just occurred to her. "I think the estate could do with some youngsters running about the grounds again, Mr. Hobson, do not you?"

He shook his head and grinned. "Ah, Miss Hawke, you have quite persuaded me, as you knew you would. One mention of bairns and I am hopeless, I am afraid."

"Mr. Hobson," she said quietly, thinking of the three years Jack had lost to ensuring her safety. "I owe a great debt to you and your son. I am blessed to have such loyalty as you have always shown to my family. My parents and I could not find better stewards of Darlington. Allow me to keep you both nearby. I cannot afford to lose either of you."

The older man was making a sound deep in his throat now. He reached into his pocket for an oversized handkerchief and blew his nose into it with a good deal of force and a rather loud honking sound. Sophia was pleased he had shown this informality in her presence at last. Perhaps he was finally becoming more comfortable with her.

"When I think," he said brokenly, and stopped to blow his nose again. Sophia waited patiently. He was staring at his boots when he resumed. "When I think about your parents, Miss Hawke, I think about how fortunate I was to come to work at Darlington as a lad. There was no messing about with your father or his father neither, but they were fair men, honest men. Sent me to school, paid me a good wage."

Sophia nodded. She knew his story well.

"But you, Miss," Mr. Hobson said, haltingly. "When we all heard what you had done, leading your sister out of the fire, then going back again for the servants, and you just a wee thing yourself, well, there was nothing we would not do for you."

Sophia was certain her shock was written clearly across her face. That night felt so very long ago. It belonged to another life. Mr. Hobson smiled then, a sweet, sad, fatherly smile, and took her chin gently in one large hand.

"I did not stay for your parents, Miss Sophia," he said hoarsely. "As good as they were to me, they were gone." He waited until her eyes met his. "I stayed for you. Had your uncle succeeded, he would have found empty tenant cottages and fields without workers." He removed his hand as though he had not realized where it was, and stood abruptly. "I accept your gracious offer, ma'am, and Jack and I will begin to work out the transition while you are away." He picked up the stack of paper Sophia had handed him at the beginning of their meeting. "A bit early, but happy Christmas to you both." He walked to the door where he stopped but did not look back. He tapped the wall twice with the palm of his hand, and disappeared into the hall with a swipe at his eyes and a light step.

Chapter Six

A FORTNIGHT AFTER receiving the Hawkes'
acceptance, Elizabeth and Georgiana stepped
outside into a chilly December afternoon to greet the
Hawke carriage as it stopped in the drive. After a
moment, the door was opened slowly and a
Pemberley footman handed down a small, dark
woman with a flawless complexion. Her wavy black
hair was woven into a complicated braid that had
been caught up into a bun. Soft dark curls framed her
face. She appeared to be everything beautiful and
proper, and was therefore a bit of a disappointment
to Elizabeth, who had been expecting something
rather different. Colonel Fitzwilliam had described
Evelyn Hawke as both quietly charming and
something of a bluestocking, always in a book about

medicine or midwifery, clearly inappropriate subject matter for a young unmarried gentlewoman. He had said nothing of her beauty. The colonel had tried to describe her sister as well but was less successful. He had finally shrugged and admitted that Sophia Hawke was a lovely but complicated woman who defied easy description. He had merely said, with a wink, that he thought she and Elizabeth would get along well. The young woman turned to wait for her sister, and Elizabeth hoped that Sophia Hawke would be as challenging a character to sketch as the colonel's words promised.

The second woman stepped from the carriage and Georgiana could not help but stifle a giggle and press Elizabeth's hand in a shared sense of expectation. The sisters could not have been more varied in looks, Elizabeth thought, as a small smile began to tug at the corners of her mouth. She and her sister Jane also looked different, but there was at least some resemblance. Despite their different coloring and figures, they were the same height, more or less, and shared the same high cheekbones, the same nose, the same hands and long, graceful fingers, though Elizabeth was convinced that Jane's hands were far more elegant than her own.

The Hawke sisters were almost entirely dissimilar. The younger was finely built and diminutive though in possession of a womanly figure with fashionably pale and unblemished porcelain skin. Her hair was as dark as a moonless midnight, several shades darker than Elizabeth's. The elder was taller even than Georgiana, with hair the color of gold gathered in a simple but very flattering arrangement of curls. Her skin was perhaps a little darker than her sister's, and her figure, though long and lithe, could not be termed willowy. Her shoulders were a bit too broad for that, though they tapered to an enticingly slim and feminine waist. Most of her height was in her long legs, and yet she was well-proportioned. Rather than simply beautiful, Elizabeth thought, Sophia Hawke was something rarer, something she could not quite place—lovely, certainly, but more than that, there was a warmth and intelligence that radiated from her without words, something that made her seem at once both innocent and wise. Elizabeth began to understand Richard's inability to describe the woman.

The one physical trait the Hawke sisters shared was their striking eyes. They were blue, deep blue, the blue of a lake at rest, a startling shade Elizabeth was quite sure she had never before seen. *The sun and the moon*, she thought, smiling. *Day and night*. When the woman she realized must be Sophia glanced up at them with no smile but a twinkling glint in those unusual eyes, Elizabeth liked her instantly.

The introductions were quickly made, and Georgiana exchanged a few pleasantries with Miss Evelyn. She was happy to take the young woman's arm and lead her inside. It did not escape Elizabeth's notice that Sophia Hawke's eyes followed the two with both affection and apprehension.

"Well, Miss Hawke," she said brightly as they walked slowly up the stairs, "we shall have your mount moved to the stable so you may ride in the morning. Our groomsman will take excellent care of her."

Sophia Hawke smiled demurely and offered her thanks, then continued. "Him. He is a thoroughbred, one of my first purchases when we resided briefly at Matlock. I admit I am very fond of him."

"What is his name?" Elizabeth asked as they entered the house, sure that the name would tell her something wonderfully appealing about the enigmatic Sophia Hawke.

"Rady," was the reply. Sophia Hawke was looking at her with those eyes that seemed to see through her, awaiting her response.

"Rady?" Elizabeth tried to keep the disenchantment from her voice, but Miss Hawke was raising her eyebrows in a teasing way. She was not as forthcoming as Elizabeth had hoped.

"Oh, Sophia," sighed her sister, who was already removing her gloves and bonnet. "Do stop with the puzzling answers." She smiled at Elizabeth and Georgiana, and Elizabeth had to smile in return. Goodness, even Miss Evelyn's teeth were perfect. "My sister never gives out information unless it is pulled from her. So I will spoil her fun and tell you both that the horse's name is Rhadamanthus. Rather a mouthful, I am aware, but though Sophia eschews most reading that does not add to the profit of Darlington, she is partial to the Greek myths."

Georgiana smiled uneasily. She considered the name, screwing up her face, trying to recall it, but Elizabeth was charmed. "The judge," she said sweetly, raising her own eyebrows at Miss Hawke. "That is an unusual choice."

"He was a king, and Rady is a thoroughbred. Further, madam, I am an admirer of justice tempered by wisdom," said Miss Hawke calmly, removing her second glove finger by finger, "and I admit to enjoying the looks I receive when I am asked his name."

Elizabeth nearly laughed outright. *Caught.* Oh yes, she liked this woman a good deal. Miss Hawke said nothing, but her eyes sparkled with good humor.

"Well," Elizabeth said, flashing a quick grin at Georgiana, "I feel as though we are going to be very good friends, Miss Hawke, Miss Evelyn. Would you two like to come into the drawing room for some tea, or would you prefer to refresh yourselves first?" She was so pleased to have company that she was more talkative than normal, and she continued before allowing a response. "I am sorry my husband was not here to greet you. Unfortunately, the tenants have little to do this time of year, so they have contrived to fill the time with the arguments they allowed to fester during harvest. They have kept Mr. Darcy quite busy of late."

Miss Hawke smiled a small, thoughtful smile. "I am pleased to hear that this is not only occurring at Darlington, Mrs. Darcy." She paused, a little uncertain how to proceed. "May I also say how pleased we were to receive the invitation for an extended visit to Pemberley? I have been so busy this autumn that my poor sister has been quite isolated at Darlington. We have both looked very much forward to meeting you all."

Miss Evelyn quietly added, "May I speak for us both, Sophia, and answer Mrs. Darcy's original question?" Sophia nodded, chagrined that she had neglected it herself. "I believe," Evelyn said softly, "that we should be happy to sit down to tea. The ride is not a terribly long one, and I for one should like to become better acquainted."

Elizabeth nodded and led the way into the drawing room, and when the tea arrived, Georgiana began to pour. Both the Hawkes silently observed the break with propriety, Sophia because she noticed everything, filing away unconnected pieces of information until they made sense, and Evelyn because she saw that Mrs. Darcy did not eat. Sophia had not shared the particulars of their invitation with her sister, and so it was only now that Evelyn realized that their hostess was increasing. She thought it might explain both why Mrs. Darcy did not preside over tea and why she was so very pleased to have company. It might be the ebullient emotions of the middle months, or she might simply be reacting to a long winter confinement.

"I could not help but notice, Mrs. Darcy," Evelyn said in her soft, genteel voice, "that you are increasing yet not eating. Are you still feeling ill this far into your pregnancy?"

Georgiana's eyes opened wide and while the hand holding a small plate of food to pass to her guests hung unmoving in the air, she glanced at her sister, flushed with embarrassment. Elizabeth was visibly startled at the direct address of such a private topic, but was also silently elated. The forward question was jarring, particularly as it was set against the low, musical tone of the woman's voice. This was the Evelyn Hawke she had been hoping to meet.

Noting that both Darcy women had temporarily lost the ability to speak, Sophia Hawke sighed. She reached into the folds of her dress where a chain was draped, withdrew a gleaming gold watch from a small pocket, and opened the cover to check the time.

"Well done, my dear," she said to Evelyn drily, "I believe this is the quickest you have ever reduced a room to silence."

As Darcy stood in the entrance hall, handing his hat, gloves, and riding crop off to James, a sudden burst of laughter came from the drawing room, not the demure, tinkling titters of London, but rather a sound more akin to a roar. He recognized the laughter of his wife and sister.

"I presume that the Hawkes have arrived, James?" he asked with a shake of his head as he removed his greatcoat.

"Yes, sir," replied James, who was valiantly repressing a smile, "they have."

Chapter Seven

DARCY CLOSED THE DOOR to his study and poured himself a glass of brandy. He eased into a chair by the fire and closed his eyes as he sipped his drink and reveled in the solitude. The Hawke sisters were intelligent and witty, but it did require some fortitude to withstand their company. Sophia Hawke was nearly as reticent as he but as willing to tease as his wife. It could be difficult, however, to understand that she had been teasing until a few moments had passed and the conversation had moved on. Where Elizabeth's wit was playful, Sophia Hawke's was dry and incisive, though entirely without malice.

Then there was the shock of her younger sister's conversation. One could be discussing something as mundane as the weather or the state of the roads and yet be abruptly subject to a softly voiced statement so completely inappropriate as to make a grown man blush. Evelyn Hawke's shocking references to the medical knowledge she had gained through her reading did not seem intended to distress. They were delivered in the same melodic tones as everything else she said. It was perhaps the nature of the statements, delivered as though she was remarking upon the color of a flower in the garden, that so shook his equanimity. Now that he thought about it, those statements functioned in much the same way as Sophia Hawke's teasing. One was nearly past it before realizing what had been said.

Far from being shaken, Elizabeth was enchanted with the Hawkes, and he could see her making fast friends with them. She clearly admired Sophia Hawke and while she was as shocked as he at Evelyn Hawke's references to various remedies and the conditions that required them, she seemed comfortable with them both. Perhaps it was her position as second of five sisters, but she seemed to understand them better than either he or Georgiana. Despite his own hesitation, he had not seen his wife so lively in months, and for that, he would endure far worse tortures than dinner in such company. Georgiana was clearly diverted by the conversation but was perhaps the most unsettled of them all, blushing profusely at Miss Evelyn's commentary, recovering only when a kind jest or quiet observation from Miss Hawke or Elizabeth would redirect the conversation into more appropriate channels.

The larger problem, he thought with a groan, was that he would be entirely on his own with this houseful of women until either the earl or Richard were able to arrive just prior to the holiday, possibly not for another fortnight. He sipped at his brandy and considered options for remaining out of the house as much as possible. As he had not yet located a suitable replacement for Harrison, the steward who had fled over the summer, he had work enough to occupy his time. That must serve as his excuse. If it proved insufficient, he could always take his horse and remain out of doors for a time on the pretense of tending to tenant disputes. Lord knows he had dealt with several of those already this year.

Darcy's thoughts drifted to the thoroughbred Sophia Hawke had brought with her from Darlington. John Briggs, Pemberley's head groomsman, had been keen to display the animal upon his return to the stable this afternoon. He was a beautiful creature with exquisite lines, one he would not mind riding himself, as he appeared to be trained for both a woman's saddle and a man's. That was not a surprise to him. Richard had told him that

Miss Hawke rode astride when she was out on her own lands. John had mentioned that she had brought a side-saddle with her, and Darcy was grateful for her discretion. The servants were already chattering about her rifle. Apparently she did not travel without it. It was certainly unusual—though not unheard of— for a woman to participate in sport, but the man who stored it had noticed immediately that it was a Baker rifle, more commonly used as a military weapon. He had been both envious of the weapon and curious about its provenance. While he knew he need not comment on the weapon at all, Darcy had thought it best to plant the seed of an explanation, remarking in an off-handed manner that her steward's son had fought with the 95th. He would need to have Elizabeth relate this information to her new friend.

The door opened slowly and a soft laugh filled his ears. The small footsteps were undoubtedly Elizabeth's, and he lifted his eyelids slightly to peer at her.

"Have we worn you out already, dearest?" she said sweetly, placing a kiss on his forehead. "I'm afraid I have trapped you with the four of us rather effectively, though I assure you it was not my intention. I had thought that the viscount at least would be here this week to help you bear our company." She moved to the settee, her favorite perch near the fireplace, and he moved to sit beside her. He put his arm around her shoulders as she laid her head on his chest and sighed when Darcy drew a finger lovingly through one of her curls. Phillip had sent his regrets a few days earlier, stating he would be arriving later, most likely with his parents and young son.

"I know they are very different, William," she said gently. "But I like them. There is no artifice there, only rather a lack of diplomacy on Miss Evelyn's part and a habit of restraint on Miss Hawke's, understandable given their experiences. Miss Hawke does make the attempt to correct her sister, but she is gentle. Miss Evelyn seems to delight in resisting correction, not unlike every younger sister I have had the fortune to know." She placed her hand atop her husband's, and he flipped his hand, palm up, to capture it. He brought her hand to his lips for a kiss, and she hummed happily. "I feel we are in a fair way to become very good friends."

Darcy studied his wife's wan face. "How are you feeling, Elizabeth?" he asked. "Are you weary?"

She smiled dreamily. "No. I will allow that I was ill this morning, and I still cannot eat much, but I am not tired."

He continued to meet her gaze, waiting. "At the least," she conceded, "not as tired as I have been."

He grunted softly and pressed a kiss on the back of her neck. Any sign of improvement, no matter how small, was agreeable to him.

"Are you ready to retire, my love?" he asked, placing a kiss on the top of her head and a hand lightly on her stomach.

"Oh!" she cried, her hand flying to his, and he instantly pulled away.

"What is it? Did I hurt you?" he asked, startled. He had barely touched her.

"No, dearest, no! Did you not feel that?" Elizabeth was glowing.

"Feel what?"

Elizabeth shot her husband a look and fought not to roll her eyes. "The babe! He kicked me!"

"Surely not, Elizabeth," was his response, but it was said with wonder. Elizabeth did not truly take offense, though she did make a small impertinent noise something between a huff and a cough. She positioned both her hands on the spot where his had been.

"Here, William, here," she said, holding his hand over the spot. She waited a moment and then exclaimed, "There!"

He hated to do it, but he shrugged. He had felt nothing. Elizabeth was visibly disappointed.

"Perhaps it was not hard enough," he ventured. She glared at him.

"I assure you that it was quite hard enough. *You* will never have to endure someone kicking you from the inside," she said resentfully, and swung herself upright. She smoothed her skirts with three long strokes of her hands and said, "I am headed upstairs, William. You may join me or not, as you prefer."

With this pronouncement, reminiscent, he thought, of the child Georgiana used to be, she swept from the room, leaving Darcy to ruminate on the wearying transformation of his quiet home. Where was his level-headed, practical wife? He picked up his glass and finished off the brandy.

"A fortnight," he grumbled. "I cannot survive a fortnight. Richard had best be here soon."

Chapter Eight

EVELYN HAWKE POKED her head around the door of her sister's chambers. "Sophia?" she called.

Sophia was in the process of neatly removing the linens from her bed, and Evelyn moved fully into the room. "What are you doing?"

Sophia made a face. "I am afraid I cannot sleep with these bedclothes," she whispered, "but I do not wish to cause a fuss. I will ask for replacements tomorrow."

"You never make a fuss about anything, Sophia." Evelyn's tone was just shy of petulant. "What is wrong?"

Sophia wrinkled her nose in such an exaggerated manner that Evelyn laughed. "They smell like lily of the valley."

"So?"

"I cannot abide that scent."

"Whyever not?"

Sophia glanced at her sister and opened her mouth as though to speak, but closed it again without uttering a word. She began to gnaw, just a little, on her lower lip, an unladylike habit upon which her sister had often remarked. "No reason. I just detest it."

Evelyn stepped over to smell the pillow. Her eyebrows pinched together and she took a deeper, longer sniff. "It is there, but it is so faint, Sophia. How can that bother you? I know you believe you can smell everything, but this is taking things a bit far." Evelyn tilted her head and her hair, which had already been taken down, swept across her shoulder in a cascade of dark curls.

"I can smell it. Trust me, I will not sleep tonight unless I find something not doused in lily of the valley."

Evelyn shook her head. "Doused. Honestly. Here, come to my room and we can exchange. I do not believe my linens are scented."

Sophia glanced at her. "Thank you."

The two women walked through the connecting sitting room and into Evelyn's chambers. Evelyn immediately began to remove the bedclothes, but Sophia held one end up and took a deep breath. She gagged and stepped away.

"No, it is here as well."

Evelyn tossed down the sheet she was holding. "For heaven's sake, Sophia, what a spectacle. Just call the maid; she will find linens you can sleep in. I never thought you so particular. You are worse than a woman with child because you smell everything *all* the time. Perhaps you are part hound?"

Sophia blinked, but ignored the insult. She shook her head impatiently. "I am not going to wake a chambermaid to change my bed," she said sharply. "Do not be absurd." She frowned at her sister. "You do not remember?" Sophia asked.

"Remember what?" Evelyn asked, opening up her wardrobe and reaching to the shelf at the very top for an extra blanket. Sophia watched her sister teeter on her toes for a moment before easily reaching over Evie's head and pulling out the blanket. She took a long breath, her face in the wool. Nothing.

Sophia sighed, relieved. "No scent. I shall use the blanket in my room as well and be very warm tonight. Thank you, Evie."

"Is something the matter?" came a quiet voice. Miss Darcy was standing in the doorway holding a candle. She flushed when the attention of the sisters turned to her. "I heard voices as I was walking to my room," she explained.

"Oh no, Miss Darcy," Sophia replied quickly, "We are perfectly well, thank you."

Miss Darcy smiled and glanced down at her toes for a moment before lifting her gaze. "I know we have only been acquainted for a short time, but I do not believe I have ever laughed so much in my entire life. Between the two of you and my sister, I have no doubt we shall have a marvelous holiday, particularly when the Fitzwilliams arrive." She paused, battling her shyness for a moment, but then saying in a clear, confident voice, "I should like it very much if you would both call me Georgiana."

Evelyn looked at her sister. Sophia nodded and smiled. "We would be honored, Georgiana. You must return the honor, though, and address us by our Christian names. I am Sophia, and my sister is Evelyn."

"I am only Evelyn when I am doing everything correctly, Georgiana," Evelyn said with her eyes sparkling and her hands on her hips. She turned to face Sophia. "When I have said something shocking, I am called 'my dear.'" The sisters laughed softly together. "I do hope you will not often find it necessary to use the second appellation, but I am sure to respond to it."

"I shall endeavor to recall that," replied Georgiana with a giggle. "Is there a problem with your accommodations, Miss. . . Sophia?"

Sophia shook her head, but Evelyn was quicker. "She apparently cannot abide the scent of lily of the valley, Georgiana. I believe she was about to tell me why."

Sophia felt a flash of irritation. Did her sister think she kept stories to herself for no reason? "Oh no, Evie. If I tell this story, it will be with a full audience, including Mr. and Mrs. Darcy. I look foolish in it, as do you, and therefore would hope to maintain control of it by telling it myself, if I must." She had meant only to put her sister off the tale, but realized her mistake as she saw Georgiana's face light up with interest. She groaned quietly. "I shall tell it only once."

Evelyn was sure her sister was only trying to get out of relating something unpleasant. She would remember were she was a part of such a tale. She pursed her lips and replied, "I am not afraid of you, sister. I believe Georgiana and I would keep your confidence."

Sophia was uncertain, but thought perhaps Evelyn did recall and truly did not mind. She tapped her foot absently against the wood floor. Evie was so very difficult to understand.

"You may as well tell us, Sophia," said Evelyn, striking a rather commanding stance. Sophia found this entertaining. Her sister was much smaller than she and the air of authority she tried to impose upon others made her seem even younger than she was.

"Oh no, *my dear*," Sophia chuckled, reaching out to touch the end of her sister's nose affectionately. "You have insisted, so I shall tell the story, but another time. It is late."

Georgiana was observing the verbal jousting of the sisters, rather perplexed but thoroughly diverted. "Is there anything I can do tonight to make you more comfortable, Sophia? Evelyn?"

"Not tonight, Georgiana, I thank you," replied Sophia. "Although, I ought to have asked this afternoon, at what time does Mrs. Darcy normally rise? I am wondering whether I shall have time to ride before breaking my fast with you all."

Georgiana frowned. "Normally, Mrs. Darcy is quite an early riser, but she has slept later recently. She might not be downstairs until nearly midday."

Sophia's frown matched Georgiana's. She might not have Evie's knowledge of illness, but clearly Mrs.

Darcy's condition was more troublesome than she had at first surmised. The mistress of Pemberley was someone she believed might become a good friend. It was disconcerting to hear she was so indisposed and she felt a bit guilty about visiting at such a time. Mrs. Darcy had seemed fine this afternoon other than not eating much. "Thank you. I believe I shall ride early, then. Evie prefers to sleep in, particularly when the weather is cold, so I will see you both when I return."

"Very well, then," replied Georgiana softly. "I shall see you both tomorrow."

The women said their goodnights. Georgiana was curious to hear the story, but had no idea when her brother might next be coaxed into the drawing room. He had been very uncomfortable tonight. Perhaps this was Sophia's way of not telling the story at all. She might have to plead with Fitzwilliam, as she had a notion that Sophia Hawke's tale might be almost as amusing as a fearless Lizzy story, and she had no intention of missing out. Georgiana heard Sophia moving across the sitting room that connected her sister's room to her chambers and heard the door close softly before she walked to the family wing to her own.

Chapter Nine

SOPHIA HAWKE WAS AWAKE before the sun began to rise, shivering in her two blankets and unable to return to rest. She stirred up the fire a bit and then took out her riding habit. She quickly dressed herself, not wishing to wake the maid so early. Accustomed as she was to dressing herself, she was able to wriggle into her riding habit without too much trouble. She would have been entirely unable, she thought with a grin, to clothe herself in the more formal gowns she had packed for the visit. Still, while there were many moments when she missed the ease of wearing clothing that did not require assistance to don, she could not deny that dressing for dinner in her fine silk gowns was a pleasant luxury.

Her hair, however, was another matter altogether. All she could do this morning was gather her curls in a loose sort of knot at the back of her head. Even the maid had to tussle with her abundant, untidy locks. *Never mind*, she thought, as she tucked her hair up, *the hat will cover most of it*. Finally, she pulled on her boots, custom made, thicker than the typical woman's footwear, and slid her small knife into the sheath on the inside. She peeked at herself in the mirror and sighed. Passable.

She was anxious to see Rady and ride a little around the grounds. From what she could view from the carriage the day before, Pemberley consisted of a few gardens near the house and then all woods and meadows, peaks and valleys. The tenant farms must have been hidden behind the swell of the hills, but she imagined that even they were tidy and well maintained. Given the cold, she did not intend to wander far, but after spending half of the day before in a carriage and the remainder indoors, she was in desperate need of fresh air and exercise.

The grooms were already up brushing and feeding the horses when she wandered in. She did not see Rady immediately but presumed he was being brushed and contented herself by greeting some of the others. *The Darcys certainly have some fine specimens*, she thought, as she patted one long neck, then another. *Gelding. Mare. Thoroughbred. Arabian. Very well cared for, too*. A young man was working with a chestnut-colored stallion in an area a bit separated from the others, talking softly to him while he ate. *Spoiled*, she smiled. *Perhaps he has been ill or injured. Looks well enough now.*

"Heyup," she heard a flustered young voice say in a Derbyshire accent. "Oh, I mean, good morning, miss. I dinnit see you there."

Sophia turned to see the young man who was nervously shifting from one foot to the other. "Good morning. I am Miss Sophia Hawke, and I am looking for my thoroughbred. His name is Rhadamanthus and he was brought in yesterday when we arrived."

"Oh, yes, Miss," said the young man with a bit too much enthusiasm. "A beauty, he is."

"Do not let Rady hear you call him a beauty," she replied with a little laugh. "He would be highly offended. He is nothing if not entirely male."

The boy fell silent, clearly unsure how to answer such a statement, and Sophia felt a little abashed about having made it. "And who is this marvelous creature you are tending?"

"Ares, Miss," he said proudly.

"Aptly named, I am sure," she said with a smile. "Father of the Amazons," she said under her breath.

"What is your name? I cannot call you 'boy' as you are clearly quite grown."

"Harry Briggs, miss," he replied with a brief bow. His face was nearly glowing with the pleasure of her compliment.

What a wonderful boy, she thought as she watched him. "Well, Harry. Might you tell me where to find Rhadamanthus?"

Harry spoke seriously, as befitted a young man. "Oh, my father is seeing to him. They should be along shortly."

Sophia nodded. "Thank you, Harry."

Harry pulled at his cap. "Miss."

Harry returned to his work, and within a few minutes, a man who was clearly Harry's father entered the stables leading Rady. Harry had his father's build, his sandy-colored hair, and, as the man drew closer, Sophia realized that they had the same brown eyes. She met them at the door and greeted Rady with a pat and a carrot.

"You must be Miss Hawke," the man said gruffly. "Are you riding this early? It is rather cold out still."

"I am not usually quite so early, Mr. Briggs," she replied lightly, "but this morning I was anxious to see more of the grounds, and," she spoke softly near Rady's ear, "I missed this boy."

John Briggs nodded curtly. "A moment, miss."

As he led Rady off, Sophia glanced over at Harry. "Is he always so talkative?" she asked. Harry's eyes widened. Sophia shook her head. *Well done, Sophia, you have frightened him.*

"I beg your pardon, Harry," she explained, "I was only attempting a jest. A poor one, as it turns out."

Harry's eyes returned to their normal size and he let out a breath. He nodded. After a moment of silence, he said in a rush, his cheeks quite red, "My father is the very best of men, Miss Hawke."

"I am sure of it. Any man who runs a stable as well kept as this one could hardly be anything less, now could he?" She smiled. *More to the point*, she thought, *any man who has inspired such devotion in his son must have at least some good in him.* She thought of Oliver, not for the first time, and felt the familiar ache. Would he have grown up like this boy, idolizing their father? Would the two of them always have been off together, riding about the estate?

Her pronouncement cheered Harry a good deal, and while she reveled in the fresh winter air, the boy smiled widely and turned back to his work. He hummed a tune, just a bit off-key, and soon his father was back with Rady, who pawed at the ground and snorted a welcome to her.

"If you follow me, Miss Hawke," he said brusquely, "the mounting block is just around the corner there." As she reached the steps and mounted, taking control of Rady, another man appeared on a horse behind her, clearly a groomsman. She glanced questioningly at John.

"Master's orders, miss," he said in a warning tone. "Nobody rides out alone in this weather, particularly guests who might not know the estate. 'Tis easy to get lost. Freddie knows his way around."

Sophia stared at John Briggs. She truly wished not to be a bother, and intended to tell him it was not necessary to provide an escort, but her throat constricted suddenly, and she cleared it to distract herself from the tears she felt forming. *Do not be absurd*, she scolded herself, but the kindness was entirely unexpected and struck her hard. *Nobody ever cares where I go*. She had not had the opportunity to ride often at Matlock, but at Darlington she would simply leave word of her destination and head out alone. No one ever suggested that she take an escort or concerned themselves if she was late, nobody cautioned her about getting lost, although Darlington's lands had at first been only a bit more familiar to her than Pemberley's. Even Evie simply assumed that she would be fine no matter where she roamed. She was Darlington's master in every way but the name, and each soul who lived within its boundaries was beholden to her. Sophia loved her home, and it was not that she minded either the work or the independence it both offered and required; she was simply unaccustomed to having another person assume care for her. Sophia took a deep breath and nodded at John, whose eyes had narrowed as he tried to gauge her reaction.

"Very well, then. I shall be able to range a little farther afield than I had planned. Thank you, Mr. Briggs."

"John, Miss." John nodded once and stepped away.

"Very well." Sophia swallowed, attempted a smile, and then checked her seat. Once she was ready, she nodded at Freddie, a rather heavyset young man riding what appeared to be a tall gray and white Lipizzan, and they set off toward the eastern paths.

John Briggs watched them leave the stables. Miss Hawke's response to the required escort was quite unlike Mrs. Darcy's, and he was not sure what to make of it. The master had been certain the woman would protest, and John had been prepared to be firm about guests following the master's rules, but rather than making trouble, she had merely appeared startled, then acquiesced with grace and gone on her way. Perhaps she would not present the challenge the mistress did. He hoped that was the case. He had plenty of work to tend to without worrying about another headstrong woman on the grounds.

"Harry," he called and walked over to check on Ares. "How does he do today?"

***

Sophia Hawke took Rady through his paces, though there would be no galloping across the meadows today. The weather was cold, and she was worried about ice. She would leave that sort of exercise to the grooms, who knew the estate well enough to know where it might be safe to run or exercise him near the stables. For the moment, she was merely hoping to get to higher ground. She identified a likely path and started uphill. By the time she made the summit, Freddie trailing behind her, the sun was almost entirely above the horizon, and they stilled their mounts to watch the final moments of the sunrise, red and orange rays illuminating a sky that was gradually turning from gray to blue. Sophia took a deep breath in. She loved the northern counties, the deep green of the trees, the comforting scents of alder, elm, oak, walnut, the promise of wild roses and lavender, the craggy hills and rolling fields. The day was beginning unusually clear, but without the cloud cover it was also quite cold, and Sophia could feel her fingers growing numb through her gloves. Finally, she turned to Freddie with a smile and indicated they should return to the stables. He replied with a nod, and they began the descent.

Her departure had been so early that even by the time she had returned to her room to dress for the day, much of the house remained quiet. As she entered the breakfast room for some tea, Mr. Darcy was seated at the table reading a newspaper. She nodded genially at him and poured, sitting a few chairs down to allow him the privacy to continue his reading. Instead, he folded the paper politely and set it next to his plate.

"Do not feel you must entertain me, Mr. Darcy," she said lightly. "I would not wish to interrupt your morning routine."

"Not at all, Miss Hawke. Have you been out already this morning?"

She nodded as she raised a teacup to her lips. After she had taken a sip of tea and felt the welcoming warmth slide down her throat into her stomach, she said, "I was anxious to have a look around your lovely grounds, Mr. Darcy. I took Rady out for a short ride."

"Were you accompanied?" he asked nonchalantly.

She smiled. "Yes, sir. It was kind of you to think of it." She took another sip and raised an eyebrow before continuing. "I will say that John Briggs seemed prepared for an argument."

"Well, knowing my wife, Miss Hawke, he probably was expecting one."

"She enjoys her solitude, I presume."

"Indeed."

She considered that for a moment as she sipped her tea. When she spoke, it was with a mournful expression that faded nearly as soon as it appeared. "I daresay I have had a good deal more solitude than I know what to do with, Mr. Darcy. I do not object to the escort."

Darcy watched Miss Hawke rise, moving to the window to contemplate the wintery scene outside. He had thought her somewhat like Elizabeth with her teases and the way she guided her younger sister's improper speech with a kind of loving firmness. She was even more independent than Elizabeth, and she carried a quiet confidence with her in nearly everything she did. Unlike Elizabeth, she did not insist upon being treated in a certain way as a matter of principle. She simply went about her business because it needed to be done, seeming to believe that she did so entirely unnoticed. There was something in her bearing that reminded him of himself in the years just after the death of his own father, when he had at last learned enough of the estate that he could finally raise his head to see how alone he really was. Perhaps Sophia Hawke was becoming fond of Elizabeth precisely because of the ways in which they were not alike, and similar to so many other people, she gained something from his wife's cheerful spirit.

Darcy's thoughts moved upstairs to his bedchambers, where Elizabeth had already been ill this morning and had returned to sleep. He had given himself over to the worries that were his constant companions now, when the faint clinking of a teacup being placed back in its saucer broke that line of thought and he glanced up to see Miss Hawke making ready to depart. He stood.

"Mr. Darcy, I bid you a good day."

"Is that all you wish to have, Miss Hawke?"

"I will wait for the other ladies to break my fast, Mr. Darcy, but it was quite cold out, and the tea was lovely."

"Then I shall see you at dinner if not before."

"Until then, Mr. Darcy."

Darcy watched her leave the room. He thought about returning to his newspaper but left it on the table, deciding that he would check on Elizabeth again before he removed to the stables himself.

Chapter Ten

ELIZABETH WOKE TO FIND Darcy sitting on the side of the bed staring at her and caressing her cheek. She smiled weakly, but he did not return it.

"You have been weeping, Elizabeth," he said quietly, the pad of his thumb gently tracing the remnants of her tears.

"I am sorry to worry you, William," she whispered miserably. "It truly is no worse than it has been, but I have never in my life been ill for so long and I am afraid I am finding it difficult to remain patient. I am so very weary of going to bed mostly well and awaking out of sorts."

Darcy was silent as he moved his hand to stroke her hair. He felt entirely helpless in the face of her distress. Elizabeth was among the strongest women he knew. If she was being reduced to tears, her illness must be worse even than he feared. He had heard nothing from the letters he had sent nor could he reasonably expect a response for weeks. It was difficult not to consider mounting a horse and riding directly to London himself. It was closer than Edinburgh and the weather heading south would be at least marginally warmer. He began to plan the details of such a journey but stopped abruptly when he realized that they were so close to Christmas now he was likely to arrive only to find the buildings entirely vacated until after Twelfth Night. Such a trip would also mean leaving Elizabeth with only Georgiana and her guests to assist her. No, the plan was impractical, and the thought of leaving Elizabeth at such a time impossible. After the disaster of their brief separation last summer, he had promised both her and himself that he would not leave again until after the babe was born, and then only if she could travel with him. He would not break that promise; indeed, he did not think himself capable of it.

What was to be done? He leaned in to kiss her forehead. "What may I do for you, Elizabeth?" he finally asked, desperate to aid in her relief.

"Just hold me, William," she said, placing a hand lightly on his arm, "it makes me far more comfortable."

Darcy immediately eased himself onto the bed and placed an arm behind her. Elizabeth dropped her head on his chest and wrapped one arm around his waist.

"Better?" he asked hopefully, continuing to stroke her hair.

"Much," she mumbled, and quickly fell asleep.

"Oh, my darling girl," he said in a whisper, watching her breathing steady and deepen, "you must be well. I cannot do without you." He felt more than he said, but it was beyond his power to speak the words. He tightened his arm, bringing her body a little closer to his own. *It took me far too long to win you, my love. I will not allow you to leave me so soon.*

When Elizabeth's maid knocked softly on the door and entered some time later, she found her master and mistress asleep on the bed. The master was fully clothed down to the boots he had not bothered to remove, yet the mistress was still in her nightclothes, her head and one hand resting on his chest. He was holding her tightly, one arm tucked around her shoulders, the other wrapped across her waist, his cheek resting on the top of her head. The maid exited as quietly as she could, catching the attention of a chambermaid on the stairs to mention that the fire in her mistress' chamber should be built up, but to be very still about it.

***

Not for the first time, Sophia Hawke found herself searching for her sister. When she had returned from a noon ride, Evie was nowhere to be found. She was not in the still room, nor was she reading in the library. Sophia had even checked the chapel, though she did not believe Evie knew the room existed. The day had become sunny and pleasant, even mild for a December afternoon, and she next walked out into the gardens, but they too were empty.

"Like a child," Sophia muttered to herself and rubbing her forehead as if pained, "taking herself off with no word." While she enjoyed the outdoors a good deal more than Evelyn, Sophia always left word where she would be and when she expected to return. It was exasperating not to be afforded the same simple courtesy by her younger sibling, particularly as this was a topic they had broached many times. There was nothing for it. She would have to make a circuit of the house, beginning with the outside. Fortunately, her boots and riding coat were still near the back door drying from the morning's exercise. She slipped the articles back on and escaped through the kitchen without much notice being taken.

She had just turned the corner near the laundry at the very back of the manor house, on the same path she had taken to the stables earlier when she saw Evie chatting to the maids as they worked outside in the comparatively mild weather, chopping up the mottled soap, dropping soiled sheets into large pots of boiling lye. One maid added a vial of something to the hot water. As she watched, another maid lifted the linens out of the lye to immerse them in cold water. Yet two more maids worked to work them through a large wringer and then, given the cold weather, took turns walking the cleaned sheets inside to be hung near the fire. She thought the maids looks a bit impatient with her sister who was likely asking many questions about the process, but when they spied Sophia, their faces became embarrassed or knowing.

Oh, no, she thought. *What has Evie said now?*

"Evie, my dear," she called. "You are wanted inside."

Evelyn turned around to face her sister, the picture of innocence. "I cannot imagine for what, Sophia. I am just asking about the chemical process of the wash." Sophia clearly saw one of the maids roll her eyes.

This was a complication. She wished to limit whatever damage was being caused, which required extracting Evelyn without a scene.

"It will be time to dress for dinner soon. I am retrieving you so that you may have your turn with the maid first tonight." There was movement around the front corner of the house; a figure was drawing near. She saw a flash of red and nearly groaned. *What is he doing here?* Her attention swiftly returned to her sister when she heard Evelyn's response.

"Oh, that is nothing," she replied with an airy wave of her hand. "You may seek her services first."

Sophia leaned down to speak in her sister's ear and said in a low voice that was nearly a growl, "Evie, go inside. I do not wish to have this conversation here." When she lifted her eyes, she spied the colonel in conversation with one of the maids, Ruth, if she recalled. The maid was a pretty girl, perhaps seventeen years old, and seemed charmed by the colonel, dropping her head and blushing. He began to stomp his boots on the stairs and then tapped them against the risers to clear the soles of mud while Ruth moved indoors. The colonel was glancing over at the two of them with an unreadable expression on his face. Ruth, however, was gazing over her shoulder at him.

Hmmm, was Sophia's only thought.

Beside her, Evelyn's eyes had clouded over and her shoulders tensed. She turned to her sister and began to whisper angrily that she was not required to follow her sister's orders, but was cut off by Colonel Fitzwilliam's greetings.

"Miss Hawke, Miss Evelyn," he said with a bow. The two women curtsied before they stood awkwardly facing him while ignoring one another.

"Colonel," said Evelyn in a clipped tone. "You will excuse me. I shall see you at dinner?"

"I look forward to it, Miss Evelyn," he replied, a bit taken aback at her abrupt dismissal. She nodded, shot her sister what could only be called a venomous look, and walked away. Sophia watched her go, her expression a mixture of anger and embarrassment.

"My apologies, Colonel," she said softly. "I am afraid I must speak to my sister." She too turned and made for the house, too distracted to see his disappointment.

***

It was already late in the afternoon when there was a commotion in the hall and Darcy heard a powerful knock at the study door. The door flew open to reveal the horrified glance of a footman and Richard's grinning face in the doorway. The colonel stood there for a moment, leaning against the doorframe, sandy hair windswept, hazel eyes bright with mirth. After a moment to take in his cousin's surprised face, he entered the room without being invited and threw himself into a chair by the fire. Darcy nodded to the footman who retreated, leaving the door ajar, and then turned his eyes to Richard. His cousin was missing his coat, which James had likely removed and Wilkins would already be transporting to a valet for brushing. Confirming his supposition, the sounds of the old butler clucking in disapproval over the state of Richard's regimentals floated back to him through the open door. The boots that now rested on the ottoman had been cleaned, he noted with a shake of his head. Richard had clearly left his coat befouled with the dirt of the road intentionally for the benefit of aggravating his staff.

"Come right in," Darcy said dourly, despite the fact that he was overjoyed to see his cousin. "No need to be announced."

"Please, Darcy," Richard laughed, "is that any way to greet your rescuer?"

"What rescue do you intend to mount, precisely?" *Rescuing me*, Darcy thought. *That is precisely what he is doing.*

"Why, Phillip told me you were quite on your own up here with four women and not a single man to buffer you from their conversation. While that might be a boon for me, he knew well it would be a punishment for the voluble Fitzwilliam Darcy. So my brother took pity on you and asked whether I might request my leave a bit early to stand in his place." He tossed himself into the chair by the fire and put his feet up on the ottoman. "I spoke with my general, explained that what with the cold weather and the festive season upon us that there was precious little for me to do and that if he had any dispatches for the north I should be pleased to hand deliver them, and I was sent off with his thanks."

He grinned even wider at Darcy, making no attempt to temper his high spirits. Working at the War Office satisfied his need to be of use, but after being in the field for so many years, most of his days were nothing short of stifling. The unexpectedly early leave and the long ride had left him feeling a bit like a schoolboy at the end of term. He spied a twitch in Darcy's cheek.

"I can see by that slightest of cracks in your stony façade that I am correct. You *are* glad to see me." He chuckled. "You are *relieved* to see me."

Darcy stood, folded his arms across his chest, and scowled. "If you would cease your prattling even for a moment, I would tell you as much." Then he allowed the smile he had felt building since Richard's appearance to spread across his face, and he moved around his desk to shake his cousin's hand.

He rang the bell and requested tea and, in response to Richard's raised eyebrows, moved to pour some brandy as well.

"Now, William," said Richard when Darcy had shut the door and they were both seated near the fire, "shall I ask what Miss Hawke and Miss Evelyn were doing near the laundry, or is domestic investigation another of their mysterious skills?" He paused. "Actually, I think Miss Evelyn was there first, and Miss Hawke came to fetch her. Neither seemed particularly pleased with the other."

Darcy was startled. "They were near the laundry? I cannot imagine why, Richard." He paused before asking the obvious question. "Why were *you* near the laundry? You certainly did not offer your coat up for cleaning."

Richard laughed. "I have to give Wilkins some reason to disapprove or the visit would be incomplete. Best to get it out of the way at once and allow the man some peace." He waved one foot at his cousin. "I was cleaning my boots so as not to track mud across your floor. Even Wilkins does not deserve that. Consider it your Christmas gift."

Soon the men were enjoying their tea. Richard quickly dispatched several scones with jam and helped himself to the larger portion of the brandy.

"How long has it been since you have eaten, cousin?" Darcy asked with a shake of his head. "I would tell you not to spoil your dinner, but I know your appetite is sufficiently healthy." He grimaced a little, thinking of Elizabeth.

"Nearly seventy miles," Richard relied, noting the expression on Darcy's face but choosing not to remark upon it. "I broke my fast early this morning, but was hoping to deliver my final missive and reach Pemberley before dinner."

"You made good time," was the only response.

"I did indeed." Richard tossed back the last of the brandy and set down the glass. "So, my friend, how is your wife?"

As he intended, his question hit the mark. Darcy's face grew pensive.

"Not well, Richard. She puts as brave a face on it as she is able, but she is suffering and I can do nothing to help."

"Is she confined to bed? I think all this company is hardly appropriate if she is so ill."

"She is worse in the morning. It takes until nearly midday for her to rise. Then she seems to improve the longer she is downstairs, though she rarely risks appearing at dinner. The Hawkes arrived a few days ago, and I admit to some concern, but it is the happiest I have seen Elizabeth in months. She is laughing and lively with them, almost her normal self. But in the mornings she is ill again. She keeps almost nothing down." He ran a hand through his hair. "I am worried for her."

Richard was trying to compose a response when there was a soft knock on the door and Darcy called "Come."

Mrs. Reynolds opened the door, her face uncertain and apologetic. "I am sorry to disturb you, sir, but Miss Hawke was hoping to speak with the colonel."

"Now?" asked Richard, annoyed. "Cannot it wait?"

Darcy rose with a grin. "Now who needs to be rescued?" He clapped Richard on the back. "Go ahead. Let me finish my work. Billiards tonight?"

Richard eyed him warily. "I suppose that will be an improvement upon hiding in your study."

Darcy shook his head. "You know me too well, Richard," he said wryly. "Go on. I shall see you for dinner in a few hours."

The colonel nodded and strode out into the hall with Mrs. Reynolds. "Where may I find Miss Hawke?"

"She asked that you meet her by the laundry. She said you had seen her there earlier." Mrs. Reynolds appeared a little shocked that a guest would be frequenting that area of the house, but she was too well trained to say anything. Richard nodded and turned to go. *Let us get this over with so I can change and speak with William again*, he thought. Miss Hawke was one of the reasons he had been so enthusiastic about arriving early, but she had barely acknowledged his presence before running off after her sister.

He walked down the stairs and to the back of the house only to find her standing with her hands on her hips and her lips pursed in what he thought might be frustration. She was making some sort of request, it seemed, and was less than pleased with the response. He stood there for a moment, watching her. When she glanced up to see that he had arrived, he began to walk to meet her. Her face lit up in a wide smile, her light curls pulled gently away from her face to reveal those eyes, so stormy, so deeply blue they were almost black. He stopped short and felt his mouth go dry before smiling back, his good humor completely restored.

"Colonel," she said, meeting his gaze and looking reassured, "thank you for coming. I find I am in need of your assistance."

"I am at your service, madam," he said with a small bow.

"I am trying to persuade the laundry maids to provide me with an unscented set of linens."

Richard raised an eyebrow.

"I have a theory and I would like to test its accuracy," she replied in answer to his expression of curiosity. When he remained silent, she begrudgingly continued. "Yes, I know," she said with a sigh. "It is presumptuous. I have only just asked for a set for my own chambers. However, what I ask is so very simple."

"I am afraid I require an explanation, Miss Hawke."

Sophia Hawke pulled him aside to speak privately.

"I merely wish the maids to use unscented linens for Mrs. Darcy. I believe the scent may be contributing to her illness."

Richard was puzzled. "In what way?"

Miss Hawke worried her lower lip just a little, something Richard knew she often did as she ordered her thoughts.

"My sister made a comment that started me thinking."

"A dangerous pastime, no doubt," Richard teased. Sophia just shook her head.

"This is hardly a joke, Colonel Fitzwilliam."

"My apologies, Miss Hawke. What did your sister say?"

"She mentioned that women who are with child often develop a keen sense of smell, and that it can increase their nausea. She was mocking me, as I have a very keen sense of smell all the time. Thus I am aware that I must avoid certain scents. One is lily of the valley."

"That seems an unusual scent to avoid, Miss Hawke," Richard interrupted. She just sighed at his inability to remain silent and he motioned for her to continue.

"Nevertheless, the odor makes me ill. Therefore, when I noticed the linens in my room were scented with it, I had to ask the chambermaid to change them. My sister said that the scent was barely noticeable and the maid could not smell anything at all, but it is there, I promise you. So it made me connect the two. "

Richard saw where her thoughts tended. "You thought although the scent was negligible to others, in her current condition it might be enough to cause Mrs. Darcy's illness."

"To contribute to it, at least. When I was here earlier, I noticed one of the maids adding something to the washing water, and was told it was the fragrance. Evidently it makes the job easier to do as it eases the odor of the cleaning solutions." She hesitated. "I do not wish to bother Mr. or Mrs. Darcy with the notion in case it is nothing. I should not wish to raise hopes." Her voice lowered. "I should hesitate to disappoint Mr. Darcy in particular. It is easy to see how anxious he is for his wife."

Richard felt his stomach churn a bit uneasily. He had not yet seen Elizabeth. Darcy had said he was worried, but he was always worried. Was his new cousin truly as ill as all that? "Well then," Richard said with a small shrug of his shoulders, "how may I be of help?"

"The laundry maids will not give me the time of day," she said, exasperated. "Apparently they are all convinced that there is no discernible fragrance in the sheets and that I am merely being difficult."

Richard laughed. "Well, despite that being the case. . ." He held up his hands when she scowled at him.

"Ruth in particular has been blunt in her refusals," Miss Hawke said quietly, "but she seems to favor you."

Richard scoffed at that, but when he was rewarded with a frown and an arched eyebrow, he relented. "Fine."

"Ruth," he called. The ginger-haired maid stepped over to the colonel, but not until she shot a nasty look at Miss Hawke. Though he hid it well, Richard was surprised at the open hostility of her behavior.

"Yes, sir?" Ruth's face lit up when she spoke with him, but Richard tried to ignore it. He glanced uneasily at Miss Hawke to see whether she had marked it. He could see that she was schooling her features. She had observed it. Why had he not seen it himself before now? He quickly returned to the task at hand.

"Is there a reason not to comply with Miss Hawke's request?"

"Sir, we dint answer to guests, just to Mrs. Reynolds."

Sophia shook her head, clearly exasperated, though she remained polite. "Why did you not say before? I would have happily asked her. I meant only to save her the time. As it is, I had to ask her to fetch the colonel."

Ruth pointedly ignored her, focusing all of her attention on Colonel Fitzwilliam. If she was seeking an ally, she was disappointed. Richard stared at the girl until she began to look at her feet. He had never known Ruth to be less than pleasant to anyone, let alone a guest. She could easily have provided the linens. He did not understand why she had not.

He cleared his throat. "Shall I call Mrs. Reynolds from her duties to attend you?"

Ruth lifted one foot slightly, then put it down and lifted the other uncomfortably.

"Nay, sir."

"Then please provide the bedclothes to Miss Hawke and I shall escort her to Mrs. Reynolds so we may see to this personally."

"Yes, sir." Ruth was not happy to comply, but she disappeared into the laundry and returned with a large stack of linens. She thrust them at Miss Hawke.

"Thank you, Ruth," Sophia said politely. Ruth gave her a shallow curtsey and returned to her work. Sophia turned to Richard. "Thank you, Colonel."

He held out his arms. "Let me carry those for you, Miss Hawke." Behind him, Sophia could see Ruth's shoulders slump.

"One moment, please," she said, and placed her face near the bundle she carried. She sniffed each sheet and the blanket before smiling and handing them over. Neither Sophia nor Richard noticed Ruth watching them from just inside the laundry as they conversed, nor did they hear her mutter something that sounded like "Jezebel" as she disappeared indoors.

"I do not understand why this was so difficult," Richard said as he turned to walk back to the main house. "Pemberley servants are usually very accommodating, particularly for guests. Any slight such as this is a poor reflection on the mistress, and Elizabeth is highly regarded here."

Sophia stopped, lifted her shoulders. "But apparently I am not. The chambermaid even argued with me when I asked her to change my bedclothes, and I was forced to come here to collect them." She shook her head. "I do not believe I have been here long enough to offend the servants, but I must have said or done something amiss."

"I would have thought that office belonged to your sister," Richard replied before he thought about his words. He grimaced and cleared his throat. "I apologize, Miss Hawke."

"Apologize?" she asked, resigned, but with a good-natured shake of her head, "Whatever for? You and I both know it is nothing but the truth."

Richard laughed. "I suppose we are beyond false flattery, then."

"Indeed, far beyond." Her lips lifted into a small, tight smile. "But you will have to remind me of any flattery at all that has arisen from your side, sir, for surely I have not heard it."

Richard played along. "I did tell my father you were an excellent shot."

Sophia laughed then, a full, throaty sound that made Richard grin. "Well, Colonel, that is simply the truth, so it can hardly be termed flattery. I believe I can best you still. Is your cousin a better shot? Perhaps I shall have to lay in a wager so I might afford a larger house. I have great plans," she said, raising her eyebrows conspiratorially.

"If you wish to wager, Phillip is the mark," he replied teasingly. "He could not hit a bird if it was stock still and three feet from him, but he believes himself a great hunter. Even my father bags more birds."

"That is excellent intelligence, Colonel," she replied with a small smile and a shake of the head. She sobered as she considered walking to the main entrance or heading to the back of the house.

"Shall we enter through the kitchen? If we can avoid Mr. Darcy asking what we are about, I would prefer that."

"Ah, a secret mission," Richard said softly.

"You should be quite practiced at those, Colonel, working for the War Office."

"Oh, we only make plans, Miss Hawke, we do not execute them."

Sophia raised her eyebrows quizzically. "Forgive me, sir, but that does sound rather dull."

"Not at all, Miss Hawke," replied the colonel with a shrug and a lopsided grin. "We have, after all, promised one another the truth."

"So the kitchen entrance, then?"

"I think it our best option, yes."

The colonel and Sophia strolled to the side entrance and then sidled their way through the hive of activity in the kitchen, where servants were chopping, mixing, cleaning, and checking the food already being cooked in their preparations for dinner. If they earned a few curious or sidelong glances, they pretended not to notice, and soon they were out in the hall. With a brief touch of her hand to his arm and a slight, sweet smile, she disappeared in search of Mrs. Reynolds. As she slipped away, he suddenly wondered how Sophia Hawke had managed to drag him there and then abandon him to cool his heels in the servants' hall. What would he say should anyone see him and wonder why he standing here holding a stack of sheets and blankets like a chambermaid?

A few moments later, she reappeared with a young girl and he willingly handed the bundle over. The girl scurried up the back stairs, but Richard was more interested in watching Miss Hawke as she followed the girl's progress with her eyes and that unsettling, intense stare he had grown to appreciate so long as he was not the object of it. There was something underneath the glare that spoke of experiences he thought might break his heart. He had plenty of those himself.

"Thank you again, Colonel. I hope that it helps. It was all I could think to do."

"Well, at the least it cannot hurt, Miss Hawke." He offered her his arm and as she accepted it he led her back out into the public hall. "May I ask, though, if it is the scent causing the problem, would not Mrs. Darcy have already detected it and asked that it be removed?"

"I do not know, Colonel. I simply thought that if she was overwhelmed with odors, she might not be able to distinguish so well between them. As unwell as she has been, she may just not have thought of it."

"So will you tell the story of why you so detest this innocent flower?" he asked, unaccountably curious.

She laughed. "I shall be required to do so. I have already promised my sister and Georgiana. Eventually you shall all hear the sad little tale if we can keep Mr. Darcy in our company long enough. I required full attendance as I do not wish to tell the story twice."

Is it Georgiana already? That is quick work. "I see I must be my cousin's keeper," he said with a smile.

Her shoulders lifted slightly with quiet laughter. "I am afraid that we have had a good deal of pleasure at his expense. My sister realized early that her bold speech makes Mrs. Darcy laugh, so she has been rather freer with it than is even her habit. I have been serving dutifully as her foil. Unfortunately, those same remarks have sent Mr. Darcy fleeing from the drawing room more than once."

Richard laughed. "Yes, other than his wife and sister, he is not known for his fondness for female conversation."

"Oh, dear," sighed Sophia in an exaggerated but good-humored show of concern. "However then did he manage to *meet* his lovely wife?"

"That is a story for the ages," Richard began, and smiled brightly. "Do you recall Mr. Bingley?"

"Of course. The amiable man who takes prodigious care of his friends yet does not always know when to hold his tongue," she said slyly. Richard laughed and nodded.

"Well, Darcy was visiting Bingley at a country estate in Hertfordshire. . ."

Chapter Eleven

ELIZABETH OPENED HER EYES to the weak sunlight pushing its way through the gap between the curtains. She yawned and stretched a little from her position propped up on several pillows. She could not sleep flat on her back without losing her breath, but she was growing used to sleeping half-sitting up in bed. Beside her was her husband, lying on his stomach, one arm wrapped protectively around her hips just below the swell of her stomach. His face was turned down towards his feet, leaving her a view of his thick black curls. She considered, idly, that his hair had grown a little longer than he usually wore it. She smiled as she leaned back on her pillows, pulled the blanket up to her chin, and closed her eyes again, placing one hand gently on his forearm. She sighed contentedly. *Warm.*

When she woke some time later, he had turned his face up towards her. She traced his familiar features and remained very still for a few moments, trying to judge how she felt. Her stomach was still a little uneasy and her head a bit heavy, but she was not in danger of casting up her accounts. She took a deep breath. Nothing but a little flutter. The babe seemed to be asleep as well. She placed her hands on her stomach and rubbed gently before stretching both arms out wide, relishing the moment, before putting a hand on her husband's head and stroking his hair tenderly.

His eyes were immediately open and seeking hers. "Are you well, Elizabeth?" he asked.

"I am almost afraid to say it, William," she nearly whispered, his head lifting slightly to catch her words, "but I believe I am much improved."

Fitzwilliam could scarcely believe it. He had asked her the same question every morning for months. Every morning he had prayed to hear this, and every morning he had been disappointed.

"Truly?" he asked, his heart in his throat. "Do you think you could eat?"

She nodded. "A little, at least," she said softly.

His face split into a wide smile, a deep dimple showing on each cheek. "I will ring for food directly." He eased himself off the bed and leapt for his clothes. His nightshirt went flying and Elizabeth laughed merrily at her serious husband as he hopped around the room tugging his trousers up to his waist before reaching to grab a clean shirt. His valet would not be pleased.

"Just toast and tea, William. I do not want to risk anything more."

"Perhaps an egg as well, dearest?" Darcy asked hopefully.

She smiled. "I will try, William. Nothing else at present, though, please."

He nodded, and still smiling, strode back to the bed, took her face between his two hands, and kissed her soundly. Then he was out the door, having rung the bell for the maid but unwilling to wait for her. Elizabeth heard his booming voice as it traveled down the hall and shook her head.

Insufferable man, she thought affectionately. *How I do love him.*

***

"What was that ridiculous performance this morning, William?" Richard asked as he entered Darcy's study. "I do not believe the rest of the house rises at dawn, but there was no sleeping for anyone with all your caterwauling."

Darcy just smiled. It had not been dawn, but he would not have cared if it had been. Elizabeth had eaten two slices of dry toast and an egg, consumed an entire cup of tea, and had kept it all down. Not much, but a proper meal compared to her morning repast these last months. Then she had sighed contentedly and fallen asleep in his arms. It had been a wonderful morning, and not even Richard would goad him out of his good mood. He met his cousin's gaze and grinned.

"Elizabeth ate this morning. She felt a good deal better, Richard."

Richard bowed his head and had a silent little laugh. *She was right.* He wondered if she knew. He looked up to see his cousin's inquisitive gaze focused on him.

"Who was right?" Darcy asked, glancing at a letter on his desk.

"Nothing," replied Richard, waving one hand. "I was just thinking about something else."

Darcy looked up and shook his head stubbornly. "You said 'She was right.'"

He paused. "Miss Hawke had a theory."

"About?"

"Elizabeth."

"Miss Hawke was speculating about my wife?"

Richard glanced up. Darcy was not angry or offended, merely bemused.

"Apparently, Miss Hawke has a very sensitive sense of smell, and realized that the linens have been washed in a scent, lily of the valley, I think she said. It was very faint, but she has a dislike for the fragrance and requested that her linens not be scented. Then, her sister mentioned that women in Elizabeth's condition tend also to have a strong sense of smell that sometimes makes them ill. So she put the two together and asked the chambermaids to change Elizabeth's bedclothes."

"Why did she not mention this to Elizabeth?"

"She did not wish either of you to be disappointed should she be wrong."

"So the sheets were exchanged. . ."

"Yesterday," Richard replied, "before everyone went up to dress for dinner."

Darcy nodded before something occurred to him. "Is that what she was doing near the laundry?"

"Indeed. She summoned me to request assistance with the servants."

"Why?" Darcy asked with some surprise.

Richard grimaced. "They were giving her a good deal of grief. It was quite odd. Even Ruth was rather obstinate about it. They did hand them over to me directly. Though," Richard said thoughtfully, scratching his chin, "even then they did require that I threaten them with Mrs. Reynolds."

"That is rather unusual," Darcy said, unsettled by the notion that any guests at Pemberley would have trouble with the servants. Most of the staff had been even more solicitous than usual since the summer, but he knew they had lost a handful of maids and even a few of the younger footmen once the fear of the illness was past. Those who resigned their positions had, for the most part, been newer hires, brought on and trained following his marriage, and were less loyal to the family. Although he and his wife had not broached the issue, they were both aware that the epidemic and Elizabeth's unorthodox response to it had frightened them away. Some had decided to seek out factory jobs in the north or in London and a few were hired by other estates. Elizabeth had given them each good characters and had wished them well before working with Mrs. Reynolds to hire new staff in their place. She had been stronger then, not quite as thin or as tired.

Mrs. Reynolds would need to hear about this, though typically such a conversation would be Elizabeth's office. He would have to first speak to his wife. She was feeling better, but he could not be sanguine. He wanted her to rest as often as possible.

"So I thought as well," Richard was saying, bringing Darcy's attention back to the conversation. Suddenly, he realized what all of this meant.

"The bedclothes," Darcy said quietly. "Has it been that all this time?"

"I do not know for certain," Richard replied, "but if Elizabeth feels somewhat better now, is not that all that matters?"

"We had two midwives and an accoucheur here to try to help her, Richard. Even Waters could not help, but Miss Hawke figured this out in one week's time?"

"She listens and observes, William. She puts things together in unusual ways." He tapped the floor with the toes of his boot. "She remembered her sister's comment and she herself has a difficulty with the scent. However, she truly did not know whether it would make any difference at all. She merely hoped." Richard moved into the room and sat down. "I believe she is quite fond of Elizabeth."

Darcy nodded. "Elizabeth is fond of her as well." *I never gave a moment's thought to whether or not there was a scent on the linens.* He stood and moved towards the door, but Richard's voice called him back.

"William, I would ask you not to broach this topic with Miss Hawke. I was under strict orders not to reveal her part in this, and I do not wish to undergo the rebuke that is sure to come from it."

Darcy stopped and turned back to face his cousin. "Why would she not wish us to know that we have her to thank?" He added, "I would have thought it would be her sister who discovered the issue."

Richard shrugged. "Miss Evelyn," he continued, his voice growing flinty, "seems better with her books than with people." Then his voice softened. "I suspect Miss Hawke is simply not comfortable with the attention." Darcy tilted his head slightly and examined his cousin. Richard would not meet his gaze and something amusing suddenly occurred to him.

"Well," Darcy said with a grin, "if it means harassing you, I shall seek her out directly."

"William. . ." Richard turned his eyes to his boots, his face pained.

Darcy's grin widened into a smile. The normally unflappable Colonel Fitzwilliam was as close to blushing as he had ever seen. *There might be great sport in this.* When Richard finally met his mischievous gaze, his eyes widened and he took a breath to protest, but could find nothing to say. Darcy began to laugh, and when he saw panic spreading across Richard's normally teasing expression, he laughed harder. All the relief and happiness of the morning welled up in his chest begging for release, and thus Darcy's laughter was louder and lasted longer than it would have normally. He could not recall when he had last laughed at all, let alone like this, abandoning all sense of restraint. He bent over to catch his breath and released another round of deep, helpless guffaws.

"Oh, Richard," he gasped, clutching the back of a chair with one hand, trying to bring himself under some sort of control and failing entirely.

"What is it that has you so amused, cousin?" asked Richard drily.

"You are afraid of Miss Hawke."

"Afraid?" Richard scoffed. "I think not." He reached up to rub the back of his neck nervously.

Darcy straightened with some effort and tugged at his waistcoat to put himself back in a semblance of order. He continued to chuckle, watching his cousin's discomfort until a new thought struck him. *Oh, better and better*.

"Richard. . ." Darcy crowed.

"What?"

Darcy poked Richard in the chest one time with his finger. "You *fancy* Miss Hawke." It was not a question.

Richard rolled his eyes and batted Darcy's hand away. "You have become an old gossip out here with all these women, William. Do not be deluded into believing you see something that is not there."

Darcy's expression was serious now, as he took in Richard's anxious expression. "No, Richard, truly." He continued to stare at his cousin until his voice lowered and he spoke sincerely. "You are enamored of her."

Richard shrugged and slouched in his chair. "It makes no difference."

"Why not?" Darcy was genuinely curious.

"Shall I list the reasons? You know most of them already, William."

"I admit I often do not know what to make of her, Richard, but I quite admire the girl." He grunted. "And it appears I am now in her debt."

"Is this my fastidious cousin, ever concerned with appearance and propriety?"

"I am a man who once thought those things of utmost importance, cousin. I have since been better educated." He frowned. "I thought my humbling was over after I convinced Elizabeth to accept my hand, but apparently there was more to learn."

Richard rubbed at his eyes wearily. "I am sorry for being the author of that particular lesson, cousin."

"No, no. It was one well worth learning, and thankfully it was not as costly as it might have been.

Elizabeth has been ill, and I have therefore had more difficult lessons since."

Darcy motioned for Richard to sit and waited until his cousin took a seat. He gathered his thoughts, and then began to speak. "Richard, surely you must see that little else matters if you have at last found a woman you can truly esteem." Darcy stared at his cousin, whose doleful countenance was not promising, and added, "Her story is so outlandish as to be easily passed off as a fabrication should it ever be known."

Richard sank back into the chair, his head tilted up to the ceiling, his eyes closed. "Ah, but she is loyal to my father, and with his insistence on the honor of the Fitzwilliam family, he would never allow it. Even the whiff of scandal is too much for him."

"She has good reason to be loyal to Uncle Henry, Richard. You cannot fault her for that."

Richard groaned. "I do not. I cannot help but blame him, though. What would such a scandal cost, really? All they really have is a girl who had reappeared after several years abroad and is a bit unconventional—she might have been anywhere, for all they know. Scotland, Ireland—they would never know, and she is not the only woman who shoots. This business with her uncle is ridiculous. She has worked against him for years."

He shook his head and continued. "My father loves her as much as he is able. I daresay as much as he loves me." He squeezed out a bitter laugh. "Perhaps more. But he is too concerned with the pristine condition of the Fitzwilliam family honor. Even if no one else ever knew what she had done, he knows." He toyed with his glass and sighed. "What is the use of spotless reputation if you are never willing to use it in a good cause?"

Darcy considered this carefully. "Do you think Miss Hawke knows of your father's affection? He can be difficult to read."

Richard shook his head. "You know he would keep such a thing from her at all costs, William. I doubt she even suspects. I doubt he even admitted it to himself until this summer, when I inadvertently mentioned the Captain's death." *It is safe to love someone who is dead,* he thought.

Darcy leaned forward. "Can you not speak with him when he arrives next week?"

"About what?" Richard lowered his voice and said with a sneer, "'Father, I know you are hoping I make a politically advantageous marriage with an heiress who is a force in the *ton* and insipid enough never to have done anything of note in her entire life, but I would rather marry the girl who ran off to war and masqueraded as a man for three years?'"

Darcy grinned, sat back, and raised his glass. This was the sarcastic cousin he knew. "Well, she *is* an heiress."

Richard glared at his cousin, annoyed that he had chosen this conversation to be so uncharacteristically flippant. "An heiress who has literally fought for years to keep what belonged to her family. She would have to be mad to marry now and turn it all over to a husband."

Darcy grew contemplative, recalling Miss Hawke's response to being escorted on her rides. "I do not think she as opposed to marriage as you might think, provided it was a man she could trust, one she admired and loved." Quietly, he asked, "Do you love her, Richard?"

Richard ran his free hand through his hair and sighed. "I do *like* her, William. She exasperates me, ignores me, and then calls for my assistance and seems pleased to see me. She smiled at me yesterday when she saw me and it made me feel. . ."

Darcy nodded. He knew such a smile. "Happy?"

Richard groaned. "Am I speaking to my cousin or my mother?" He quietly considered Sophia Hawke. "I do not know what to make of her." He gazed out the window to the gardens beyond Darcy's study. "It is just that. . ." he shrugged and gave up. "I like her."

Darcy thought about that for a moment, wishing very much for his wife's insight. He could not be certain, but he believed Richard already lost to Miss Hawke. At the very least, he was in some danger. Perhaps he could speak with his uncle during his visit if Richard would not. If he loved her, and she reciprocated, it would bring Richard home. That alone would assure Lady Matlock's approval, if not her husband's. More than that, though, when he carefully considered the match, he could think of few women better suited for his cousin. Of course, she had her own fortune. Matched with Richard's savings and the money his parents would gift him upon marriage, they would do very well, but this went far beyond financial considerations.

Now that he was permanently assigned to London, Richard had regained much of his good humor. He put his easy manners to use, devising all manner of heroic, romantic, even comedic narratives about his time abroad meant to please his dance partners. He spun wild arguments about military strategy for the men while they smoked cigars and drank brandy, but Darcy was not fooled. *It must be exhausting to keep up such pretense,* he had thought when Richard dined with them before returning to London. *I have my mask, and Richard has his stories. It does make one see more obstacles than truly exist.*

Darcy had begun to wonder whether there was an Englishwoman in the entire country who could offer Richard what he needed. Instead, Darcy had thought that his cousin might someday find himself married to a wealthy widow from the continent, one more experienced with the consequences of war. He had hoped for that rather than a political alliance formed by the earl.

But now there was Miss Hawke. She was lovely in a way he knew Richard particularly appreciated, she was kind and intelligent if a bit somber, and she could be the perfect lady when such manners were required. She could offer him more than simpering adulation, insincere concern for his well-being, or even honest hero worship, which was the last thing Richard desired. Instead, she was a woman who could offer him keen understanding rather than vague sympathy, a woman who knew without being told that the war was not something romantic because she shared that experience with him. Darcy checked off her other attributes as he knew them: strong, physically active, and quick of wit, like his cousin. She listened more than she spoke and quietly observed, a complement to Richard's more gregarious but equally perceptive personality.

Further, she had a purpose in the rebuilding of her family estate. Richard had mentioned at times that he was unsure whether the life of a gentleman was active enough. Sitting at a desk in the War Office was a trial for him. The challenge he would face assisting Miss Hawke in reestablishing her family's legacy would not allow for indolence. In that sense, Richard would be at least as good a match for her.

Darcy watched his cousin move to the window as he next considered the possibility from an admittedly selfish perspective. This match would have Richard settled in an estate convenient to both Pemberley and Matlock with a woman of independent fortune, though even with Darlington's considerable holdings, they would need to be careful of expenses as they laid out the capital to rebuild. *Stop planning, Fitzwilliam,* he admonished himself and nearly chuckled out loud as he recognized his wife's laughing voice invading his own thoughts. *What have you done to me, Elizabeth? You have me planning a marriage, but I shall never admit it.* Finally, he spoke.

"Well, Richard, we have an entire month for you to figure this out."

The colonel turned back to the room and shook his head, resigned. "Father would never approve, and

Miss Hawke will not gainsay him. She owes him too much."

"I have never known you to be averse to risk, Richard."

His cousin shrugged.

Darcy watched Richard closely. *This type of risk is different. He has never felt as much for a woman as he does for her. I have certainly never seen him thus. Hopeless attraction.* He nearly grunted in commiseration. *That is an experience I can share with him.*

"Let us consider a plan of action when it becomes necessary." Darcy thought about how pleased his Aunt Eleanor would be to discover that her second son might finally marry. "Take the time you have, and if it seems to be more than an infatuation on both sides," he paused, debating whether to explain his thoughts to his cousin, then grinned and let them go, "perhaps we might have Elizabeth speak with your mother."

"My mother?"

Darcy skirted what he believed to be his Aunt Eleanor's first concern—keeping her second son in England and alive. Instead, he broached the second. "Come, Richard, your mother is desperate for more grandchildren. Phillip has demonstrated no interest in remarrying and you have never indicated an interest in marrying anyone before. You are the soldier here. Consider, if a frontal assault does not achieve your objective. . ."

Richard chuckled and nodded. "Attack from the flanks." He lifted an eyebrow. "I did not know you had it in you, William."

"I have been left alone for a week with four women, Richard. An entire week. I have had to turn my mind to more masculine pursuits."

"And not just any women, William." Richard raised his glass. "You are a man of great courage and fortitude. An excellent chess player."

Darcy barked out a jagged laugh and affected the Derbyshire accent he had not used since his youth. "And you, Richard, art a balmpot."

Chapter Twelve

THE DAYS FOLLOWING the discussion in Darcy's study passed quietly. Elizabeth and Fitzwilliam took to breaking their fast together above stairs in the morning, and the rest of the party was pleased to note that their hostess was downstairs a little earlier each day. As she began to grow stronger, Elizabeth desired more exertion, and the women often toured the house with her. The gallery, in particular, made for a pleasant walk. Georgiana had been required to learn a great deal of her family history as part of her studies and had an unfailing supply of stories for each portrait.

Although still uneasy about his wife's health, Darcy was beginning to feel more comfortable about her confinement. He was, however, encountering a new problem. Now that Elizabeth's vigor was increasing, so too was her desire to do more. Never an inactive woman, she was insistent that she was so much improved that she could resume many of her usual pursuits. She promised not to wander far, but she desired to walk out of doors and had already informed her husband she would be helping to gather the greenery for the house the day before Christmas so that she might partake in the decorating. Her husband, only just beginning to recover his own equanimity in terms of her heath, shook his head firmly and refused to discuss it. With each response, Elizabeth was temporarily thwarted, but she was determined that in the end she would have her way.

It was heavenly to feel a little more like herself after months of sickness. She still had moments where she was nauseous, but for the most part she had been able to keep from becoming ill. In addition, she was beginning to put on a little weight and to feel a little ungainly, though her stomach was not yet nearly so large as she knew it would become. She remembered each of her Aunt Gardiner's confinements, so she knew by the end she would be fortunate to see her own feet. She could now take the stairs on her own, though her husband would not allow it, insisting she always have a footman escort her if he was not available. Though she believed it excessive, Elizabeth could not be upset with him for this much. It was a small concession, and he had been so worried for her.

Though she tended to follow her Aunt Gardiner's advice about her condition rather than her mother's, there was something Elizabeth was feeling that her aunt had never mentioned. Now that she was well enough to eat and to get out of bed for most of the day, she had become startlingly amorous, more so than she could remember being even in the first heady days of her marriage. She thought perhaps this was a result of not having been well enough to fully engage her husband in such activities for so long. *I have stored it all up,* she thought with a giggle. *And William must be ready to burst, poor man.*

It was no more than a day after Elizabeth began to consider ways to seduce her husband that she entered his chambers late at night after he had dismissed his valet. She stood by the fire wearing only a thin red dressing gown that barely covered her stomach and was tied haphazardly by a narrow belt. Her husband's face was something she would recall forever. His eyes widened while delight, desire, need, and alarm warred against one another in his expression. The self-control was there too, though, and he managed to choke out a caution to her as he placed one hand on the wall for support and turned his face away.

"Elizabeth, are you sure you are well enough?" he asked in a low, strained voice. "Please, my love, if you have any doubts at all, you must leave *this moment*."

In response, she had freed the sash with one small tug and allowed the dressing gown to slide to the floor. Darcy, though not facing her, had heard it fall, the soft whisper of the silk against her skin then the nearly imperceptible shushing as it pooled on the floor, breaking through his last thin veneer of restraint. He approached her breathlessly, hungrily, reaching out to touch her skin gently with his fingertips, reverently tracing her shoulders, breasts, ribs, buttocks, lingering at last on her rounded abdomen. He circled their babe lightly with one hand for some time before moving both hands to the small of her back and pulling Elizabeth carefully against him. He lowered his mouth to hers and parted her lips with his tongue, exploring tentatively before engaging in a deep, heated kiss.

Elizabeth's arms slid up around the back of his neck and she plunged her hands into his hair. When she stopped to tug at the collar of his nightshirt, he tossed it over his head in one fluid movement. She gazed into his eyes as she stroked his cheek and then ran her hands up and down his chest tenderly but eagerly, at last moving tantalizingly down his abdomen, where he halted her progress by grabbing her hand and leading her to bed.

The lovemaking was careful but insistent, and it did not take long for her husband to complete the act. He murmured a nearly incoherent apology as he turned on his side and placed his arm over her waist. As he lay on his side next to her, she began to trail the fingers of one hand from his ribcage to his hip, over and over until he gave her a hopeful look and she nodded happily.

This time the lovemaking was less cautious, though still gentle. Elizabeth gasped and moaned as her husband took his time, attending to her entire body slowly, methodically. She felt her need growing steadily until she was clinging to him, pulling herself up against his hard chest, begging for him to finish as he whispered words of love in her ear. By the time he finally heeded her cries, it took only a short time more before they reached their climax, first her, then him, and they collapsed together into the pillows. As Elizabeth's breathing returned to normal, she pulled herself up a bit and then placed a hand, still shaking slightly, on her husband's head. She loved his curly hair, the only part of him that he could not keep under strict regulation.

From beneath the dark tangles, he moaned a little and grunted, "God, I love you, Elizabeth."

She smiled, sated, and mumbled as her eyelids slid closed, "I love you too, William."

***

When the room began to light up weakly in the early morning hours, Darcy opened his eyes. Elizabeth was still asleep, her lashes long, dark, and fine against the rosiness of her cheeks. He sighed contentedly and reached up to stroke her hair. Unlike the toll her condition had taken on the rest of her body, her hair had grown glossy and thick. He adored the long locks, twisting into large, soft curls that were, just now, cascading like a dark waterfall down the mountain of pillows upon which his wife reclined. He thought she looked like a fairy from one of the books he had read to Georgiana as a child, and he marveled again that he had ever thought Elizabeth beneath him. *She is ethereal.*

After some time, Elizabeth mumbled a few words he could not understand and twitched her nose. He chuckled and she opened her eyes. She looked confused for a moment but then let out a soft laugh of her own as she saw the boyish delight on his face.

"Good morning, love," he said. He blushed a little at her knowing glance, but otherwise his expression did not change. Instead, he kissed her and then laid his cheek against her stomach.

"Good morning, little one," he said in a normal tone of voice. "Are you still sleeping?"

Elizabeth giggled, and Darcy's happiness was complete to see her nearly giddy. *I might like this part of having a wife with child*, he thought, grinning.

Suddenly he felt something tap his cheek and startled, he pulled his face away.

"What was that?" he asked, placing his hand against his wife's skin.

Elizabeth began to laugh and her husband waited patiently for her to stop. He felt a great deal calmer this morning than he had in months, and it was delicious to see his wife in such good spirits.

"He kicked you, William," she said, struggling to control her mirth. "Was it hard enough for you this time?"

They lay in bed for another half an hour, talking about names, while Darcy waited to feel another kick. When he did, Elizabeth gasped.

"Oh," she breathed, her hands flying to the spot. "A strong one. We should definitely consider boy names."

"I felt it," said Darcy, swallowing hard. He kissed her stomach and said, "I would not be so certain that this is a boy, my dear. I know how strong you are—perhaps this is a girl like her mother." He paused for a moment to consider how wonderful it would be to have a little girl to spoil, one who looked like his wife.

Finally, they both decided to repair to her chambers so his bedlinens could be changed and they might break their fast. Darcy had to retrieve his nightshirt from the canopy above his bed before escorting his wife from his room and into her own. He waited until her back was turned to quickly sniff at her sheets. No lily of the valley. Smiling, he went to ring for a tray. When it arrived, he began to serve her.

"Thank you, William," she said, her cheeks flushing as he spread preserves on her toast and poured her a cup of tea. "I do not know what came over me, but I cannot say I am sorry that it did."

"Do not ever apologize for loving me, dear," he teased, with a kiss to her cheek. "I believe that the well being of all Pemberley depends upon you allowing yourself to be overcome in that way as often as possible." He handed her a plate and climbed into bed beside her. "In fact, once you have finished your meal. . ."

She laughed, lifted her face to his, and took a large bite of her toast. "That," she replied pertly, "is a grand idea, Mr. Darcy."

Chapter Thirteen

RICHARD WAITED AT the stables, rubbing his hands together for warmth, until he heard Miss Hawke's footsteps on the path. He nodded at Jacob Briggs, John's older boy, who stifled a grin and began to saddle the colonel's horse while he pulled on his gloves.

"Miss Hawke!" he called to her as she emerged from the path where it left the trees, "Good morning!" She was dressed in a riding habit with a short dark green jacket he thought outlined her figure very becomingly. A soft gray scarf was wound around her neck in deference to the cold. Two blonde curls fell free of her jaunty hat on each side, and he felt a grin begin on his own lips.

"Three days in a row, Colonel?" she asked archly. "Are you making a bid to replace Freddie?"

"He is being well compensated for allowing me to take his place, Miss Hawke."

She shook her head sadly, sending her curls into flight. "You really are incorrigible, Colonel."

He winked at her and then asked, "Is that a new riding habit?"

She scoffed at his wink and adjusted her gloves. "Your mother insisted I have three made as I ride out so often. I cannot tell you how much time we spent with her modiste while at Matlock, but it seemed an age. Thank goodness we were not shopping for a season in London or I should have drained the coffers entirely."

"My mother knows her trade, Miss Hawke. It was money well spent."

"Your mother will be happy to hear you have ascribed her the traits of a tradeswoman," was the light reply.

John Briggs walked Rhadamanthus to the mounting block.

"John," protested Richard, "you never have my mount prepared when I arrive."

John was uninterested in banter. "You tell me when you plan to be here, Colonel, and the boys will get you sorted."

Richard turned back to Miss Hawke, who was hiding a smile. "How did you manage to get John Briggs to see to you personally?"

She shook her head, her eyes lit with laughter. "He likes me, Colonel Fitzwilliam. Apparently more than he likes you." She walked quickly over to the mounting block and was soon up in her saddle and adjusting her skirt. She took the reins and then glanced back at him.

"Well, Colonel," she said a bit impatiently. "Are you coming?"

Richard swung up into his saddle and followed her out of the yard.

The past two days, they had taken a long, looping path through the lower part of the estate, through a lightly forested area and close enough to a stream that they would have heard the gurgling water had it not been turning to a slushy sort of ice. Today, Richard led them out to a flat meadow entirely exposed to the sun.

"I thought we could allow the horses a bit more exercise," he said. "The Briggs boys assure me that the meadow is safe so long as we do not try to race."

She nodded, and they trotted amiably for a time without speaking. Richard finally turned to her and began to ask a question, but stopped.

"Is there something you wish to ask, sir?" Sophia asked.

Richard eyed her carefully. He had seen her riding astride at Darlington, and he rather wished she would do the same here, but he could not help but admire her seat upon the thoroughbred. It was not the typical choice of a mount for a woman, but then, such choices were entirely typical for her.

"I wanted to ask you something about your time on the Continent," he said sheepishly, "and thought we were far enough away from the house here to talk."

She turned to him with an upraised eyebrow and fixed a serious look upon him. She shifted in the saddle, uncomfortable, but replied, "What is it you would like to know?"

He shrugged, "I only wish to know you a little better, and this seems as good a way as any. If you would, I think I know why you went, though I do still wonder at the audacity of it all."

Sophia looked away and stifled a small smile, making her lips purse into what appeared to be a pout.

"Why the 95th?"

Sophia gazed across the meadow. "I found myself in Kent after I left London. At the behest of your father, I might add. The 95th was quartered nearby."

Richard nodded. "You met my cousin Miss de Bourgh at some point while there, you told me."

Sophia slowed her mount and adjusted her hat. "Indeed. You have a good memory, Colonel. It was her notion."

Richard blanched and turned quickly in his saddle. "I beg your pardon?"

Sophia muttered something under her breath that he thought might be a curse. He had never heard her curse before, and it calmed him a bit to realize that her façade could slip, too. It did not calm him enough to forget his question.

"Miss Hawke," he said rather firmly, "I must insist you explain that comment. What notion of my cousin's?"

Sophia grimaced. "Anne is going to kill me," she groaned. "You must promise to keep what I am to say in the strictest of confidence. Otherwise I will go no further."

Anne? They are so informal?

She spoke again. "Not even to Mr. Darcy. Nobody must know."

Richard nodded.

"A little more than three years ago, your father sent me to Kent to check up on his sister, your Aunt Catherine, I presume. He was hoping to discover something about Anne's health. It was perhaps the easiest thing he had ever asked of me, and I admit, I was not in a good frame of mind at the time. The ease of the chore was welcome."

Richard felt a rush of sympathy. "After London, then?" He knew she had made a visit to London upon reaching her majority to try to assert her rights as her sister's guardian, and that her sister had turned her away.

"Yes," she said bluntly, staring ahead of her. "I simply met Anne one day as arranged by your father and listened to her complaints about her care. I made some inquiries nearby and then I recommended to your father that the physician tending her seemed more interested in keeping her ill than curing her. I daresay I learned nothing your father had not already fathomed. But your cousin was so grateful to have someone listen that we met several more times. I believe this, more than the task he gave me, was his true intent."

Richard felt a sense of guilt and indignation wash over him. "She could not confide in us? Darcy and I spent some time there every spring and we thought her well looked after."

"So you were the cousins of whom she spoke?"

"I suppose we were."

"But you were men. And one of you was meant for her, according to her mother."

Richard harrumphed. "Darcy."

"Really?" Sophia sounded surprised. "I would have thought it was you."

"Miss Hawke," Richard said, frustrated, "What do you mean?"

She glanced over at the colonel. "Anne is quite capable of acting out her wishes without her mother's knowledge. Even feeling ill, she assisted the 95th, particularly the youngest men, as they made their way past Rosings to the south. She was, at that time, rather enamored of the regiment's major-general, and he seemed taken with her as well."

"She was not," Richard said, unbelieving. This picture of his sickly, cross cousin was completely at odds with what he knew of her. For the first time in his life, he considered whether he would not be cross himself in Anne's situation. Her life, to him, seemed hopelessly constrained, yet he had believed her too ill to mind. As much as Darcy had distanced himself from Anne because he did not wish to raise her hopes, perhaps she had distanced herself from them because she did not wish to marry Darcy.

Sophia laughed. "Did I not say, when we met last summer, that women know a great deal more than the men believe?" She paused. "Though Anne really was ill, she was not on her deathbed. She wanted to be doing something of import. I hope that the new physician the earl said he would send was able to help her."

"I would not know," Richard said, shrugging. "Her mother handled Darcy's marriage rather poorly and she has not yet apologized to Elizabeth, so we have not visited since. She did not seem improved at our last meeting, but that was some time ago now."

"Oh, yes, I did survive the violence of her mother's disapprobation. I was already in uniform by then and apparently no more than an insect to be pinned to a board," she said teasingly. "You know, given some real purpose to work upon, Lady Catherine might have made a formidable general herself."

Richard shuddered at that pronouncement. "What did Anne have to do with getting you into the 95th?"

"I trusted her. I told her a little of what troubled me, and she remarked that if she were set adrift in such a way, she would do something with the freedom. Knowing my circumstances, she recommended the 95th."

Richard felt his ire rise. "Of all the things to recommend, she thought to send you off to die?"

"Such melodrama, Colonel," Sophia chided. "I am, after all, still here after three years abroad, am I not? Anne would have done it in a second, had she the chance."

Richard shook his head. "The blazes she would. Anne would never consider such a thing."

Sophia emitted something close to a snort. "Are you privy to her thoughts, Colonel? Does she confide in you?"

He had to admit, now that he considered it, that she did not.

"Anne was not capricious in her advice. She suggested I might be able to use the skills I would learn in the 95th. She believed being an excellent rifleman would allow me to protect myself and to maintain some distance from the fighting." Sophia shook her head. "She was not entirely correct about the latter."

He was silent for a few moments. "It also got you out of England," he said faintly. "At a time your uncle was likely searching for you."

She nodded. "He had men at every port. They were not, however, looking for a boy in uniform." She grinned. "Anne cut my hair and then recommended me to the major-general."

"Deuced woman!" he exclaimed with some grudging admiration. "I stand corrected, Miss Hawke. Were you women running the war, it would have been ended in our favor ten years past."

"Ah, Colonel," replied Sophia jokingly with a sly nod of her head, "you begin to see things my way at last."

"Was Hobson there, in Kent?"

"No. He returned home after London, expecting me to follow. His father had a plan to hide me, but I could not put them at that sort of risk. He learned from your father that I was in Kent, but he arrived just after I had signed up."

They rode quietly while Richard thought about what he had learned. He would never look at Georgiana and Elizabeth the same again, he thought wryly.

"I will say only one more thing, Colonel, and then I will ask that we speak of you," she sighed. "Anne's notion was singular, but it was not unique."

"What do you mean?" he asked, befuddled.

She cleared her throat. "I was not the only woman in uniform, sir. I met another, who I believe still serves," she said evenly, "and I must assume there are at least a few others."

He shook his head. It was too much to take in.

"Now," came her clear, steady voice, "I am tired of speaking about myself. How old were you when you first went to war?"

As he spoke, they wended their way across the meadow to the woods and made a large, lazy circle along the well-worn path that would take them back to the stables. The path narrowed among the trees, and Sophia took the lead. As she exited the final stand of pines, she took hold of a branch heavy with snow to move it out of her way. With one quick, mischievous look behind her, she held the branch as it bent back farther and farther before she let go.

The branch hit Richard full in the face, showering him with snow that found its way into his nose, his mouth, and his coat, melting as it slid under his cravat and down his chest.

"Bloody. . ." he bit his tongue. "Gads, woman, what are you about?" He dismounted and pulled his cravat from his neck, trying to dislodge the powdery snow.

He heard a soft thump as two boots landed on the hard-packed ground. He glanced up to see that his riding companion had dismounted and was walking back to him, unwinding her scarf from her neck, laughing but with a sincere apology on her face. He froze.

"I *am* sorry, Colonel," she was saying, "I had no idea it would be such a direct hit." She had the wool scarf in her hand and without a word, began to dust the snow from his shoulders. He stood stock still, trying not to react to his increased heartbeat as her hand brushed against the skin of his neck. *She only means to touch your coat*, he told himself, *do not react.* But then she moved to wipe the water from his bare throat and he had to shut his eyes. *Self-control, man*, he thought sternly. When he forced himself to open his eyes again, he saw a look of confusion on Miss Hawke's face as she dabbed the water away. Meekly, she offered him the scarf for his face.

He took the damp scarf as she held it out without meeting his eyes, grazing her gloved hand as he did. *Blast all this winter clothing*, he thought, but as Miss Hawke stepped back and swallowed, eyes on the ground, he felt something akin to euphoria soar through him.

When he had finished and returned her scarf, Sophia glanced around for a log she might use to remount.

Now or never, Colonel, he told himself, moving to escort her.

"Allow me," he said gently, Sophia faced him but would not meet his eye as he placed his hands on her waist and counted. "One, two. . . three." She pushed up with her legs at the same time he lifted, and she was quickly back on her saddle, adjusting her skirt.

Richard released her waist, but she caught one hand as he pulled away.

"Thank you," she said, almost shyly, and Richard could have cheered.

I am not alone, he thought jubilantly, as he walked back to his horse, turning to steal a last look at her reddened cheeks. *She feels something too.*

Chapter Fourteen

THE CANDLELIGHT LIT the small dining room brightly, though the edges still fell into shadows. The sound of gentle laughter just reached the hallway. Servants walked crisply in and out of doors bringing more food and wine, though the footmen who normally stood in their positions along one wall had been dismissed. Both ends of the table had been abandoned to the informality of a family gathering. Sophia was pestered to tell her story and though she demurred at first, she smiled tightly once she accepted that she would not be left alone.

"Very well, I capitulate," said Sophia, raising her hands, palms out, to deflect the insistent pleas of Evelyn and Georgiana. "In honor of Mrs. Darcy being able to join us again at table," she lifted her wineglass slightly in tribute to her hostess, who blushed under the approbation of her beaming husband, "I shall tell my story, though I am afraid it is a paltry thing and will not live up to the expectations you are now placing on it, Georgiana."

"Nevertheless," Georgiana said with a breezy laugh from her position next to the colonel, who sat directly opposite Miss Hawke, "you must honor your promises."

"And I shall." Sophia cast her eyes momentarily to the ceiling and bit her lower lip, stopping when she noticed that her sister had silently raised an eyebrow. She took a breath and began.

"At the extremely advanced age of nine, I felt myself quite mature enough to take my wayward younger sister in hand whilst my mother and the nanny prepared a little tea and cake in honor of said sister's sixth birthday. I had been so honored at my own celebration many times and therefore was quite certain I knew all there was to know about such things."

Evelyn's face was completely blank. Despite her sister's earlier warning, she had not truly believed she would figure in this story, and she was attempting to recall anything to do with her sixth birthday. Sophia raised an eyebrow of her own and nodded, saying, with some playful emphasis, "You asked for this story *particularly*, Evie. Now you must reap what you have sown."

Everyone laughed good-humoredly, except for Evelyn, who blushed and looked at her plate. She did not enjoy being the subject of their laughter. It was safer to say outrageous things and have people focus on what she offered up for ridicule than it was to allow others to choose her as their target.

"I told Evie that I would go with her wherever she wished as it was her birthday. Of course, I was rather hoping she would wish to visit the stables." Here Sophia looked around the room, her eyes flashing with merriment. "We had both been given beautiful mounts. Evie's was a white pony, quite a striking creature, and I had been gifted a lovely chestnut mare in anticipation of my own birthday though it was not for several months yet." Sophia's voice was wistful, remembering. "She was beautiful, though in my very mature opinion entirely too gentle." There was more laughter around the table and Evie relaxed. Sophia noted her sister's response out of the corner of her eyes before returning to her story.

"Alas, my sister, even then, preferred the still room."

Evelyn interrupted. "Did mother allow me in the still room?"

Sophia nodded. "Of course. She could hardly keep you away. You were forever concocting potions and cures. Of course, at the time, you had no idea what you were doing." Sophia made a face. "She had a special apron made to cover your dresses, and the smells were atrocious."

Even Evelyn had to laugh at that. Sophia smiled at her sister and gazed around the table. Mrs. Darcy and Georgiana were waiting with some anticipation and Evelyn waited with what seemed to be anxiety. Even Mr. Darcy and Colonel Fitzwilliam were graciously attending her gently delivered narrative, nodding in appropriate places. Sophia felt a sudden warmth suffuse her body, a sincere pleasure in belonging to a group of people she could call her friends. She took a quick breath and continued.

"I sat down and allowed her to bustle rather importantly around the room as though she knew what she was about. She asked me to fetch two teacups and declared we would have tea together. I mentioned that we would have tea upstairs and she nodded, but said that as my gift to her, we would drink the tea she made."

"Oh, no. . ." groaned the colonel, who had an inkling where this might be headed.

Sophia shook her head, the skin at the corner of her eyes crinkling in a rare full smile. *Of course he would see immediately where this was headed.*

"Indeed, Colonel. Perhaps you would like to complete the tale?"

He cleared his throat and waved her off. "No, no. Pray forgive the interruption."

"I am afraid of the answer," said Evelyn, rather quietly, her mind racing at the possibilities, "but pray tell, what did I give you in the way of tea?"

"Oh, you brewed a fine stout black tea, my dear."

"Then what. . ."

Sophia shook her head ruefully. "I am afraid it was very strong. It tasted awful and I said as much. I was not very gracious about it. In fact, I was rather cruel and poured it out, insisting we go outside to visit our horses instead. You made the same face you make now when you are displeased, and stomped around to prepare another cup. You were, in fact, growing dangerously close to throwing a rather spectacular tantrum. I was concerned I might be punished for upsetting you on your birthday." She tilted her head and gazed at her sister. "So I did my duty. I took the second cup, and drank it down without delay. Disgusting stuff."

Evelyn waited to hear the rest, but Sophia seemed unwilling to continue.

"What was wrong with it?" prompted Georgiana.

Sophia shook her head with a genuine smile. "Probably nothing, with the first cup, other than the taste. Had I simply been a kind elder sister, Evie would have eventually forgiven me for calling it terrible."

"Then what . . . ?" Evelyn faltered. Sophia could see the tension in her sister's wrinkled brow, so she took a deep breath and continued.

"You apparently crushed something a little extra into the second cup."

Evelyn's eyes widened in shock and dismay. "Lily of the valley?" There was a small intake of breath from Elizabeth's end of the table.

Sophia nodded. "Lily of the valley. This time the tea was not only very strong, but as I was swallowing it, I realized that it smelled terribly as well. However, I knew I was in the wrong for being so rude to my little sister, on her birthday of all days, and so I plugged my nose and drank it down."

"Is that all, Miss Hawke?" joked the colonel. "I was rather thinking there was more to it than that."

Mrs. Darcy opened her mouth to speak and Sophia moved to respond first, but her sister anticipated them both.

"There is, Colonel," replied Evelyn, abashed.

"I thought you did not recall the event, Evelyn," said Georgiana, confused.

"No, Georgiana, I do not." She pursed her lips and looked apologetically at her older sister. "However, I do know that lily of the valley, while lovely as a scent," she lifted her shoulders in a tiny shrug, "can be poisonous if ingested."

Mr. Darcy glanced at his wife, who appeared rather horrified but offered him a small nod.

Georgiana's eyes nearly bulged out of her face. "Oh. . ." she said breathlessly.

Sophia laughed aloud. It was a true laugh, not a forced one, and shook her head at the shocked expressions of her audience. "I was never ill as a child, so I had no idea why I felt so wretched. I was forced to remain in the nursery through the real tea and cakes because my mother thought I was making a scene to attract attention away from Evie on her special day. It was not until I was quite violently ill that she actually deigned to believe me."

Evelyn was contrite. "Sophia, while this is obviously quite a belated apology, apologize I must. I am sure at that age I did not know what I had given you. Truly, I do not even remember it." She gazed at her sister earnestly and was relieved to see only affection in Sophia's face.

Mr. Darcy cleared his throat. "I am afraid this story does not strike me as exactly *humorous*, Miss Hawke. Were you quite all right?" His wife smiled at him from across the table.

"Oh, Mr. Darcy, you are too kind," chuckled Sophia, touched by his concern. *It must be a family trait*, she thought distractedly. "As you see, I appear before you in the best of health. I am afraid that I was put out primarily because Evie tricked me into drinking something she knew would not only taste awful but offend my sense of smell. It was incredibly humbling for the wise older sister to be bobbed by a little thing of barely six."

The colonel nodded and attempted to assist Sophia in lightening the mood. "I am afraid we younger brothers and sisters must fend for ourselves, Miss Evelyn," he said with feigned seriousness, "Apparently, Miss Hawke had been quite lording it over you and I am sure she only reaped what she had sown."

For a moment, there was silence as the colonel's appropriation of Miss Hawke's tease was digested, but then the laughter began to build. In the end, even Evelyn was laughing. The only one who did not was Sophia Hawke, who watched everyone with a self-effacing roll of the eyes, lips curled up slightly at the corners, quite pleased with herself.

Sophia had been more than ill, though she would never burden her sister with that knowledge. For the first few days she had, in fact, been in some danger. Even Oliver, who detested being indoors and who at eight years of age felt himself far too old to display affection for his sisters, had crept into her bed and tossed his arms around her, desperately worried because he had overheard the servants talking about her parents' fears. It did not surprise her that Evie would not remember this. She had been quite young, after all.

Even though she was several years older, Sophia did not herself remember everything about being so very stricken, but a few precious threads of memory remained. Her brother's tears, his golden hair soft against her neck, the weight of his head resting against her chest, the warmth of his body and the smell of horses on his clothes. Her mother's melodious voice reading and singing, the rustle of silk skirts, the scent of rosewater. Her father's rumbling bass, the odors of tobacco and brandy and wheat, the feel of his hand on her cheek and his lips on her forehead. Sometimes when she closed her eyes at night, she could feel them with her still.

She wondered briefly whether Evie had any such memories to keep her company. Her lips straightened out a bit and her eyes lost focus for a moment, but when she released the beloved phantoms to the misty recesses of her mind, she happened to glance at the colonel and found that his eyes were searching her face with some apprehension. He lifted an eyebrow as if to ask if she was well, and she gave his the slightest of nods in response and returned to the tale.

"In the end, Colonel Fitzwilliam," she announced with some impertinence and a good deal of relish, "I was the winner. For you see, my poor mother felt so much guilt for believing her oldest and most responsible child would prevaricate about being ill that she treated me quite like a queen for months after."

Evelyn nodded thoughtfully. "That part I do remember. I am ashamed to admit I was quite jealous." She had been, as her birthday had been thoroughly overshadowed and nobody would tell her why, or where her sister had gone.

"I earned a fine new saddle to adorn my mare and a promise from my father to let me ride his stallion with him when I was recovered. So you see, my friends," Sophia said jokingly, "I am willing to go to any length to best my sister. She may have all the cleverness, but I am twice as stubborn."

Georgiana giggled. "We have not the slightest idea what that might look like at Pemberley, Sophia.

I am afraid there is not a single stubborn person in the entire Darcy or Fitzwilliam families."

Elizabeth hooted gaily at this display on Georgiana's part and held up her hands in mock dismay. "Georgiana, I hardly know you. I think the Hawkes are a terrible influence."

"Oh we are, Mrs. Darcy," laughed Sophia. "We are indeed."

"You should attend my sister, Miss Hawke," Mr. Darcy said quietly, gravely, as was his wont. "We suffered so much for a want of stubbornness at Pemberley I was forced to seek it out in a wife."

Mrs. Darcy wadded up her table napkin and made the entirely indecorous decision to throw it at her husband across the table. Colonel Fitzwilliam watched with delight to see his solemn cousin so beset.

"I find myself among friends, then, sir?" asked Sophia cheerfully.

"You do indeed, Miss Hawke." Mr. Darcy removed his wife's napkin from his shoulder without comment and dropped it on the table, offering her a clandestine wink. Mrs. Darcy met his gaze and held it lovingly for a moment, the others looking away, Sophia and Colonel Fitzwilliam to offer the couple their privacy, Evelyn because she was embarrassed. Georgiana watched her brother and sister just a bit longer than the others before dropping her eyes, a satisfied smile playing on her lips. Eventually, Mr. Darcy's hand moved to his wineglass, which he lifted. As he stood, the others realized he meant to make a toast and followed suit.

"As often happens," he said in a sonorous voice, "I find myself at a loss for the correct words. At such times, Miss Hawke, Miss Evelyn, I wisely consult those whose facility with language far exceeds my own. Thus, as Shakespeare has so aptly written, 'I count myself in nothing else so happy as in a soul remembering my good friends.'" He raised his glass a little higher. "We are very pleased to have you both here with us."

From her seat across the table, Elizabeth smiled up at her husband. It was just like him, she thought, her heart swelling with pride, to deliver such an eloquent toast while insisting he had no talent for words. The rest of the company lifted their glasses in salute and drank before the conversation returned to a gentle hum.

Elizabeth stretched her leg out under the table and tapped her husband's leg just above his boot. He glanced at her, surprised, and then looked down, clearly pleased. She quickly replaced her slipper and concentrated on her own plate, cheeks flushed.

Chapter Fifteen

EVELYN HAWKE FELT her cheeks grow warm, then heard Sophia thank Mr. Darcy for his kindness and his wife for her hospitality. Evelyn nodded her assent absently and then turned back to her own plate, though she ate little. This story she had goaded her sister into telling had shaken her deeply. For years, she had believed unstintingly in her own superiority of person, having been complimented excessively on her physical appearance and well educated by her uncle. He had shown great trust in her by not constraining her education in any way. Her desire to know everything about treating illnesses and injuries, she knew, was neither proper nor ladylike and was far worse, she thought for the first time, than the little habits over which she scolded Sophia.

Evelyn was very aware that she was clever—so clever, in fact, that she keenly felt the need to hide the extent of her intelligence from other people. She spoke several languages where her sister spoke only English and French. She was extraordinarily well read in the classics and the philosophers and had even taught herself a little Latin and Greek to try to read them in their original languages. It was frustrating when Sophia was at a loss when Evelyn wanted to discuss philosophical theories or different translations of a work. Sophia was of a mathematical bent, able to keep accounts, and track harvest numbers. She had also been learning a good deal about investments. However, she was not versed in the higher study of mathematics nor in science, unless it was agricultural in nature. More irritating still, Sophia had asked Evelyn to find more general subjects of conversation so that their guests, few as they were, might participate in the discussion. Evelyn had complied, but released her bitterness over the need to conceal so much of herself in slightly inappropriate remarks and occasionally impertinent, though never, she had thought, terribly damaging behavior.

How foolish I have been, she thought. Evelyn remembered with a grimace comments she had let fall to remind Sophia of her lack of formal education, how she did not read what Evelyn considered challenging books or seem willing to engage in the life of the mind beyond her newspapers and political tracts. She had teased Sophia about following the war news rather than reading Shakespeare or her older sister's inability to keep straight all the medicines in Evelyn's book of receipts and what each was used to treat. *You live too much in the world*, she had told Sophia derisively, and only now began to consider how cruel that statement had been.

She had made pointed remarks about any tiny variation from proper London behavior on Sophia's part either with a disapproving glance or sharp remonstrance. Yet she had carelessly spoken before the Darlington staff about private matters, not just her own but also Sophia's, and all her sister had done was point to the potential evils of such behavior and request that she desist. Sophia had waited until a moment came when they were alone and would not be interrupted, and she had been kind with her corrections. Even Evelyn had to begrudgingly admit her error, and then she had done it again here at Pemberley by voicing complaints to the laundry maids. The girl called Ruth had been unusually interested in her remarks, yet even that had not encouraged silence. Evelyn was embarrassed to find the habit of giving voice to her disappointments more difficult to break than she had anticipated.

Later, after she had bid everyone a good night, Evelyn closed the door to her room and sat at the vanity as the maid unpinned her hair. Able to finally think in depth about her behavior over the past half-year, the ache in her stomach began to grow stronger. She had to admit to herself that she had made light of the numbingly tedious details required to run Darlington, that she had treated her sister as being simply dull rather than industrious and burdened with responsibility, interested in coarse financial matters to the absolute exclusion of all finer feelings, while she herself had been quite willing to live comfortably on everything Sophia had provided through those endeavors. She had, at times, been openly resentful that Sophia had not revealed where she had been after she left their uncle's house so long ago, but how could Sophia trust her discretion when she had demonstrated none? Yet Sophia loved her regardless, forgiving her freely and repeatedly. At dinner, she had for the first time felt, and believed now with all her heart, that Mr. Darcy's lovely toast could have been made only for Sophia. She herself had done nothing to deserve such friendship.

The youngest Hawke had not known many people in her circumscribed life, but she was now convinced that even should she meet a new person every day for as long as she lived, her older sister would remain one of best she knew. Evelyn had, in the company of the Darcys, begun to better understand her own character as selfish, unfeeling, even petty in her continued efforts to demonstrate her own excellent understanding. The behavior of the Darcys and Colonel Fitzwilliam, with their genuine care for one another, was a clear reminder of how a family was meant to act.

Evelyn's throat constricted with the knowledge that her uncle, who had encouraged her behavior, had not loved her in any way that was not also tied to his own comfort, while Sophia loved her despite the pain her sister caused her. Sophia had tried to explain the danger their uncle represented, but to her everlasting shame, Evelyn had spurned her sister's increasingly desperate offers to leave Uncle Archibald's house, to live together under Sophia's guardianship, to reside again as sisters. She had seen the look on Sophia's face when at last she had been forced to flee, but at the time had given it little thought, only unhappy to have been so imposed upon. Now, when she closed her eyes and tried to recall her sister's expression, it came to her in terrible, vivid detail. She could only call it despair.

Not only was she now humiliated by her inability to discern her uncle's malicious intentions, she was abjectly miserable to learn what she had done to Sophia's tea. *You were a child then*, she thought. *You cannot blame those actions on your uncle.* Though Sophia had brushed away her apology and made a joke of the incident, Evelyn knew how ill even a small portion of a lily of the valley plant would have made a young girl. She hoped, with some trepidation, that she had not been aware of the consequences, that she had hoped only to make the tea taste bitter, but so little did she feel she knew herself that she could not be sure. The fact that Sophia had forgiven even this, had in fact saved her life in the fire a few years later, that she had, even tonight, made light of her own suffering, was a shock. Evelyn knew enough of her own character to realize that she would not have been so forbearing. Considering her own behavior as a child and now as an adult, Evelyn believed that Sophia's love for her was nothing short of a miracle.

Sophia was far from perfect, she knew. Evelyn had been witness to bouts of anger and resentment, primarily aimed at their uncle, but also at the men who had worked for him. She suspected even some lingering resentment aimed at the earl. Sophia could be impatient, particularly when she had too much to learn and could not manage to absorb it all at once. She could be unreasonably stubborn and at times played the elder sister as though Evie was twelve rather than one and twenty. Still, as she thought of Sophia making pleasant conversation with genuine amiability only moments after offering up a rather horrible story as a pleasant dinnertime diversion after being forced into the disclosure, Evelyn made a resolution. *There is but one way forward. I must strive to be worthy of such devotion*, she told herself firmly. Then she threw herself on a small settee near the fire with an unladylike energy. *How, though? How?*

Chapter Sixteen

COLONEL FITZWILLIAM DISMISSED his batman for the night once his boots had been removed, for he wished no other company. He removed his cravat and tossed it across the back of a chair, sitting heavily on the side of the bed as he removed his waistcoat. He was fighting a deepening dislike of Miss Evelyn Hawke and he tried to shake it.

Through her gentle corrections and habitual considerations for Miss Evelyn's comfort, it was clear that Miss Hawke loved her sister as much as Darcy loved Georgiana. Yet he could not keep from thinking that Miss Evelyn was entirely undeserving. After witnessing their behavior near the laundry, he had been rather attuned to any discussion between the sisters. While he observed much to admire in Miss

Hawke, he had heard in Miss Evelyn's conversation a condescension he found difficult to bear. Even tonight, she had made a face at her sister. The insults were airily done, and he wondered if anyone else had even noticed, particularly given that Sophia had stoutly refused to take offense. *Sophia*, he thought, aggravated. *Careful. It is still Miss Hawke to you.* The waistcoat landed on the chair next to his cravat.

Richard rubbed his forehead. He was not only aggravated, he was close to outright anger, something that would have to been kept in check. It would not do to display his temper here. He was not among his recruits, and Miss Hawke would not thank him for it. He was not blind to the fact that he already felt irrationally protective of her. He closed his eyes, remembering the touch of her hand through her glove.

His shirt followed the waistcoat and he stripped off the rest of his clothes without much concern for their state, grabbing the nightshirt laid out on the bed for him and sliding it over his head. This unsettled feeling was not going to go away. He wanted courtship. He wanted more. Sophia was stubborn and impatient and desperately seeking goodness, teasing and serious and joyful, abrupt, prideful, and yet perfect in her imperfections. And she felt something for him. He was sure of it.

As Richard curled up in the softest bed he had slept on in months, he shut his eyes and relived the smile Sophia Hawke had bestowed upon him when he answered her summons and appeared outside the laundry. She was attractive, with her golden hair and deep blue eyes, but that smile had transformed her into a stunning beauty. He groaned and attempted to punch his pillow into shape. *I shall never sleep tonight.*

***

The sun was up, though it was still early when Richard decided to abandon his bed and dress for the day. He rang for his batman only to find that Black, having taken to his bed earlier than normal the night before, was already up and preparing his ablutions.

"No scent, Black," he said absently, as the man clucked over the wrinkled clothing from the night before and poured out hot water for a shave.

"Yes, Colonel," Black replied. "Mr. Darcy has been quite clear about that."

"He spoke with the servants?"

Black nodded. "He had Mrs. Reynolds explain that they were not to use scent at all, not on their persons, not in the laundry, not anywhere."

"Did he? Good for him," the colonel said quietly, wondering if he had told his wife first.

"Indeed. I am told the laundry maids liked the way it removed the smell of lye and that they believed it could not possibly be detected once the sheets dried. New girls, evidently, since the summer. I expect they will remove it now."

Richard leaned back for his shave, closing his eyes. Black was a godsend. He did not think he could ever put up with a proper valet who could not tell the difference between gossip and information or who made him read between the lines of some properly oblique statement.

Richard felt the sharp blade of the razor grazing his throat, then his face, and shortly thereafter the warmth of a hot towel. He sighed with the contentment of a shave in his own large, comfortable chambers. The warm towel relaxed him and he gave into the simple pleasure, thinking that he would have himself quite talked out of going back to the War Office at all before long, though he was not quite ready to take that step. Above all, he would have to refrain from saying anything in front of the Darcys, any of them.

After he was prepared for the day, dressed every bit the gentleman in dark brown trousers and a new shirt, dark blue and brown waistcoat, blue coat, and his now highly polished Hessian boots, he strode down the stairs towards the breakfast room. As he stepped from the final stair, he thought he caught a bit of yellow skirt fluttering around a corner and curious, he followed.

It was, as he had hoped, Miss Hawke. She evidently had not gone for a ride this morning, as she was dressed in a lovely morning dress with her hair up and curled. As she walked, she pulled a blue shawl tightly around her shoulders, and Richard could just detect a Greek pattern around the border done in yellow and white. She strode with the confidence of habit and entered a room at the end of the hall that Richard remembered as the family chapel. He had not been in it himself since the day of George Darcy's funeral. He took careful steps and slipped into the room without alerting her. She was already sitting in the second pew from the altar in the small room, arms resting on the back of the first, her hands clasped together firmly, eyes closed, lips moving silently. Her shoulders rocked back and forth gently as she spoke just below his hearing.

Richard slipped into the pew nearest the door and gazed at the scene. He spent a little time admiring her figure, so unlike the many pale, overly thin women he had met in London. She was tall and strong, yet still feminine. She had put on a little weight since the summer when she had been injured, he thought approvingly, and her softer figure, longer, styled hair, and new dresses chased away all but the faintest outline of the boy soldier he had met. Suddenly the impropriety of what he was doing struck him and he flushed. *Churl. You are ogling her in a church.*

Sophia had told him she prayed back on that dreadful summer day they had traveled to Matlock. He remembered being shocked, believing that having survived both the repeated attempts on her life by her uncle and the horrors of the battlefield, she would have as little use for the church as he had himself. Obviously, he had been wrong. She prayed for a long time, at one point laying her head entirely down upon her outstretched arms, intent on something as her lips continued to move. At one point, he thought she had whispered her sister's name, and in another moment, he flushed to hear his own. He felt suddenly wrong, sitting there, and he stood to leave. She must have heard the movement, though he had intended to leave silently, for she turned her head and looked hazily into his eyes.

The moment passed quickly and he felt himself being minutely scrutinized, evaluated, and found wanting. Her eyes were alight with what he believed might be annoyance. His discomfort rose as she stood to greet him.

"I see you have discovered my secret, Colonel," she said cheerfully, confusing him. "It has been very good to be able to just walk downstairs. At home, I must venture out onto the grounds to reach the chapel, even when the weather is poor."

"I am afraid I followed you here, Miss Hawke," Richard said quietly. "I saw you walking down this hallway and was curious as to your destination."

She smiled at him. "You might simply have asked, Colonel," she said lightly. She turned and bent to the seat of the pew to pick up a piece of paper. "I am going through my list, as I do each morning."

"Your list?"

"Yes, my prayer list." She held it in both hands, running a thumb along the edge nervously. "My mother had one, though it was a good deal longer."

"And who do you pray for, Miss Hawke, if I may be so bold?"

"It is bold, Colonel." She stood silently for a moment before her shoulders slumped and she shook her head. She looked a bit embarrassed, but met his gaze. "My sister, my tenants, my staff, the Tildens, the Darcys, the earl, the countess, and you, Colonel. I shall probably add your brother and his son once I have met them."

"You pray for me?"

"Yes."

"I did not ask for you to do that." His cravat felt tight against his throat. He and God were not on speaking terms. He did not wish for her to pray for him.

"I do not believe I require your permission, sir," she said resolutely but without malice.

"Do you pray for yourself, then? Or are you beyond the need?" He asked coldly.

She winced a little at the tone, but was unmoved. She took a deep breath and pulled herself to her full height before saying, "I pray for myself most of all, I think."

"You think? Do you not know?"

She was not looking at him now, but over his shoulder. "In praying for those I love, I am praying primarily for myself," she said quietly. "It may be egotistical and weak, but I have been happy in these past months, and my fear rises equal to that happiness."

"What are you afraid of, Miss Hawke?" Richard asked, surprising himself with the haughtiness in his voice. *What are you doing, man? You sound like William.*

She looked askance at him, as though she thought him a simpleton.

"Everything, Colonel."

He was startled by such a reply. She had never appeared afraid of anything in the time he had known her.

"Surely not, Miss Hawke."

"The more one has, the more one has to lose," she said to her feet before raising her head and continuing. "You asked the question, Colonel," she said stiffly, appearing both unhappy and a little angry at his unexpected response to her revelations. Richard berated himself. He had followed *her* to the chapel, after all. She had not coerced him to attend her, indeed she had not even invited him. Finally, she said in a clipped tone, "Do not fault me should the answer not be to your liking." She folded the page. Richard noticed that the paper looked rather worn at the creases. When he looked up, she was moving towards the door.

"Do not let me interrupt you," he said, suddenly apologetic. Despite his pique, he did not wish to keep her from her routine. He felt torn, confused by his irritation, but attempted to shrug it off. *The prayer must help her in some way,* he thought, though it made little sense to him.

"No, I am finished," she said a little too quickly. She stopped as drew close to him. Her eyebrows pinched together in thought as she considered how to explain something she did not fully comprehend herself. "It is not piety that draws me to the chapel each morning, Colonel. I would not have you think that I consider myself. . ." her voice trailed off. She made another start. "I am not. . ." For a moment it seemed as though she would continue, but with a small, frustrated huff, Sophia Hawke left the room.

Richard was left feeling heartily ashamed of himself as Miss Hawke swept past him and out of the chapel. If a woman of whom he thought highly wished to pray for him, what was the harm? He was unaccountably perturbed that he was on the list with the rest of his family and hers. He pushed both hands through his hair and groaned softly in exasperation.

Why was he forever making a hash of things with her? Last summer, he had accused her of deceit, of luring not only him but Darcy and Bingley into danger with that blasted letter. At Matlock, his father had commanded most of his attention, leaving him precious little time to make his farewell at Darlington before removing to Pemberley and London. They had made polite conversation, but not much else. Now he had teased her about being the cause of rude servants, had assisted her only reluctantly with her plan to help Elizabeth, and had been peevish with her this morning over what any normal man would have seen as a sweet gesture. Why could he charm every woman who did not matter but only confuse and insult the one who did? *The maids are charmed by me*, he thought sourly, *but Miss Hawke must think me a cad.*

During their residence at Matlock, his mother had quickly determined that the Hawke girls both required a mother, and having only sons, had been very happy to take on that role. She loved both girls, he thought, but rather doted on the eldest. Sophia Hawke had even broken through his father's icy reserve, albeit temporarily. Darcy admired her; Elizabeth and Georgiana were well on the way to loving her. What was wrong with him? His fingers gripped the back of the pew tightly for a moment before he released his hold with an impatient grunt. *Sophia Hawke is in every way too good for you, you stupid mud.*

Chapter Seventeen

THE REST OF THE DAY passed without incident. Already in possession of a list from Lambton, Elizabeth had asked her husband to request a list of any remaining families in the Kympton parish who required aid through the winter season. She thought it would make a nice diversion for the ladies to work together on baskets, though she harbored no hopes that she would be allowed to help deliver them. Mrs. Reynolds had already asked the cook, Mrs. Cronk, to lay in the food they would need, and despite her illness, Elizabeth, along with Georgiana, had managed to sew quite a few simple garments for the younger children and infants. This morning, Miss Evelyn had offered to help embroider the gowns and had proven to excel at the art. Miss Hawke had smiled and offered to do any utilitarian sewing. She would not try a fancy stitch or attempt to embroider, she laughed, for her rosettes wound up looking like spiders and she had no desire to frighten the children or their parents. Miss Evelyn smiled and agreed, but pointed out that her sister's stiches were not only quick, small, and neat, they were actually beautiful.

"Much nicer than mine," she smiled genuinely. "Therefore, we make a good pair."

Elizabeth could only shake her head at the conflicting manners of Miss Evelyn. She saw love between the Hawkes, but it was a complicated, often uneasy love, not without bitterness or resentment, with the lighter, easier feelings she took for granted with most of her own sisters only occasionally breaking through. *It must be wearisome*, she thought, *to always protect one's heart from a sister. What would I have done without Jane to rely on?* She thought briefly of Lydia, but even her youngest sister was nothing if not entirely consistent, her thoughtless remarks and self-involved ruminations always simple to read and guard against. That was not the case with Evelyn Hawke.

***

Richard rode out to visit the parsonage with Darcy to collect the requested names, as his cousin would not hear of Elizabeth leaving the house, even well bundled, in a carriage, with footmen to attend her. She had frowned at her husband but acquiesced. Richard shook his head, thinking that if Darcy did not offer her a little freedom, she would soon take it on her own. Knowing his newest cousin, she would then take on more than she ought. Clearly she was feeling better. What was the harm of a walk? *He should bundle up his wife and take her outside himself.* She would be pleased, he would enjoy having her to himself, and they would both be outside, where they were happiest. *It is simpler to see what others should do than do it yourself,* he thought wryly, thinking of his own errors that morning. He would try to say something about Elizabeth to Darcy after dinner. *Not that he will care for my advice.*

As the entire party assembled for the last dinner before the expected arrival of their other guests, Richard sidled up to Miss Hawke to offer an apology for his earlier behavior. It was not the most private of encounters, but he had been thinking about his reaction all day, even on his ride, and could wait no longer. She glanced at the others before leading him to a corner of the room where they might have a bit more privacy.

Elizabeth noted their movement to a quieter part of the room and glanced at her husband. She thought

Sophia Hawke and Richard a good match if only they would see it, but she had not discussed this with her husband. Staunchly unwilling to act her mother's part, Elizabeth was determined not to interfere. Other than creating opportunities that allowed them to be in company together, she would engage in no matchmaking. The looks the two were wearing did not offer her hope that this was a romantic conversation, but it did at least hint that there was a relationship of some sort building between the two. Perhaps it would serve as a beginning.

Before her own marriage, her husband had explained the earl's devotion to maintaining his family's unsullied image as a reason for his initial concern about their engagement. She had very nearly scoffed out loud at such a ridiculous presumption. Lady Catherine, she had pointed out, had consistently and overtly made a mockery of decorum and propriety, sending out vitriolic letters to every contact she had left in the *haut ton* to insist that Elizabeth Darcy, "the usurper," never be admitted to the best drawing rooms in London. If there were to be a blemish on the family honor, it would be from that quarter, not from hers. Fortunately, the letters had forced the earl to avoid a public breach in the family by publicly supporting his nephew's marriage and privately censuring his sister. As a result, he had, in less time than she had expected, come first to acknowledge her as his nephew's wife and then to appreciate her as a niece.

The family honor, Elizabeth believed, would not be blighted should Richard come to care for Sophia Hawke. Even if it did acquire a little tarnish, she told herself, it would be thoroughly worth it if the consequence were to have Richard happily settled in England. Savvier now than in the past, she rejected outright the notion that there would be an issue with acceptance by either the *ton* or the earl's political allies. Unless both his brother and nephew perished before him, Richard would only ever have a courtesy title. He was neither in line for nor interested in a seat in Parliament, proclaiming he had been a soldier too long to be a politician. Sophia Hawke was a largely unknown heiress in possession of a significant fortune. Having an uncle with political enemies would mean little if her husband sought no such power, and as merely the second son of the Earl of Matlock and the daughter of a wealthy, untitled Staffordshire gentleman, it would be an entirely eligible, unremarkable match. *It is absurd*, she thought, with a shake of her head, *as a more truly remarkable couple would be difficult to find*. In any case, it did not signify. She herself had faced more scrutiny than she believed Richard and Sophia would encounter. The earl, she knew, would be more skeptical in his analysis of such a match, as he had long planned to increase his political connections with his younger son's marriage. She pondered that for a moment before recognizing another difference between her own situation and theirs. *They are both of age, and Miss Hawke has Darlington. Richard did fall for a woman of fortune after all.* She recalled with humor Richard's farewell to Darcy as they set out upon their wedding tour to warmer climes.

"I am truly happy for you, you lucky sot," Richard had said with a grin and a clap on his cousin's shoulder.

Elizabeth thought perhaps Richard had stumbled into a bit of luck himself.

***

Not oblivious to the silent but avid speculation their brief conversation was begetting around the room, Richard and Sophia stood speaking to one another in low, urgent tones. Sophia's face was drawn, closed, demonstrating her consternation and unease, while Richard's searching gaze indicated not love or even admiration, but contrition. Of course, there was nobody in company who would be so improper as to openly watch the two, but neither

Richard nor Sophia had any doubt they were being observed.

Richard swallowed nervously. "I simply wished to apologize for my rudeness earlier today. I am not a religious man. I am not accustomed to being an object of prayer, and I responded rudely. At the risk of behaving inconsistently, I must beg your forgiveness." He tried to meet Miss Hawke's eyes, but she would not look at him. Her face remained pinched, thoughtful, and it pained him to see it. He held his breath and awaited her reply. After a few excruciating moments, it came in a voice so soft he had to lean in to hear it.

"I cannot speak of this here, Colonel, but I wish to make you understand. I have said I am not a pious woman. I do, however, have faith. I must." Finally, she lifted her eyes to meet his. "You are of course forgiven. You must promise, however, to allow me a further explanation at a more appropriate time."

Richard let out his breath in a rush and her lips curled upwards. "Of course. Tomorrow morning?" he asked. "In the chapel?"

She nodded once.

"Thank you, Miss Hawke," he said, and offered her his arm. Quietly, they returned to the rest of the company.

Chapter Eighteen

RICHARD PULLED ANXIOUSLY at his cravat as he made his way to the chapel, his hands red with chilled. He had risen before the fire in his chambers was built back up and the weather outside was achingly cold. A few inches of powdery snow had fallen overnight, and he briefly wondered whether his parents' travel would be affected.

As he approached the chapel, his thoughts focused more fully on the conversation ahead, and he stepped inside to see Miss Hawke already at prayer. He watched this time with feelings softened by familiarity, and while he had no desire to join her, his eyes did briefly flit to the crucifix upon the wall. He knew precisely when he had given up prayer, not that he had ever been devout. His Sunday visits to church as a child he recalled as excruciatingly dull, a set time each week when he could not move a finger without reprimand while an old man in black clothing droned on about the kind of proper behaviors in which he had little interest.

Richard had given up genuine prayer altogether after the battle at Roleia. Although he had been in the Army for some time, it was at Roleia that he had watched a young boy, no more than fifteen, perhaps, cut nearly asunder by cannon fire. The moment was frozen in time, the image indelibly marked on his memory. It was at that instant he knew with a resounding certainty that a loving God could never countenance such slaughter. He believed in God, he told himself. He just had no use for Him. Any prayers he uttered now before heading to battle were more out of superstition than faith.

It was only a few moments later that Miss Hawke stood and turned to greet him. She was wearing a long-sleeved gown. and was wrapped in a jonquil shawl, but still appeared to be cold. He offered her his arm.

"Perhaps we should seek the warmth of a fire in the breakfast room? I think it should be some time before anyone rises. I expect my cousin will watch his wife eat before gracing us with his presence this morning."

She smiled a little at that, a satisfied smile he thought, before she nodded her agreement. She accepted his arm and they strolled to the room where, as Richard had surmised, the fire had been built up, the wood crackling merrily in the grate. The room had not yet had time to completely warm, but it was far more comfortable than the chapel and there were no servants about. Richard drew a few chairs to face the hearth and held hers for her while she sat. Then he took his own chair, prepared to hear her recriminations in full. *It is the least I can do,* he thought pensively.

"When do your parents arrive, Colonel?" she asked politely.

"After breakfast, Miss Hawke, if the weather cooperates. I do not," he continued, "believe we are here to discuss travel plans."

"Indeed. This will not take long, Colonel," said Sophia quietly. "I simply could not discuss it in a drawing room with four other people in attendance." She sat, her fingers tangling and untangling the fringe at one end of her shawl while she spoke. "I do not pray because I am particularly pious, Colonel, as I have said before."

He nodded, understanding that this was not a time for interruption.

Her eyes closed, and he watched as some indefinable emotion flit across her face. He felt his stomach constrict as he recognized the kind of pain he knew he carried. It passed soon enough, however, and he was relieved when she opened her eyes again to stare into his.

"It is no great mystery, sir. I had nothing, not so long ago. Nearly nothing, I suppose I must say. But now," she shook her head, "it is almost too much." She tried to smile, but it appeared more a grimace. "I could not sleep in the bed at Matlock, did you know? It was far too soft. I was fortunate that it was summer, for I slept upon the floor."

He grunted and nodded. He knew the feeling, when one was gone too long, how unused to any sort of luxury one became. How uncomfortable it became.

"So you see, then, I had nothing. I had less than nothing. I could not even accept that which had been provided for me."

Richard said nothing, waiting for her to continue.

"Now, in the space of a few months, I have so much. An embarrassment of riches, really. I have everything." She paused again, thinking her words through. "But because I have so much, I am very afraid. . . *very afraid*, of losing it. When I had nothing, there was less to fear. I was concerned only with myself. Then, when Jack decided it was his duty to protect me," she said affectionately, "I was concerned for him as well. But now. . ." Her eyebrows knitted in concentration.

Richard rubbed the bridge of his nose. He knew now what she was going to say, should have known yesterday when she had mentioned being afraid. It made perfect sense.

"Even when I had little in the way of possessions or friends, I was afraid of losing what I did have. I was afraid to lose Evie." Her forehead wrinkled in thought and the rest spilled out in a rush. "Then I thought I *had* lost Evie, but was afraid for Jack, and you, then Evie again, and Mr. Darcy and Mr. Bingley. Now I must add Mrs. Darcy and Georgiana, for they are wonderful friends, so much better than I had even imagined them." She thought for a moment and then said firmly, "I even worry for your parents, little though they need it." Her lips twisted in concentration. "I have seen how fragile, how dangerous life can be, so the fear, the worry, the concern, the love I feel is too big, too. . . heavy, I suppose, for me to carry on my own. When I pray, I am asking for a little help to bear the load." She smiled bashfully. "Perhaps more than a little help." She cleared her throat. "I have done things," she murmured, "as you have done things, and I feel unworthy, but I rather selfishly ask anyway. And it does—help, I mean." She sighed deeply and closed her eyes, suddenly very vulnerable, and said, weakly, "I am rambling. Did any of that make sense?"

The revelation of her struggles, so like his own, struck Richard silent. She was better, so much better than he. To his shame, he had faced his fear by refusing to feel it, succeeding in most cases by convincing himself that he was the only one in danger, that he need not fear loss in the way he knew his family feared they might lose him. While he was away, he could manage it tolerably well. When he returned, even he could not shut the fear away entirely, so he hid it, dishonestly, behind stories and jests.

It was at its worst in the brief period when his ship was in sight of English shores but before it had docked, suspending him between dread and uncertainty. Would everyone he left at home still be there to greet his arrival? What had he missed in the time he had been away? Since the last letter? It had been on one of these returns he had appeared at the estate only to find his brother's wife had been dead for nearly six months. He had liked her though they had not been able to spend much time together. Rebecca had made Phillip a little less self-important, a little more human and a good deal happier. Together they had doted on their young son. She had been quite young herself, healthy enough that he would never have believed a fever could carry her off so quickly, so unexpectedly, on what Phillip had only meant to be a brief visit to London. The shock of that loss and his guilt at not being with his brother the entire first half of his mourning remained with him still. As in so many things, it had been Darcy, so well acquainted with grieving for loved ones, who had stepped in to support Phillip.

Richard had no desire to lower the walls that protected him against further loss and he had learned the maneuver well as a son of the Earl of Matlock. Yet Sophia had not put up walls, tucking her emotions away in a bid to remain strong. She had faced her fears, accepted them, and asked for help. It was an act of faith so simple yet so incredibly difficult that he could not help but deeply admire her for it.

He bowed his head. He more than admired her, and he thought she might admire him. What a terrible dance this was, to wait for a surety that might never arrive. He remembered his cousin's words: *I never knew you to be averse to risk, Richard.* Could he take a chance with this woman? Would she even want him? He had thought she might, only a short time ago. He shut his eyes, squeezing them tight, hoping, perhaps, for an epiphany, but all that came was what he already knew, that every day he felt more, desired more.

A hand gently touched his arm and he opened his eyes. Her face was turned to his, her gaze intense but warm, and his heart began to beat a little faster. He wished to play with the errant lock of her hair falling across her cheek and had to make a fist to keep his hand still. *We are running out of time and I am out of patience. I must know one way or another, before I make another stupid misjudgment or father arrives. He will never let us alone otherwise.* If he wanted to know whether he stood a chance, he would need to ask. Discomfited by his prolonged silence, Sophia began to withdraw her hand from his arm, but his hand reached up quickly to catch and hold it, in much the same way she had held his when he had lifted her onto her horse. She was startled, but made no move to pull away.

"Miss Hawke," Richard said earnestly, "I know there are certain obstacles we must work our way through, not the least of which is my own obtuseness," he saw her smile demurely at this and felt his lips tugging upwards in answer, "but might you do me the singular honor of allowing me to court you?"

He gazed at her face and was abashed to realize she was genuinely astonished by his request.

"But," she sputtered, "your father said. . ."

In for a penny, Richard thought, letting out the breath he had been holding. He gently brushed her cheek with his free hand, toying with the golden strand of her hair that teased him. "My father wishes for more political influence and hopes I will marry a titled woman of the ton. Unfortunately for him, I have no use for a young lady who wishes for seasons in town with silk gowns and balls, dinner parties and gossip. In fact, the older I grow, the more like my dour cousin I become, for I can think of few things more certain to torture me." He paused. "I have not been a good man, Miss Hawke. I have not been. . ." he paused here, uncertain how to give voice to what he meant to say, but she shook her head at him, a few blonde curls bobbing merrily. She had the impertinence to look amused.

"Chaste?" she interjected with a sudden grin and upraised eyebrows.

Richard felt the tips of his ears grow hot and his face began to flush as it had not since he was a very young man. That was not what he had meant, but he was grateful for the humor in her interruption. Besides, this too was true. He nodded. Never had his exploits felt more entirely ridiculous than they did now.

Miss Hawke seemed to consider his acknowledgement. "Will I ever have to meet them?" she asked seriously.

"No," he said simply. He had at least been discreet.

"And you are," she asked, blushing, "healthy?"

He nodded numbly. He must be offering a courtship to the only maid in the kingdom who would ask such a question, who would even know to ask. Given his past, though, he thought sourly, she was wise to do so. Still, there was something rather humorous, even absurd, about the two of them standing here with bright red faces.

"Well then," she said quietly. "In return for such a confession, I must tell you something as well."

He swallowed hard when he realized she had not yet answered him. "What is it, Miss Hawke?" A million awful possibilities crowded his mind, so many that he could barely hear her over the cacophony in his head.

She glanced to her right, to her left, behind the chair to be certain the room was clear. Then she leaned in very close to him. He smelled a faint odor of pine in her hair as she hovered just an inch from him. He shivered as she spoke, still in very low tones, directly in his ear.

"I can shoot an apple hanging from a branch three hundred feet away."

He snorted and she laughed softly. He rubbed his ear absentmindedly.

"I stand warned," he replied with a smirk.

He wanted to laugh aloud at the ridiculousness of their situation, the deucedly odd exchange in which they were engaging, but he was too anxious to hear her reply. He grasped her other hand, looked her full in the face, and asked, "Well?"

She examined his face curiously. "I had not expected this. Not at all."

He squeezed her hands gently. "And yet you will accept, will you not?"

She pursed her lips. "Your father will be displeased."

He smiled. "My mother will be ecstatic."

Sophia tilted her head quizzically. "It will bring disquiet into the Darcys' home over the holiday."

Blast, thought Richard. *She will run out of excuses eventually, will she not?* "Darcy is the one who told me I was a fool not to ask."

Her eyes widened in surprise. "Truly?"

Richard grinned. "Truly."

She stood quietly and Richard stood too, hoping he had at last convinced her. Then she sighed and asked, "What of your career? Should we eventually marry, I would not wish to be left on my own in Staffordshire." Her meditative expression warmed him. *Progress*, he thought.

"Sophia," he said, unthinkingly taking the liberty before she had offered it, "I can only promise we will discuss it. The decision may not be entirely my own."

Her lips twitched at his use of her Christian name, but she did not address it. "You would give serious consideration to selling your commission, then, at the least?"

He nodded and she began to worry her bottom lip. He tried not to watch, as it made him wish to make her stop by pressing his own lips to hers.

She hesitated, then said, her voice wavering slightly, "And my uncle?"

Richard considered that. Of course she would be concerned, his own father had told her it was an impediment to any man who might wish to marry her. He had a wicked thought.

"What a joy it would be for Archibald Hawke to hear that you are a Fitzwilliam."

She looked at her feet instead of him, and he could wait no longer.

"The only question remaining, Miss Hawke," Richard said softly, moving a little closer and leaning in to speak in her ear, "is whether you might be able to love a broken-down old soldier like me?"

She lifted her face to his, smiling the full, bright smile that had stunned him as she stood near the laundry awaiting his help, then laughingly replied, "I can if you can."

"Yes?" he asked, his chest filling with something he could not entirely identify but felt like joy.

"Yes," she said firmly, and nodded her head. "Yes."

He gently placed her hand on his chest, against his heart. It was beating very quickly. She began to breathe a little faster, and Richard imagined her own heart beating in tune with his.

"I believed it would be far more difficult to get you to agree," he admitted ruefully.

"Well," she responded teasingly, "I do have other questions. . ."

He laughed and placed a finger gently on her lips.

"Stop," he said, his voice falling almost to a whisper. "Allow me to savor my victory first."

As she began to protest, he leaned down to brush her lips with his own. Her breath stopped for a moment and she stood very still.

"Are you all right?" Richard asked with a gentle laugh.

She blinked twice, then put her lips up to his in answer.

Chapter Nineteen

D O YOU THINK," Elizabeth asked her husband between delicate bites of toast and egg, "that Richard will ask her soon?" She carefully placed her fork on her plate and leaned back into the cushions of the settee in her sitting room.

Darcy was still so pleased to watch his wife eat that he was barely listening. "Ask who what?" Now that she had finished her breakfast, he set down his cup and moved to fill his own plate from what remained on the tray.

Elizabeth laughed and took a small sip of tea. She was feeling a great deal better now. She still felt the need to eat slowly and take very small meals, but she had only been ill once over the past several days. Being able to return to the dinner table had been a tremendous boon to her confidence. She was more than pleased that the timing was so fortuitous. Now she would be able to truly perform her role as hostess for Lord and Lady Matlock.

"Do you think Richard will ask Miss Hawke for a courtship? If he means to, he ought to decide soon. He has little time left before he must return to London and he shall have to share that time with his family."

"Now I know you are feeling better," her husband said flatly, though with some amusement in his tone, "for you are back to asking impertinent questions."

"Well, I presume he has mentioned something to you," she said, arching one eyebrow at him. "It is difficult not to notice that he was out of her favor yesterday, before escorting her and Miss Evelyn in to dinner."

"I have no idea about the topic of that discussion, Elizabeth, nor have I any desire to know," he said firmly. "Surely you do not mean to have me disrupt their privacy?"

She smiled. "If you are chastising, you must be feeling more sure of me," she teased, patting his cheek. "Certainly you see the aptness of the match despite the fastidiousness of your uncle?"

Darcy shook his head at her. He was not honestly upset, not at all. Her humor was returning, and she already looked healthier to him, better fed and better rested. She was eating only small amounts but had taken several small meals and tea yesterday without incident. She was still easily fatigued, but she was clearly improving, and the terrible knot in his stomach was easing a bit. He owed Miss Hawke a great deal and would be pleased to call her cousin, but it was not his decision to make. His support, however, they would both have, should Richard ever request it.

"I think it best to leave that determination to Richard and Miss Hawke, my dear. They are both of age and have been for some time. Should they wish it, there is little the earl can do without making a family breach public, and as you know," he shook his head, remembering, "he despises the public demonstration of private strife. The real question is how much loyalty Miss Hawke feels to the earl. She may not desire to thwart his wishes."

Elizabeth considered this for a moment before saying, quite seriously, "I believe you men may be surprised at the answer to that question, William. Particularly the earl."

***

The cold and snow had indeed slowed their travel, but the rest of the Fitzwilliam family arrived around three in the afternoon. Darcy, Georgiana, and Richard were outside to meet them. Elizabeth, at her husband's insistence, was indoors. When she began to protest that she had met the Hawkes' carriage, he set his jaw and glared at her.

"You were not here to advise, William," she said pertly, "and in the excitement of my guests' company, until this moment I had quite forgotten."

"Convenient, Mrs. Darcy," he replied gruffly. "It is freezing outside. Please just wait in the drawing room where it is warm. Nobody will fault you for not venturing out of doors." With this, he turned on his heel and strode to the front hall where he was handed his coat.

Elizabeth crossed her arms across her chest. "Maddening man," she grumbled quietly. She turned on her heel in an imitation of her husband and walked, under protest, to the drawing room doors. She took a breath, nodded at the footman to turn the knobs, and was let into the room where the two Hawke women were seated, waiting for the arrival of the remaining guests. Miss Evelyn was concentrating on a piece of embroidery, but Miss Hawke looked up from the infant's gown she was stitching with silent sympathy in her face. Elizabeth twisted her lips into a wry grin that felt more like a frown and wandered to a chair, sitting carefully to wait.

It was no more than a quarter of an hour before the Fitzwilliams were ushered into the room and Elizabeth rose to greet them. Lady Matlock opened her arms wide and gave Elizabeth a warm but gentle embrace.

"How good it is to see you, my dear!" she said enthusiastically. "I trust you are well and are prepared for the onslaught?"

Elizabeth smiled. "Indeed, Aunt Eleanor. We have all been eagerly anticipating your visit."

As the countess smiled and turned to hug Georgiana and greet the Hawkes, the earl stepped up to take her hands. "We must thank you, my dear, for the invitation to Pemberley," he said in his deep, gravelly voice. "It has been years since we have had the family together for the holiday."

"You are all very welcome, Uncle Henry," she said sweetly, noting that apparently, Lady Catherine and Anne were not included as family. Elizabeth did like the earl, but she thought it might take more time to feel entirely comfortable with him. For his wife, she already felt a great fondness. She spied Phillip conversing with his brother and her husband crouching to speak at eye's level with Pembroke, Phillip's young son.

"And who have we here?" she asked gleefully. Darcy turned his head to bestow a cheerful smile upon his wife, his blue eyes twinkling with mischief, and she knew he would take great pleasure spoiling Pembroke while he was with them. She pondered whether he would do the same for his own child. *No, she thought, a Darcy child would not be spoiled. Well, perhaps not a Darcy son.* She felt a great warmth well up in her chest as she thought about how the stern Fitzwilliam Darcy would behave with a daughter and nearly laughed aloud at the thought. *Indulged,* she thought fondly, *terribly indulged. But not spoiled.*

Pembroke was bouncing up and down now, and broke away from Darcy to race to his newest cousin. They had met twice, once only briefly and again for a fortnight in the country, and he had found in her a most obliging playmate. When his father had mentioned they were invited to Pemberley for Christmas, his only question had been whether his cousin Elizabeth would be there.

Darcy, worried that the boy's enthusiasm might be too rough for Elizabeth, said urgently, "Pembroke, have a care!" The boy, hearing such harsh words, immediately tried to stop, but found himself skidding, the rug folding up like a fan before him.

Fortunately, the earl was in his path, and the boy was safely swept up into his grandfather's arms.

Darcy stood and brushed the palms of his hands on his waistcoat nervously.

"Thank you, Uncle Henry," Elizabeth said gaily, then turned her attention to the boy. His sandy hair and hazel eyes reminded her more of Richard than Phillip, as did his behavior.

"You have grown a good deal since last we met, my friend," she said as he held a leg out for her inspection. "Soon you shall be as tall as your cousin William."

"Taller!" cried the boy merrily, tossing a lock of hair out of his eyes. "I shall best them all, Cousin Lizzy, you will see!"

"Shall you begin by giving me a kiss, then?" She held out her cheek, but he shook his head and hid his face in his grandfather's coat.

"No!" he yelled, "No kisses!" They all laughed, Elizabeth included.

"Well then, Master Pembroke," she concluded, "as you are so opposed, I shall not force you. We shall play some games tomorrow, though. There are some wonderful toys in the nursery just waiting for a boy like you to play with them. Are you interested?"

Phillip approached Elizabeth and placed a kiss on her cheek. "Thank you, Elizabeth. We are pleased to be here. Shall I take this rascal upstairs and get him settled?"

Elizabeth nodded. "Before you go, Master Pembroke, I must have a handshake since you have refused me a kiss."

Pembroke nodded and held out his hand, which Elizabeth shook heartily. He giggled, showing two missing front teeth, and Elizabeth felt truly happy. *A child's laughter is the very best sound in the world*, she thought. Phillip grinned and took his son from the earl.

"Come, my boy," he said, "let us see what wonders await us in your rooms." The viscount set his son on his feet before taking Pembroke's hand and leading him out of the room.

Richard glanced at Sophia while everyone's attention was on Pembroke. She was watching the boy with a wistful expression, full of longing, and while he was not yet entirely accustomed to her acceptance of a courtship, he began to consider what must eventually follow marriage. He had never thought to marry, let alone have children of his own, but he now suspected that a family, a family with Sophia, would answer all his dearest wishes.

Lady Matlock was charmed by her grandson's conversation with Elizabeth, and she smiled to see her nephew so pleased to have his family near. Her gaze next traveled to her younger son, thinking, as she often did, what a wonderful father he would be someday. However, when she glanced his way, Richard was not watching Pembroke as William was. He was gazing in quite the opposite direction. Without moving her head, his mother slid her eyes to the left to confirm that he was, in fact, drinking in the face of Sophia Hawke. In his countenance was a tenderness that caused a surge of hope in her breast. *Could it be, finally? After all this time?* The Countess of Matlock turned her eyes back to her grandson lest she be discovered. *Well, we shall have to help this along.* She heard Elizabeth mention that their rooms were ready, and she did wish to change out of her travelling clothes. Her youngest son walked over to his mother to escort her to her chambers and she patted his arm lovingly. *I must speak with Elizabeth. There is some work to be done.*

***

When Sophia emerged from her room dressed for dinner, the colonel was waiting for her in the hall. He eyed her approvingly, in a sage gown with a rounded neck and fitted long sleeves, adorned with a wide ribbon in a darker green. A thin gold chain with a teardrop emerald enhanced the simple, elegant lines of her figure. Her hair was up with one long, thick curl left to trail enticingly down her back. It reached a few inches below her shoulders now, he noted with satisfaction. Hairpins adorned with pearls held the style in place.

"Am I late?" she asked lightly, when it appeared he was content to study her rather than speak.

"You know you are not," he replied with a shake of his head. "But I did not wish to miss the opportunity to escort you."

"Then you ought to begin, do not you think?"

He paused. "Shall we wait for your sister?"

"Evie went down long ago," Sophia said ruefully. "She does not require the same level of maintenance."

He smiled, taking her hand and bending over it for a kiss. "You are beautiful now, but you are stunning in your riding habit, accosting me with snow-laden branches."

She laughed a little at that and rolled her eyes. "How very kind of you to note that I appear to best advantage if I do nothing."

"That," he said with a wink, "is exactly what I mean."

She did not blush, but she did avert her eyes for a moment, embarrassed by the compliment.

"Sophia," he said quietly.

"Yes?" she asked without raising her eyes.

Richard cocked his head to the side, trying to make eye contact. "You must learn to accept praise from me."

She would not look up. "I do."

He gave a short, disbelieving groan. "Prove it."

She glanced up at that. "How?"

"I will offer a compliment," he proposed, "and you will simply say 'Thank you.'"

She shook her head at him. "Do not be ridiculous."

He refused to be swayed. "I am completely in earnest. Let us try." He tipped her chin up to face him. "You look beautiful this evening, Sophia." He waited.

She stammered a little. "This is foolish."

He shook his head at her. "Wrong answer. Try again. You are beautiful this evening, Sophia."

She squirmed a little, but met his gaze and said, weakly, "Thank you."

He chuckled. "Now, say it as though you believe it. Accept that you are a beautiful woman, Sophia. It is nothing more than the truth."

Finally, she looked up into his face, her dark eyes searching his, and in them Richard saw, for the first time, a vulnerability. He gazed back, trying to show her in his expression that his admiration was sincere.

She bit her bottom lip lightly and he said once more, "You are beautiful tonight, my dear."

"Thank you," she whispered.

"That will do for now," he said appreciatively. He offered his arm and she took it. As they walked, she quickly changed the subject.

"Have you spoken with your father?" she asked with some trepidation, and he shook his head.

He had thought about this all afternoon. "I believe I will speak with William first. He will undoubtedly tell Elizabeth, who will inform my mother, and then we will have my father surrounded."

"An ambush, Colonel?" she asked skeptically, "I know he will be displeased." She pursed her lips. "Still, reinforcements are clearly called for."

Richard shrugged. "I believe he thinks more highly of you than you suppose."

"Perhaps," she allowed, "but not well enough to wish to have me as a daughter."

"You cannot know that," Richard said with more hope than confidence.

"No?" Sophia asked, arching an eyebrow. "I believe he told me so himself."

"No," he stated emphatically. "In any case, I shall not be asking for a blessing, not permission. His is not needed."

Sophia considered this. "No," she finally agreed with a satisfied nod. "It is not."

Chapter Twenty

IT WAS THE FOLLOWING morning before Richard could get his cousin alone. He knocked and entered Darcy's study without waiting for a response.

"I do not know why you even bother knocking," came the surly greeting from Darcy, who, despite facing away from the door, knew exactly who had entered. He was standing by one of the tall oak bookcases where he had been searching for a specific ledger and was in the process of removing it from the shelf.

"You work too much, William," Richard responded lightly. "I am here to give you sport instead."

That caught Darcy's attention, and he turned to face his cousin. "Sport?"

Richard chuckled a little and shrugged. "I have asked Miss Hawke for a courtship."

Elizabeth will be pleased. "Excellent, Richard," said Darcy with a grin. He tossed the ledger on his desk and moved to shake his cousin's hand. "I thought you would go right for the engagement, but I suppose you military men like to proceed cautiously."

"Honestly, William, can you not just be happy for me?" Richard asked laughingly but not entirely joking. Darcy's grin vanished.

"I am happy for you, Richard," he said softly. "Are you here to discuss your father?"

"I am. I knew that once I told you, you would tell your lovely wife."

"Of course," Darcy replied with a wave of his hand. "In any case, I do not think anyone is unaware of your mutual affection. Every woman in the house seems to be awaiting your declaration."

Except perhaps her own sister, Richard thought dismissively. He cringed as he realized what William had just said. Had he been so obvious? "Must you make it sound like a novel, William?"

Darcy smiled and shook his head. "I am not the one waiting for her at the stables every morning, Richard." Richard's eyes narrowed in displeasure.

"None of that, now. John Briggs works for me, not you."

Richard shook his head while his cousin continued, "And for once, I am not the one saying precisely the wrong thing at every juncture." Darcy clapped his embarrassed cousin on the shoulder. "I would never have thought to see you turn into such a bumbling lover, cousin, but I am thoroughly enjoying it."

"It is my pleasure to provide you such entertainment, William," Richard said with a frown. "Just let Elizabeth know that it is all right to tell my mother about this."

Darcy looked troubled. "You may want to approach your father directly, Richard. He may not take this well should it come from anyone else."

Richard nodded. "I plan to do just that, but I want my reinforcements in place beforehand."

"What do you plan to do if he objects?" Darcy asked. Richard did not need the earl's permission, but his acquiescence would ease the way.

"I plan to make her my wife, William," Richard said seriously. "The only person who can keep that from happening is Sophia Hawke."

***

The drawing room was bright with winter sunlight, and Sophia Hawke sat upon a chair nearest the window as she worked her way through a pile of baby clothing. Her sister was right to say that her stitching was quick and sure, and she had made a good deal of progress with the basket she shared with her sister. Evelyn, though very accomplished in her decorations, was a good deal slower in her work, particularly since she had been distracted by the immense library down the hall. As Christmas was quickly approaching, Sophia realized she would have to press her sister to put off her reading for a few days so that the gifts would be ready before Boxing Day. She had heard from Georgiana that while Mrs. Darcy distributed the traditional gift of money to the servants in the house, Georgiana and her Aunt Eleanor would take the clothing out to the tenant homes. Four families were expecting new arrivals, and the clothing the women had generated would be more than ample should they be finished in time. Sophia continued to work, as she thought it would not go amiss to have additional gifts to use during the final months of Mrs. Darcy's confinement, when she might not wish to be doing such work. This way, no tenant would feel slighted. In any case, it kept her busy.

As she whipped the final stitch through a tiny gown, she gazed around the room. Georgiana was working on an infant's cap and Mrs. Darcy was reading and trying to pretend she was not nodding off. Sophia smiled and shook her head. The mistress of the house was still quite young and now appeared like a little girl trying not to be sent to the nursery. Sophia waited until she caught Georgiana's eye and then nodded once towards her hostess.

Georgiana touched her sister's shoulder and said, in a low voice, "You are about to slide off your chair, Elizabeth. Go back to bed if you are weary. We are well able to entertain ourselves."

For a moment, it appeared as though she might protest, but she stopped, her face flushing in embarrassment. She laughed at herself a little, nodded, and stood.

"I beg you would both excuse me," she said cheerfully, "but it appears the little one wishes me abed. I will see you all for tea."

"Good afternoon, Mrs. Darcy," said Sophia blandly, as though she had noticed nothing.

"Good afternoon, Elizabeth," called Georgiana as her sister made her exit.

After Mrs. Darcy departed, Sophia laid the gown on top of her pile and moved to sit beside Georgiana. She leaned over to take a cap from her basket, but they were all completed as well. She admired the small, even stitching and set the cap back down, before spotting a basket of large material scraps. A few of them were of a finer linen than the clothing she had been working on, and she pulled them out, smoothing them against her leg. She took a pair of scissors and began to cut in order to preserve the largest pieces for the scrap basket. When she was finished, she had two handkerchief-sized squares. She quickly folded the edges and sewed them down. Then she began to think about what she would like to embroider. She could ask Evie to do this part, but she wanted to make them a gift for Richard.

It did not take long for her to decide upon the decoration, and she selected her thread. She could not offer the colonel a gift while they were only courting, but her skills being what they were, she would be optimistic and begin now. Sophia could not say exactly why she had so much faith in her suitor. Being with him simply felt natural, and despite her jaundiced view of the world, her cynicism did not apply to him. She was sure they would not be courting for long. Richard would either convince his father or he would not, but either way, they would proceed to an engagement before he left. She would not allow herself to believe otherwise. *Richard*, she thought, the name sounding foreign in her mind. She had never allowed herself to think of him as anything but "the colonel." *Richard*. It began to feel a bit more natural. Perhaps with time, she would not think of him as anything else.

"Well, is this not a lovely sight?" came a woman's voice from the doorway. Both younger women glanced up to see Lady Matlock striding into the room. "So quietly engaged in your good work," she said, raising her eyebrows approvingly.

Georgiana laughed lightly. "We are nearly finished, Aunt Eleanor. Sophia has started some other project, I think."

Sophia looked at the work in her hands and tried not to blush. She had not realized Georgiana was watching her so carefully.

"Well, and what is it you are working on, my dear?" asked Lady Matlock, walking over to Sophia and sitting next to her. She took the linen from Sophia's hand to inspect it. It did not look like much yet. "A gift for my son?"

Georgiana's eyes grew round as her head shot up from her work. "Sophia," she gasped. "Do you have an understanding with Richard?"

Sophia heart raced and she felt her cheeks growing warm. *Ambush*, she thought in a panic. *Good Lord, even his mother is a soldier.*

"Why would you ask such a question, Lady Matlock?" Sophia asked, stalling for time to form a coherent answer. Would Richard care if she confirmed his mother's guess? Georgiana raised her eyebrows, impatiently awaiting an answer to the question still hanging in the air.

The woman smiled and placed a pudgy hand on Sophia's leg to give it a loving pat. "Oh, my dear, it was all over his face. And now," she added meaningfully, "it is all over yours." She inspected the cloth she still held. "It is too large for a woman, so it is not for your sister. The linen is too coarse for a woman's handkerchief in any case."

Wretched idea, to make them here in a public room, Sophia chastised herself. She had only meant to keep her hands busy, but making something for Richard had seemed so normal a thing to do, she had not considered the need for secrecy. She wished he were here to speak to his mother. Yet, had he not mentioned he would like her blessing before he approached his father? She ought to have told Evie by now. She would have to remedy that soon

She drew in a deep breath and looked Lady Matlock in the eye. "Your son asked me to accept a courtship shortly before you arrived."

Lady Matlock clapped her hands together with an enthusiasm that surprised Sophia. Richard had assured her that his mother would be delighted to hear he was courting her, but she had not truly believed it until now. Her heart leapt and she felt tears pooling in her eyes, but she fought them down.

"And you said yes, Sophia, did you not?" Georgiana asked insistently.

Sophia nodded. "I did."

Georgiana squealed and tossed the infant's cap down on the settee as she leapt across the floor to hug her friend. "Oh, Sophia, we shall be cousins! How wonderful!"

"I hope so, Georgiana," Sophia said quietly. She was certain that if she tried to speak in her ordinary voice that it would fail her completely. Everything was so difficult with Evie, and Georgiana's affection was so exuberant, so uncomplicated.

"Richard will propose, my dear," Lady Matlock said confidently. "Anyone with eyes can see how besotted he is with you." She smiled broadly. "And I shall at last see him wed." She still held Sophia's hands and gave them a squeeze. She leaned in to bestow a kiss on Sophia's cheek.

As Lady Matlock pulled away, Sophia smelled rosewater and felt a rush of longing so intense that it entirely overwhelmed her. She closed her eyes and bowed her head, stiffening against an onslaught of emotions she had not allowed herself to feel in many years.

"Sophia, dear, are you all right?" She heard Lady Matlock ask, but Sophia could not answer. She feared she might burst into tears if she tried. When people were cruel or indifferent, it was a simple matter to remain placid, but kindness of any kind seemed to undo her. *Take control of yourself, Sophia,* she chanted to herself. *Gain control lest they all think you mad.* So engaged was she in trying to keep her tears from escaping that she entirely missed several other people entering the room. There was the sound of hurried footsteps and then someone spoke.

"Sophia?" came a low voice from directly before her. A large, warm hand took her cold one. "Love, what is it?"

Sophia shook her head and concentrated on the roughness of the hand as she struggled to regain control. Finally, she gasped out, "Rosewater."

Richard spoke gently, as though she was a spooked horse. "I do not understand." She wanted to laugh, but the sound died in her throat.

Sophia clutched his hand and cleared her throat, shook her head, and finally opened her eyes. He was kneeling on the ground before her so that he could better view her face. Her heart was pounding so hard with the memories the scent evoked it was painful.

He placed his free hand on her cheek and she instinctively tilted her face to meet his palm.

"There is nothing wrong, truly," she said, placing a hand over his own. "It is only that," she cast a shy glance at Lady Matlock, "my mother wore rosewater, too."

Richard was watching her with no less concern for her disjointed explanation, but Lady Matlock let out a breath she seemed to have been holding and threw her arms around the girl.

"Oh, Sophia," she exclaimed, beginning to cry noisily. "Did I remind you of your mother just now?"

Sophia nodded tightly. *Do not cry. Do not cry.*

Only Richard saw the wetness gathering in the corners of her eyes. He kissed her hand and the dam broke. Sophia cried silently, as she had learned to do, but the tears would not stop. They simply slipped from her eyes and rolled down her cheeks. Her arms slowly, gingerly rose to embrace Lady Matlock. She felt Richard's hand move to the small of her back, knowing he was completely bemused but that he felt a need to remain close.

"I am all right," she told him, but the ache in her voice was unmistakable.

"Well, my dear," sniffed Lady Matlock, straightening her skirts after she loosened her arms and sat back. "I shall be very happy to be your mother once you and Richard are wed."

Before anyone, including her son, could recover from their shock at such a bold pronouncement, a deep voice barked from the doorway, "What the devil is going on in here?"

Sophia froze as Richard slowly stood and turned to face the voice. There, in the doorway, stood a red-faced Lord Matlock.

Chapter Twenty-One

DARCY, IN A VOICE that brooked no argument, declared that everyone should go about their business and the men would repair to his study after dinner to answer the earl's question. Mrs. Cronk's food was as delicious as ever, and Mrs. Darcy had made certain to include the favorite dishes of her guests. Still, the atmosphere was strained and tense, a stark contrast to the conviviality of the evenings prior to the Fitzwilliams' arrival.

After the final course was cleared, the members of the party gratefully retired from the table, the women to the music room, the men to the study. Richard caught Sophia's wrist and held her behind as the others left the dining room. He clasped Sophia's hand and pressed a kiss to it.

"I have something to ask you," he whispered.

"What could you have to ask me?" she asked suspiciously, her volume matching his.

He grinned. "Will you marry me?"

"Richard, honestly," she sighed, still in hushed tones. "You ask me *now*? Is this the best proposal you can contrive?"

His lips curled up in amusement. *Will I never have a simple answer from this woman?* "I will offer you a proper proposal later. I just need your consent to dispense with this courtship nonsense. I think we are both old enough to know our own minds. Since I must go battle the old dragon anyway, I might as well tell him what it is I truly want. What we want."

Instead of answering directly, she asked drily, "Your father is a dragon now? Do you have your sword?"

"That," he replied seriously, "might not be a good idea."

Sophia looked up into Richard's unusually dark hazel eyes. In this light, they looked more green than brown. This was not how she had expected her proposal, but she knew her answer. She nodded.

"Of course. I accept."

He smiled widely before schooling his features for the discussion to come. "I will speak to you in the morning," he said quietly. "Do not wait up."

They entered the hallway together. Richard turned towards the study, and Sophia waited as he closed the door softly behind him. It was only the briefest of moments before the yelling began. She recognized the deep bass of the earl and felt a moment of misgiving. She knew that the policies Henry Fitzwilliam had pushed in Parliament had, over the years, saved thousands of people from poverty, made working conditions better in the cities, helped stave off many of the riots that had taken place in the factories of the north, even some nearby in Derbyshire. He was a good man. Still, she thought that with as much power as he had amassed, simply telling a few truths about her acrimonious relationship with Archibald Hawke would not interfere unduly with his work. The earl had asked much of her and she had fulfilled his requests every time. *Is it not my turn, finally?* It might be selfish, it was selfish, but there it was. *Nobody is going to give me my happiness. I shall just have to take it.* With this thought and the cheering image of the colonel, resplendent in his regimentals, facing down the sputtering fire of a recalcitrant dragon, she turned her back to the shouting and walked to the music room.

***

Richard entered the study quietly, but with a dogged sense of determination and no small amount of anger. It was too much, he thought resentfully, to have his father pay attention to him only when he sought to deny him something he wanted. And he did want Sophia as his wife. Desperately. The earl had never done anything for him to earn such a sacrifice on his part, and because he knew for certain he would never give in, he began to plan.

First, he told himself, *I must allow the old man to blow out all his hot air, and then, in the morning, I will write the general again. I will resign the commission from here and they can come drag me away if they must. They have men enough. They can roust Little Boney without me.* His thoughts continued in this way for some time while his father's raised voice crashed down all around him but did not break through.

"Richard!" shouted his father, his posture nearly rigid with anger. He had at last asked something of Richard but his son did not hear, so focused was he on plotting out the life he meant to have. He glanced around the room. Darcy was standing in front of his desk, arms crossed over his chest, lips drawn in a straight line, a posture Richard knew meant his cousin was holding in some anger of his own. Phillip stood a few feet from his father and had apparently been attempting to calm him. Richard gave him a grateful look and his brother lifted his shoulders ever so slightly in a sign of unity. He turned to face the earl.

"Yes, father?" he asked with some resignation.

"I asked you what you hope to accomplish with this alliance?" The earl was nearly growling.

Richard shrugged. "A marriage, father." He paused. "A happy marriage."

"You could have that with any number of the women your mother has lined up to meet you."

Richard shook his head. "No. I could not."

The earl was nearly apoplectic. "No? That is all you have to say to me? After going against your promise?"

Richard shook his head. "What promise would that be, father?"

His father growled, "You promised not to look to Sophia Hawke or her sister for a bride."

Richard was truly confused now. "Father, you never asked for such a promise, and I certainly would never have agreed to it."

"I did, Richard. I asked you and her as well. She promised."

"She has said you never asked such a thing, sir. What you said to me at the time agrees with her understanding—that you told her Jack Hobson was her only choice apart from spinsterhood. Rather presumptuous of you, really."

"Richard," hissed Phillip.

Richard turned to his brother. "What, Phillip?" he asked, upset and hurt. "What is it I am supposed to do here? The man has ignored me my entire life and only wishes to become a father and make pronouncements from on high when I choose a bride he does not like?"

"I knew it," sneered his father. "You are jealous of Phillip."

Richard shook his head, exasperated. "I have never wanted to be the first son. Phillip and Pembroke are more than welcome to the earldom." He looked directly at his brother. "Phillip knows I am not made to be a politician."

Phillip grinned at him despite his father's irritation.

"Phillip, you cannot agree with this. It will compromise your position."

"Father, everyone knows my brother is a little addled," Phillip said, trying to neutralize the situation with humor. "Too much time abroad, you know." He tapped a finger against his temple while Richard shot him a look of gratitude.

"No, Richard," grumbled the earl, thumping his fist against the back of a chair. "You made me a promise."

"As did you, father," Richard replied, his voice strained. "You told me that you loved me." Both Darcy and Phillip turned their eyes away from the pair. "Was that true? Or do you love me only when it is convenient?"

The raised voices and agitated rejoinders continued for several hours, but the more his father said, the less Richard understood. The earl had invented a history out of whole cloth. He insisted that Richard had said and done things that had never occurred, and that he had done them with the intent to injure the family's spotless reputation. Richard stopped arguing after a time, not knowing what to say to the fanciful stories his father was weaving. He could not defend himself other than to say that his father was mistaken, which only sent the earl into another lather over his disloyalty.

Darcy watched his uncle carefully. The man's insistence that the pair had made him a promise not to wed was outlandish considering Richard's continued denials. Richard would not have made such a promise about any woman, feeling he had earned the right to choose his own bride. Shooting a look at Phillip, he could see that his older cousin's thinking was in concert with his own. Nor did he believe Sophia Hawke would make and then break such a vow. She had shown herself honest and honorable in everything she had done since he had known her. During the discussion, a conversation that was largely a diatribe, a sense of dread began to gnaw at him. Darcy paced the room, sat in one of the wingback chairs, stood again, and finally grabbed the edge of his desk before leaning back against it. He had seen this behavior before, in the grandfather of a Cambridge friend.

"Uncle Henry," he said as calmly as he could manage, "when did you say Richard made this promise?"

Phillip and Richard looked at their cousin, unsure why he would ask such a thing. With a barely perceptible shake of his head, Darcy urged them to wait for the answer.

The earl was flustered. "I do not recall. . . April, it must have been. April. After he came home from Rosings."

The room was suddenly silent. "Father," said Richard quietly, "I did not meet Sophia until June."

Darcy cleared his throat gently. "Nobody went to Rosings last April, uncle. Richard was in Spain," he glanced over at his cousin, "or Portugal?" he looked back at his uncle, "and Lady Catherine has not yet apologized to Elizabeth. We will not return until she does."

"It must have been when Richard came home, then. I do not recall the exact date, for heaven's sake. What is the matter with you, Darcy?" The earl glared at his nephew suspiciously.

"Nothing, sir," replied Darcy, as he exchanged a look with Phillip, whose face was now a good deal paler than normal. *He is seeing what I see*, Darcy thought, a sense of melancholy beginning to gather like a misty fog. *Soon it will be Phillip arguing policy.*

"Father," said Richard, trying to hide a hitch in his voice and looking, Darcy thought, more than a little ill himself, "I think you have said everything there is to say." He tugged the bottom of his waistcoat. "I should like you to know that I will marry Miss Hawke. She has agreed to be my wife. My honor is engaged and I will not recant or withdraw." He took his father's hand. "I hope that you can wish me happy."

The earl snatched his hand away. "You are no son of mine," he said bitterly. "Leave me, all of you."

Darcy felt a wave of anger on Richard's behalf, but bit back the retort he wanted to give, that this was *his* study, and that if anyone was to leave, it should be the earl. There was no worry for his uncle now, not like there had been for Georgiana two summers before, Richard when he was abroad, or Elizabeth at the worst of her illness. Instead, he felt only a deep and abiding sadness for what would happen to a man who had always appeared larger than life, not only to him, but to the entire country. It would not be long before the family would have to face the fact that Uncle Henry was only human, and that all humans were mortal.

The other men wandered out into the hall and moved towards the stairs. A footman approached from the other end of the hall to ask whether they ought to snuff the candles lighting the hall and staircases once they were gone. Darcy, thinking that his uncle would likely remain in the study until dawn, nodded his acquiescence.

As they reached the top of the stairs, Richard broke the silence by smiling weakly at his brother and cousin and asking, "Well, will *you* two at least wish me joy?"

"Of course, Richard," said Darcy, extending his hand. "You are a lucky man. She is a fine woman."

Richard took Darcy's hand and nodded. "Thank you, William."

Phillip clapped his brother on the shoulder. "I have not had much time to get to know my new sister," he said with a restrained smile, "but she puts up with your nonsense and is easy on the eyes. I cannot help but think well of her."

Richard pushed his brother away. "A fine thing to say about my betrothed." The men chuckled, but their hearts were elsewhere. Richard felt a petty resentment flare, that after all this time he could not feel the joy he should in his betrothal nor feel free to lay out his grievances to his father. To do so would be unconscionable given what they all believed was happening to the man. He should feel sympathy, and he did, to an extent. But there were other feelings, not at all noble, and he would have to sort through them on his own, as usual.

He was stopped on his way to his room by a footman who presented him a letter on a silver tray. It was late to be receiving post.

"It was here this afternoon, sir," the man said apologetically, "but I was asked not to interrupt you. I would have waited until morning, but thought it might be important."

"Thank you," said Richard with a nod. He removed the letter and went to his room.

When he broke the seal and unfolded the missive, he saw it was a very short note.

Colonel Fitzwilliam, it read, *your bird located in Calais, backed at pushing school.*

Richard sighed. It would have been helpful to have this before spending hours arguing with his father.

Chapter Twenty-Two

IT WAS LATE. Sophia and Evelyn were sitting in the latter's bedchamber as Evie changed into her nightclothes. It had been a difficult discussion, and while much had been revealed about Sophia's relationship with Lord Matlock, she had not explained her whereabouts for the past three years, nor the circumstances of her return. Evie was impatient to hear the rest of the story, but schooled herself to be patient. Sophia would tell her in time, she thought, and she tried not to feel slighted.

Sophia had not been introduced to the Matlocks as a friend of the family, as Evie had long supposed. While their father had met the earl, they were no closer than might be expected of neighbors thirty miles apart, particularly as the earl was so often in

London. Instead, Sophia had approached the man after leaving their uncle's house and had essentially worked for him, though no money had changed hands. At first, she had helped the earl thwart their uncle, who was a corrupt and ruthless man. Then, as her uncle's power waned, she had been asked to perform other, less dangerous tasks, using the same skills Uncle Archibald had taught his eldest niece. She gathered information and ran private messages, and in return, the earl helped keep her hidden and had been of material use in preserving their fortune.

Still difficult to believe, she sighed, though she had slowly come to trust her sister. Remembering her uncle's behavior, not only from the past summer but her entire life, the little moments of pique and anger, the disparagement of a father and mother she barely remembered, and especially his tirades about her sister, should have made his intentions clear long ago. Compared to her sister's diligence and occasionally blunt honesty, it was clear now who deserved her loyalty. Evie was abashed to hear that part of the deal Sophia had made with Lord Matlock was to send in a servant to check on her. There had nearly always been at least one on staff being paid to assure her physical welfare. Always someone watching for her safety, and she had never known.

During their long conversation, they had heard angry voices from below stairs. Evelyn had winced, for once concerned about the servants hearing, but Sophia's face was a mask of calm. Evelyn was certain that she would have been furious if she were in Sophia's place. How could the earl decide for his grown son who he was to marry? How could he, of all people, have objections to Sophia? Had he not found her exceptionally capable? If not, why would he have asked for her help for so many years?

She almost smiled when she realized that her impulse now was to defend her stubborn, inscrutable sister. It felt good. Perhaps, she thought, analyzing her new emotions, she wanted the pleasure of criticizing her sister saved only for herself. *No,* she thought, *that is no longer the case. He has some nerve to treat my sister this way after all she has done for him.* She decided that she would dislike him for Sophia's sake. Lady Matlock had been as lovely as ever, and Evelyn found herself hoping that the earl would be receiving an earful from his affectionate wife.

It seemed hours before the voices downstairs quieted, but the sisters talked for another hour or two after the house fell silent. Now Evelyn was too tired to continue, and Sophia kissed her sister and slipped out into the hallway. As she blew out her candle, Evie wondered why her sister had not gone through the sitting room, but her mind was busy with other things. It was some time before sleep dampened her swirling thoughts. The last determination she formed was that if Sophia might finally have a chance to be happy, she would do whatever she could to help.

***

Sophia slipped out her sister's room in the small hours of the morning. She was sure she would find herself alone, but immediately spied Richard standing in front of her bedchamber. He turned, not at all shocked to see her awake, and handed her a note. He held his candle close so she could read it.

"So," she said softly, a weight lifting from her shoulders, "dead in a French brothel. I can think of no better end for such a man." She glanced up at Richard. "I hope this will not make things more difficult with your father."

"I will discuss it with him tomorrow," was the response. "I am to bed, dearest, and you should retire as well." He kissed her hand and walked away, taking the letter with him.

Distracted as he was, Richard remained unaware that Sophia had not entered her bedchamber. Instead, she stood in the dark hallway for some minutes, assuring herself that everyone else was now either asleep or in their own rooms. *Except one.* She tiptoed down the stairs in her house slippers to the drawing room where she had last seen Richard and the earl arguing while Mr. Darcy and the viscount tried to mediate between the warring parties. Their meeting now concluded, she knew the earl would not have retreated to his rooms.

The drawing room was empty, so she moved to the study, where a flickering light glowed in the small space between door and floor. Stealthily, she slipped inside and closed the door behind her with an audible click. As she thought, the only light came from the fire in the hearth, and she could see Lord Matlock sitting on a settee, staring aimlessly into the flames. She noted, briefly, how much older he looked than when she first met him. His hair had still been mostly the same sandy color as his sons, with only a scattering of gray, but now there was more silver than anything else. Deep lines ploughed grooves into his cheeks, and more lines appeared on his forehead, which was furrowed in contemplation.

"I have been waiting for you, Sophia," he said in a hoarse, pained voice.

"You are angry," she said evenly.

"No," he groused. "I am disappointed."

Sophia grimaced. *So it is to be guilt*, she thought. *For such an accomplished politician, he has chosen a terrible line of argument.*

"You did not expect this," she replied flatly.

"How could I expect it?" he asked harshly, his voice rising a bit. "We spoke at Matlock, Sophia. You turned down the only sensible match for you. You chose to remain alone, but with an estate to run, an estate I secured for you. Now to promise yourself to my son? What were you thinking?"

Sophia felt her face heat and focused on her breathing. Animosity was usually easy to deal with, but her bitterness ran deep. She ignored his question and instead posed one of her own.

"What is it," she asked in a controlled, steady voice, "that you believe I owe you?"

Lord Matlock stood up then in agitation, stretching himself to his full height.

"What do you *not* owe me, child?" His face was haughty, proud.

"What do you not owe *me*, my lord?" was her sharp reply. "Who removed my uncle from your path? Who cleared your way to advancement? Despite your political prowess it was not something you accomplished entirely on your own."

The earl snorted and reached for his brandy. "After I saved you from his house."

Sophia actually laughed then, a brief, sardonic laugh. "You saved me to use me. Is that the reason you do not want me in the family? You do not wish to be reminded that you are not the perfect man so many believe you to be?"

He waved her away. "Do not be ridiculous," he snorted. "I do what must be done. I have reasons enough, but my image is not one of them."

"There are so many reasons you would object, I am not certain which one you think the worst," she said flatly. "But remember this, Lord Matlock. I was a girl of sixteen. I had few choices." Her voice shook with suppressed anger, and she could feel a headache beginning at her temples. "You had so many resources at your command. I was very grateful for your help, at first."

"Only at first?" he asked, bitterness seeping into his tone.

"You did only what would benefit you, *my lord*," she said. "Everything you did, protecting me, protecting Darlington, you did so I would help you." She shook her head. "I cannot have expected more than that. It does not follow that I did not wish for more. My life might have been quite different had you shown any consideration for my position outside of what it might gain for you. The emotion you bestowed upon me in your greeting last summer was as unusual as it was fleeting. I was a child, Lord Matlock, younger than your own niece, and you took advantage."

The earl would not look anywhere but into the fire. "I find it difficult to accept this ingratitude, Miss Hawke. You have not worked for me in three years, yet last summer I offered you and your sister a haven, men to escort you, a place to remain safe. That was not to benefit me. My own son put his life in danger for you, not to mention my nephew and his friend."

She knew he had a point, but so did she. "I grant that you offered asylum for us, and I thank you for that. However, you were otherwise little involved. You merely arranged to pass information to your son. In that, you used him too, put him in as much danger as I."

The earl flushed, though Sophia could not tell whether it was from anger or embarrassment. He sat, wearily this time, and Sophia caught a glance of the clock on the mantle. It was close to three in the morning.

"You are a liability, Sophia," the earl said, almost sadly. "I do not wish you or your sister ill, but to align my family with yours is to put everything at risk. Your uncle is a traitor."

Sophia shook her head. "He may be a traitor, but I worked very hard to keep him out of power. One word from you to the right people in London and all will be rightly understood."

The earl rested his head on the back of the settee and spoke to the ceiling. "It would require calling in every significant favor I hold, and even then, success is not assured. I thought you understood this. I thought your good sense and a modicum of gratitude would help you see."

Sophia shook her head. "Let us not confuse gratitude with obligation. You offered me safety, both physical and financial, but you also gained much from me. It was not a friendship you offered, but a partnership, and I have fulfilled my end. I will forever be grateful, I will even always love you for it, but I do not owe the rest of my life to you."

The earl remained silent.

Sophia closed her eyes and shook her head. *Stubborn man.* "I am of age, as is your son. If you deny him the financial settlement you have promised should he not marry where you choose, so be it. My father provided enough for us both, and I have no doubt that Richard and I will be able to increase Darlington's profits together. He seeks a partnership of a different sort, sir, one I happily anticipate." Her anger softened a bit, and she added, "We should, however, be pleased to have your blessing."

Half-heartedly, he replied, "I can have your money frozen. I have access to all the accounts."

She sighed. "I can hear that you do not really mean that, so I will pretend it was never said. However, you should know that my first order of business at Darlington last fall was to remove all of my funds from the accounts you set up." She moved a little closer to the fire. "I must have solicitors and bankers who are loyal to me and mine. *You* taught me that. And make no mistake about it, my lord," she finished softly, "my family will soon include Richard."

He was silent. Not wanting to leave it with such a stern pronouncement, she unknowingly asked the same question as her betrothed. "If you will not call in your favors, will you not at least give up this pretense and wish us happy?"

The earl did not respond, though the slight movement of his head when she mentioned removing her funds told her he had not known and that he was shocked that she had accomplished such a thing without his knowledge. *Mr. Hobson may not be an earl, but he has friends too*, she thought, touching a hand briefly to her head, which had begun to throb. She moved to the earl's side and bent to kiss his cheek. He remained still as she straightened, squared her shoulders, and exited, leaving the door wide open.

The earl sat in the same attitude, nursing his drink, until the sun began to rise and the footsteps of the servants drove him upstairs.

Chapter Twenty-Three

ELIZABETH WAS STILL SEATED at the breakfast table when Sophia Hawke entered uncharacteristically late. She sipped her tea as her guest smiled sincerely and moved to fill her plate. Elizabeth was mortified for Richard and Miss Hawke after the events of the previous night and was determined to return the visit to its previous level of ease and comfort. Christmas was only two days away, and she was adamant that nobody, not even Lord Matlock, would ruin the celebration.

"How are you this morning, Miss Hawke?" she asked as the woman set her plate on the table and shook her head ruefully when a footman appeared to smoothly draw out her chair.

"Well rested and growing quite spoiled, Mrs. Darcy," was the jovial reply.

Elizabeth smiled, pleased. Miss Hawke seemed none the worse for wear, though last night's argument must have been painful to hear.

The earl and Lady Matlock were the only guests still abed. Elizabeth believed her aunt was having a serious conversation with her husband. From what her husband had said when at last he had dragged himself into her chambers after midnight, even Phillip had not seen a problem with the match, though he understood more fully than the others what it might cost his father if not handled correctly. His offer to plan strategy with the earl had been summarily dismissed.

The men were out riding, allowing Richard to work off his excess anger from the argument the night before. Georgiana had taken Pembroke out for a walk around the lake, Miss Evelyn was in the library, and thus Elizabeth had been left to enjoy a peaceful, unusually extended morning meal. Better even than the joy of eating was the look on her Fitzwilliam's face when she had insisted on eating breakfast with the others. She could see his panic at last subsiding, that he finally looked happy despite the upheaval with his uncle. *Uncles,* she thought sourly, *who would believe they could cause such problems*? The thought made her long for Uncle and Aunt Gardiner. She wondered what they were doing today and whether the children were excited for Christmas dinner. Her thoughts then turned to Christmas holidays in the past, at Longbourn with all her sisters.

She gazed at Miss Hawke over the rim of her teacup and considered how very different the two Hawke sisters had proved themselves to be. It was not just their appearance but their personalities, and she felt all the sympathy of an older sister who had, with limited success, attempted to correct the behavior of the younger. The circumstances were certainly different, she allowed—Miss Hawke's sister threw everything into her intellectual pursuits while her own youngest sister did everything to avoid them—but the results were, in the end, similar. Miss Evelyn was deeply knowledgeable, but Elizabeth, who did enjoy the woman's conversation, was not entirely sure she was a friend to be trusted. It was an unsettling feeling, and she chastised herself for it, but it simply would not go away. Sophia Hawke's conversation might not be as deep or as varied as her sister's, but she was certainly knowledgeable about the world, clearly an intelligent woman, and more importantly, she was kind. Both her words and behavior inspired trust.

As they had prepared for sleep some nights before, Fitzwilliam had made a quiet remark to her that while he would never be less than civil, that he too preferred Sophia Hawke to her sister, a sentiment apparently shared by all the men. The earl and Richard, of course, already knew Miss Hawke, and while Phillip clearly appreciated Miss Evelyn's beauty, even he found her behavior off-putting. Elizabeth had been unable to dissent, but attempted to explain away Miss Evelyn's distraction in company as a lack of exposure to society and polite conversation rather than a sign of her flawed character. Because she had witnessed at least a few coldly condescending remarks meant to target her sister, though, Elizabeth could not help feeling that she might have been rather disingenuous in her defense. Angry and frustrated as she had been with her own sisters at times, she did love them and was never unkind.

She heard Miss Hawke speak but had not been attending. "Oh, pardon me, Miss Hawke," she said with a little blush. "I was woolgathering, I am afraid."

"No need for apologies, Mrs. Darcy," was the calm reply followed by a sip of tea and a flicker of dark blue eyes. "I merely stated that it was very nice to see you at the breakfast table, even as tardy as I am this morning."

"Yes, it seems my appetite has returned," Elizabeth said with some relief.

"That is excellent news. I am told," Miss Hawke continued, "that you are by habit an early riser. I am happy to hear of another such as me."

"It is true," Elizabeth replied. "I am accustomed to rising not long after my husband and breaking my fast with him. However, of late I have been rather lazy whereas I believe Georgiana rose quite early this morning as she had promised Pembroke a walk in the snow." She set her teacup back carefully in its saucer, glancing longingly out the window. *It has been ages since I was out of doors. I believe I too could walk today, even if just for a short while.*

Taking a sip from her own teacup, Miss Hawke paused and made a request. "It appears that all of my riding attire has been removed from my chambers, for cleaning no doubt. I was therefore considering a walk rather than a ride this morning myself, Mrs. Darcy. I was hoping you might point out a suitable trail that will not take me too far out of the way. John Briggs seems to be under orders to have me followed everywhere if I am not with the colonel, but surely a short walk in the gardens or down to the lake with the mistress of the estate would not require an escort from the stables?"

Elizabeth was too pleased with this unexpected offer to feel any guilt about how transparent her wishes had been. Surely her husband could find nothing wrong with a short walk should she be with Miss Hawke. With all the tension of last night's argument still permeating the house, she was desperate to go outside. She had stopped herself only because she forced herself to remember the most important lesson of the past summer, to better judge her own limitations. Reluctantly she had admitted to herself that she should not venture out alone.

"I think a short stroll down the lake and back would be wonderful, Miss Hawke, if you would be willing to have a bit of company. I have been very much confined to the house given the weather."

"Of course, Mrs. Darcy. It would be my pleasure to have your company." The women sat in companionable silence until both had eaten their fill.

Miss Hawke rose, noting that Elizabeth had pushed her plate away. "I am finished here, Mrs. Darcy. Would you like to call your maid to fetch your things? I shall have mine brought down as well."

Elizabeth smiled to herself. Miss Hawke must see, as did she, that were they to wait for the men to return and tell Fitzwilliam where they were headed, he would insist she remain indoors. She was not insensitive to his concerns for her welfare, but she could not bear one more suggestion that she instead stroll around the conservatory. She was not herself, it was true, but she was much stronger than she had been. The lake was along a gentle path less than a quarter of an hour away, and she promised him silently that she would not even attempt to walk around it.

"We will stop any time you wish to return to the house, Mrs. Darcy," Miss Hawke assured her. "You must not overdo, but I recognize when someone must remove out of doors or risk going quite mad." She raised her eyebrows and smiled, leaning in to say in a low voice, "It is a disorder with which I am familiar."

Elizabeth nodded with a small smile and a deep breath. "Thank you, Miss Hawke."

Sophia Hawke stood, then gazed at her feet for a moment before saying, "Do you not think it is time you call me by my Christian name? We are friends, are we not, and I hope we will soon be cousins. If you are comfortable, I should much prefer Sophia."

Elizabeth had hoped for just such an invitation for days. She was somewhat envious that Georgiana, of all people, had made the request first. As the hostess, she felt that she should wait until her guest requested the informality, but she had been impatient for it.

"I would be more than happy to call you Sophia. I am Elizabeth. Or," she added almost shyly, "Lizzy." Sophia's answering smile was broad, and Elizabeth felt the contentment of making a new, but very good friend. Now not only would the Bingleys be settled nearby but the Fitzwilliams only a bit farther. They should all be able to meet very often. She placed a hand on her stomach and indulged in a few daydreams about a horde of children standing in the streams fishing, learning to ride on their ponies, on spring picnics in the meadows or stifled laughter and loud "shushes" emanating from the nursery long after bedtime. She released a happy little sigh.

She and Sophia were soon donning their heavy coats and slipping outside to the lake path. The moment she emerged from the house to the outdoors, a frigid blast of air hit Elizabeth in the face like a slap, but she quickly accustomed herself to it, listening with glee to the crunch of the fallen snow under her boots. She breathed deeply, savoring the sharp, clean air. Sophia had her arm, but her touch was so light Elizabeth felt no constraint, only the promise of strength should she require it. She had not before realized how strong Sophia was, though of course it made sense.

Although it had been Sophia's idea to walk, she said nothing as they strolled, though Elizabeth spied her friend glancing at her every so often to be sure they should continue. When they reached the edge of the lake, they both stood silently for a few minutes, listening to the sounds of wildlife going about winter's business. Somewhere in the stand of woods farther down the shore, voices floated back to them. *Georgiana and Pembroke must not be far*, she thought.

"Look," came a whispered voice, deep and awed. Sophia was pointing to the eastern sky, where a stand of evergreens towered high against the line of the horizon. There was a dark cloud forming before their eyes. It was moving, a black mass swiftly changing shape.

"Starlings," she informed Sophia. Then, almost reverently, she whispered, "a murmuration of starlings." Together they watched the flock of birds dipping, rolling, pivoting in a rhythmic dance, the darkness contrasting with the white dusting of snow on the ground, the slate gray of the sky, the dusky green of the trees. Elizabeth took a deep breath and expelled it, feeling all of her frustration and illness dissipating with it. She glanced at Sophia's face to see a similar sense of ease relaxing her features. Elizabeth turned her eyes back to the spectacle before her and absently caressed her protruding stomach with one hand as she watched. After a time, she realized that her nose was growing cold, and she turned away, prepared to call their foray outside a success and return to the house. Sophia turned with her, carefully linking her arm through Elizabeth's.

They had taken no more than five steps back along the path when they heard Georgiana say, quite clearly and with some exasperation, "Pembroke, that is enough."

The women stopped and turned back even as Georgiana's next statement was ringing loudly through the thin winter air. "Pembroke, I said no. It is not safe!"

The next moments were a blur. Elizabeth watched it all as time slowed around her. A flash of color breaking from the trees and skidding across the ice of the lake perhaps twenty yards away, Pembroke waving, flashing a toothy grin at his cousin, Georgiana's strained, suddenly frightened voice as she begged him to come back off the ice, his teasing steps farther out towards the center of the small lake, his jump to prove the surface was sound, and then, at last, the shattering of the ice as it broke in pieces under his weight. Pembroke's red scarf flew up, hiding his face as his small body plunged, feet first, into the water. Then she was moving, starting to run, until she was grabbed from behind and held motionless.

"Let me go, he is in the water!" she cried, horrified.

"Elizabeth," gasped Sophia. In her panic, Elizabeth had driven an elbow into her friend's midsection, but she stilled as she spied Georgiana pushing out onto the ice nearly in Pembroke's own tracks, onto a surface not fully formed, certainly not solid, to reach him. From somewhere far away she heard Sophia yelling at Georgiana to stay where she was, not to advance, that the ice was weak. Either Georgiana did not hear her, so intent upon her mission that the words did not carry, or she simply ignored them in pursuit of her goal.

"No, no," moaned Elizabeth, trying to twist away once more, stretching out her arms towards the two, as though she might draw them away from the lake with nothing more than wishes. "Let me go, Sophia!"

Elizabeth was released momentarily only to be grasped by her upper arms as Sophia gently but firmly turned Elizabeth to face her. There was a comforting resolve in Sophia's gaze. When her friend spoke, it was distinct, careful, and very quick.

"Lizzy," she said, and the name startled Elizabeth into attending. "You are not yourself. If you go out there, I will be pulling you from the water as well. I need you to wait for the boy, then take him inside.

Then I will try to get Georgiana off the ice. You must send help once you are indoors."

Elizabeth began to speak, but she was abruptly cut off.

"Do not even think about putting the babe at risk, do you hear?" Sophia said harshly as she turned her head to view the lake behind her, returning her gaze to Elizabeth while delivering her *coup de grâce*: "If any harm were to come to the child, you would never forgive yourself."

It was, perhaps, the only argument that would have stopped her from immediately attempting to affect a rescue. Elizabeth nodded silently, just one bob of her head, and suddenly her arms were free. She watched Sophia stretch into a run, skirt drawn up into one hand to allow her a longer stride, racing along the shore towards the break in the ice, tossing her bonnet aside, tearing her gloves off with her teeth and dropping them behind her, unwinding her scarf, shrugging off her coat, leaving a trail of her clothing as she rushed to the point at the shore where she could better judge her approach. Elizabeth had not seen any women move like this, with such speed or purpose, and she watched with a sense of relief. She picked her way more cautiously towards the shore, gathering the discarded items and, now that she walked alone, feeling the muscles in her legs begin to quiver with fear and exertion. How correct Sophia had been to stop her! She would not make such a mistake again; she would follow directions and wait for the moment she could gather up Pembroke and rush him to the house. Despite her outward appearance of calm, her heart was pounding painfully in her chest, her throat constricting with an attempt to swallow her fears.

Georgiana had reached Pembroke now and was grasping one arm, but the boy was thrashing, hitting her, frightened and uncontrolled, expending a great deal of energy yelling and crying. She was having a terrible time keeping his head above water and was struggling to avoid being pulled in with him. His clothing was adding significant weight to his small frame, and she tried to free one hand to remove his scarf, while his little hat floated a few feet away, crown down, dipping and spinning like a rudderless ship.

"Oh please," Elizabeth whispered, horrified, "Phillip cannot..." The words died in her throat. She wanted desperately to close her eyes but could not bring herself to do it.

Sophia was lying flat on the ice, using her arms and feet to slide out carefully, her movements not constrained by heavy clothing, but also unprotected without it. She approached the pair from the opposite side of the gap, choosing a pathway where the ice was evidently more solidly frozen than the place where Pembroke had broken through and Georgiana was struggling now. Elizabeth watched her rapid progress anxiously, the cerulean blue dress and black walking boots bright against the ice. She focused on regulating her breathing. *A friend, a cousin, a sister, all in danger. Should I not be doing more? How can I just stand here? Should I not go to alert the house, find William, find Phillip, locate someone with rope or boards?* She had to force herself to stop the spiraling panic by recalling the resolution made only moments before. She had been given calm, calculated directions and though she was near to pulling out her own hair in the agitation it caused her, she had promised to follow them. She stood still, waiting, while her breaths came in ragged gasps. She knew that Sophia would succeed, that she would help Georgiana save Pembroke and then guide Georgiana off the ice. She believed it. She had to believe it. The quarter of an hour or more it would take her to get back to the house on her own would be far too long to do anyone out on the lake any good at all, even if it took that help less than another quarter of an hour to arrive.

"Please," she mumbled, lifting herself slowly up on her toes and then lowering herself down again as she watched their progress. It was the only word she could force out between the hands that were clasped to her mouth, and it became a chant. "Please, please, please..."

Pembroke's movements were becoming more sluggish, but by the time Sophia glided about ten feet from the edge of the break, Georgiana had succeeded in pulling him to her and he was trying to climb up next to her.

"No," cried Sophia, pushing a little faster to reach them. "Not that side, Georgiana, do not let him try to..."

"I have him!" snapped Georgiana, cutting her off with some irritation. "He is nearly out!"

Pembroke pushed up feebly with both little hands on the jagged edge of the ice, trying to toss one leg up on the surface just to the side of where Georgiana was sprawled out, trying to distribute her weight evenly. Her left hand fisted the back of his trousers, and she pulled him up as he tried to lift himself out of the freezing water with his arms.

For a second, Elizabeth watched as Pembroke emerged from the water. He had lifted his body halfway out of the water, his knee coming up to rest upon the slick surface. Georgiana had a firm grip on the back his clothes and was hauling him in like a hooked fish. For a moment, she felt intense relief, her muscles relaxing ever so slightly. Pembroke leaned forward, putting his knee down and slapping the surface of the ice as his hands came down clumsily. Sophia called out again sharply, but her head was positioned away from shore, towards Georgiana, and Elizabeth could not hear what she was saying. She moved further down the shore, preparing herself to grab Pembroke and whisk him away to the house as quickly as possible. *Finally*, she thought, *finally*. She inched steadily closer in anticipation of having a task at last when she heard the loud grinding groan of ice giving way.

Her heart began to pound wildly. There were now two bodies in the water.

Chapter Twenty-Four

ELIZABETH COULD NOT HAVE said who had screamed, but she heard it, an earsplitting, keening, paralyzing cry that she was sure would travel over the brittle winter air to the edges of the park, ten miles around though it might be. When the cloud of fear cleared, she recognized Georgie in the water supporting Pembroke, Sophia reaching out, calling out orders of some kind, and then Georgie was pushing the boy up from beneath as Sophia simultaneously grabbed the back of his trousers and pulled. Suddenly, he was on his stomach, spinning slowly on the ice next to her, spluttering and huffing and shaking. Sophia said something to him, but he flipped over on his back and did not move. Then she positioned him carefully near her legs, turned onto her own back, placed the soles of her feet on the boy's side and gently but firmly shoved him away, yelling harshly at him to get to the edge of the lake so he could go home. He slid for perhaps ten or fifteen feet and then slowly turned himself over onto his hands and knees, crawling blindly across the additional ten feet or so of slippery surface to Elizabeth as she encouraged him, grateful to be helping at last.

"Pembroke, you must reach me," she called. "Your father wants you home. Come, Pembroke, you cannot give up. What would your papa say?"

She saw the boy talking to himself as he crawled, slipped, crawled further. In less than a minute he was close enough for her to grasp his hands, though it seemed to take hours. As she held his small fingers and felt how cold they were, he gazed into her face with his dark brown eyes and said in a small, tinny, stuttering voice as he shivered, "Papa says a gentleman must be brave." His face was so pale as to be nearly bloodless, and Elizabeth's chest tightened at the sight of him. She wanted nothing more than to scold him for worrying them all in such a way, but he was a child and already paying for his disobedience.

"He will be so proud of you, dearest," Elizabeth told him as she lifted him to his feet. She stripped the boy's jacket and scarf from him and bundled him up in Sophia's thick coat, careful not to step on the material that spread out on the ground behind him like a train. Hurriedly, she hustled him off towards the house, noting with eerie clarity the white hands, the bluish tinge to his lips, the pale skin making the light dusting of freckles across his cheeks stand out prominently. His steps were small and lethargic, and she nearly dragged him along, one hand under each of his arms, knowing she could not carry him but that he needed to be out of the cold immediately. A frigid wind was kicking up, and the sooner she got Pembroke to the house, the sooner she could send more help. She glanced back only once, and saw that Sophia had Georgiana by the arms and was speaking to her.

It was with an intense sense of gratitude that she heard horses approaching in haste as they headed up the incline towards the house. The men must have been returning to the stables from their morning ride.

"Elizabeth!" called Darcy, his normally calm voice strained with alarm. "We heard a scream. . ."

Phillip was already off his horse, gathering Pembroke to his chest. Without a word, he had swung the two of them up into his saddle and was wheeling around for the house.

"The lake," she said, breathlessly, pointing behind her. "Georgiana. Sophia is trying to get her out." Richard spurred his horse and was gone.

"Go back to the house, Elizabeth," Darcy said, almost angrily. "We will meet you there." He paused for a moment, and his voice softened. "Be careful how you step."

Elizabeth nodded, too weary to speak, and her husband disappeared after his cousin. She said a silent little prayer as she trudged back to the house.

***

From the corner of her eye, Sophia could see Elizabeth hurrying Pembroke up the trail towards the house. *Thank God*, she thought, grasping Georgiana's forearms and trying to guide her up onto the thicker ice. She tugged, stopped, tugged again. Something was caught.

"Is it your dress?" she grunted. Her strength was at last beginning to wane in the cold as she lay on the ice without a coat and her arms partly submerged.

Georgiana's light hair was lifting away in wisps from her forehead as the breeze grew stronger. She still wore her bonnet, but Sophia shifted, reaching out with one hand to remove it and toss it aside, the knot in the ribbon too wet to be undone. Georgiana had not gone completely under, but the bonnet was restricting her ability to see.

"I cannot tell," the younger girl forced out between frozen lips. "My legs are entirely numb. Either my dress or my boot is caught."

Sophia swore softly. Georgiana only had a few minutes before she would lose all feeling and be unable to aid in her own rescue. At least one of those minutes was already past. She could not wait for the help Elizabeth would send. She grimaced and felt her fear blossoming. Acting in spite of it was something with which she had a good deal of practice, at least. She remembered what it was to be a soldier, and as she looked at Georgiana's frightened face, she felt her heart swell with love for the girl. *You know how to act. Admit the fear and push it away.*

"Georgiana," she said calmly, "This is what we are going to do..."

***

Darcy caught up to Richard as he bolted down the lake's western shore. They had expected two women, one on the ice, one in the water, but they could see only Georgiana, clinging tenuously to the edge of a jagged gash in the ice roughly eight feet across and nearly thirty feet from shore. On one side of the break was the weaker, white ice, the other side a mixture of white and clear.

As they pulled their mounts to a halt, they saw a head break the surface of the water. Richard cursed loudly beside him as they both watched Sophia Hawke take a deep breath and disappear from view.

"Sophia. . . what the blazes. . ." Richard sputtered.

Darcy was off his mount in seconds, grabbing a rope from his saddlebag, tying a small hand axe around the end to serve as an anchor, then wrapping the other end around a tree and tossing it underhand, out as far as he could. It was an accurate toss, the axe skittering nearly to the rope's full extension about ten feet from the great gaping hole in the ice. Richard moved to follow it out, but Darcy placed a hand to his chest to stop him.

"You will go in, too, Richard. This is snow ice. It could not even hold Pembroke. I should appreciate it if *every* person now in residence did not go for a swim today." His voice was low but firm. "We must trust that she will be able to get Georgiana out."

"William," Richard said, "neither of them have much time in that water. If Sophia does not have Georgie out in one minute, I am going out there. Fish me out or leave me to freeze, I will not remain on the shore." He felt a surge of guilt as he vented his anger on his cousin, for it was not a moment after the words were out of his mouth he calmed just enough to recognize, beyond the stoic set of his jaw, the nearly wild anguish displayed on Darcy's face.

Sophia Hawke's head again broke the surface of the water.

"Why is this taking so long?" Richard asked, his entire body trembling with the need to slide out on the ice.

Darcy shook his head. "Georgiana must be caught somehow." His baritone was taut with anxiety. He pulled the knot on the tree tighter as the seconds ticked away. Richard was preparing to make his way out to the ice when Darcy stopped him by placing a hand on his shoulder. "Richard, I think she has it."

As Darcy watched, Sophia Hawke's arm hovered briefly over the ice before jabbing something into it. She said something to Georgiana and swam behind the girl. Suddenly, his sister was being shoved from underneath, reaching out to grab what looked like a knife's hilt. He waited for her to slide out and grab the rope, preparing to pull her in, nearly twitching with anticipation. With Miss Hawke's continued assistance, Georgie shakily leveraged herself and rolled onto the ice, the rope at last within her grasp. She lay still for a moment, and Darcy's heart squeezed with dread. Then Georgiana stretched out one trembling, nearly translucent hand to fully grab the end of the hand axe. The second hand came up and she wrapped the rope around her arm. Then Darcy was pulling her in, careful to not yank too hard or too fast for her fragile grip, yet needing to get her inside and out of the growing wind as soon as possible.

Richard guided the rope and put his arms out for his young cousin as Darcy pulled Georgiana to shore, but his eyes also watched the last figure in the water, the only one that he suspected had gone in voluntarily. It was indeed a knife, he saw, that she had stuck in the ice, a small one. It had not sunk deeply in the ice, but it was enough. She placed one shaking hand on the hilt, one flat palm on the ice, and half lifted, half rolled herself out of the water. Sophia lay there, panting, stomach on the surface, shaking but otherwise unmoving, and suddenly Richard realized that Georgiana was in his embrace. He lifted her gently and passed her to Darcy, who grabbed his sister and removed her pelisse before peeling off his own greatcoat and covering her with it.

"Can you manage with Miss Hawke?" Darcy called to Richard as he ushered Georgiana to his horse.

"Yes," Richard replied, already sliding the axe across the ice to Sophia, who wrapped the rope around her right arm and held on with her left, allowing herself to be pulled along the ice, her legs limp but her grip secure. Behind him, Richard heard the hooves of Darcy's horse as he raced Georgiana back to the house.

The wind was picking up powerfully, beginning to howl as it rushed through the trees, and then she was in his arms, alert but soaked from head to toe, skirts stiff with ice, her eyebrows and the strands of her curls already frozen white, her entire body shaking violently. She had no coat, no scarf or gloves. He stripped off his greatcoat as Darcy had done and wrapped her in it, hoping his body heat had warmed it enough to do some good.

"I suppose," she forced out, shuddering so hard he thought she might not be able to stand, "I will be riding this morning after all." She tried to smile, but he was not in a mood to return it. He helped her to her feet and half assisted, half dragged her to his horse. She was no child nor was she slight like Georgiana, but she was hoisted into the saddle in a trice and they were away.

Sophia leaned against his chest and closed her eyes. She should be worried about the boy, she thought. She should be concerned about Georgiana.

But now that they were out of the water, all she could think of was how the wind was tearing at her, how it felt as though her head had frozen into solid block of ice, how numb her feet were in boots full of water, and how wonderful Richard's greatcoat smelled, of horse and evergreen and something else she could not place. *Does he always smell like this?* she thought, her mind beginning to cloud over as the overwhelming imperative to act drained away, leaving her wrung out, exhausted. *How wonderful.*

***

Richard held Sophia close as he urged his horse to the house. He felt the very moment her body began to sag against him and counted. *One, two, three. . .* By six, they were at the front steps; by eleven, they were in the grand entrance hall. Her eyes were closed, her lips were blue, and her skin was cold, so cold. She had stopped shivering. *Not a good sign*, he thought frantically. Richard held her upright in a chair with one hand and ripped off her boots with the other, cursing softly at streams of water leaking from them as they fell, the liquid pooling on the marble floor. Sophia's hair, warmed by the temperature of the house, began to thaw, and he idly noted that some of the melted ice was sliding down her neck. He adjusted her so that she could sit up on her own, though she slumped to the side and was held up primarily by the wing of the chair.

The servants were moving with efficiency and speed through the halls. No doubt Mrs. Reynolds had them preparing baths and fires. He was handed a towel and he had begun to dry her hair when someone else forced a glass of brandy into his hand.

"Sophia," he said sharply, trying to stay calm but unable to entirely banish the fear from his voice. "Sophia, open your eyes. You must remain awake for the doctor. Open your eyes."

She moaned a little, but did not stir. He lifted the glass to her mouth anyway and was grateful that she accepted a little of the liquor. He tried again with a more success, and her eyes opened a fraction to fix on him.

"Tired," she whispered.

"I know, love," Richard replied, "but try to stay awake. We shall get you warm shortly."

Mrs. Reynolds came halfway down the stairs and waved them up. He grunted a bit as he shifted to lift her, and she tried, numbly, to put her arm around his neck to lighten the load. He held her tight and climbed the stairs, following the housekeeper to the sitting room shared by Miss Hawke and Miss Evelyn. A bath was being filled in the adjacent dressing room. He laid her down on a chaise and two maids immediately began to remove her clothing. He turned his back and followed Mrs. Reynolds out of the room.

"Will you need help getting her into the bath?" he asked gruffly.

Mrs. Reynolds shook her head. "No, sir, we will take care of Miss Hawke. You should change clothes yourself. I have alerted your valet and he awaits you in your chambers."

Black will be rather irritated to be called a valet, he thought with grim humor.

"Do not make the water too hot at first," he warned. "She is very cold. We do not want to put too much strain on her body to warm all at once."

"Yes, sir," responded Mrs. Reynolds in a soothing tone he nevertheless understood meant that she knew her business and did not require his advice. It was humbling to be so pleasantly put in his place, but it did not remain with him long. It suddenly occurred to him that someone was missing.

"Where is her sister?" he blurted out.

"We do not know," Mrs. Reynolds said quietly, glancing back to the room they had vacated. "We thought her in the library and then checked the still room, but she is not in either place. I would have thought she had heard everyone coming in, but if she was not nearby, it is not so difficult to fathom."

"Thank you," Richard replied. He should repair to his chambers to change, he knew, but there had been enough disquiet for the day. He thought he might just check the library once more. Miss Hawke would like to have her sister nearby and the servants were all quite busy enough without the need to mount a search. After being informed that both Pembroke and Georgiana were already in warm baths and being seen to, and that the older Briggs boys had been sent to fetch Mr. Waters for all three, he took the stairs to the now silent main hall.

He reached the ground floor quickly and entered the library without knocking. A summary glance around the room revealed nothing, but he stepped inside to see whether she might have walked through the outside door into the gardens. There were no tracks in the light dusting of snow that had fallen overnight. As he turned to leave, he saw one delicate pink slipper dangling over the arm of a sofa.

"How is it possible she slept through all that noise?" he asked himself aloud in a voice only a hint above a whisper. He cleared his throat. Loudly. Nothing. He did it again, a little louder, and the foot disappeared. It was only a moment before her dark tresses preceded blue eyes peering around the corner of the sofa, her face pale and sleepy against the deep burgundy of the brocade.

"Miss Evelyn," Richard said with a curt bow. "I am sorry to disturb you, but there has been an accident, and your sister requires your presence."

He was surprised but gratified to see Miss Evelyn's eyes widen in alarm before settling into an expression of resolve. She stood and began to walk towards the library door.

"Where is she, sir? Take me to her at once."

Richard shook his head at the imperious tone of her voice and his reply was spoken to her back. "She is in her chambers, Miss Evelyn. I know she will be more comfortable with you near. I will check on you both later, if you will allow it."

He was startled when she suddenly stopped. Her shoulders drooped as she turned and she let out a small sigh before lifting her face to his. Her gaze was sincerely remorseful.

"My apologies, Colonel. I was terribly rude just now. It is just that I am worried for my sister. Would you walk upstairs with me and tell me what has happened?"

Richard lifted his eyebrows. He was surprised by the civility in her tone following her brusque initial response to his news. *She is trying*, he thought. He recalled from Jack Hobson that Miss Evelyn had nursed her sister most faithfully upon Sophia's return to London. *That must be in her favor*, he thought warily. He swept his arm before him, indicating that she should precede him through the entrance, and moved to her side once they were in the hallway.

"Mr. Darcy, the viscount, and I were finishing our ride this morning when we heard a terrible scream," he began, proceeding to tell her all he knew. She nodded, her face turning pale when he suggested that her sister had intentionally gone into the water to cut Georgiana free, but she nodded.

"My sister cares for everyone's life above her own," she said quietly. "It can be difficult to live with someone so selfless, Colonel."

Ah, there was the Evelyn Hawke he knew. "Difficult, Miss Evelyn?" Richard asked stiffly.

As they reached the guest chambers, she clarified, "It is only that I have truly known Sophia for so short a time. I am afraid I am learning that despite what my uncle has told me, my character rather suffers in comparison to hers. It can be rather a blow to one's vanity to have such a sister." She smiled at him with a queer, melancholy smile, and disappeared behind the door in a soft swish of muslin.

Richard stood in the hallway for a moment, still damp and cold, shocked at such a frank admission. He remained longer than he should, trying to detect any sound in the room, but there was nothing more than the soft hum of muffled voices. After willing himself not to open the door, he laid the palm of his hand on the wood briefly before straightening, turning, and heading to his room to change.

Chapter Twenty-Five

DARCY WALKED TOWARDS Georgiana's room after having first checked in on Pembroke. The fire in the nursery hearth was burning at a high heat. The boy had been taken from a warm bath, wrapped in dry clothes and thick blankets, and upon Mr. Waters' orders, was being spoon fed hot tea and soup by his grandmother. Liquids, the apothecary had insisted, were more important than food at this point. Lord Matlock had remained in the room long enough to be assured that his grandson was doing well before removing himself with a nod to his wife and son. Lady Matlock watched him go, a mixture of pain and pity on her face, before she returned to her task.

Pembroke had regained some of his color but was drowsy and befuddled, making it difficult to get him to drink. One small hand grasped his father's larger one, and Phillip refused to be moved from his son's side, every so often brushing his free hand gently over Pembroke's head and cupping his cheek. As Darcy knocked and opened the door to his sister's chamber, he saw a similar scene, though his sister, while clearly fatigued, was holding a quiet conversation with Elizabeth.

The temperature of her room, like the one in the nursery, was warm almost beyond what he could bear. Georgiana heard his entrance, turning her head towards him and offering a small smile. He felt a great weight lifting from his shoulders as he smiled in return and moved to sit by her side. He heard footsteps behind him and recognized them as Richard's, but did not turn to greet his cousin.

"How are you feeling, Georgiana?" he asked, taking her hand in his own. It was warm, he noted with satisfaction.

"I am well, William," she sighed just a bit impatiently. "I am simply tired, but I remained awake as I thought you might wish to speak with me."

Elizabeth met her husband's troubled glance with an arched eyebrow. "I believe that you were mistaken when you said I was the only stubborn one living here at Pemberley."

She must be doing well if Elizabeth is teasing me, he thought.

"If you feel up to it, Georgie. If you are weary, it can wait."

"I would rather have it done, brother," she replied, sinking a little further into the bank of pillows.

"Elizabeth has told us that Pembroke disobeyed you to run out on the ice?"

"He did. He was very excited about the snow, William. I was trying to explain to him that snow ice is not as solid as the clear, but he was. . . unable to attend."

Darcy heard a snort behind him. "That is a kind way to express it, Georgiana," came Richard's voice. "He has been spoiled by a grieving father and he must be corrected."

"Richard," came Elizabeth's mild reproof. "Perhaps we should allow Georgiana to continue so that she may rest."

Richard nodded. "My apologies, Georgie."

Georgiana simply nodded once and continued. "I told him that it was not safe. When he ran out on the ice and it held him, he was sure he was in the right and moved farther out, despite my directions." She paused to take a sip of the tea Elizabeth held out for her, smiling her thanks. "He then jumped on the surface to show me that it was sound. Of course, it was not."

Darcy frowned. *Good God, Elizabeth did not mention that. The boy did everything he could to insure he would go through the ice. Richard may have the right of it after all.*

"Worse yet, I went out on the same ice to retrieve him, though I could hear Sophia telling me not to proceed." She grimaced, whether in pain or embarrassment Darcy could not say, but his sister waved off his concern with a weak flick of her wrist.

Elizabeth cleared her throat. "You must not blame yourself, Georgie. Even I immediately made for the ice, but Sophia held me back. I should like to believe I would have stopped once I had my wits about me, but I cannot say that for certain."

Darcy heard a surprised huff behind him as he stared at his wife incredulously. "Elizabeth," he breathed. "Are you mad?"

She lifted her shoulders, an apology plainly written on her features as she met his horrified gaze. "I believe I may have been. It was but a momentary panic, William, but Sophia held me back until my senses returned. I promise, it was only seconds." She turned to Georgiana and patted the hand her husband was not holding. "So you see, Georgiana, it was simply an instinct. You are not to be blamed for wishing to reach Pembroke as soon as possible."

Georgiana closed her eyes briefly before opening them again. "I ignored her again when I was trying to pull Pembroke out of the water. I nearly had him, but she told me not to pull him up onto my side of the ice." She stopped again.

Elizabeth added that Sophia had taken a circuitous route out to the hole in the ice, following the clear ice as much as possible. Georgiana nodded.

"When I fell in, Pembroke was very frightened, thrashing, but not as much as he had before. Sophia told me to push him from underneath and she pulled at the same time. Then she pushed him across the ice with her feet so he would have a shorter way to crawl. Elizabeth talked to him from there, encouraging him to reach the shore. I did not hear what she was saying, but she would not allow him to stop." Darcy watched as Georgiana squeezed his wife's hand.

"When Sophia tried to lift me onto the ice, I was caught." Darcy nodded. He felt, rather than saw, Richard move farther into the room and sit in an empty chair near the foot of the bed. Georgiana shivered and Elizabeth adjusted her covers, tucking them in tightly around her. "I could not tell where. Sophia told me she would cut me free and I was too cold to object. She took a knife from her boot and slid into the water." She closed her eyes again. "I believe you know the rest."

Darcy finally turned his head to look at his cousin. Richard was sitting in the last available chair in the room, leaning forward, head down, forearms on his knees and his hands clasped together so hard the knuckles were turning white. He recognized the rigid set of Richard's jaw as he rubbed his own. *These women, Richard*, he thought, exhausted. *They will be the death of us for certain.*

Elizabeth was speaking now, in low tones. "I am sorry for leaving the house without informing you, William," she was saying, Darcy only looking up at the sound of his name. "But I could not stay inside a moment longer. Sophia was with me the entire time, and we had only planned to walk to the lake and back, a half hour at most." She stood and walked around the bed to put her hand lightly on Darcy's shoulder and he reached up to cover it with his own.

"No, Elizabeth," he said stolidly, fighting against the inclination to rail at her for acting before thinking. *That can come later, when I am calmer.* "It was fortunate the two of you were there."

"Especially Sophia," she murmured. "Now that you are here, I should like to see how she is getting on. Mr. Waters should be finished with his examination by now."

Richard stood. "Stay here, William. I would like to hear how Sophia fares, and I know you would like to remain with Georgiana until she sleeps."

Darcy nodded, and after they kissed Georgina and said their goodnights, his wife and cousin left the room.

***

Mr. Waters knocked before entering the final bedchamber of the afternoon. He heard a female voice telling him to enter, and he stepped inside.

"I am Mr. Waters," he said, "I understand Miss Hawke was also in the water today?"

"She was," came a soft, musical voice from the foot of the bed. Waters turned to face it and was struck by the beauty of the young woman before him. She was a small woman, perfectly proportioned with dark hair pinned up in perfect curls, clear pale skin and unusual dark blue eyes. He stared for a few seconds before her lifted eyebrows required he recover his equanimity. He cleared his throat.

The woman spoke. "I am Miss Hawke's sister, Miss Evelyn Hawke."

"Miss Evelyn," Mr. Waters said with a short bow, "I am at your service."

***

Mr. Waters was stepping out of Sophia's room as Elizabeth and Richard approached. He stopped to greet them, shutting the door behind him.

"Mrs. Darcy," he said seriously, glancing at the colonel, "I presume you are here to discuss Miss Hawke?"

"Yes," Elizabeth replied, glancing around the hall. "This is my cousin, Colonel Fitzwilliam. Shall we step into the sitting room?"

"Certainly," nodded the apothecary. He lifted his hand to beckon a servant and spoke a few words in the man's ear before turning to follow Elizabeth. Richard trailed them both. Once inside, Elizabeth sat heavily in the first chair. Richard stood beside her, his foot tapping anxiously on the floor.

Mr. Waters cleared his throat. "Miss Hawke is as well as I might expect. She is slowly warming and her organs do not seem to be involved." He turned to Richard. "It is a good thing you got her inside so quickly, Colonel Fitzwilliam."

Elizabeth sent a reassuring look to Richard who merely frowned. Mr. Waters caught the exchange and reluctantly added, "There is an inflammation in her chest but her lungs sound clear so far. She is not yet entirely lucid, but this is common in such cases. We shall watch both and hope for the best. I have a poultice for the inflammation and she should be given fluids, with an invalid feeder if necessary."

Richard nodded and turned to his cousin. "Elizabeth, I wish to help with her recuperation."

Elizabeth smiled wanly at Mr. Waters. "Miss Hawke is the colonel's betrothed."

The apothecary nodded. "Congratulations, Colonel."

Richard nodded absently.

Elizabeth gazed at him with concern. Richard was standing with his arms crossed tightly across his chest, his foot tapping even more quickly now than it had before. It was clear he would not be able to wait until the morning, but she could not in good conscience allow him to spend the night in Sophia's room.

"Richard," she said gently, reaching up to touch his arm, "I believe her sister is with her now and we will have a maid sit with her tonight. Perhaps you might return in the morning."

He shook his head. Elizabeth sighed. "What if you see her now and then return in the morning?"

He considered this for a moment, then nodded, and his foot at last stilled. "Is there anything else we should know, Mr. Waters?" he asked gruffly.

"No, Colonel," Mr. Waters replied with a shake of his head. "Now we wait." He turned to Elizabeth.

"Mrs. Darcy, I would like to stay the night if possible. I will need to check on all three of my patients in the morning."

"Of course, Mr. Waters. I have already had a room prepared. You need not sleep in the ballroom this time," Elizabeth said with a weak attempt at humor. "Please wait here for Mrs. Reynolds."

"Thank you, Mrs. Darcy," he replied.

Elizabeth stood wearily, and he added, "You should really get some rest now, Mrs. Darcy. We have things well in hand."

Elizabeth frowned. "You seem always to be offering me the same advice, Mr. Waters." Her shoulders slumped a little. "Unfortunately, my husband has said the same thing several times today and I fear you are both correct. Richard, please give my regards to the Hawkes. I have ordered a tray sent up tonight and will check in on them in the morning. If they require anything when you visit, will you please call for it?"

"Of course," he said, and offered her his arm as she stood.

She waved him off. "I know you are desperate to see her. Go on."

"Get some help on the stairs, Elizabeth," he said in a low voice and she nodded.

"Go," she repeated, shooing him away.

***

Richard knocked on the door to Sophia's room. He waited only a moment before Miss Evelyn opened the door. She stood unmoving, surprised to see him.

"I would like to see Sophia, Miss Evelyn."

"She is sleeping, Colonel," Evelyn replied uncertainly. She glanced back into the room.

"Please, Miss Evelyn," Richard said solemnly. "I will not take long."

With a quick nod, Evelyn opened the door and allowed Richard inside. Like the other bedchambers, the fire was burning hot, warming the entire room. He moved directly to the bed where Sophia was curled up, knees to her chest, shaking, though not as hard as she had been when he pulled her off the ice.

"Why is she still shivering?" Richard asked. She was facing away from him but he could see that her eyes were closed. He reached for her hand.

"Her body has not yet recognized she is warm. Mr. Waters believes the shivering will slow and then stop over the next few hours. You can feel that her skin is no longer as cold. She is making good progress."

Sophia's hair had been plaited after her bath, but a few stray pieces had escaped. Richard reached to brush them away from her face, touching the back of his hand to her cheek. She was much warmer than she had been, but considering how hot the room was, he thought she ought to have been warmer. As he listened, he could hear a slight rasp in her breathing.

He turned to face Miss Evelyn, whose expression was pensive. "Has she been taking tea or water?" he asked.

"Not as much as I would like," was the honest answer.

Richard returned his gaze to Sophia. The shivering unnerved him, but the bluish hue of her lips was gone. He leaned in close to her ear and said her name softly. There was no response, and he said it again. She moaned a little, and turned towards his voice, her eyes opening just a little, and he smiled gently.

"Sophia, love, you should drink. Do you think you can sit up?"

Evelyn said nothing, just stared at Richard for a few moments, but then walked to the table and picked something up. She handed him an invalid feeder.

"We have just received this from the kitchen," she told him. "It should help."

Richard set the feeder on the bed while he tried to prop Sophia a little higher up on her pillows. She mumbled but did not offer any assistance, and her eyes were open but unfocused. He was unsure whether she was truly aware that he was there. Evelyn suddenly appeared on the other side of the bed to push pillows behind her sister as Richard lifted her up. Between the two of them, they maneuvered Sophia into a reclining position to take a little warm tea. After a few minutes, she refused more and sank back into sleep, and Richard could not delay his departure any further. He kissed Sophia's hand and nodded at Evelyn.

"Have me summoned should she need anything. I will return first thing in the morning."

"Thank you, Colonel."

He executed a small, stiff bow, and with one final, troubled look at the figure on the bed, he departed.

It was after midnight when Evelyn finally retired, leaving instructions for Polly to rouse her should her sister require anything. She kissed Sophia on the forehead, noting with satisfaction that she was sleeping peacefully. Evelyn was asleep nearly the moment she stretched out upon her own bed.

***

Sophia heard voices all around her, but they were indistinct, blurred, producing only a sort of buzzing noise that could not keep her entirely awake. She was sure she heard her at least two female voices, but sleep dragged her away from the sound, and when she finally woke, there was only silence. She turned on her side, sluggishly attempting to discover what it was that had awakened her. After some time puzzling it out, she realized that she was cold. She sat slowly, gathering her blanket around her and stood. Her legs trembled beneath her but held, and she was too tired to wonder why she felt so unsteady.

The night sky outside the window was lightening to gray as Sophia made her way listlessly to the hearth. It took her two attempts to grab the poker, which felt rather heavier than she remembered. She stirred the coals and numbly dropped some tinder on top to restart the blaze, grateful the box resting next to the stones had been filled and a few larger pieces of wood were stacked nearby. She had not realized she was shaking, but her trembling limbs were not supporting her desire to rise from the floor, and she decided to remain close to the warmth and continue to feed the flames for a time.

I must be ill, she told herself, surprise breaking through the haze that surrounded her thoughts. *I am never ill.* She raised her eyes to the bell pull, but did not believe she could stand up to reach it. *One of the maids will come to help me eventually*, she thought, and closed her eyes, leaning against the back of the settee. Her eyelids grew heavier as the fire began to warm her, and shoving one last log clumsily into the grate, she tucked herself into her blanket, stretched out upon the floor, and fell asleep.

She was not sure how much later it was that she felt herself being lifted and carried back to the soft bed, where she curled into a ball. A few moments later, a bedwarmer was tucked under the blankets at the far end of the bed, and she sighed contentedly. The deep breath she took caught, tickled, and resulted in a long bout of coughing. Still, she was too sleepy to open her eyes. Her chest hurt, and now she could hear more buzzing in a low, angry timbre. Not a woman's voice this time, she decided, pleased with herself for discerning so much, but unhappy she could not decipher what was being said. She took short, shallow breaths to avoid coughing more and was not happy to feel herself being hauled up and forced to drink. She turned her head when she felt something touch her lips, fighting against the icy liquid being forced down her aching throat.

"No," she managed to say, twisting away with a cough. Even in her head it sounded garbled. "Too cold."

There were more voices, one rising above the others.

"Tea," said a familiar voice, barking out an order rather than making a request.

"Richard," she whispered, disoriented. She felt a rough hand on her cheek.

"I am here, love," said a voice near her ear. "We will get you something warm to drink. Rest until then."

A simple order to follow, she thought disjointedly, and allowed herself to drift away.

Chapter Twenty-Six

RICHARD WAS LIVID. He had arrived at Sophia's room nearly as soon as the sun was fully up in the sky, determined to be at her side as soon as possible. He knocked, stood quietly, knocked again. When there was no response to his third knock, he feared that the maid had fallen asleep and stepped into the room to check. What he found was worse than he had presumed. The maid meant to be stoking the fire and tending to Sophia was not sleeping. She was simply not in the room at all.

Richard's eyes flew to the bed where he expected to find his betrothed, but only rumpled sheets provided proof she had been there at all. Had she been moved? Rapidly yet methodically, he canvassed the room with his eyes, finding no sign of Sophia until he turned to check the fire. It had died down, and he thought the room too cool. Then he saw a blonde curl, just one, peeking out behind the settee positioned before the hearth and his heart began to thump against his chest so hard he heard the rushing of blood in his ears. He grabbed one end of the heavy sofa and it slid out of his way, the back legs groaning and scraping loudly across the wood floor.

"Sophia," he whispered as he saw her balled up before the fire, a single blanket tucked haphazardly around her, not quite covering her feet. An iron poker was on the hearth, next to her hand. He lifted her, moving her quickly back into the bed, tucking her in completely and grabbing more blankets from a small stack that had been piled on the writing desk, leaving an inkbottle spinning in his haste. Next, he filled the bedwarmer with new coals and slid it under the blankets. Once he was sure she was warm, he applied himself furiously to the bell pull, not stopping until Mrs. Reynolds herself was standing at the door.

"Mr. Waters," he said shortly, so angry he could not trust himself to say more. The older woman nodded, but before turning away, searched the room with her eyes. Richard saw her quizzical expression and forced himself to add, "She is not here, Mrs. Reynolds. There is no one here."

He was gratified to watch Mrs. Reynolds' expression transition quickly from shock to indignation to something as close to fury as he had ever seen on her face before she regained her composure, nodded, and said, "I shall fetch Mr. Waters at once, sir." She was gone before he could thank her.

Sophia began to cough then, a long, hacking cough that increased his concern and brought several servants into the room. Evelyn trailed behind them in a morning dress, her eyes reddened from lack of sleep, hair pulled up in a simple knot. She glanced around the room as Mrs. Reynolds had, her eyes narrowing when she did not locate the face she had expected. Richard ordered tea brought up, and Evelyn moved to the other side of the bed as she had the previous evening. She waited as one servant hurried away to fetch the tea and the other stoked the fire before curtseying and removing herself from the room.

"Colonel," Evelyn said quietly, placing a hand on her sister's forehead and grimacing. Sophia had been warm but not hot the night before, now she clearly had a fever. "What has happened?"

"What time did you retire last night, Miss Evelyn?" he inquired, his voice rough with worry.

Evelyn took his question as an accusation. "Not until the early hours of the morning, Colonel," she said defensively. "I had been here since the morning and Sophia was resting well. I meant to take a few hours repose and return to her this morning."

Richard silently calculated the hours. "I should have remained with her," he said guiltily, "and damn propriety."

Evelyn took this as proof of his condemnation. "I assure you, Colonel. . ." she began, but he interrupted her.

"Forgive me, Miss Evelyn," he said, though he did not sound apologetic. "I am merely trying to discover how long your sister was left alone."

"What do you mean, left alone?" she said, clearly dismayed. "Was not Polly with her?"

"Excellent," Richard growled. "Now I have a name."

"Richard?" came a soft voice from the door. "Is everything all right?" He turned to see Elizabeth enter the chamber through the wide-open door. She was dressed simply, hurriedly, and he remembered that she had probably spent the night on her own as Darcy had wished to remain with Georgiana. He ran a hand through his hair, running through a long string of curses in his mind. What had he been thinking? In the service of proper manners, he had allowed Sophia to be left to fend for herself. He knew there had been trouble of some sort between her and the servants. He had let himself forget it. *I should have stayed.*

"No," he said, strained and tired. Elizabeth opened her mouth to reply but was prevented by the hasty arrival of Mr. Waters, who brushed past her to examine his patient. Mrs. Reynolds appeared behind him, remaining in the doorway and signaling to the mistress that she was needed elsewhere. Elizabeth was torn. She could see that her friend was not well, but saw also that she was being attended by her sister, Richard, and now Mr. Waters. Nodding once at the housekeeper, she reluctantly turned away, shutting the door behind her.

***

Elizabeth could not believe what she was hearing. Mrs. Reynolds was speaking in a quiet, urgent voice that managed to be at once ashamed and angry as the woman paced the small space behind the desk in her office.

"*Never*, Mrs. Darcy," the elderly housekeeper was saying, more agitated than Elizabeth suspected she had ever been, "never in all my years at Pemberley has the staff been so entirely disrespectful to any guest, let alone one who has been injured." She muttered something under her breath and then said more clearly, "Miss Hawke, of all people. It is unconscionable." She met Elizabeth's somber gaze, both women thinking of Georgiana. Then Mrs. Reynolds straightened her thin shoulders, took a deep breath and released it before delivering the statement for which she had requested Elizabeth's presence. "Polly is young, perhaps not the brightest of girls, but she only needed to tend the fire and summon Mr. Waters if necessary." She shook her head. "For some reason, she left Miss Hawke unattended after her sister retired. Judging from the colonel's reaction, Miss Hawke has thus come to harm. I am fully prepared to resign my post should you desire it." The older woman's voice quavered slightly, but she stood straight and looked her mistress in the eye.

Elizabeth's eyebrows pinched together in contemplation as she waved her hand and shook her head. "I am sure that will not be necessary." She tipped her head to the side for a moment before saying, "However, we might use the threat of such an action to shake up the staff a bit."

Mrs. Reynolds peered at the mistress, puzzled, and Elizabeth sighed.

"I think you will agree there is something going on beyond one maid not doing as she is told."

Elizabeth stood quietly, contemplating. "Mr. Darcy mentioned the problem with the bedlinens, and just yesterday there was some issue about Miss Hawke's riding clothes, though I have not had time to inquire about it."

Mrs. Reynolds nodded. "I have noticed some animosity directed at Miss Hawke, though I have been unable to discern the source and I confess I had mistaken it as a petty dislike. I spoke with the offending party and believed the matter resolved. Now. . ."

"Was the offending party Polly?" Elizabeth asked, bemused. She had thought Polly above stairs only because so many of the maids had been pressed into service after the accident.

"No, Mrs. Darcy. It was Ruth."

Elizabeth considered that, but could fathom no reason for Ruth to have spent any time with Sophia, let alone take a dislike to her. She considered how to approach the dilemma. "The staff knows that I would not allow you to resign for any reason other than retirement. Only a calamitous event would see Mrs. Reynolds removed from her position unwillingly," she said thoughtfully, tapping a finger on the arm of her chair.

"Ma'am?" the faithful housekeeper asked, confused.

"I had thought us beyond such performances, but there it is, I am afraid." Elizabeth spoke to herself as much as to Mrs. Reynolds. She leaned back in the chair, still thinking. "We could handle this quietly, but I fear we may need to make a bit of a scene or we may forever be wasting time on petty grievances." Elizabeth closed her eyes as a plan began to form in her mind. After a few minutes, she stood and took the housekeeper's hand. "I want you to just follow along. Simply agree and look suitably chagrined. Although I may say things that mislead, I will not entirely prevaricate." She caught Mrs. Reynolds' eyes and held them. "Do you understand? I plan to get to the root of these problems. It may not be an entirely honorable course, but I hope it will be a productive one. Will you trust me?"

Mrs. Reynolds blinked. "Yes, ma'am."

"Have no fear, Mrs. Reynolds," Elizabeth said calmly, a sly smile on her face. "I shall not allow you to fall on your sword for this." Her expression grew hard, and she released the housekeeper's hand. "Let us proceed. Will you ask all the staff who can be spared to assemble in the servants' hall in one hour? Please make certain that Polly and Ruth are among them. I wish to speak with Lady Matlock."

"Of course, ma'am," stated Mrs. Reynolds with a firm nod. She waited for Elizabeth to walk out of her office before she set off to spread the word.

***

Precisely one and one-quarter hour later, Elizabeth Darcy entered the servants' hall. As she turned to face her staff, there were a few sharp intakes of breath before the offenders were hushed.

Everyone employed in the house at Pemberley was at least aware of Mrs. Darcy. A few of the upper servants had even worked with her on occasion when Mrs. Reynolds asked for their expertise. She was known as a fair and generous mistress, if a bit young. Truth be told, she had a reputation of being perhaps a little too kind, a little too giving, her unwavering devotion to those who lived on the estate and had fallen ill the previous summer only the most well-known example. During her own illness over the autumn, most had lost sight of the mistress entirely, and while the more established staff felt deeply loyal to Mrs. Darcy and would never attempt to take advantage of her absence, the same could not be said for those not long in Pemberley's service. When the mistress had reappeared among them a few weeks earlier, there had even been a bit of grumbling, though it had been put down quickly by Mrs. Reynolds.

Before them stood someone very few had ever seen: a proud, stately woman in the process of haughtily assessing them with cold eyes. She was dressed in a long-sleeved gown made of ivory silk and trimmed with dark coquelicot and gold embroidery at both the neckline and the elegantly turned cuffs. The waist was beaded with tiny white pearls, the motif repeated on the hem with small glass beads that reflected the morning sunlight. Satin house slippers peeped out from beneath her skirt. Atop the gown she wore a coquelicot silk spencer that tapered neatly at her waist, nearly hiding the tell-tale swell of her abdomen, its wide lapels embroidered with an intricate flower and wheat design in fine gold thread. Her long, dark chestnut hair had been swept up into thick curls held in place by sparkling ruby hairpins and accented with a thin golden tiara, a small circular ruby set in the center.

The woman who stood before them today was not the young bride, the generous mistress, the sweet-natured country lass their master had brought home. That woman appeared in clothing that, while quite fine, was better suited to visiting tenants or strolling in the woods. That woman wore her hair up in styles becoming but not sophisticated, a few wispy curls always escaping their ordinary pins. That woman had a smile and a kind word for everyone. This woman was Mrs. Fitzwilliam Darcy, the mistress of one of the finest estates in all of England. This was a woman whose grandeur would make her not only an accepted member of the *ton*, but an influential leader. This was a woman of power and significance, and judging by their pale faces and shuffling feet, her staff, young and old alike, was suitably intimidated.

Elizabeth let them stew for a bit before speaking.

"As you should all be aware," she began in a strong, clear voice, "we had an eventful morning yesterday. As a result, Miss Darcy, Miss Hawke, and Master Pembroke are currently confined to their beds."

She stopped, staring at the assembled group. She saw a few confused nods.

"Miss Hawke," Elizabeth continued, "as you may *not* know, was walking with me when the accident happened, and was instrumental in pulling both Miss Darcy and Master Pembroke from the lake. She put her own health at risk to save them." Elizabeth again paused, intentionally dragging out the length of her speech.

"Miss Darcy and Master Pembroke, as you are likely aware, are very important to the Darcy family, and we are greatly indebted to Miss Hawke for their recovery."

Now they were all uncomfortable, waiting to hear the real reason their mistress had called them together. The tension in the room was growing with each sentence, and as the more the mistress spoke, the clearer it was becoming that this was not to be a pleasant Christmas greeting. The group gathered in the hall looked to Mrs. Reynolds for some hint or reassurance, but the housekeeper gave nothing away, standing quietly to the left and behind her mistress, hands clasped before her, staring straight ahead, making eye contact with no one, a frown settled on her face.

Elizabeth began again, allowing her indignation to show. "Imagine my surprise, then, to find this morning that the Pemberley maid assigned to assist Miss Hawke overnight had abandoned her post without a word to anyone." She swept the room with her disapproving glare, her line of vision falling on a young maid trying to unobtrusively step behind the crowd to escape notice. "This would be a weighty insult to the Darcy family even were our guest not ill, but due to our negligence, Miss Hawke's condition is significantly worse this morning. Not only have we failed to provide the most basic hospitality to an honored guest, we have actively caused harm." She waited another moment to deliver her iciest proclamation. "Upon making this discovery, Mrs. Reynolds offered her resignation, and I am considering it."

This time, the gasps were audible and intense, and she was certain the upper servants were aghast. The hiss of increasing whispers was cut off as Elizabeth spoke again.

"Should that occur, I put you all on notice that the next housekeeper of Pemberley will not be selected from among your ranks."

Now not only was the anxiety in the room palpable, there was real fear. A position at Pemberley was prestigious not only because of the wealth and longevity of the family but because Mrs. Reynolds helped make a life of service comfortable and rewarding for those who worked hard. Her rapport with the family went a long way towards easing the common difficulties staff encountered. Children were welcome here, and even marriages between the servants, while not encouraged, were not actively discouraged if the couple continued to perform their duties well. A new housekeeper, a stranger, might not see the advantage in such arrangements and would doubtless be more inclined to let staff go for what might be now be considered minor infractions.

"Before I make that decision," said Mrs. Darcy flatly, "I would know the origin of this staff's disdain for Miss Hawke. I am fully aware she has not been treated as a guest ought to be, and I will hear the substance of the hostility leveled against her. If you know of anything that would help me to this end, report to Mrs. Reynolds' office where she and I will await you." Elizabeth then observed coolly, "Should nobody be inclined to come forward, I will call each of you in for an interview individually and make staffing decisions accordingly."

Mrs. Darcy turned slowly, about to make a grand exit before halting. She glanced back at the assembled workers, seemingly lost in thought before she leveled her final salvo, one upon which Lady Matlock had insisted.

"You should know that Miss Hawke is not only of recent importance to the Darcy and Fitzwilliam families," she said emphatically. "She was a ward of the Fitzwilliam family until she came of age." *It is true in essentials*, she consoled herself. "And although no formal announcement has been made, Mr. Darcy has recently informed me that Miss Hawke is Colonel Fitzwilliam's betrothed." She smiled, but there was no mirth in it. "I think you will all agree that the colonel may not be best pleased with our performance and will seek to address it. It behooves us all to prevent the need for any response on his part." Her eyes moved to the back of the room where Polly stood, eyes downcast, and caught sight of Ruth, a young woman who had worked very hard in the laundry during the epidemic over the past summer, her arms crossed over her chest and her pale face defiant, angry. The servants closest to her had edged away.

Elizabeth continued her graceful retreat, followed closely by Mrs. Reynolds, who turned at the door to announce, "Polly, you will attend me this afternoon. I will send for you."

Once outside the room, the two women nodded at one another.

"I will meet you in a quarter of an hour, Mrs. Reynolds," Elizabeth said quietly. "I expect we will soon hear the truth of it."

"As you wish, ma'am," said Mrs. Reynolds, her face pinched. "I shall see you then."

When the imperial Mrs. Darcy arrived at the appointed time, there were five maids and three footmen waiting in the passageway.

Chapter Twenty-Seven

ELIZABETH AND MRS. REYNOLDS spent all morning in interviews with the maids, as Mrs. Reynolds had asked Wilkins, the butler, to interview the men. Over the course of the morning, they learned a good deal of what was occurring below stairs. Mrs. Darcy's unusual address had prompted confessions of gossip about Miss Hawke, but also on completely unrelated and thankfully inconsequential matters. At the end, the source of the current problem had been identified.

"Well, Mrs. Reynolds," she said grimly as the door closed behind the last of them, "it appears we must speak first to Miss Evelyn."

"I find it difficult to believe that she would have said such things about her sister, Mrs. Darcy," the housekeeper said, shaking her head. "I believe it more likely that the slander we are hearing must have been exaggerated, though I cannot imagine why."

"Still," Elizabeth replied, pressing one finger along an eyebrow, uncomfortable with what she had learned, "I must speak to her about this before the final two interviews."

"Polly and Ruth, ma'am?"

"Ruth," Elizabeth sighed. "I would never have thought Ruth would engage in such behavior. She worked so diligently for us last summer and has never given us cause for alarm, but the look on her face today gave me pause."

Mrs. Reynolds shook her head. "She has been with us several years but is still quite young, and she can be terribly judgmental when she believes someone has committed a sin."

"'It is mine to avenge; I will repay,' says the Lord," Elizabeth intoned softly, recalling her childhood instruction. Elizabeth's thoughts flitted briefly to her sister Mary's penchant for insensitive sermonizing. "The contradiction of proclaiming such judgments is lost upon her, I assume?"

Mrs. Reynolds pulled a face before responding. "Quite lost, Mrs. Darcy."

At that moment, a tea tray arrived, and the women stopped speaking while they at last broke their fast. Afterwards, Elizabeth slipped upstairs to speak to her husband, leaving Mrs. Reynolds to alert the two maids that their presence was expected later that afternoon.

***

Elizabeth found her husband in his chambers belatedly attending to his ablutions. She waited for his valet to complete his shave before asking for a few moments of his time. Darcy sent his man away and drew her into his lap.

"You are dressed in a good deal of finery for a morning indoors, Elizabeth," he said by way of a greeting. One arm circled her waist as his long fingers lightly traced first the embroidery on her spencer and then the pearls on her gown. "I cannot say I am not enjoying it a great deal, but it does make me question what you are about?"

"Merely a demonstration for the staff, William," was the reply. She placed a hand on his cheek and kissed him quickly on the lips, eliciting a low growl and a short laugh.

"I do not believe you should start anything you may not wish to finish, Mrs. Darcy," he said playfully, laying his forehead on her shoulder and putting his arms around her waist.

"I have come to speak to you about my morning," she said in a tone that was almost plaintive.

"I presume this has something to do with Miss Hawke?" he asked.

Elizabeth nodded. "It does. Am I to understand you heard what happened last night?"

"Mmm. As much as Richard could tell me. He was angrier than I believe I have ever seen him," Darcy said softly, "and I have seen him very angry indeed."

"Of course he is angry," she replied emphatically. "None of us is ever so upset as when a wrong has been perpetrated upon a loved one." They both sat for a moment, remembering before Elizabeth continued. "Clearly there is an issue with the staff." She considered what to say next, but decided she was too tired to be anything but blunt. "Mrs. Reynolds came to me this morning quite distraught about it. She offered to step down and leave Pemberley."

Darcy froze briefly, his face still hidden, and then asked, carefully, "And what did you say?"

Elizabeth had been thinking of the interviews she was yet to hear and was startled by the fear she thought she heard in his voice. She slapped his arm lightly.

"Do not be absurd, William. A yawning chasm would have to open up beneath us and swallow

Pemberley whole before I would consent to such a thing."

She felt her husband shake his head a little before he said, "A simple 'no' would have sufficed, love." He put his other arm around her.

"Humph," was her distracted response. "It was the correct thing for her to offer, given the infraction, and I do believe it was sincere. She would have stepped aside." After reflecting on Mrs. Reynolds for a moment, Elizabeth added, "there is such a difference between the experienced staff and the new, William." She had always regretted the staff who had resigned after the epidemic. "I am afraid much of that is my doing."

He lifted his head to search her face before saying, "What is done is done, my love, and it was done for the best." He laughed, a little in relief at hearing his wife's support for Mrs. Reynolds and a little at the intentional echo of words once delivered in a less affectionate manner. He peeked up at her and she rolled her eyes.

Better, he thought fondly, and kissed her neck just below her ear. *I hate to see her so distressed.*

Elizabeth sighed happily, stroking his hair before laying her forehead down to the top of his head. "We may have to debate that later. For now, may I speak of this quandary?"

He let out a sigh of his own. "How may I help?"

Elizabeth lifted her head and her husband straightened up. "It seems that nearly the entire staff has heard certain slanders about Miss Hawke. The untruths do have a seed of veracity, though unless the story you have told me is lacking in some fundamental way, they have been wildly exaggerated. The more pious among the maids determined that such an unrepentant sinner should receive no notice from them despite her mysterious sponsorship by the Darcy and Fitzwilliam families."

Darcy pulled away from his wife, his hands now gently grasping her waist. He met her gaze, and his face was troubled, stormy. "The Pemberley staff does not gossip, madam, let alone treat a guest based such slander. Who is the source?"

Elizabeth sighed. "I have a plan, William. I shall tell you, but for now I ask only advice on your part, not action."

"That, my dear, I cannot promise until I know what you have to say." Darcy's face was as closed and shuttered as it had been when his wife first knew him, and she dreaded what that might portend.

"The house staff is mine to deal with, William. I assure you that on that score, I will not give way."

He offered her one very small nod, though his expression did not soften. "If there is aught else to be done. . ."

"Miss Evelyn," Elizabeth blurted out, interrupting him.

"What?" Darcy asked, nonplussed.

"Miss Evelyn appears to have been the original source."

Darcy shook his head, not quite believing his wife's information. "Miss Evelyn slandered her own sister? Would not that implicate her as well?"

Elizabeth turned her face to the ceiling with a small huff. "It makes little sense, William, but we have both seen how she behaves. There is discord there, and I am unhappy to say that I do not think Miss Evelyn would have much care for the reputation of her own character should she feel the need to expose her sister's."

Darcy closed his eyes. "What a mess. Richard is half mad with worry, and he has been assisting Waters and Miss Evelyn in Miss Hawke's care. To tell him now. . ."

"Indeed," was his wife's reply. She reached up with one hand and gently stroked his hair again. "Shall we wait to inform him?"

He nodded, then smiled softly. "I would dearly love to run my hands through your hair as well, dearest, but it looks as though this style took a great deal of effort," he teased, trying to redirect the conversation. "What were you about, going in all your state to speak to Mrs. Reynolds?"

Elizabeth smiled though she knew he could not see it. "I did not only go to see Mrs. Reynolds, William. I addressed nearly the entire staff."

"Ah," he said, understanding at last dawning. "You were introducing them to Mrs. Darcy. Our aunt's idea?"

"Mine, though she supported it." She took his hand. "They know Mrs. Darcy, William," she said in a quiet voice. "At least, they know Miss Elizabeth. I do not believe they have ever met Mrs. Fitzwilliam Darcy." She sat up, pulling her head back until she could look her husband in the eye. "I thought it was time they did."

Darcy chuckled and shook his head. "I would have liked to have seen that." His eyes lit up as he contemplated the scene. "I should have liked to see that very much indeed."

"You would have found a good deal to please you, I think," she said, still in that quiet, firm voice. "However, it would not have been nearly as effective had you been there with me."

Darcy took her face in both hands and kissed her forehead. "Mrs. Fitzwilliam Darcy." He grinned mischievously at her. "I rather like the way that sounds."

Elizabeth kissed his cheek. "I believe I must speak to Miss Evelyn, though I will do so privately. Eventually, Richard must be told, but I believe it should come from you, dear, and you are correct that it should be delayed."

Darcy sobered quickly, considering how irate Richard would be and hoping Miss Hawke would be much recovered before he was forced to speak with his cousin.

"Very well, wife."

She shook her head again at him. "You speak as though I am the one in charge, William," she said primly, removing herself from his lap and smoothing down her skirts.

His eyebrows lifted as he studied her figure. "Are you not?" he asked.

She tilted her head at him and her brown eyes sparkled with recognition. "I suppose I am," she said with wonder, and then with confidence. "Yes. I am."

***

Elizabeth walked with quick strides to Sophia's room. She had first checked in on Pembroke, who seemed to need nothing more than to blow his nose every so often. He was sitting up in bed playing with the old pewter soldiers that had been packed away in the nursery since her husband's boyhood. His father and grandfather were fully engaged in helping him best Napoleon. She had never seen the earl willing to engage in child's play, but then he did adore Pembroke. *Only for a grandson in line for the earldom*, she thought with a little bitterness. *He would not do so much for Richard.* She felt no animosity towards the boy, but knew well enough that he would be better served should he face some sort of punishment rather than rewarded with increased attention and a game.

Next, she had entered Georgiana's room after knocking and receiving an invitation to enter. Aunt Eleanor was sitting with Georgiana, who was still tired, but better, her color improved and her conversation stronger. The pair invited her for tea, but Elizabeth declined, citing a general need to finish some tasks that had been neglected the day before.

Finally, her feet at last slowing, she made her way to Sophia Hawke's chamber, where before she could inquire after the patient she heard the raspy, rattling cough of its occupant. She opened the door without waiting for anyone to let her in and saw with some relief that Mr. Waters and Miss Evelyn were working on something together over by the fire. She could hear the soft hum of their voices but not what they were saying.

Richard was supporting Sophia's back as she coughed and expelled something into a basin. Elizabeth's fragile stomach turned before she regained control and walked into the room.

"I came to check on Sophia, Richard," she said, laying a hand on his shoulder. "But I can see that she is not well."

He was silent as he settled his betrothed back onto the pillows.

Sophia's face was red with the exertion of coughing, but the blood in her cheeks faded away until she was almost white. Her breathing was shallow, as though she feared to breathe too deeply, and her eyelids were half-closed. She was exhausted, clearly very ill.

It took some time for Richard to position Sophia as he wanted, but once he did, he half turned his head to say, over his shoulder, "I will not leave her tonight, Elizabeth. I will not leave until she is well. Do not even attempt to persuade me otherwise. I have no energy to argue it, but I will not be moved."

Elizabeth thought to protest, but stopped herself, considered the result of such an action, and nodded. "I will not make the attempt, Richard."

He nodded stiffly. "Thank you."

"I shall have a cot sent up for you to sleep on tonight. I will insist that a maid be present."

Richard snorted. "For all the good that will do."

Elizabeth made a humming sound. "I am handling that situation, Richard. I promise that there will be fewer servants on the Pemberley staff this evening."

He turned to gaze at her then, appraising the bejeweled hair, the fine dress, the silk spencer, the satin slippers, and made a guttural sound deep in his throat that Elizabeth recognized as approval. "Reviewing the troops, general?"

"I learned from listening to you, cousin."

Richard reached out to take her hand and press it for a moment, then turned his attention back towards the bed. Elizabeth moved over to the hearth, where two dark heads were bent together, still talking in hushed tones. Evelyn filled a small pot with water from a pitcher and Mr. Waters took it from her to hang over the fire. Three more were already positioned over the flames.

Mr. Waters noted Elizabeth's interest. "When they are boiling, we will take them off one at a time, then refill and reheat them as they cool. Steam will help her clear the phlegm from Miss Hawke's lungs more effectively," he told her in a clipped, professional tone. Evelyn nodded and glanced admiringly at Mr. Waters. Elizabeth saw the look, but said nothing.

"Mr. Waters has explained the properties to me, Mrs. Darcy," Miss Evelyn said enthusiastically. "It is the heat more than anything. A bath would also work, but we cannot risk the chill she might take when the water turns cold or she is removed into a much cooler room. This is a simple solution but I think an effective one."

Mr. Waters nodded, a small smile on his face as he watched Miss Evelyn speak. "It is often the simplest solutions that are the most effective," he agreed. Miss Evelyn returned the smile and he turned back to his task.

"Miss Evelyn," Elizabeth said quietly. "Might I have a word in private?"

Chapter Twenty-Eight

ELIZABETH WATCHED AS Miss Evelyn's perfect brow wrinkled in consternation and she glanced back at Mr. Waters. He nodded and motioned that they should go, that he had things in hand, and the two women stepped into the adjoining sitting room. Another fire was burning brightly here, though it was cooler than the sickroom. Elizabeth waited for her guest to sit.

Miss Evelyn remained on her feet, clearly uncomfortable to be away from her sister, gazing at the door to the room repeatedly before turning her attention to her hostess.

"How may I help you, Mrs. Darcy?" she asked somewhat curtly.

Elizabeth was used to Miss Evelyn's moods by now and gestured calmly to a chair.

"We should be seated, Miss Evelyn."

The younger woman smoothed her skirt behind her before lowering herself onto the chair to which Elizabeth had gestured. She clasped her hands in her lap and waited expectantly. She was clearly at a loss as to the reason she had been called away.

Elizabeth kept her voice low and soothing. "Miss Evelyn, I am trying to ascertain what exactly happened last night."

Miss Evelyn's flawless nose wrinkled in disdain, though her anger was targeted in the proper direction. "I think we know precisely what happened last night, Mrs. Darcy. For some reason, Polly did not think my sister important enough to remain in her room, and my sister was left to fend for herself." Large blue eyes met Elizabeth's own before flickering back towards the bedchamber. "She might at least have come to fetch me. I would have stayed."

Elizabeth waited patiently, thinking that Evelyn Hawke would continue to speak, but she did not. The woman was clearly upset, genuinely worried about her sister, and Elizabeth was pleased and relieved to see it. She had been increasingly concerned over the course of the morning that the younger sister had slandered the elder maliciously. She knew this would be the opinion of others in their party, but she had held out hope that Miss Evelyn had behaved thoughtlessly but without spite.

"I cannot disagree, Miss Evelyn," she replied after a long pause. "That is indeed what I have come to speak to you about."

This ignited some interest, and Evelyn leaned forward. "Have you determined why she left, Mrs. Darcy?"

She has not an inkling of the damage she has done. "We are still speaking with the staff," was the response, but Elizabeth hesitated, considering without much success how best to explain the events of the morning. As the silence deepened, Evelyn Hawke grew impatient, rubbing her hands together and then lacing and unlacing her fingers.

"Well?" she asked, jarring Elizabeth from her thoughts. It was a gentle inquiry that somehow also managed to be abrupt.

"It seems," Elizabeth sighed, "that you said something about your sister to the maids gathered outside the laundry, and that it gave birth to some rather cruel gossip. The maid last night heard that gossip, and it may be why she did not remain in the room. It does not," she added quickly, to avoid the impression that she was excusing the behavior, "explain why she would not wake you to take her place, though I suspect she did not wish to make her absence known."

Evelyn sat back in her chair, thinking of the time she had spent outside the laundry watching the girls work. She shook her head. What had she said? She had spoken about chemicals and their properties and Sophia had come to take her back inside. *No, before that,* she thought. *I spoke to Ruth about Uncle Archibald and. . .*

Elizabeth watched as Miss Evelyn dredged up the memory of her interactions with the laundry maids. *Perhaps she does not recall, or perhaps she is feigning concern.* Suddenly, the blood drained from the woman's face, and she knew that Sophia's sister was not dissembling, that she had indeed remembered.

"It is important that I hear from you what was said, Miss Evelyn," she said quietly. "I will speak with the maid involved, but I need to know exactly what you said."

Evelyn closed her eyes. *How could I have been so stupid?* "One of the girls asked if I had always lived at Darlington and I told her I lived with my uncle in London until Sophia came home."

Elizabeth nodded encouragingly. She already had some idea where this was headed, but she needed to hear it. When Evelyn did not continue, she spoke again.

"And?" she prompted.

"Ruth asked where Sophia had been." Her voice dropped to a whisper, her eyes still shut. "It was just simple conversation while they worked. I never thought. . ." She grimaced, shook her head, her tone turning sour. "You never do think it through, do you, Evie?" she said harshly, as though there was nobody else in the room.

"Miss Evelyn," Elizabeth said reassuringly, "it will help me to know."

"I told Ruth I had no idea where she had been, that she and I were only recently reunited." She opened her eyes and met Elizabeth's steady gaze. "I never meant anything by it," she said, almost pleadingly. "For all they knew, she might have been with the Tildens or other friends of the family."

Elizabeth cleared her throat. *Highly open to suggestion*, she thought, *but not as bad as it might have been. Repairable.* "I need to know whether those were your exact words, Miss Evelyn, if I am to correct this. Please take a moment to consider."

She watched as Miss Evelyn's dreamy blue eyes clouded over in contemplation before she said, suddenly, without preamble, "Sophia left my uncle's house when I was twelve. I have no idea where she has been. She has not told me, and we have only recently been reunited."

This version was less benign, but Elizabeth did believe that this was the worst of it. She took a moment to consider the information. *She sounds a runaway, a wanton, but with Lady Matlock's assistance, we can explain Sophia's disappearance with the story about her being a Fitzwilliam ward. The earl did take responsibility for her safety.* She paused, wondering idly whether that was as true as she hoped. *At least the enmity between Uncle Henry and Mr. Hawke is well known and will explain much.*

"Thank you, Miss Evelyn." She stood, placing a hand on the other woman's shoulder in a bid to offer some small comfort. "I will see to the maids. You should return to your sister."

"Mrs. Darcy, what is it that is being said about my sister?" Evelyn was determined to hear it.

"Your words were unfortunately rather careless, Miss Evelyn. The maids who spoke to us are under the impression that your sister was a runaway and that she is ruined."

Miss Evelyn remained in her chair, though she nodded. *Sophia warned me to hold my tongue.* She heard Elizabeth leave and for a minute, she arched her neck and leaned her head against the back of her seat. She was exhausted, but being able to help Sophia had allowed her to push her tiredness aside. Now she felt all of the worry, the distress of the day descend upon her. *Sophia might have fallen ill in any case*, she tried to tell herself, but discarded that thought immediately as unworthy of the person she wished to become. *You know,* she told herself reproachfully, *that hours spent on the floor tending to the fire had to have hurt her. You did that.*

She wiped an angry fist at the tears on her cheeks and sternly told herself that she had no right to cry. Accepting the consequences of her actions was new to her, and she was quite displeased with the feeling. *It is all your fault*, she told herself. *Entirely your fault.*

***

Elizabeth was headed to meet Mrs. Reynolds again when she spied her husband striding through the hall, speaking to a footman who bowed and hurried away as she approached. She walked directly to Fitzwilliam and put her arms around his waist. He bent to kiss the top of her head.

"Are you well, Elizabeth?" he asked, sounding weary.

"I miss Jane," she mumbled into his chest. "I miss my sister."

He held her for a minute, uncomfortable with this sign of affection out in the open when the house was so busy, but clearly his wife required comfort.

"Come," he said, and before anyone could see, he wrapped one arm around her shoulders, leading her an empty guest room a few steps away. Once the door was shut behind them, he sat her on the bed, kneeled before her, and took her hands in his own. "I take it the meeting with Miss Evelyn did not go well?"

With a small lift of her shoulders, Elizabeth replied, "As well as could be expected, William. I believe she spoke unguardedly, and though her words themselves were not slanderous, they left Miss Hawke vulnerable to gossip. I am thankful I thought to ask for Aunt Eleanor's help. Nobody knows how to turn the tide of gossip like your aunt. I just never expected to need to use her talent in my own household."

Darcy touched her hands to his forehead before lowering them for a kiss. "This holiday has not turned out quite the way we planned, has it?" he asked ruefully. "Here it is, the day before Christmas, and we have a houseful of invalids and a war of words to win."

This elicited a small sigh from his wife and a weak laugh. "*This* is not a houseful of invalids, William. Last summer was a houseful of invalids."

He feigned insult, pleased to see her humor restored, even in small measure. "Regardless, you had no wish for me to be here, so there is no way for me to make a fair comparison."

"I did not want you then," she said, all trace of teasing gone, "but I am very happy to have you here now."

"Was it only a few days ago," he pondered, "that our most pressing concern was you going out to collect greenery?"

"Oh," she said with an arched eyebrow and steely resolve, "I will still be doing that."

"Elizabeth," he began, a growl beginning to build in his throat. He glared at his wife, only to see her lips begin to tremble. For the briefest of moments, he believed her about to cry, something he dreaded and yet had come to expect. Instead, as she struggled for composure, a choked laugh escaped and he shook his head at her, relieved and annoyed.

"Oh, William," she said lovingly, leaning in to kiss his cheek. "Your face, dear. Like a great forbidding grizzly."

"I knew I should not have taken you to the Menagerie," he grumbled, and she laughed again. A deep breath helped clear her melancholy, and she moved to stand.

"Thank you, William," she said with a chuckle, "I always feel better when I speak with you."

"So I need not send the carriage to collect Jane?" he joked, offering his hand to assist her from the bed.

"Not yet," she replied saucily, "but I shall require a substantial donation to the fund for expresses. I cannot be expected to wait even a week between letters."

"Yes, my dear," he said, sounding put upon, but ruining the effect with a warm smile. "I know you must speak with the maids, but please, after that, you must rest before dinner. Even I am tired and I have not your burden to carry."

"I will," she promised, for as many trips up and down the stairs she had been required to make today, she was already craving her bed.

Her husband peered at her suspiciously.

"What is it?" she asked.

"I am not one to question my good fortune," he began, "but you are being rather agreeable. I cannot help but wonder what you have done with my wife?"

"You should take full advantage while you may," she retorted tartly, with a tilt of her chin. Just as quickly she leaned against him, placing a hand over his heart, and said softly, "I am still heartily ashamed of myself for my actions yesterday, William."

Darcy hesitated. "For going out when I asked you not to do so?" He wanted to be clear to which infraction she referred. Her mouth twisted in irritation and he quietly berated himself. *Wrong again, apparently.*

"No, I am not apologizing for going out of doors, William. I have had quite enough of being held prisoner inside, even in such a large and lovely home as Pemberley."

He groaned inwardly. The conversation had been going so well. One question and they were returned to the quarrel. "Elizabeth. . ." he began

"No," she said determinedly, wrapping her arms around him as she had in the hall. "I am sorry for thinking, even for a moment, that I could help on the ice. It was a completely selfish, foolish notion, to think that I must always be the best one to help. It lasted but a moment, but it was wrong. It delayed Sophia and I would have done nothing but make more work for everyone." She placed a hand on her stomach and said wryly, "I am not particularly buoyant just now."

Darcy took a quick look at the door. He wanted to speak with Waters to see how Miss Hawke fared, and he particularly wished to check on Richard. Still, there was something that he needed to explain to his enchanting, infuriating wife, and she had just provided him the best opportunity he was likely to have. He returned his gaze to her and took both of her hands in his.

"Elizabeth," he said, swallowing hard and suddenly very serious, "when I heard that scream, I knew immediately it was you." He grimaced before continuing. "I did not know where you were or what had happened, but I immediately thought the worst." He took in a very deep breath and released it slowly, his head dropping. "I think that scream may have taken ten years from my life." He met her apologetic gaze with his own steady, appraising one.

He moved one hand to her stomach and said, "I could not bear it should anything happen to you or our child." Elizabeth felt the warmth of his hand and placed hers over his, but did not try to look away. His voice was hoarse as he continued to speak, staring straight into her eyes, "Everything I need most in the world stands before me."

His other hand came up to cup her cheek before he said, earnestly, "I may appear overbearing to you, my love, and I daresay I am, but please, I beg of you," his eyes remained locked with hers, and in them she saw vulnerability, pain, "have mercy."

Elizabeth threw her arms impulsively around his neck and he encircled her with his arms. Her husband's admission of weakness was awful and endearing and she felt some guilt for forcing him to it. He had taken so much upon himself since she had been ill. Elizabeth had long understood that she must curtail some of her own independence to support her marriage, but it now struck her in a far deeper way what her responsibilities to him must entail.

"I will do my best not to worry you, William," she said in a low voice close to his ear. "My temper may not always be under good regulation, but I love you very much, and I promise to do nothing that will put us at risk." Her husband responded only with a slight tightening of his embrace.

They remained that way for some time, but eventually Darcy straightened, tugged his waistcoat to pull out the wrinkles, and took her arm. She watched with tenderness as he composed himself and said, "Then allow me to escort you downstairs, my dear."

Chapter Twenty-Nine

THEY PARTED AT THE BOTTOM of the staircase, Elizabeth to Mrs. Reynolds' office, Fitzwilliam to see Mr. Waters. She doubted that their paths would cross again until dinner, which they would dutifully attend with their sadly diminished party. In short order, Elizabeth had gained Lady Matlock's approval and assistance and turned her steps to Mrs. Reynold's office.

When she arrived, the housekeeper was waiting.

"We shall proceed as we did this morning, Mrs. Reynolds," Elizabeth said, "I will not interfere with the interviews unless I feel I must, but I do wish to be present."

Mrs. Reynolds left, returning with Polly. The girl stood awkwardly, shifting nervously from one foot to the other and wringing her hands. She did not look up when she entered, but bobbed a curtsey in Elizabeth's direction.

"Polly," Mrs. Reynolds said coldly, once she stood before them, "tell us why you are here."

The maid did not look up, but said, in a small voice, "I left Miss Hawke's room last night."

"I have to say that I am disappointed," Mrs. Reynolds said in a voice brimming with disdain. "You have insulted both the Darcy family and myself by directly disobeying your charge as you have."

"Yes, Mrs. Reynolds."

"What could have possessed you to leave that room, Polly?"

Polly was silent. Elizabeth and Mrs. Reynolds waited for what seemed a very long time before the housekeeper added, "Well?"

"Mr. Redding, Mrs. Darcy," Polly almost whispered, "he preaches about fallen women and says they pollute. . ."

Elizabeth interrupted before the maid could finish. Her eyes flashed with fire. "What can you mean, Polly?"

Polly swallowed anxiously, "Only that Miss Hawke ran away from home. Her sister said. . ."

Elizabeth raised an eyebrow at Polly. The kindly rector who held the living at Kympton did preach about avoiding sin, but in her dealings with him he had never shown anything but compassion for the sinner.

Mrs. Reynolds said coldly, "Leaving Mr. Redding aside, do you believe that Mr. and Mrs. Darcy would host such a person as a guest in this house?"

"Well, no ma'am, but they mightn't know, you see," chirped Polly anxiously.

Mrs. Reynolds slapped the palm of her hand on her desk, producing a sharp noise that made the girl jump. "Do you think Mrs. Darcy, or I for that matter, would know less about the guests in this house than you?"

Still in a very soft voice, Polly added, as though by rote, "Sometimes the servants, we hears things, ma'am, that the family might not."

Elizabeth was grateful Mrs. Reynolds had spoken first or she could not have been sure her words would have been wise. She was now quite sure that the girl had been prepared for this meeting. "Clearly," Elizabeth stated acidly, "though I suspect what you have heard and we have not is gossip and slander of the basest kind."

The girl shook her head obstinately while Mrs. Reynolds, for all her years and tenacious grip on propriety looked as though she might leap over her desk to force Polly to stop.

Elizabeth placed a gentle restraining hand on Mrs. Reynold's arm. She was in control of her fury at this show of disrespect, but it was a near thing. She told herself that the girl was very young and had been misled. "What you believe you know," she said, "has been fueled by an erroneous interpretation of Miss Evelyn's words."

Polly stopped shaking her head, though she still looked doubtful. *Stupid girl*, Elizabeth thought incredulously, to hold so tightly to misinformation as though the consequences of her infraction might be eased by such behavior.

"Miss Hawke did leave her uncle's house," Mrs. Reynolds replied, "but as the mistress said this morning, she was taken in by Lord and Lady Matlock. She is not ruined."

Elizabeth felt the tiniest twinge at misrepresenting the relationship, but Sophia was neither wanton nor ruined and she focused on that. Polly still had no right to leave Sophia's room with no word, no excuse. She watched the maid fidget but saw no comprehension of her situation.

Then something occurred to her in a rush of understanding. Polly was not malicious enough, indeed hardly even clever enough, to have conceived this abandonment on her own.

"Was it Ruth who told you to leave the room, Polly?" she asked harshly, sure of the answer before she had even phrased the inquiry. Mrs. Reynolds looked surprised, then closed her eyes, lowered her head, and crossed her arms over her chest as if to hold herself in place.

"No, ma'am," replied the girl. "She told me it would'na be good for my soul to be there, tending to such a one, but she dinna tell me to leave. Always whispering in our ears, she is."

Mrs. Reynolds followed up on this statement while Elizabeth was still contemplating Polly's response. "Ruth said your soul was in danger if you sat with Miss Hawke?"

"Yes, ma'am," replied the maid, with a twitch of her nose. "She said that the lady ran away and her sister had not seen her in years." Then she added, "And that her own sister did not know where she was."

Mrs. Reynolds opened her mouth to speak again, but Elizabeth caught her eye and shook her head ever so slightly. The housekeeper closed her mouth and pressed her lips together until they were nearly white.

"Was that all you heard?" Elizabeth asked.

Polly played with the cuff of her dress, and Elizabeth focused on her.

"Polly?"

"Ruth said there was only one reason to run away, ma'am, that she left for a man, that she was ruined and a. . . a. . ." the girl blushed deeply, her cheeks flushing the same color as Elizabeth's spencer.

"Never mind, Polly," Elizabeth said, cutting her off. "You are telling me Ruth said this?"

Polly nodded solemnly. "She said Miss Hawke were wicked and good at hiding it. Said we needed to save the family and the colonel from her."

Mrs. Reynolds groaned aloud and shook her head. "Mrs. Darcy," she said quietly. "Ruth is rather sweet on the colonel."

Elizabeth touched a hand to her forehead and sighed. Suddenly so many things made sense. Ruth fancied Richard. Though she knew he was out of reach for her, she had to know, Richard had always been kind and respectful to the maids. He had also been very proper, but for a young woman whose position in life meant she was often ignored, his charm and kindness might have appeared to be admiration.

Elizabeth had no doubt that not only the betrothal but Lord Matlock's opposition to it had been disseminated widely below stairs by the unusually loud argument between Lord Matlock and his younger son. Elizabeth rubbed the back of her neck absently.

Ruth had heard some rather general complaints from Miss Evelyn and had ascribed the worst possible meaning to them because it served her purpose. She had then spread what she presented as evidence to insist that Sophia Hawke was not a maiden and should be treated with contempt. She had been clever, though, careful, in not directly telling the Polly to leave her work last night.

Though perhaps Ruth was not the only one to hear Evelyn Hawke's statements, according to the eight servants who had come forward, she had been the one who had perpetuated the gossip about Sophia. Ruth wanted to hurt Sophia Hawke, and had found a way through a young, easily manipulated girl.

As Elizabeth was ruminating, she heard Mrs. Reynolds clear her throat.

"Did you plan to come back to the room in the morning, Polly?" the housekeeper asked.

Elizabeth frowned. *That,* she thought, *is an excellent question.*

There was no hesitation in the reply. "Ruth said I ought to tell the morning maid I had come downstairs when she woke," Polly admitted, "but Colonel Fitzwilliam rang the bell before I could."

"Ruth may have suggested many things to you, Polly," Mrs. Reynolds said unsympathetically, "but this was your charge, not Ruth's."

"Yes, ma'am," Polly replied, her teary eyes indicating her misery.

"Step out into the hall for a moment, Polly," said Mrs. Reynolds firmly.

As the door closed behind the maid, Elizabeth spoke. "I believe we agree what must happen here. Regardless of Ruth, Polly ignored her charge and intended deceit."

Mrs. Reynolds nodded and called the girl back in.

"Polly," Elizabeth said carefully and clearly, "I want you to understand what is going to happen now."

The girl looked up at Elizabeth meekly, meeting her eyes for the first time.

"We cannot keep you here. You have directly disobeyed Mrs. Reynolds. Your actions have hurt a guest and you have therefore brought shame to this house."

The girl gasped a bit. *Did she think she was safe?* Elizabeth wondered. *Did Ruth tell her she would be safe?*

"Mrs. Reynolds," Elizabeth asked, "shall we send Polly home tomorrow morning in the sleigh?"

"Sent home on Christmas," mused Mrs. Reynolds. "That seems fitting."

The girl's shoulders slumped, knowing that not only was she to be sent home in disgrace on Christmas, but that she would miss Boxing Day entirely.

Elizabeth thought she would need to sit for a time before calling Ruth to attend them. Her lower back was sore and she was emotionally spent. As if she could hear the mistress' thoughts, Mrs. Reynolds ushered the distraught Polly out of the room and pulled out a chair, motioning for her to sit.

"Shall I call for tea, Mrs. Darcy?" she asked cautiously. "Perhaps we should wait until tomorrow to see Ruth?"

"No thank you, Mrs. Reynolds," Elizabeth replied, lifting her feet slightly and flexing them. "I just need a moment off of my feet."

Mrs. Reynolds nodded. "All of this upset is not good for you, ma'am, but I must say that I would not like to see it wait until the morning either. I am afraid neither of us would get any sleep at all."

"You are correct, Mrs. Reynolds," replied Elizabeth, putting her hands on her lower back and arching a bit to stretch the muscles there. "I would like this at an end." She leaned back in the chair. "There has been so much going on in this house in the past months that I fear we have both been remiss, but we are correcting that now," Elizabeth said thoughtfully and then, affectionately, "Do not attempt to deny that you have been quite preoccupied with my care, Mrs. Reynolds, nor that you have spent an inordinate amount of time soothing the fears to which my husband will never admit."

"I shall not deny it, ma'am, but it is still my job to keep things running properly." Mrs. Reynolds did not appear distressed, simply stoic, though the one finger tapping on the desk gave her away.

"Things will happen, Mrs. Reynolds," Elizabeth responded seriously. "This was terrible, to be sure, but not even you can be perfect all of the time, particularly when someone has put so much effort into subterfuge. We are not accustomed to that at Pemberley."

"No ma'am, we are not," said Mrs. Reynolds, her voice steady and unyielding. "But we shall be prepared in future."

"That is all I ask," nodded Elizabeth. She leaned back into the chair. "Shall we call for Ruth?"

***

The interview with Ruth was unsatisfying. Mrs. Reynolds had taken the lead, and for the first half of the encounter, Elizabeth silently observed the exchange with a sense of incredulity bordering on astonishment. The maid focused her dark eyes on Mrs. Reynolds and answered the housekeeper's questions in a clear voice, unrepentant about the consequences of her actions.

"I said nothing that was not true, Mrs. Reynolds," she said stoutly. "Her own sister said she was wanton."

Elizabeth chose this moment to speak. "I have heard her exact words, Ruth. Miss Evelyn said she did not know where her sister had been. As there was a break in the family, this is not surprising. Removing herself from the house of her uncle does not make Miss Hawke wanton." *In fact, she left his house to avoid such a fate.* "Is it possible, Ruth," she continued, "that you simply heard what you wished?"

The maid was silent and still. "I know what I heard, ma'am," she said stubbornly, but less emphatically than she had before.

"Ruth," Elizabeth said, nearly bleary with fatigue, "I must say learning that you were the author of such a terrible slander has shocked and disappointed me." She waited until Ruth's eyes met hers before adding, "Do you have a sister, Ruth?"

Ruth hesitated. "Three, ma'am."

"Do you always get along with your sisters?" Elizabeth knew enough of sisters to know this was impossible. Even angelic Jane could be stubborn when she believed herself in the right.

Ruth shook her head.

"Is it not possible that Miss Evelyn was angry at her sister when she said what she did?"

Ruth shrugged. Mrs. Reynolds said authoritatively, "Answer the mistress, girl."

"Anything is possible, ma'am."

Elizabeth squelched a smile. "*Anything*, Ruth?"

"Yes, ma'am."

"Then it is possible you were mistaken, is it not?"

Ruth was silent for a moment, clearly warring between the logical answer and the one she wished to give.

"I suppose, ma'am."

"And if that is the case, you have engaged in nothing less than gossip about and slander of an esteemed guest in this house?"

Ruth clenched her jaw before replying, "Yes, ma'am."

"Very well, I am glad we see things in the same way." Elizabeth turned to Mrs. Reynolds. "Mrs. Reynolds, I am ending Ruth's employment here immediately. Given her infraction, I cannot offer her a character."

Ruth paled. Without a character, it was unlikely she would ever find work in service again. Her lips parted as if to speak, but Mrs. Darcy was not yet finished.

"Ruth," she said with a shake of her head, "I would not wish for anyone to starve, but I cannot recommend you for a place in another house. You have caused great harm to a guest of this house. Even were she not both a great friend to both the Darcy and Fitzwilliam families and a particular friend of mine, you must see that what you have done is deeply wrong." She continued to gaze at the girl who was, at last, showing signs of fear, though still no contrition.

"You say," Elizabeth continued, "that you spread the story about Miss Hawke because you are a Christian?"

Ruth looked away. "Yes, ma'am."

Elizabeth shook her head. "I am convinced you do not know what it means to be a Christian, Ruth."

"But I do, ma'am!" Ruth burst out, agitated. Mrs. Reynolds stepped forward to grab the girl and toss her out on her ear, but Mrs. Darcy shook her head.

"Is it a Christian act to abandon the ill, Ruth?" she asked.

She was met by a single shake of the girl's head.

"Do you know your Proverbs, Ruth?" Elizabeth continued.

Ruth looked baffled. Elizabeth was very familiar with the Proverbs, as she had recited certain ones to herself many times after receiving a letter from her now-husband that had painfully revealed her own errors in judgment and behavior.

Elizabeth's voice was both angry and sorrowful as she said, "Miss Hawke is a virtuous woman, Ruth, and you have perpetuated gossip and slander about her." Ruth turned her gaze to her feet. "You profess an interest in Christian virtue and the purity of one's soul. You insist that Miss Hawke has sinned." She sighed a little. "Yet somehow you do not know the proverb that reads 'Whoever belittles his neighbor lacks sense, but a man of understanding remains silent. Whoever goes about slandering reveals secrets, but he who is trustworthy in spirit keeps a thing covered.' Gossip," she finished tiredly, "is also a sin."

What can I do? Elizabeth thought, taking in the scene before her. *I cannot in good conscience send the girl out to prostitute herself. We should have been more aware of what was happening below stairs, so I must bear some portion of the blame.* She gazed at Ruth, who still stood, head down, before her. *She is perhaps a little older than Polly, but still so young. Can she learn?*

Perhaps it was that Christmas was only one day away, or perhaps it was her unwillingness to be the cause of harm to a young woman, no matter how well deserved, or perhaps it was even that she did not think Sophia would approve of sending Ruth away without recourse, but for whatever reason, Elizabeth was loathe to cut even Ruth loose from all ties with Pemberley. How would she ever improve were she cast out in such a way?

"There is another way, Ruth, but it will not be easy." The girl lifted her head. "If you wish, we shall send you to the parsonage tomorrow with a letter for Mr. Redding. You can work cleaning the church and their home in exchange for Bible lessons. If he will take you on, and you truly dedicate yourself to learning where you have erred and how to live as a Christian, then I may reconsider my decision about the character." She paused, hopeful that this dreadful afternoon was nearly at an end. "I must include everything that has happened in any such letter. Should Mr. Redding have a good report on your progress, he may write one for you as well." She paused. "It is your choice, Ruth, and I daresay it will take quite a long time to prove yourself, but I am certain Mr. and Mrs. Redding will have work enough for you to exchange for your keep."

Ruth swallowed this humiliation with a small portion of relief and nodded. "Yes, ma'am. I will go to the parsonage if they will have me."

I shall have to ask William to supplement the Reddings' pay to accommodate both the increased board and the aggravation they shall certainly bear, Elizabeth thought, but if anyone can teach Ruth the error of her ways, it is Mr. and Mrs. Redding.

"Very well," was all Elizabeth said. She nodded at Mrs. Reynolds. "I will write the letter. Will you finish here and collect it in an hour?"

"Yes, Mrs. Darcy," Mrs. Reynolds said, admiring her mistress yet again. *More than the girl deserves by fa*r, she thought crossly, *but everything I would expect from such a fine woman as Mrs. Darcy.*

Ruth and Mrs. Reynolds watched as Mrs. Darcy exited the room.

Mrs. Reynolds sat in the chair at her desk, leaving Ruth to stand, and looked her over disdainfully. "I understand," she said directly, "that Colonel Fitzwilliam is a favorite of yours."

Ruth did not respond overtly, but almost imperceptibly, her eyes widened, and Mrs. Reynolds saw it. "Do you think he would approve of your behavior?"

Ruth's face clouded over. "I was trying to protect him."

Mrs. Reynolds laughed, but there was no humor in it. "Do you honestly believe a colonel, a man who has fought in the Regulars for many years, has any need of your protection?" she asked, making a valiant attempt not to sneer. "Do you think so little of him? Would the man you admire be fooled by, indeed promise himself, to a wanton woman?"

Ruth said nothing, but Mrs. Reynolds watched as the girl battled against the truth.

"That man loves Miss Hawke nearly as much as the master loves the mistress," she said bluntly, knowing it was skirting propriety to state it out loud but equally aware that the Darcys' love match, at least, was no secret at Pemberley. "And when they wed, I do not doubt that he will love his wife every bit as much as Mr. Darcy loves his own."

Mrs. Reynolds glared at the maid, whose face was now nearly ashen, and delivered the final blow.

"The colonel will eventually learn what you have done," she told Ruth, "and he will not be as forgiving as Mrs. Darcy." She sighed. "Go now, pack your things. You have been given an extraordinary Christmas gift. You will leave for the parsonage at first light."

Chapter Thirty

DARCY CLIMBED THE STAIRS to the guest wing hurriedly. The weather outside was growing colder, and if there was a need to send someone to Waters' shop in Lambton, it would have to be soon. He approached the door to Miss Hawke's chamber and knocked firmly. It was not long before Mr. Waters stepped outside.

"Mr. Darcy," he said quietly.

Darcy examined the man's face. There were circles under his eyes though they were not yet too dark, and his forehead was crossed with lines. *Worried,* he thought, and his heart went out to his cousin.

"I came to say that Miss Darcy and Master Pembroke continue to improve," Darcy told Mr.

Waters. "Miss Darcy would like to leave her bed tomorrow."

Mr. Waters smiled. "She wanted to leave it today, I suspect, but was persuaded to wait?"

Darcy nodded once. "Master Pembroke seems pleased to remain abed."

Mr. Waters chuckled at this. "He enjoys the attention, I imagine." He stifled a yawn. "Forgive me, Mr. Darcy." He pulled himself up straight. "Both were well when I saw them this morning. I will visit each again tomorrow morning and can offer my recommendations then. For now, if I am needed, you can send a footman to this room."

"How does Miss Hawke fare?" Darcy asked.

"She is not as well as I would like, sir," Mr. Waters replied honestly. "She is having more trouble with her lungs, and I am afraid it has developed into pneumonia."

Winter fever, Darcy thought, dismayed. He had hoped that Miss Hawke was improving like the others and was troubled to hear she was worse.

"Do you think this is a result of last night?" he asked seriously.

Mr. Waters lifted his shoulders a bit. "It did not help, to be sure, but it may not be the primary cause. Her immersion in the water simply left her susceptible."

"Do you have everything you need?" Darcy asked. "If we are to send for anything, we should do so before the temperature drops further."

Mr. Waters nodded. "I have a short list. Let me retrieve it."

Darcy nodded and waved a footman over. "Peter, Mr. Waters has a list of supplies he needs from Lambton. Take it out to John and have him send two of the boys to collect everything. Make it clear that nobody is to ride alone in this weather. If they cannot make it back safely tonight, they are to delay until morning."

Peter nodded and stood with his hands behind his back until Mr. Waters appeared with the list. The apothecary appeared to have heard the last of Darcy's instructions.

"There is none of this urgent," Mr. Waters affirmed as he handed it over to the young man. "Have Mr. Reynolds or one of the girls check the still room first. If you need to ride to Lambton, returning tomorrow early will be fine. The boys can even sleep in my quarters if there is a need." Peter waited for the nod from Mr. Darcy before he turned and walked hastily away, leaving the two men alone again.

"Mr. Waters," Darcy said, "may I speak with my cousin?"

"I will try to pry him away, Mr. Darcy," was the reply. Mr. Waters disappeared back into the room, leaving Darcy to wait. Although he knew it would be improper and he had no interest in seeing any woman in her bedchamber other than his sister or his wife, he could not help but wish to observe Miss Hawke's condition for himself. He had long admired Sophia Hawke's courage and integrity if not always her judgment. The assistance she had extended to Elizabeth had earned his gratitude and friendship, her betrothal to Richard his loyalty. Her quick thinking at the scene of the accident, though, where she had acted so decisively to save his family had earned her his love, the same kind of love he felt for Richard and Georgiana, Aunt Eleanor and Uncle Henry, and Phillip. *Even Pembroke*, he thought grudgingly, *though the boy deserves a sound whipping for his disobedience*. That she had come to harm while a guest in his home grieved him deeply.

He waited what felt like a long time before Richard came out to meet him, still shrugging on his coat. Darcy eyed him critically.

Richard's face was haggard. He clearly had not slept much the night before. His hair was rumpled, his waistcoat wrinkled, his shoulders slumped, his hazel eyes bloodshot. Darcy was reminded, forcefully, of his cousin's appearance at Bingley's

London townhouse nearly six months earlier, when he was still ill from his own injuries, yet determined to find Miss Evelyn Hawke. Even then he had looked better. Then he had been worried and frustrated. Now he was afraid.

Darcy sighed and ran a hand through his own hair. "I came to ask after you and Miss Hawke, but I think your appearance is enough to satisfy that inquiry."

Richard frowned. "She is quite ill, William. Her breathing is labored and she has a pain in her side now that Waters says signifies pneumonia. She is young and strong, and that is in her favor. . ."

"It does not help to hear that, I suspect," Darcy grunted. He sympathized, having so recently been through this with Elizabeth. Waters had said the same thing to him at the worst of it. It had not alleviated his worry.

"No." Richard leaned back against the wall. "How are the others?" he asked, trying to change the topic of conversation.

"Well. Georgie is complaining to your mother that she is ready to leave her bed and Pembroke is happy playing with his father and grandfather."

"Pembroke," Richard growled. "I should like to wring his scrawny neck."

Darcy nodded but thought the less said about that subject the better.

Richard rolled his shoulders to loosen tight muscles. "Any word on the maid who disappeared last night?" he asked warily.

Darcy shook his head. "Elizabeth and Mrs. Reynolds are handling it now. I believe she will not be in residence long."

Richard met his cousin's gaze. "You still do not know why?"

Darcy shook his head again. "I will let you know when I do."

"Not that it matters much now," Richard replied, and Darcy nearly flinched at the pain in his voice. "The damage is done."

"Richard," he said, "I know you do not wish to hear this, but if you plan to remain with Miss Hawke tonight, you will need to rest. Let me bring your mother to relieve you for a time. I will sit with Georgie."

"I cannot leave her, William," Richard said softly. "I will sleep in the room."

"Richard," Darcy said warningly, "you cannot sleep in her room."

"Your wife has already approved."

Darcy felt a flash of irritation with his wife. *She should have told me. I would have refused to allow this*. He looked at his cousin again and knew that Elizabeth's soft heart could not withstand Richard's insistence. They were betrothed, at least, all of Uncle Henry's protests aside. *Still, she should have consulted with me.* He sighed. *Of course, we have been rather preoccupied.* He frowned, but let it go.

"Then sleep now while your mother watches. Miss Evelyn should also sleep so she can spell Waters later."

Richard grunted in assent. "I will tell her as much." He glanced back at the room behind him and Darcy motioned towards the door.

"Go on back to her then," he said in a low voice. "I will collect your mother."

Richard looked him full in the face and Darcy could not remember a time when he had seen his cousin, his friend, looking so entirely lost.

"She will be well, Richard," he said, sounding more hopeful than he felt.

"You cannot know that," was the colonel's grim reply. Then he was gone and Darcy was again alone in the hall, sending up a small prayer for both for Richard and the woman he meant to wed. When he was finished, he turned to seek out his aunt.

***

He found Georgiana reading, a maid sitting in a chair near the window working on some mending. Aunt Eleanor was not in the room.

"Where is Aunt, Georgie?" he asked, surprised.

"Oh, I made her leave, William. She was getting quite stiff sitting in this chair. She said she would walk over to see Pembroke." Darcy nodded and took a few more steps into the room.

"How are you feeling?" he asked, standing with his hands behind his back.

"I am fine. Once I was warm and had a full night's sleep, I was well, truly, brother. Please tell me you will allow me to leave my bed tomorrow. I do not think I can stand another day confined to my chambers." Her face was soft, pleading, and Darcy gave her a little smile.

"Mr. Waters will visit you in the morning. If he allows it, yes, you will be able to leave your room. Mind, if he says you should remain, you shall."

Georgiana sighed. "I am nowhere near as ill as I was this summer, William. I promise. I do not wish to spend Christmas stuck up here."

Darcy moved fully into the room then and perched himself on the side of Georgiana's bed.

"I am afraid there will not be much of a celebration, dear, just a quiet dinner."

"Why not?" Georgiana's hand flew to her mouth. "Is Pembroke very ill?"

Darcy shook his head. "No, sweetling. He is well and enjoying his father's care."

Georgiana frowned. "I am not certain I like the sound of that. When he is out of bed, I will be having a talk with him."

Darcy would have liked to begin such a conversation himself, but it was not his place. "Such a talk is really the province of his father, Georgie."

"If he is well, then why. . ." Georgiana closed her eyes briefly and bent her head. "Sophia is ill."

"Yes."

She shook her head, opened her eyes, and said, "I do not know why I did not consider it. Sophia is so very strong. I thought that if I was well, she must be well."

Darcy took her hand lightly. "She was completely submerged, Georgie, and half-frozen by the time Richard got her up to the house."

"Poor Sophia," she breathed. "Is her sister with her?"

"Yes."

"And Richard?"

A pause. "Yes."

Georgiana nodded. "I expected as much. He loves her, that much is clear." She glanced almost shyly at her brother. "They *must* marry now, even if Uncle Henry is set against them."

Darcy's frown twisted upwards in a pained sort of grin. *Of course.* "I suspect that is why my wife allowed it."

"Oh, and Richard can plead his case quite prettily when he wants something," replied Georgiana in an amused tone. Then she grew solemn. "Is she *very* ill?"

Darcy did not want to answer that question, but he knew he must. "Yes. In fact, Richard plans to sit up with Miss Hawke tonight. I came to find Aunt Eleanor to sit with her now so he can sleep."

"Oh," exclaimed Georgina, reaching over to give him a push. "Go find her, then. I am merely bored, but Richard must be exhausted."

"I believe he is," Darcy said, releasing her hand and rising. He gave her a tired smile. "Try to get some sleep, Georgie."

***

The door to Pembroke's room was wide open, but there was an intense conversation going on. Darcy waited outside, trying not to listen, but his aunt's voice was very clear, and knowing his business was with her, he did not wish to leave. Finally, he showed himself in the doorway and announced his presence by clearing his throat.

"William," his aunt greeted him in her sweet voice.

"Aunt," he replied, "Phillip."

Phillip and his mother were standing near the window, Aunt Eleanor looking as calm and pleasant as ever, Phillip looking impeccably dressed but thoroughly disgruntled. Pembroke was fast asleep, the pink in his cheeks revealing him to be every bit as healthy as he had when he first arrived.

"I was simply explaining to my son that my grandson will require significant correction for his behavior," she elaborated, as Phillip's face turned an unhealthy shade of red.

"I believe the decisions about my son fall to me, mother. There is no reason to speak to me about my duty or to involve my cousin."

Darcy nodded without comment but silently applauded his aunt. "Aunt Eleanor, I have come to fetch you for Richard. He wishes to sit up with Miss Hawke tonight. That being the case, I offered to take you to sit in his stead while he sleeps this afternoon."

Lady Matlock's face grew grave. "Is she so ill?"

Darcy nodded dourly. "Waters says pneumonia."

Neither of them noticed Phillip's face softening.

"How is Richard?" she asked softly.

"Fearful."

She nodded. "I will come at once," she said, turning to her eldest. "There must be correction, Phillip, and you are indeed the one to do it. To neglect it will do more harm to your son in the long run. I know that Rebecca would agree."

Phillip turned to face the window. "She always said boys learned to be men while they were young." He thought about that for a few seconds, then added, "And that it was the father's job to teach him."

"Your son," Lady Matlock sighed, "disobeyed his cousin and deliberately put himself and others at risk, and now Miss Hawke is ill. You cannot excuse him from responsibility because he injured himself as well. In point of fact, you have rewarded him." Her expression was not reproving but compassionate. Her words, however, were blunt. "I have raised two boys of my own, Phillip, and I am saying that to allow your relief to overwhelm your good sense will only encourage such behavior in future." She patted her son's cheek and gave him a kiss before stepping away.

"Come, William," she said, lined face resolute, "let us go."

Darcy indicated she should go before him, and she moved to take the lead, her silk skirts swishing gracefully. "From one son to the other," she said in what was meant to be a cheerful voice. Neither Phillip nor Darcy was fooled.

***

Darcy escorted his aunt to Miss Hawke's chamber and was suddenly seized with a desire to see his wife. When he entered her bedchamber, Sarah was removing the jeweled pins from her hair.

"Oh, that is a shame," he said, leaning against the doorjamb, his arms folded across his chest. She turned to take him in, her eyes weary but questioning.

"What is it that distresses you so, dear?" she asked innocently, the failed attempt to control her smile giving her away.

"Those hairpins are quite lovely," he responded. "It is a shame to remove them."

She shook her head at him. "I cannot sleep with hairpins, William. I shall have to change into a nightgown as I find myself in great need of rest."

He took several long steps to stand behind her.

"I will help Mrs. Darcy from here, Sarah," he told his wife's maid, who promptly curtsied and scurried out of the room. She was quite used to her master's peremptory dismissals, and once she realized it meant her work was lightened, quite looked forward to them.

Darcy gently plucked the remaining pins from his wife's hair and kissed her neck.

"William," she said slowly, "I would love to, but I am truly very tired."

"I know, love," he said in a husky voice. "I shall help you prepare and then I will hold you. Perhaps I will sleep as well."

"That sounds nice," sighed Elizabeth.

"Was it very bad downstairs?" he asked distractedly as he helped his wife stand and began to unbutton her dress.

"It was awful," she said with a little moan, and told him the story.

"Good Lord," he said disbelievingly when she had at last done, "Miss Hawke's life continues to unfold like a terrible novel."

"With the exception that she has not yet reached her happy ending," added his wife.

"She will, my love," said Darcy, determined that she would, that Richard would. It was a unique position for him to occupy. He was not used to being an optimist.

His wife was giving him a rather odd look. *Optimist*, he thought, *is normally her role.*

"You cannot know that, William," she said in a forbidding echo of Richard, and allowed him to slip her nightgown over her head.

"I believe it, though," he insisted, gently guiding first one of her arms and then the other through the sleeves and allowing the garment to flutter down around her.

Elizabeth touched his hand and nodded. "Then I shall believe it too," she assured him, no hint of irony in her voice.

He led his wife to bed and held her while she slept. As he watched her breathe in an easy, untroubled rhythm, he thought of Miss Hawke, how she had given him back his wife not once, but twice, and he held Elizabeth just a little tighter.

Chapter Thirty-One

RICHARD TURNED AS his mother entered the bedchamber and he tried to offer her a smile. She moved to his side directly and kissed his cheek.

"How is she?" she asked quietly, gazing at Sophia who was at last sleeping, her golden hair pulled away from her face in a plait.

"No worse, I suppose," he replied gloomily, glancing at Waters, who nodded. *Awful,* he thought. *Weak, pale, feverish.*

He felt his mother's eyes upon him, evaluating his appearance. "You look terrible, son," she told him. "Please go, get some rest. I will take care of her."

A swell of fear rose from his stomach and he nodded at the cot in the corner. "I will rest here."

His mother took his face in her soft hands. "That will not do," she said firmly.

Richard pulled away. "I will rest here, mother. I do not care about appearances." *I cannot be away from her. What if she needs me?*

Lady Matlock clucked at him, something she had not done since he was young. "For heaven's sake, Richard, I think that much is obvious. You cannot remain here without getting some sleep in a real bed. Perhaps you ought to walk around the house a bit beforehand. It is quite warm in here." She released him and tapped on Miss Evelyn's shoulder. "You too, miss."

Miss Evelyn smiled and shook her head, black curls a little frayed from the steam. "I will remain," she said. *At last we agree on something,* Richard thought.

"No," said Lady Matlock, raising her voice. "You have both made it clear that you will be returning tonight. For now, you must leave." The two looked at her blankly. "You do her no favors wearing yourselves down like this," she warned. "To be of use to her, you must take care of yourselves." She jabbed a thick finger in her son's chest. "You may use that cot tonight, not before." Then she glared at Evelyn, "I know you, Miss Evelyn, and I am large enough to bodily toss you out of this room. I hope you will not require me to resort to such vulgar behavior."

The increase in volume had awakened Sophia, and when Richard glanced over at her, he shook his head. "I apologize, love," he said, moving to sit on the side of the bed and take her hand. "The Fitzwilliam family does not do anything quietly."

A ghost of a smile crossed Sophia's pale face. She squeezed his hand a little.

"For the sake of my sleep if nothing else," she said, pausing to catch her breath, "get out." Another small smile. "My sister, too." She waited, took a shallow breath. "I am in good hands."

His expression must have revealed his hesitation, because she shook her head. "I do not have enough air to repeat myself, Richard." She took a few shallow breaths this time and he gently ran the pad of his thumb over her bottom lip, grateful to note that the bluish tinge that had returned with the onset of the cough was again replaced with a light pink. "I will see you both tonight."

She closed her eyes and he leaned over to brush a kiss on her forehead. Sophia Hawke was the only one who had the power to remove him from the room, and she had invoked it. Reluctantly he stood, bowed to his mother, and walked out without another word.

He wandered aimlessly along the corridor before he thought to see whether Elizabeth was about. He was hoping to hear that the situation below stairs had been resolved, though he was truly too wrapped up in Sophia's recovery to think on it much now. If Elizabeth happened to be available, he would ask. It did feel good to walk after hours of stooping and bending.

Elizabeth was not to be found. The downstairs was nearly deserted. Darcy was not in his study, his wife not in her own, or the drawing room, or the small parlor off the entryway where she sometimes curled up on a settee to watch the weather, not even in the library, where she had admitted she often took refuge from the hustle of guests. He had one foot on the bottom stair, ready to ascend to his room when he thought he saw a yellow skirt disappear around a corner.

"Hello?" he called "Is anyone there?" He then remembered seeing Sophia disappear in just such a way not long ago, and snorted. "Now I am seeing phantoms. Marvelous." Still, he removed his foot from the stairs and walked in the direction of the chapel. He hovered in the doorway, almost hoping that she was here though he knew she was not. The room was cold, and in the twilight of the darkening afternoon, it was difficult to see. He reached over to the nearest sconce and removed the candle, then walked back to main hall and found one already lit. He touched the wick to the flame and returned to the small room at the end of the hall.

Carefully he entered and placed the candle in an empty sconce along the wall. It gave off a weak, flickering light, but it was enough to see where he was stepping. He slid into one of the oak pews somewhere in the middle of the room and crossed his arms defiantly across his chest. He felt no different in this room.

"Why am I even here?" he asked aloud, frustrated. "It is Sophia who prays to you and now she is ill." He shifted in his seat. "I do not like you," he said, raising his voice the way his mother had raised hers. "I might even hate you." He uncrossed his arms and leaned forward. After taking a breath, he stretched his arms straight out, resting them on the pew in front of him, hands clasped as he had seen Sophia do before, and tried to think of something to say, something to pray for, something to ask. Nothing came.

Nothing, that is, except the anger and the terror he had held in all day. *To finally have love only to have to face its loss. It is too much.* He felt the first sob tear through him, and he was powerless against it. He wept for a long time there in the almost dark with nobody to watch, nobody to criticize. He wept without regard for quiet now that there was nobody to protect, his shoulders shaking with fear and grief. He wept until the effort racked his body and left him weary, spent.

He never saw the tall, regal figure in the shadowy doorway, who took one step into the room before changing his mind and walking away.

***

Not long after the colonel had vacated Sophia's room, Evelyn Hawke followed. After attempting to sleep in her room and being entirely unable to rest, she changed back into her gown, pulled her house slippers over dainty feet, and went for a stroll about the house. The air outside Sophia's room still felt frigid against her skin after hours of draping a blanket over her sister's head and helping her breathe in the steam from pots of boiling water. Sophia was exhausted and in pain, her sister knew, yet she had done everything she was asked without complaint. The men had spent the afternoon hauling small, heavy pots, one after another, placing each in its turn upon the floor beside the bed, removing each as they cooled only to refill them and hang them again over the fire. It did seem to help with Sophia's breathing, but only so long as there was steam. In the breaks Mr. Waters deemed necessary, the cold air brought on Sophia's cough again, and then the colonel would support her back and help her hold the basin on her lap.

Evelyn watched them carefully, all day long, her sister's hand resting lightly on the colonel's wrist as she coughed, how he whispered in her ear as she fell back against his chest, drained, how he touched her hair or stroked her cheek after replacing one pot for another. Everything she had observed was building up inside of her but it took removing herself from the room for the realization to finally settle upon her. *It is no great epiphany, you stupid girl,* she scolded herself silently. *It must have been like this between mother and father. This is love. Not that tripe in the novels, but difficult, untidy love. Real love.* Not for the first time on this visit, she felt the stirrings of jealousy, but this time she squashed it down brutally as soon as she recognized it. *Sophia loves you,* she told herself*, and you love her.* An idea formed itself in her head. *I cannot speak to her now, cannot apologize as I would like. But I can speak to him.*

***

The drawing room was deserted apart from the earl, who stood with his hands clasped tightly behind his back, staring out the window into the falling snow.

"I am not in the mood for more debate," he said gruffly without turning.

"Then it is good," came the soft, musical voice of Miss Evelyn, "that I am not here to argue."

The earl's cheeks puffed out as he released a large sigh, but he did not turn. He had expected his wife, or perhaps his son, to enter. He had given no thought at all to Miss Evelyn.

"Are you looking for Mrs. Darcy?" he asked sharply. "I believe she is above stairs."

"I expect," she continued, "that you thought the colonel would be here to speak with you? I believe he is resting. Your wife was adamant that he leave the sickroom."

The earl's eyebrows lowered gloomily.

"Yes, Sophia is ill," Evelyn continued smoothly. "Thank you for inquiring after her health. She is ill because she helped to save your stubborn grandson, I am told, and then not only remained to assist Miss Darcy out of the water, but dove in headfirst to cut her free. That is the character of the woman you reject as a wife for your son."

The earl did not reply.

Miss Evelyn joined him at the window, staring out instead of looking at him. She ignored his question completely, instead beginning a different line of conversation. "In fact, Lord Matlock," she said calmly, "I came in search of you. I would speak to you."

"I cannot imagine you have more to say," was the irritated retort.

She ignored him. "We are not so different, you and I," she stated with a directness that nettled the older man further.

"How is that, Miss Evelyn?" he asked, turning his face just far enough to scowl down at her.

Evelyn Hawke met the man's stern hazel eyes without a qualm, and replied, "We are both of us loved more than we have earned."

The earl continued to scowl, and Evelyn smiled. It was a bitter little smile, and it faded quickly.

"Do you think I am frightened by your stony demeanor, my lord?" She shook her head slowly. "I have far too inflated a sense of my own worth to be intimidated by you. Pack up your House of Lords face; it is unlikely you will need it much longer."

The earl felt the affront deeply. "How dare you," he hissed.

"I dare because it is the truth, sir," she said without sympathy, "and I do not believe there is anyone who heard tell of your display the other night who remains unaware." She made a pretense of checking her sleeve for dust. "Tell me, will the country be tending you in your illness? Will it even care that you are gone?"

"I am painfully aware that we are all of us expendable," he said, his gravelly voice surprisingly reflective.

Evelyn nodded. "Then perhaps it would be best to tell those who *do* love you and who *will* care for you that you love them as well."

The earl grunted, but whether this was meant to signal assent or dissent was unclear. He gazed out at the falling snow, considering briefly how it made everything look different, foreign.

"I told Richard when you returned last summer that I love him. I do not say it often but he understands," said the earl gruffly. "To show love too overtly is a weakness." The statement sounded practiced, but the earl's characteristic confidence was lacking.

"This is the way in which we are most alike," Evelyn responded firmly. "We have both felt love a weakness, yet are surrounded by people who see love as a strength. Who is happier, my lord?"

"Happy," he scoffed, though the severe expression soon melted away.

"Indeed," she said, unruffled. "Happiness. If not for yourself, you might at least seek it for your son. Is it such an astonishing thing for which to ask?" She tugged at her cuff and then allowed her arm to drop. "I am under the impression he has neither requested nor received much else from you."

"You have said quite enough, Miss Evelyn," grumbled the earl. "You may leave me now." He returned his gaze to the scene outside.

"May I?" asked Miss Evelyn, even now unperturbed. "One thing more before I do, sir." She tapped the windowsill idly with one elegant finger. "There is another thing we share."

The Earl of Matlock closed his eyes briefly. "Well?" he asked in a voice tinged with exasperation.

"You are a courageous man in many ways, but not in the most important one." Evelyn paused, considering the words she might use to explain, and put her small hand on his arm. It was a gesture of commiseration rather than condemnation, and his rigid shoulders relaxed a bit. He opened his eyes and turned his head ever so slightly towards her to indicate he was listening.

"Love requires courage," she said in a harmonic tone at odds with the stark message. "Are you are brave enough to seek it?" She idly drew an interlocked S and E in the condensation on the window. "I, at least, am making the attempt."

Without waiting for an answer, Evelyn Hawke turned and gracefully exited the room, leaving the earl to stare outside as the landscape was entirely transformed.

***

It was, the staff agreed later, perhaps the strangest Christmas Eve they had ever spent at Pemberley. Mr. and Mrs. Darcy presided over the table but were subdued, even when the small group of guests insisted that Mrs. Darcy have the honor of sitting on the Yule log, and when it came time to light it, Mr. Darcy's speech was pleasant but brief. The young boy assigned to watching the flame was called in rather quickly thereafter. Young Master Pembroke was not allowed to attend, and while Miss Darcy did join them for dinner, she was whisked upstairs immediately after. The colonel and the Hawkes were not in attendance.

The only guest who did not make a swift return to one of the bedchambers was Lord Matlock, who had taken possession of the master's study. While his actions were certainly curious given the date, the staff did not question why he was penning a succession of letters nor did they murmur a word of protest when he insisted they must be sent express at first light, holiday be damned. They were, in truth, no longer of a mind to speak about the strange doings of the gentry or aristocracy, not even among themselves. Word had spread that two maids were being sent away, on Christmas no less, and word that there might be more. There was universal relief when Mrs. Reynolds announced she would not be leaving, and every remaining member of the house staff from the scullery maids to the housekeeper herself said a little prayer before falling asleep that night that the worst was now over.

Mrs. Reynolds was up very early Christmas morning to watch two young women climb into the sleigh. Wilkins the butler was also awake, handing a small stack of letters to the driver, who noted the earl's seal and the word *frank* across the back of one before tucking them into his coat and giving the reins a shake.

Chapter Thirty-Two

SOPHIA WAS MISERABLE. There was a tremendous pressure on her chest that made it difficult to breathe. Any deep breaths set off long bouts of coughing that tore at her throat and made her head ache. She tried to take shorter, shallower breaths to avoid the coughing altogether, but that left her gasping for air. However, every so often, Mr. Waters or her sister would insist that she breathe deeply without the steam that soothed her throat so that she could cough to clear whatever might build up in her lungs. It was painful and wearying, and she just wanted it all to stop. She was warm and peevish, and her sister finally admonished her for being such a terrible patient. She glared at Evie only to hear her sister laugh—a small laugh to be sure, but an honest one, and Sophia thought it a wonderful sound.

"So," Evie said mildly, "you are not perfect after all."

"Never," gasped Sophia, responding to the tease as she finally felt the heaviness of sleep descending, "have been."

When Sophia next opened her eyes, the weak light of the new day was trickling through her windows. She was still fatigued and had nearly allowed her eyelids to close again when she heard a soft snort from beside the bed. She forced herself to turn her head and tried not to groan at the pain in her side. She gazed at the figure in a wingback chair she did not recall belonging to the room. Richard was slumped to one side, his cravat and jacket removed, his sleeves rolled up, snoring. One arm was on the bed and when she glanced down, she saw that he still held her hand in the palm of his, though his fingers had relaxed their hold. She loved the feel of his calloused hand and wished she felt well enough to enjoy all the liberties he had been taking. *Of course, if you were well, he would not take them,* she told herself.

The back of her neck was uncomfortably hot, and she tried to move to a cooler part of the pillow, but her face was warm too, and though her thoughts were fuzzy, she determined that removing the blanket might help. She propped herself up on one elbow, unable this time to keep from moaning a little at the pain the movement caused, and laboriously peeled the blanket away.

That helps a bit, she thought, collapsing back on the pillows and let her eyelids drop, relieved.

Richard woke in the middle of a snore. He sat up trying to determine what had disturbed his sleep when he saw Sophia breathing quick, shallow breaths on her pillow, blanket tossed aside. Her cheeks were flushed, and he reached out to touch his cool hand to her forehead. Suddenly he felt his own breath begin to quicken. She had been running a fever since the day before, but it had remained manageable. Now she was burning up. He took a clean cloth from a pile near the bed and reached over to the water pitcher to pour some of the cold liquid over it. He laid it on her forehead, but was afraid to do much more. She had been subjected to the shock brought on by the cold too many times. Waters had already mentioned that to put her in a cold bath, even a lukewarm one, might be too great a strain on her system. Waters. He should fetch Waters.

He stood, cursing himself for sending Miss Evelyn to bed and touched the arm of the maid who was sleeping on the cot Elizabeth had provided for him. "Emily, I am going for Mr. Waters. Please sit with Miss Hawke while I am gone."

Emily nodded sleepily and rose, dropping herself into the chair near the bed but drawing herself up a little straighter when she saw Miss Hawke's brightened cheeks. She reached over to flip the cold cloth and clucked a little under her breath.

"Ay 'eck, me duck," she crooned. "Whatstha thinkitis? You oughtn't be making us worry so."

Mrs. Reynolds had chosen Emily because she often cared for her numerous younger siblings, and though barely twenty, she seemed the elder sister here, practiced in the sickroom. Elizabeth had approved Emily particularly, as had Mr. Waters. Richard was grateful for her. Still he watched, making sure the girl was fully awake before moving out of the room to roust the apothecary from his slumber.

Mr. Waters already had one arm in his coat when Richard knocked. He did not wait for an explanation but walked directly out of the room, indicating they could speak as they made their way back to Miss Hawke's chambers. He had been done in yesterday, but now had a full night's sleep and was feeling sharper. He heard the news of the increased fever with concern, not panic, and Richard was reassured.

"It is not necessarily a bad sign, Colonel," Mr. Waters said, his inflection carefully neutral. "Her body is fighting whatever infection has manifested itself. We will just need to keep it in check."

Richard ran a hand through his already disheveled hair. He had wept all his tears yesterday, wept as he never had, not even as a child, not even when he was wounded and in pain. He was out of tears and ready again to fight.

"Just tell me what to do," he said.

***

Phillip Fitzwilliam stood quietly watching his son sleep for a few minutes before stooping to place a hand on the boy's shoulder.

"Pembroke, wake up," he said somberly. The boy stretched and rubbed his eyes before sitting up.

"Happy Christmas, Papa," he said, confused.

"Happy Christmas, son," Phillip replied. "I think you know what it is I am here to discuss with you."

Pembroke's face fell. "I think so, Papa."

"You were sick before, but now it is time to speak about what you have done," Phillip said sternly, fighting to keep from brushing the boy's hair from his forehead.

"Yes, Papa," Pembroke replied in a meek voice.

"What is it that you have done wrong, my boy?" Phillip asked, his voice low and even.

Pembroke hung his head. "I disobeyed Cousin Georgiana."

Phillip nodded. "You have, son, and that disobedience has hurt both your cousin and Miss Hawke."

Pembroke's eyes grew wide. "Yes, sir."

"You are no longer a child, son. If you are old enough to disobey, you are old enough to take responsibility for your actions. Get dressed and meet me in my room."

Pembroke's voice shook, but he lifted his chin and replied, "Yes, sir."

***

Pembroke stood before his father's door nervously, raising his hand and knocking twice.

"Come," called a familiar voice. The boy took a deep breath and entered.

The viscount was sitting near the fire, one leg crossed over the other. He set down the book he was holding and beckoned to his son to approach and stand before him. Pembroke obeyed and stood silently, his hands clasped before him. Phillip gazed at his boy, his hazel eyes grave. "Now, son," he said firmly. "Tell me again. What did you do that was wrong?"

"I disobeyed my cousin, sir, and put her at risk. I am also re. . . responsible," he stuttered, the word difficult for him to say, "for Miss Hawke being ill." He screwed up his face and thought for a moment. "I went out on the ice when I should not have. I jumped on the ice when I should not have. Other people had to rescue me which hurt them."

"You missed a few people, son, but that is a good beginning," said Phillip after he realized his son was finished. "You also put your cousin Elizabeth at risk. She is increasing—do you know what that means?"

Pembroke shook his head.

"It means she is with child. It is a time during which it is easier for a woman to be hurt. Your cousin needed to remain out in the cold longer than she should have to wait for you. She then had to physically pull you along to get you to the house. If your Uncle Richard and Cousin Darcy and I had not arrived, she would likely have had to haul you up the front stairs to get you indoors. Is that something she should have to do?"

"No, sir," replied Pembroke, hanging his head.

"You are also responsible for the fatigue and worry both your Uncle Richard and Miss Evelyn are feeling, because they are nursing Miss Hawke day and night." He stopped. Pembroke was so very young. He wanted his son to be happy, to retain the joyousness he displayed every day. Above all, Phillip did not wish to continue this conversation. But then he thought of his wife. *Pembroke's future includes a title and its burdens.* This was a lesson best learned immediately.

"My boy," he said quietly, "every decision you make in this life will have consequences. You are a Fitzwilliam, you are my heir, and someday, like your grandfather, you will sit in the House of Lords, helping to make decisions for the entire country." He leaned forward, put his hand under the boy's chin, and tipped it up gently until Pembroke met his gaze. "You must do all that you can to make your decisions carefully, thoroughly considering how they will affect other people."

Pembroke whispered, "Yes, sir."

Now the hard part. "Pembroke, you will receive two strikes with the paddle for each person who has been adversely affected by your poor decision. Wait for me behind the screen in the corner and pull down your breeches."

"Yes, Papa," sniffled Pembroke. He pursed his lips and walked, not quickly but not slowly, to do as his father bid.

Phillip rose to do his duty, and not for the first time, wished his wife would be waiting for him when it was over.

***

Sophia heard someone entering her room and turned her head, searching. When her eyes found Richard, she tried to smile, but she simply did not have the energy.

"There you are," he said gently, moving to the far side of the bed, leaving room for Waters.

Mr. Waters smiled at Sophia, but her attention was given entirely to Richard, watching his face for clues. She heard a question but not the words.

"Mr. Waters wishes to know how you are feeling, Sophia," Richard said quietly.

Sophia gathered her strength. "Tired." She closed her eyes. "Hot."

She felt Mr. Waters touch her side and she winced.

"That answers my other question," he said calmly. "Well, Colonel, Miss Hawke is indeed ill, but this is not unexpected. If she promises to sleep when she needs it and takes fluids when we ask, she will feel better soon."

Sophia was watching Richard's face. His lips had twisted into a frown, but when he realized she was watching him again, he forced them into a slight smile.

He does not believe Mr. Waters, she thought, *and neither do I.*

"Sophia," she heard in her ear, "he is trying to trick you into health."

She wanted to laugh, but could manage only a very soft snort. A low, rumbling laugh tickled her ear.

"I am told he is an excellent physician, not just an apothecary," the gentle, teasing voice continued, "so we shall just have to put up with his lies." There was an exaggerated grunt of offense from the other side of the bed that finally earned a thin, tight-lipped smile from the patient.

She rolled her head a little to the side to nestle against Richard's cheek, rough with stubble. *It feels so good*, she thought, *to have someone to depend upon.* She heard him let out a contented sigh and felt him kiss her ear.

"Hate being sick," she wheezed.

"I hate it when you are sick, too, love," was the whispered reply. "So hurry up and get well."

"Will do my best," Sophia coughed, and closed her eyes.

"Fight this for me, Sophia," she heard as she drifted off to sleep.

***

Elizabeth entered Sophia's sickroom silently, her silk slippers making barely a sound as she sidled up to the bed. It had been three days since Sophia's fever had grown so high, three days and three very long nights of a fever that raged, subsided, returned. Sophia had been unnaturally quiet as she battled, and Elizabeth could not tell whether enduring the silence, broken only at odd intervals by a few inaudible words and groans, was better or worse than delirium. Richard had been stalwart, but he watched Sophia so carefully, so intent on each breath, so frightened if the next breath was not quick to follow the previous, that she was sure he was in agony. Without fail, he coaxed Sophia to drink, to take some broth, to breath in the steam. He worked without complaint, taking orders from Miss Evelyn when necessary, giving them when he thought there might be a better way to accomplish something. Elizabeth had always known the colonel was a soldier, but she had truly never seen that part of him until now.

The day after Christmas, messages arrived for Mr. Waters. He had other patients to tend, and Miss Hawke was now in good hands at Pemberley. When he arrived to examine her each morning, he remained in conference primarily with Miss Evelyn and then made his report to Mr. and Mrs. Darcy.

Elizabeth saw that Richard could not be bothered to hear that Sophia was still ill and there was nothing to do but continue with their treatments and wait. He was already aware.

Elizabeth had taken a shift each day at Sophia's bedside as had Lady Matlock. Even Georgiana, who was much recovered, came to sit awhile, and of course Miss Evelyn was nearly always about, but even with all these willing attendants, it had been nearly impossible to get Richard to leave for more than a hurried trip to take care of his most basic requirements. Black had managed to stop him only twice, once to shave and once to bathe, but he had not been able to persuade the colonel to rest in his own room. Richard had instead stretched out on the cot in Sophia's room, falling into a dreamless sleep when he was at last too tired even sit up in a chair.

Darcy tried to get Richard out of the room for a short time, to go out for a brief ride as soon as the storm blew through and the sun returned, but he was rewarded with an irritated scowl and a pointed refusal. Elizabeth took her husband's arm and leaned against him as Richard disappeared again into Sophia's bedchamber.

"You must pardon him, dear," she said, trying to placate him. "Richard is a man in love, and he is worried."

"You forget," Darcy replied, not in the least offended, "that I have recently suffered the same fears." He bent to kiss the top of her head. "I worry for Richard as well."

Elizabeth took her husband's hand. "Let us go for a walk out of doors, William. I think it would do both of us good."

He hesitated, but nodded. "Be sure to wrap up well, Elizabeth, or I shall do it for you," he demanded, his tease at odds with the seriousness of his tone. Only a slight twitch at the corner of his mouth gave him away. Elizabeth put her hands on her hips and fixed him with a ferocious glare he found amusing.

"Mr. Darcy," she said sharply, "I do believe I know how to dress myself." She put one hand on her stomach, and her eyes twinkled. "I am nearly a mother myself, you know."

His lips stretched into a genuine smile and Elizabeth felt the familiar flutter in her chest at the sight of it. "Indeed you are," he grumbled. "I will meet you here in a quarter of an hour."

She counted. *One. . . two. . . three.* Then she matched him word for word as he uttered the familiar refrain: "Do not try to take the stairs yourself."

"Impertinent miss," he growled.

"Stubborn man," she replied.

"Elizabeth," he warned, "if you continue in this way we shall not make it outside."

"Scandalous, sir," she replied saucily, raising her eyebrows. She truly did wish to stroll outside with her handsome husband, and for the moment, Sophia was being cared for, so with a flurry of muslin Elizabeth whirled away to gather her things.

***

Fire. There was fire and heat and smoke, and she could not find Evie. Her lungs burned as she called for her sister, coughing, crawling from room to room, all of them empty. After searching everywhere, she saw them, all of them, grouped together on the other side of the stairs near the master's chambers. Father stood with his hand on Oliver's shoulder, both wearing their riding coats and breeches, their boots polished to a high sheen, mother in her blue silk ball gown and sapphires, an eight year-old Evie in a rose morning dress, one hand held by mother and the other clutching a bedraggled stuffed horse by its frayed tail. She tried to make her way to them, but the fire was too hot, too high. Oliver offered her a wide, brilliant smile and held up a hand, but then she was falling, falling away from everyone she loved. She heard Richard calling her name in a steady voice, a loving voice, but she could not see him, could not find anyone in the dark. She was alone, and felt tears welling up. I do not wish to be alone, *she tried to say,* please come back. *But there was nothing. Just the dark. The dark and the fire.*

Then, through the blackness, she heard it. A voice, calling to her. Evie's voice. Then Richard's, both telling her what she most needed to hear. She was not alone.

When at last she clawed her way out of the nightmare, Sophia slowly opened her eyes. Her chest hurt, but perhaps a little less than it had. Her side was not as tender, her breathing not as difficult. She still had a wheezy cough, but she could take a slightly deeper breath without triggering it. Her head felt clearer, too. She used her arms, weak but also improving, to push herself into a semi-sitting position on the pillows before leaning back to catch her breath and glancing about the room.

The light was bright as it streamed through the window. *Late morning?* She thought. When she turned to her left, she saw Richard asleep in his chair, his head on the bed as though it was just too heavy to hold up. Emily sat near the window with her sewing, and another figure was sitting in a chair near the door, his back ramrod straight, his hazel eyes wide open, watching her. She met his gaze, raised her eyebrows, and offered a tired smile, the corners of her mouth barely moving. He stood abruptly and strode over to Richard, putting his hand on his son's shoulder.

"Richard," he said.

Richard started, instantly awake. "Sophia?" he asked, then saw her awake, watching him, and grasped her hand with both of his with such an expression of relief that it made Sophia's heart constrict. *What I have put him though,* she sighed to herself. She placed her other hand gently over his, but looked up at the imposing figure towering over her betrothed.

"My lord," she whispered.

Lord Matlock offered her a low bow before retreating. When he reached the door, he stopped, gazing back to see that both Sophia and his son were watching him, Sophia with forgiveness and his son with a wary hope. He offered both a small smile.

"I am glad to see you feeling a bit better, Sophia," he said, and it did not sound forced. "We were all worried."

"Thank you, sir," she said, still in a whisper.

"Richard," he said, looking at the wall now instead of his son, "when you can tear yourself away, I have some things to discuss with you. This afternoon, perhaps."

"Yes, father," was the quiet reply.

Henry Fitzwilliam nodded brusquely and was gone.

Richard kissed Sophia's hands, both ignoring Emily's dancing eyes darting quickly between them and her work. "What do you suppose he wants?"

Sophia tested her lungs, taking just a bit more air than she thought she should. She felt a tickle. "To give me away?" she asked pertly.

Richard chuckled. "Yes, but to me?" He touched his forehead to hers. "Do not ever do that again, Sophia," he said solemnly. "Any swimming in icy lakes must be done by someone else in future."

"I can make that promise," she said, making it nearly to the end before Richard heard a catch in her breathing.

"Enough now," he fussed. "Would you like some tea?"

She nodded.

Richard stood to pull the bell, shaking his head at Emily, who was rising from her chair. If he was to remain in the room, she must stay as well. His neck and shoulders were sore, he had not slept well in days, and his back felt as though it was one large, intricate Gordian knot.

He had never felt better.

Chapter Thirty-Three

MR. WATERS ARRIVED in the afternoon and was very pleased to find his patient not only awake but having tea with Colonel Fitzwilliam.

"There now," the apothecary said with a genial smile. "I think we can all agree that Mr. Waters is not a prevaricator." Evie stifled a snort from her position near the fire. Emily, as always, was quiet and watchful.

Richard just shook his head and watched as Sophia gave Waters a skeptical look.

"You may glare at me all you like, Miss Hawke," he said pleasantly. "I am pleased to bear the brunt of your displeasure as it means you are clearly on the mend." He patted her hand and began his examination, gently prodding her side, listening to her lungs, forcing her to cough. Finally, he said with a satisfied nod, "With the colonel and Miss Evelyn working on your behalf, it would have taken something worse than this to carry you off."

Richard swallowed uncomfortably, and Mr. Waters noticed. He quickly changed the subject as he turned to include Evie. His voice softened. "Please do keep working with the steam, Miss Evelyn, though as your sister's breathing improves, we shall begin increasing the intervals." He turned to Richard. "Now that she can take nourishment on her own, you should see a steadier improvement. She will still need to remain abed for another week or two."

"*She*," complained Sophia, "is in the room with you."

Mr. Waters laughed. "Indeed she is. My apologies, Miss Hawke." He stood, bowed to his patient and then nodded to Evie. "Miss Evelyn, I have an herb to add to your sister's tea. Would you walk me out?"

Evie met Mr. Waters' gaze and held it for a moment, her weary expression softening into an expression of girlish delight, before she nodded and led him from the room.

Sophia's eyes narrowed as the two departed. "Richard," she wheezed, bemused but suspicious, "What do you know about Mr. Waters?"

***

Darcy watched as Richard entered his study trying to stifle a yawn. The earl had assured them all that Miss Hawke had taken a turn for the better, and an appearance by his cousin downstairs seemed to confirm it. Only a few moments ago Elizabeth had caught his arm and cheerfully informed him that Miss Hawke had banished her betrothed from her room and insisted he not return until the next morning. She laughingly added that Richard had been torn between arguing and relief at being set free for a good long sleep in his own bed.

Richard glanced around the study, his face indicating surprise, and Darcy realized he had been expecting only his father. The earl had asked both he and Phillip to join him.

"Father?" Richard asked with some trepidation. "What is all this, then?"

The earl stood, pulled the bottom of his waistcoat, and looked Richard in the eye. When he spoke, it was as though he had practiced the speech. "I may be an old fool, but when I am wrong, I am man enough to admit it," he began.

He is nervous, thought Darcy. He could read the same disbelief in the face of his cousin.

"My complaints were made in this company, Richard. My apologies should be as well."

The tension seemed to dissipate from the room. Darcy and Phillip visibly relaxed, and Richard's keen eye discerned it.

"I have had a rather enlightening discussion with Miss Evelyn, or rather, she had a discussion with me." The earl ran a hand through his silver hair. "Rang a rather elegant peal over my head, if you want the truth of it."

Richard did not respond, but Darcy and Phillip shared a look.

"She was not kind."

This they had no trouble imagining. Richard even grinned a little, and Darcy nodded, thinking it about time Miss Evelyn had turned her incisive censure on someone more deserving than her sister.

"Yes, Richard, I thought you would find that amusing," the earl frowned. Richard wiped the smile from his face.

"Sorry, father," he said, though everyone in the room knew he was not.

"Never mind, son. I deserved it, though she was only the final and most direct female in this house to speak with me." His gaze faltered a bit, but he coughed and continued. "I have some things to discuss with you all." He held out his hand to Darcy, who lifted a small stack of letters from his desk and handed them to his uncle. Lord Matlock shuffled them until he found what he wanted.

"Phillip, this first involves you."

Phillip's brow creased, but he remained silent.

"I will remain in the House for now, but as it was recently pointed out to me, I may not have much time left there," Lord Matlock stated roughly. "I have written as much to Lord Charles Grey, who has agreed to keep my confidence and use my proxy vote when the time arrives. When I die, he will release the proxy and you will take my seat."

The stark pronouncement fell heavily upon the three younger men. Henry Fitzwilliam's death would mean the end of an era. He had always been a looming presence in their lives, whether for good or ill, and it struck them, suddenly, that the mantle would be passed to them to carry on in his stead. Phillip reluctantly took the letter from his father's hand.

The earl nodded and next held up a small bundle of letters. "These are for my eyes only, boys, but suffice to say, certain favors have been called." Darcy watched as Richard clenched his jaw, and he felt his own back stiffen. Richard had asked for exactly this, but it had taken being set down by Miss Evelyn to move his father to action. Richard's own request had fallen on deaf ears.

"I believe, Richard, you had made some inquiries of your own on the matter of the elder Hawke?"

For a moment, Richard looked confused, as if he wondered why his father would mention Sophia, but his face cleared and he straightened his shoulders. "Archibald Hawke. Yes, I have."

"Either I am getting old or you have gotten very good at this in your time in London, Richard," his father said approvingly. "I was unaware such an investigation was proceeding." He frowned, and yet seemed pleased, too.

Darcy found this an opportune moment to pour out four glasses of brandy and pass them around. Lord Matlock thanked his nephew but set his glass down on the table beside him without taking a sip. He was not yet finished.

"You already had the plan in motion, Richard, which made my job easier. I believe you were informed of Hawke's whereabouts?"

"Not until a few days ago, sir," was the stoic reply. "I received word the evening before the accident."

"Archibald Hawke," continued the earl for the benefit of Darcy and Phillip, "left the country and fled to France, where he was summarily dismissed by his previous government contacts, as he no longer had either the connections or the funds to be of any interest to Boney. He was found dead a few months ago." The earl stopped there.

Richard fidgeted, drawing Darcy's attention.

"In a Calais brothel," Richard added, clearly unable to resist.

"Yes, well. Obviously, this news should be kept quiet, gentlemen," said Henry with a shake of his head at his younger son. "And I have ensured that a different story will gradually make its way around town." He cleared his throat. "Hawke left the Home Office, returned to his home in Mayfair to pack, left for a trip north with his niece, was taken ill and died. His illness was the reason for his resignation. The elder Miss Hawke, who had been estranged from her uncle, retrieved her sister and took her home."

Darcy sighed. The story followed Hawke's true movements until he fled alone to Dover. He was unhappy with the deception but pleased for his cousin. "A dull story. Not even a crumb for the gossip-mongers."

Phillip nodded and slapped his brother on the back.

"That is the idea," replied Matlock. He pulled another letter from the pile. "I wrote your general, Richard." Darcy's heart sank as he watched Richard's expression harden and the blood rush to his face.

"You did *what*?" he asked in a dangerously low voice.

"Never mind, Richard," said the earl waving him off, "I told him you had asked me to pen the letter for you as you were tending your betrothed. I may also have mentioned that since your brother shows no inclination to remarry that you or your issue may be the spare. "Therefore," he continued, "you should not be risking your life abroad." Phillip's face was impassive, but his father either did not notice or did not care. "He was not happy, but has agreed to allow you to sell out."

"I cannot believe you had the gall to speak for me on this matter," Richard said bitterly, despite having meant to do the same thing himself. "Is there any part of my life that you do not feel free to direct?"

"I have one more bit of direction for you," his father said, appearing not at all discomfited. "Be so good as to tell me should you wish to send this one back."

He returned the other letters to his pocket and held the final one out to Richard.

"What is this?" he asked, moving to take it from his father's hand. His father said nothing, just motioned for Richard to open it. Darcy had seen the seal on the letter and hoped he was correct about the contents.

Richard opened the missive, blinked twice, then narrowed his eyes suspiciously at his father. "This is a special license."

The earl nodded. "I am relieved to hear it. I would have hated laying out all my shortcomings as a father to the Archbishop and paying what amounts to a small fortune for anything less." He paused. "I made the case that your betrothed was likely to be restricted to the house by her recovery for some time and that you wished to wed soon. I did not scandalize the man with the tale of your sickroom heroics."

Phillip swallowed a laugh and Darcy allowed himself a small smile, but Richard just stood there, stunned, the license held firmly between his thumb and index finger. Darcy's smile dropped from his face and he felt a flash of genuine anger on Richard's behalf. It was clear that such a kindness on the part of the earl was so unexpected that Richard was deeply shocked. Recalling his own father's fondness for Wickham, he thought he at least could sympathize with Richard on that score. *Not really*, he reminded himself. *Papa still spent time with me, even told me he loved me. I was rarely just ignored.*

The earl was watching his son's face, too, and his own seemed to crumple under the weight of a similar realization. Phillip put a hand on his brother's shoulder, waking him from whatever lethargy had overtaken him. Darcy watched as Richard looked up from the license and slowly but deliberately held out his hand to his father. The earl brightened considerably at this and held out his own. They shook, and then Richard pulled his father in for a short embrace, embarrassing them both. As they stepped back, Richard took a deep breath.

"You have no idea what this means to me, father," he said, his voice sharp, jagged.

"But I should have," muttered the earl, and forced a grin. He tugged at his coat sleeves and announced, "That is all, gentlemen." He lifted his brandy and drank it straight down. "I will leave you now." He returned his glass to the table with a soft *thunk*, nodded at them all, and walked out.

The three remaining men stood silently for a time before Phillip slapped his brother on the back again and proclaimed, "Richard, I never thought I would see you leg-shackled. Truly, it is a miracle of epic proportions. Miss Hawke must have some sort of unearthly power to convince you to settle down."

Darcy laughed. "I rather suspect he had to convince *her* to settle down."

Richard's face was a mixture of chagrin and astonishment. "You are both correct." He gazed at the license in his hand and shook his head. "I could not have done this for her," he said softly. "Father is the only one who could convince the Archbishop. . ."

Darcy nodded. A special license was available primarily to peers and sometimes their children. It could be granted under exceptional conditions to others as well, but such licenses were almost never granted. They were expensive and quite rare, and this one had clearly been expedited. It was an extraordinary gift. *A peace offering.*

Richard shook his head, still incredulous. "I suppose I ought to speak with Sophia."

Darcy smiled, so very pleased for them both. "I suppose you should."

"But first," Phillip interrupted, "A toast to your lovely bride." He held up his glass and the other two men lifted theirs. They touched glasses, drank, and then Phillip said one final thing. "Treasure your wives, lads," he said. "And do not hesitate to tell them that you do."

With that, the viscount strode from the room.

Richard folded the license and held it firmly. "William, I wish to show this to Sophia, but afterwards I should like to keep it in your safe if you have no objection."

"Richard," replied Darcy seriously, "You need not even ask."

"I know, William," Richard replied gratefully. He met his cousin's somber gaze and said, "With you, I always know."

Chapter Thirty-Four

SOPHIA WAS QUIETLY THRILLED to see the special license, and when she heard that her sister had taken the earl to task, she sat very still, holding Richard's hand tightly until she could master her emotions.

"I did not think," she said to him in a weary, nearly inaudible voice, "that she would ever be able to love me."

"Apparently, she does," Richard reassured her with a smile, "I am told she held nothing back."

"Good for her," murmured Sophia. Despite her best efforts, a few tears escaped, and she brushed at them impatiently. "We do need to speak with Mr. Waters, Richard. I would like to know whether his interest in Evie is genuine." She took a breath. "I would not normally think of an apothecary for her, but he seems a very clever man and it does make a sort of sense, do you not think?" She took a deep breath, setting off a cough.

"That is quite a speech from you, my dear," Richard replied gently, "but you have done enough for today." He shook his head at her frown. "It is entirely self-serving. The sooner you are well, the sooner I can marry you." Sophia opened her mouth to protest, but Richard kissed her nose and said, "I promise, I will ask Mr. Waters to join us tomorrow."

Sophia shook her head at him. "Do not forget," she murmured, "you still owe me a real proposal." Her eyelids were growing heavy and she leaned back against her pillows.

"I have not forgotten, love," he said with a smile. "Sleep now."

At last she acquiesced, curling up under the blanket and closing her eyes. Richard sat on the side of her bed and gazed down at her, lifting a stray strand of her hair back away from her eyes and tucking it gently behind her ear

"You are a treasure, Sophia," he said softly, "and I will always remember to tell you so."

***

It took more than a week to finally meet with Mr. Waters. The man himself was willing, but Evie blocked their efforts at every turn. Ultimately, her suitor took her aside to assure her he did not mind, and she nervously gave way. Not unlike Sophia's discussion with the earl, Evie reminded Mr. Waters that she was of age and did not require her sister's consent. Still, she did finally admit she would like her sister's blessing.

Sophia had many questions for Mr. Waters, but while she had improved enough to be allowed to sit in her private sitting room for a short time each day, Richard was still worried about her overexerting herself. After a short fit of pique, she relented, compromising with a written list that Richard would read. He told her he would ask follow-up questions as well, and she nodded approvingly. When their conference was complete, they had the story that Elizabeth had wanted to hear in the summer but that Waters had kept private.

The third son of an impoverished earl, Adam Waters had denied his father's wishes that he take orders, instead choosing to attend the medical college in Edinburgh. At nearly the end of his second year, he had been sent down for "radical beliefs." He drew out that phrase and gave Sophia and Richard a smile, demonstrating that he was not at all unhappy with the designation.

"I told them," he said, clearly enjoying the conversation, "that it was not only ridiculous but also atrocious that a physician should believe himself above actually treating his patient. What good is the knowledge if you do not apply it?"

He had gone into business as an apothecary, he said, because he could still bring his new skills to bear while treating those he thought needed it most. He had been fortunate to meet Mr. Darcy in Lambton when old Dr. Gordon had first taken ill and unable to attend a houseguest. They had spoken at length about his treatment theories and Mr. Darcy was willing to offer him a chance to tend to those at Pemberley. From there, his reputation had grown and flourished.

Despite the propensity of old Mr. Waters to spend more than he earned, his wife had left each of her four sons an equal portion of her dowry. "Her father, my grandfather, insisted that only the interest on the money be made available to the earl," he told Richard and Sophia. "There were other properties that went to my father upon their marriage so it did not seem a loss to him at the time. Once he had gone through all the other money he attempted to access the dowry, but the marriage settlement was well written and my mother never relented. We each received ten thousand pounds upon her death, and I live quite comfortably on the interest and what I earn." He smiled, his thoughts far away now. "Between the famers' wives who feed me and the tailor who clothes me and the cobbler who repairs my shoes in exchange for my medicines, I have hardly anything to spend my money on, and have been able to put some aside." He paused. "I will of course take a proper house once I am wed, and Miss Evelyn has indicated I should advertise as a physician, but we will discuss that together when the time comes. Otherwise I think my working life will change very little, except. . ."

He paused, his fingers interlocked, thumbs tapping against one another. "I know that Miss Evelyn is used to rather a more lavish lifestyle than I can provide, but she has assured me that she would be happy with what I can offer so long as she might assist with my practice." His voice sounded almost reverent by the end, as though he had never thought to find a woman interested in his life's work.

Sophia smiled at that, and nodded. "I believe that," she said, her voice nearly at a normal volume. "There is no life that would better suit Evie." Richard out a hand on her arm and she shook her head at him.

"So long as you can keep her safe and happy, Mr. Waters."

Richard stared at Waters until the younger man cleared his throat and looked away. He waited just a bit longer until the apothecary glanced up again. "Her happiness is important to Miss Hawke, Waters, and Miss Hawke's happiness is important to me. Do you understand?"

"Yes, Colonel," said Waters hurriedly, all traces of good humor gone. "I understand."

"Good," said Richard in a voice so cold Sophia hardly recognized him. She allowed Mr. Waters just enough time to leave the room before giving her betrothed a kiss on the cheek.

"You will be a good brother," she said softly.

"I would rather be a good husband," he responded with a smile.

"We have the license," she said, laying her head on his shoulder. "Perhaps you should call Mr. Redding to come to the house tomorrow."

"You are not well enough, Sophia."

"I am well enough to wed. We may have to wait a bit for. . . other things."

He grinned. "Other things?"

Sophia blushed and Richard's grin grew wider. He loved making her blush, and it was not an easy thing to do. *I do enjoy a challenge*, he thought.

"Let me send a message to the parsonage," he said, "and see when Mr. Redding is available. Will that do?"

Sophia nodded.

"Come," he said and held out his arm. "Let us see if Waters has gathered the courage to propose yet."

"I rather doubt it," was Sophia's languid reply. "Evie insists on being courted first."

Richard threw his head back and released a single barking laugh. "Of course she does," he said with a knowing shake of his head, "of course she does."

***

At dinner, Richard reported that Mr. Redding would not be available until the following week, and Sophia was disappointed but resigned. When she woke the next morning, rested and feeling better than she had since the accident, her maid asked whether she could practice the hairstyle she had in mind for the wedding, and Sophia had agreed, thinking that it would at least pass the time. When her hair was finished, she thought it looked nice and told her maid so before dismissing her. She spent an hour finally finishing Richard's handkerchiefs and wrapped them in neatly folded brown paper.

Evie appeared at her door with a gown in her hands and asked cheerfully, "May I come in?"

"Of course," Sophia replied. Evie smiled and walked over to her sister before holding up a mazurine blue silk gown that Sophia had ordered while staying with Lady Matlock but had yet to wear. She had brought it to Pemberley thinking it would do for Christmas Eve. She wondered why her sister had it out but then realized that the bodice, the neckline, and the hem had been beautifully embroidered with tiny yellow roses linked with sprigs of heather. The work was exquisite.

"Do you like it?" Evie said, coming as close to gushing as her older sister had ever seen. "I thought when you and the colonel marry, you might like to wear this as your dress." When Sophia remained silent, she began to babble, "Of course, if you do not care for it you should wear something else. I just thought. . ." She stopped as Sophia shook her head.

"It is possibly the loveliest dress I have ever seen, Evie," said Sophia as she reached out a tentative hand to touch the flowers. "The work must have taken a great deal of time."

"I had plenty of time while you were ill," Evie shrugged. "And I wanted to give this to you as a wedding gift."

"You had faith I would recover?" her sister teased.

Evie nodded. "I had faith in you."

Sophia raised her eyebrows and continued to eye her sister silently. Evie flushed and added, "I also had faith in Mr. Waters."

Sophia laughed softly as she lifted the hem to examine it. "As well you should. Thank you, Evie. This is truly a work of art."

"Try it on," her sister urged. "Please? I cannot wait a minute more to see it on you."

Believing that her wedding day would be soon enough, but not wishing to deny her sister the sight of her hard work being appreciated, Sophia agreed. Evie helped her change and was ebullient when she saw the gown on.

"Oh, Sophia," Evie whispered. "You look. . ." She took her sister's hand and led her to the mirror in their sitting room.

Sophia stood before the mirror. Lady Matlock had insisted on the purchase of so many dresses that she did not ever remember wearing this one, not even for a final fitting. The shade was a blue so deep it was nearly violet, which made her eyes appear even darker than normal. The bodice was cut close, tucking in sharply at her waist, the neckline low without being too revealing, the skirt barely skimming her hips before falling in a straight line to the floor. The embroidery added a bit of light to the fabric, the yellow roses reflecting the color of Sophia's golden curls.

"Oh, Evie," she said, breathless not with illness but pleasure. "I have never had a more beautiful gown."

There was no response. As Sophia turned her head to determine why that was so, Evie nearly skipped through the doorway from her sister's room carrying the matching slippers.

"Try these on as well," she smiled. "Oh, it is just marvelous, Sophia." She knelt before her sister to change her slippers and then glanced in the mirror again. She clapped her hands excitedly. "Georgiana should see this. Please do not change yet!" Sophia lifted her shoulders in a gesture that indicated acceptance, and Evie scampered off to locate their friend.

Evie is acting like the girl I once knew, she thought to herself with a smile. *Though I must admit*, she thought as she looked in the mirror, *it is by far the nicest gown I have ever had and I feel beautiful in it.* After a moment, she thought she would sit to wait as it did not appear that Georgiana was close at hand. She sat on the settee closest to the window, careful to arrange her skirt so it would not wrinkle, and pulled her legs up to rest lengthwise on the cushions. She laid her head on her arm with her face to the light and thought about what Richard would say when he saw her dressed this way.

She heard steps and turned to greet her visitor. It was neither Evie nor Georgiana. Instead, as though her thoughts had summoned him, Richard was standing at the end of the settee. Sophia startled a bit and then could do nothing but stare.

Richard was dressed more formally than she had ever seen him in a black tailcoat and pressed trousers, a crisp white shirt and cravat, and a waistcoat shot through with gold and violet threads that shimmered in the light.

"Oh," was all she could say.

"Have I left you speechless?" he teased. When all she could do was nod, the expression on his face softened and his gaze grew intense. He offered her a hand and she stood, but he shook his head and helped her sit properly, both feet on the floor, facing him. Without releasing her hand, he went down on one knee before her.

"I believe I owe you something," he said warmly, "and I always pay my debts."

Sophia smiled widely. She was gratified to see Richard struck dumb for a moment before he shook himself and began.

"My dearest Sophia," he began, "I do not believe there are any two people in this world who have had a more unusual beginning than us."

Sophia's eyes sparkled, and she pressed her lips together tightly to avoid laughing. This was one speech she did not intend to interrupt.

"From that meeting came the most difficult period of my life, and that is saying quite a bit considering what my life has been like since I left home." He lifted Sophia's hand to his lips and bestowed a gentle kiss. "You are unlike any woman I have ever known. You are maddeningly stubborn, frustratingly brave, clever, funny, wise, beautiful." He grinned up into her flushed face. "When you smile at me like you did a moment ago, I cannot think, I cannot even breathe. I love you truly, faithfully, ardently. Sophia Hawke," he asked, "will you do me the very great honor of becoming my wife?"

Sophia smiled and nodded. "Yes, Richard, I would be very happy to marry you."

Richard heaved a great sigh and removed a thin rectangular box from his jacket. "I have something for you to wear with your gown," he said happily, lifting the lid and showing her the contents.

Sophia exhaled a little too quickly, which caused a small cough.

Richard frowned. "Are you all right?"

She nodded. "Fine, Richard, truly." She reached out with one finger to touch the necklace he was holding for her. It was a strong gold chain, not too thick, at the end of which was a single, perfect white pearl. "I love it," she said, and put a hand to his cheek. "I love it, and I love you."

Richard put the box down and drew the necklace out. He undid the clasp and stood. Sophia stood as well and turned her back to him as he draped it around her neck and closed the clasp. When she turned back to him, the white pearl nearly glowing against the dark background of the fabric, Richard could fully view the gown and the woman wearing it for the first time. He stepped back to take it all in and shook his head.

"I am a very fortunate man," he said, gazing at her longingly.

"I am sure all the credit goes to Evelyn and your mother's modiste," added Sophia with a tilt of her head. She took his hands and leaned into his chest. "I cannot wait to marry you, Richard."

"Well," he mused, "why do we not go downstairs and see whether Mr. Redding might be in residence?"

"You said he was not available," replied Sophia, at last beginning to feel suspicious.

"Perhaps I did," Richard said in her ear, "but I cannot really recall." He offered his arm. "Shall we go see?"

Richard had expected a pert remark or a complaint about his disguise, but she merely looked up at him, her deep blue eyes nearly violet against the color of her gown, and nodded.

Chapter Thirty-Five

BY THE TIME Sophia and Richard descended the stairs and walked to the chapel, it was no surprise to her to find Mr. Redding standing at the front of the room.

"I will wait for you right over there," Richard smiled, indicating the place next to the pastor. In a low voice, he asked, "I hope you do not mind if my father gives you away? I thought William, perhaps, but father wanted. . . and William will stand up with me instead."

"I do not mind," Sophia said with a tiny sigh, anxious to begin.

Richard kissed her hand, beckoned his father over to take Sophia's arm, and hurried to stand in his place. There was nobody at the front of the church on the bride's side and Sophia sought out her sister. With her eyes, she indicated where Evie should be standing, and the bright smile that broke out across Evie's face made Sophia shake her head. *Who else?* she mouthed at Evie as her sister sidled out of the pew. She felt a warm hand cover her own and looked up into the face of Lord Matlock, who gave her a small smile and a nod before turning his face towards the altar.

In deference to the health of the bride, Mr. Redding performed a short service, moving rapidly to the vows. When they had both said "I will," and the ring was on Sophia's finger, the bride held her husband still for a fleeting moment after they signed the register and turned to face their families. She wanted to remember this day, this moment, for the rest of her life. Lady Matlock, Georgiana, and Elizabeth were standing together near Phillip and Pembroke, the earl slightly separated from them on the left. She turned her head to see a quietly smiling Mr. Darcy standing beside Richard. To her other side was Evie, eyes bright as she reached out to press her sister's hand. She closed her eyes, imagining her parents and Oliver standing in the last pew, and then leaned on Richard's arm and allowed him to escort her to their wedding breakfast.

Richard led her directly to a sofa where she was to receive their well-wishers, few as there were, and Sophia had to admit she was grateful for his forethought. She had not considered that there would be a breakfast at all, but she shook her head and laughed to herself. This was Pemberley. Of course there would be a wedding breakfast.

After about an hour, Richard could see that Sophia was blinking to keep her eyes open. He made his way over to her and held out his hand. After a few hasty farewells and a tasteless joke from Phillip that earned the viscount a swat on the arm from his mother, the newlywed couple headed upstairs together.

"Was Phillip unhappy that you asked Mr. Darcy to stand up for you?" Sophia asked as they reached the first landing.

Richard shook his head. "Phillip is six years my senior. By the time I was old enough to be interesting to him, he was away at school. William has always been my brother, and Phillip knows it. He expected it would be this way."

Richard took a hallway that led away from Sophia's room. "Where are we going?" she asked.

"To our chambers," he said with a warm smile. "Did you think we would remain in your room next to your sister?"

Sophia blushed again and Richard grinned. *Three blushes in one day*, he thought, *I am learning*.

"I do not expect that we will do anything but sleep, love," he said in her ear. Sophia shivered a little in response to his nearness. "But I will be happy to be able to hold you in our bed instead of trying to rest on one of those terrible cots Elizabeth had brought up."

"Perhaps she was sending you a message," Sophia replied archly.

"Perhaps she was," agreed Richard amiably, "but I was in no mood to receive it."

They reached their new chambers at last and Richard led Sophia into the room. Inside was an enormous canopy bed centered on the interior wall. There were heavy, rich brown bedcurtains and coverings over the large windows, too, to keep out the cold. In the far corner of the room, a fire burned high and hot in the hearth. The walls had been papered in a sky blue and ivory. The room was perfect, Sophia thought, but she could easily forgo any additional exploration. She desperately wanted to change out of her lovely gown and go to sleep. Before she knew it, Richard was helping remove her hairpins and undressing her so that she could.

She briefly considered brushing out her hair, but decided she would be asleep before she could finish.

"Are all my things here?" she asked as Richard reached around her neck to remove the necklace.

"I think so," he said, placing a kiss on her forehead and helping her don her nightgown. She sleepily walked to a table where she had seen a few of her personal items and found the package for which she was searching. She picked it up and held it out to him.

"It is not much," she said with a yawn, "but I wanted to make you something, and I had the entire week."

He smiled sweetly at her and took the gift. "Bed," he said, gently scolding, and Sophia thought she had never been so pleasantly censured.

Richard dropped the gift on the bed and settled her under several blankets before preparing himself to join her.

"Do you mean to sleep all day with me?" Sophia teased. To her surprise, he nodded.

"I do indeed. I still have sleep to catch up on as well, my dear, but even were I wide awake, I would not be separated from you today. You are at last my wife, and nobody will be able to chase me out of your room again."

"Except me," Sophia said drowsily as she settled her head on a pillow.

"Perhaps," grinned Richard. He watched his wife's eyelids flutter and fall. Soon she was breathing evenly if not deeply, something he did not believe he would ever again take for granted. He opened his trunk and withdrew a crumpled bit of fabric that resembled a bonnet. He glanced at it, poking a finger through two holes at its crown before walking to the fire and tossing it in.

Richard returned to the bed, picking up the package his wife had given him and then stretching out beside Sophia, his back supported by the headboard. He slipped one arm beneath her shoulders and lifted her gently so that her head was resting on his chest and one of her arms was draped across his stomach. Then he unwrapped his gift. He could not help but laugh, though he stifled it so as not to wake his wife. Nestled inside the paper were two handkerchiefs, rather well embroidered, with his initials above a pine bough laden with snow.

***

Although he would officially remain Colonel Fitzwilliam until his commission was sold, Richard asked that his military title no longer be used. Thus, it was the Honourable Richard Fitzwilliam and his wife Sophia who remained at Pemberley longer than either had originally intended. Sophia required nearly two months to fully recover her strength. Her desire for her husband, however, could not wait nearly as long. When, some two weeks after the wedding, Darcy saw the staff bustling trays of food up and down the stairs and recalled that he had not seen Richard in some time, he was happy his wife had had the foresight to locate the pair on the otherwise uninhabited third floor.

Henry and Eleanor Fitzwilliam returned to London shortly after Twelfth Night for the parliamentary session, Phillip and Pembroke in tow. However, with Miss Evelyn being courted and Georgiana beginning to prepare for her coming out in a year's time, life at Pemberley was not much quieter for the loss. In February, with Elizabeth's confinement nearly upon her, both Georgiana and Miss Evelyn were sent to London to stay with the Matlocks and Darcy thought with some relief that he finally had his home back, at least for a short time. Mr. Waters had asked that Miss Evelyn be allowed to remain and assist if necessary, but Elizabeth had selected a midwife recommended by Mrs. Redding to assist. Miss Evelyn was still an unmarried woman, and the mistress of Pemberley felt there had been enough flaunting of convention in the past year.

***

Elizabeth's eyes flew open. The room was dark, and she was uncertain what had awakened her until she felt a strong pressure spread across her stomach. She breathed a sigh of relief and trepidation and whispered, "At last."

Her husband was sleeping soundly beside her. The new midwife, a Mrs. Peters, had informed Elizabeth as a part of a detailed explanation of what she ought to expect that first births often took a full day or more. Feeling she might later require rest, Elizabeth closed her eyes and tried to sleep, pretending that her pains were not progressing. She spent several hours in a fitful kind of sleep before the involuntary contractions began to grow more regular and increasingly intense. When the tightening of her abdominal muscles made her sit up, she groaned softly and waited for it to pass.

When it did, she said, "William." Elizabeth touched her husband's arm, but he did not move. "William," she said again, raising her voice.

Darcy sat up suddenly and blinked. "Elizabeth?" he asked urgently, turning to her.

"My pains have started, William. I think you should send for Mrs. Peters." In the dark room, they both heard a slight, almost inaudible *pop,* and Elizabeth felt liquid on her legs. "Oh," she said quietly, trying to remain calm and remember what she had been told. "William, my waters have broken."

Darcy nearly flew from the bed, but once he was safely away he reached back to touch her cheek. "I love you, Elizabeth," he said, and turned to grab his trousers from the chair where he had taken to leaving them the past week. He tossed his nightshirt off and pulled on a clean shirt, pulling on his stockings and shoving his feet into shoes. "I will send a maid to change the linens."

"I do not think you need to rush, dear," she said laughingly, but the tease was cut short as the next contraction arrived. "Oh!"

Darcy waited, his hand on hers until the tightness passed, then strode purposefully out the door.

In the absence of Jane, who was still in London awaiting her own confinement, and Mrs. Bennet, who had been delayed by design, Elizabeth had asked Sophia to sit with her. Though Sophia was not experienced with childbirth, she was close at hand and was at least married. Half an hour after Darcy had left his wife, Sophia came shuffling into Elizabeth's room, hastily dressed and rubbing her eyes. Elizabeth was sitting on a chair near the bed as the maids replaced the linens.

"Good morning, Elizabeth," Sophia said with a smile. "Mrs. Peters thought you should walk early on. Are you feeling up to it?"

Elizabeth nodded, and Sophia held out both hands to help her rise from the chair.

"I thought you might," said Sophia, teasing. "You do enjoy your walks."

"Sophia," warned Elizabeth, "I am not in the best of moods."

"Well done, Elizabeth," Sophia replied cheerfully, "send all that ire my way. I am strong enough to handle it."

They walked through the room into the sitting room, then into the hall and back again in a repetitious circular path. Elizabeth hardly remembered walking at all by the end of the day. She heard Mrs. Peters arriving, and then Mrs. Redding, Sophia excusing herself to take a few hours of rest before returning, her husband's worried voice from the doorway on multiple occasions, but for the most part, her thoughts had turned inward.

Despite the intensity of Elizabeth's early labor, it was indeed nearly twenty hours before Mrs. Peters at last ordered her to push. Elizabeth was gray with exhaustion and her throat was sore from screaming, but she held Sophia's hand and tried.

"You have to push harder than that, Mrs. Darcy," clucked Mrs. Peters. "You are nearly there."

"I cannot," Elizabeth panted.

"You can," said Sophia encouragingly. "You are strong, Elizabeth. You can do this."

Elizabeth took a breath and bore down, too tired even to scream or cry. At the end of the push, she gasped for air.

"Excellent, Mrs. Darcy," said Mrs. Peters approvingly. "Now rest up for a moment and when I tell you, push again."

This was met by a strangely deep, guttural curse, and Sophia planted a kiss on Elizabeth's temple.

"I will not tell your husband you know that word if you can offer us another push," she teased.

"Someday," Elizabeth growled threateningly, "you will be going through this and saying far worse."

"Ah," Sophia agreed, "but *my* husband will not be in the least bit shocked."

"*Now,* Mrs. Darcy," came the command from Mrs. Peters.

Elizabeth bore down again, this time letting go and releasing a high-pitched screech.

"You are nearly there, Mrs. Darcy," said Mrs. Peters calmly.

Elizabeth snapped, "Stop saying that unless it is true!"

Mrs. Peters and Mrs. Redding exchanged amused looks while Sophia's face indicated her agreement with Elizabeth. This went on for nearly three-quarters of an hour before the midwife could ease a little head out, cautiously maneuver a set of rather broad shoulders, and catch a slippery, wriggling little body that opened its mouth to mewl as Elizabeth cried out one last time and fell back against her pillows.

"Oh, Elizabeth," crowed Sophia. "You have done it!"

Elizabeth cracked one eye open and trained it on the midwife, who smiled.

"Indeed, Mrs. Darcy, you have a lovely baby boy." Mrs. Peters completed her work, cutting the cord while Mrs. Redding wiped the baby clean. The pastor's wife wrapped the babe tightly in a blanket and placed him in his mother's outstretched arms. Elizabeth's tired eyes stared at her child adoringly.

"Sophia," she began, but trailed off.

Sophia was watching the infant, mesmerized, but shook herself at the sound of her name. "I will fetch him right away, Elizabeth." She sighed. "Your son is just perfect." With one last look at the little boy, she went to collect his father.

When he appeared at the door not five minutes later, it was apparent to the women that he had not been waiting neither in his study nor in the library, but somewhere very close by. Sophia whispered to the others that she had met him already halfway up the stairs, Richard following behind trying to catch him. She took Mrs. Redding's hand and they slipped out together. Mrs. Peters fussed a little over mother and child for a minute before announcing that she would step out for a short time as well.

Darcy was still standing in the doorway, gazing intently at both Elizabeth and the tiny bundle in her arms.

"William," she said softly, no fatigue in her voice at all, "come meet your son."

He let out a breath she did not realize he had been holding and was across the room in four long strides.

"A son." He sat gingerly on the side of the bed and shook his head. "Somehow I had expected a girl."

"Are you disappointed?" Elizabeth asked playfully.

He shook his head again. "Joyful," he said solemnly. "You are both well." He reached out tentatively to trace his wife's face. "How do you feel, love?"

"Perfect," she replied. "I am tired and sore but so very happy."

"I did not expect him to be so small," he whispered, touching a tiny nose. "It has been a long time since Georgiana was born. I did not remember."

"Small?" Elizabeth asked, irritated. "Have you seen the width of his shoulders? *You* try forcing something that wide out of your body, Mr. Darcy."

Darcy hung his head and allowed himself a little laugh. "I apologize, dearest. This is only one of numerous occasions I have been happy not to be a woman."

Elizabeth's eyes narrowed and he kissed her forehead to delay the retort he could see forming. "Your job is so much more difficult than mine," he finished quietly, lifting a single finger to stroke his son's cheek.

Elizabeth swallowed her frustrated response without uttering it when she heard the sincerity in her husband's voice and softened even further as she watched him fall in love with his son. *I am too tired to argue in any case,* she thought with a smile, observing a kind of peace she had never before seen settling over her husband's features.

Without looking away from the infant's face, he asked, "Bennet?"

Elizabeth relaxed, allowing the weariness she had been feeling all day to at last wash over her. "His name?" she asked.

Darcy nodded. "Yes."

She smiled, a weary smile, but a wide one. "Yes." As her husband bent to capture her lips, she added, "Thank you."

"For what, my dear?" he inquired, touching his forehead to hers and kissing her eyelids.

She sighed contentedly. "For choosing me. For loving me."

He chuckled, and they both stared at their perfect son. Soon enough, they heard the door begin to open as Mrs. Peters re-entered the room.

"You are welcome, Elizabeth," Darcy said, gazing directly into his wife's eyes. "But in the end, there was no choice for me, none at all. It has always been you."

Epilogue

EVELYN HAWKE AND Mr. Waters married the summer after the Fitzwilliams' wedding at Pemberley. Because they had met and courted in Lambton, Evie requested that their small ceremony be held there. Mr. Redding was delighted to pronounce the vows. Mrs. Redding and young Ruth spent hours decorating the church, but when it was at last time to begin, Ruth could not bear to remain in the company of Mrs. Darcy and Mrs. Fitzwilliam. She retired quietly to the parsonage without so much as a glance at anyone. She was not missed.

While never blessed with children of her own, Evelyn Waters became, over the years, a beloved presence in the birthing rooms of Lambton. Many children and their mothers were said to owe their lives to the lovely Mrs. Waters, and she was a godmother many times over. Despite the disappointment of never having a family of their own, she and her husband lived long, full lives, working together to apply the most advanced medical knowledge of their time for the benefit of all their patients.

About the same time Evelyn Hawke was marrying in Lambton, Lord Matlock authorized Lord Charles Grey to perform as his proxy in the House of Lords before retiring to the Matlock estate. Lady Matlock was a tender and loving nurse and Phillip sat with his father a few hours each day to speak about politics, even when Lord Matlock's memories of his political victories began to merge and wane. The rest of the family made regular visits as they were able.

Young Pembroke accompanied his father on his daily visits, and when the time came that his grandfather no longer recalled the faces around him, it was the boy who woke him up gently each morning with a tray of food, a cup of tea, and a cheerful recitation of any introduction deemed necessary. Even to the last, Pembroke was welcome in his grandfather's room, and he was present, along with the adults of the family, to hear the great man's final, unexpectedly lucid words.

Sophia and Richard Fitzwilliam spent the first months of their marriage concerned that Richard's unsold commission meant he would be called back to service. Finally, after Napoleon's incarceration on Elba, the commission was bought up at a loss and the Fitzwilliams decided to take a wedding trip. Their hope was that by the time they returned, the manor house would at last be complete, as Richard worried that the constant construction stirring up dust and debris was irritating Sophia's lungs and might endanger her health. They completed all outstanding estate business and, leaving the building and all other Darlington business in the capable hands of the Hobsons, departed at the end of harvest for what they intended to be a year-long journey.

Sophia had requested that Richard take her somewhere "at the ends of the earth" where they might enjoy complete privacy with no estate responsibilities, and Richard knew just the place. Their carriage crossed into Scotland just as the news of Napoleon's escape reached London; by the time the news reached Darlington, the Fitzwilliams were completely isolated from the outside world in a house on the Outer Hebrides, just off the coast of Northern Scotland. It was many months before word of Boney's escape and new campaign reached them. By the time Richard could get them both to London,

Waterloo was already imminent, and he was turned away when he made his terribly belated appearance at the War Office to offer his services. Neither Richard nor Sophia ever complained that while every member of their family had known their location, not one had seen fit to alert them.

When they left London and returned home to Staffordshire, Darlington's new manor house was completed, appearing as if it had sprung directly from Sophia's sketches. Just in time, too, for less than five months after their return from London, Sophia gave birth to Oliver, the first of their three sons. After listening to his wife's screams for nearly sixteen hours, Richard was at last convinced that Sophia's lungs were fully healed. Their life together was a good one, with a home rich in childish mischief. Sophia was not surprised that the ringleader was often Richard, who enjoyed teaching the boys many ways to tease their mother. While Richard taught the boys how to climb trees, catch frogs, and ride their horses, it was Sophia who taught them to shoot. And every day for the rest of their lives, Richard worked to earn at least one blush from his lovely wife.

After the return of her cousins from Scotland, Georgiana Darcy officially entered society. However, it was not until the beginning of her third season that she met a young man she liked well enough to entice her to leave the felicity of life at Pemberley. The young Earl of Shrewsbury had noticed her in her first season, but as he had just assumed the title at the age of twenty-two, he was not yet searching for a wife and did not seek an introduction. In her second, the earl heard Georgiana play the pianoforte. He was entranced, and though still insisting he was not in the market for a wife, began to show up at every event where she was expected. He stared at her from across the room for months, but only sought an introduction a few weeks before the Darcys were scheduled to leave the city for Pemberley.

Finally, in her third season, thoroughly annoyed by the man and hoping for someone just as handsome but far less aggravating to arrive and court her, Georgiana accepted coldly when the earl requested a dance at the first ball of the season. After soundly berating him for his earlier ungentlemanly behavior, he apologized clumsily yet so earnestly that she reluctantly forgave him. After another particularly fraught quarrel, the young man had been left standing in the street with a bouquet of flowers in his hand, and Elizabeth was forced to make the request that Georgiana invite the earl inside so as not to make sport for their neighbors. Although Darcy would have been just as happy had his sister left the young man on the steps, Georgiana at last relented and agreed to allow him to call. They were married just after Georgiana's twenty-first birthday. By all accounts, the marriage was a very happy one, though the formerly timid girl who grew up to become Lady Shrewsbury took great pleasure in confounding her besotted husband.

Fitzwilliam and Elizabeth Darcy had four more children after Bennet—Jane, Anna, Henry, and Sophia. Bennet grew to look very much like his father, but his sense of adventure and ease in social situations were gifts from his mother. Unfortunately, by the time he was ready to enter society as the heir to Pemberley, it was necessary to adopt a bit of his father's reticence in female company. To his father's exasperation, his mother's delight, and his sisters' amusement, he spent the fortnight prior to his first ball practicing the famous Darcy scowl in his dressing room mirror. Only Henry, the one blond in the brood, remained unmoved by his brother's predicament, offering an eye roll in response to his brother's newly acquired, rather stoic mask.

Of the Darcy girls, it was Sophia, arriving last and as quite a surprise, who was her mother's exact copy, from her chestnut curls and fine eyes to her daring nature and sharp wit. This, combined with a precarious delivery for both Elizabeth and the infant, made Sophia quite the most spoiled of all the Darcy children, not only by her infatuated father and rather more sensible mother, but also her thoroughly enchanted but more reserved siblings. Or rather, as her father would insist, *indulged, not spoiled.*

The proximity of the Darcy, Fitzwilliam, and Bingley estates made regular visits relatively simple, and it was never a surprise to Darcy when, upon his return from a business trip to London, there were more than a dozen children racing through the park, holding picnics near the lake, and crowding into Pemberley's nursery, talking and laughing long past their bedtime.

Having so many people to care for and worry about came quite naturally to Darcy, and of course he and Elizabeth had their share of arguments, vexation, and sorrow. But when they were at loggerheads, when they feared for their children or for one another, when they sat together mourning a loss or feeling uncertain about the future of Pemberley in an age of machinery and ready capital, they reminded each other of Henry Fitzwilliam's final words. "Love requires courage," he had said. "And courage requires love."

Excerpt from *Headstrong,* A Modern *Pride and Prejudice* Variation, Coming Fall 2017

SGT. ELIZABETH BENNET looked up with a grin as Major Fitzwilliam appeared next to her table. The restaurant was already crowded with students and tourists, but she'd arrived early to grab her favorite booth, the only seating tucked behind the front door as it opened. While it was out of the direct line of sight for the other patrons, it had a clear view of most of the restaurant, perfect for playing her game. She had perched on the end of the bench to identify the different citizenships while she waited—French, British, Italian, Greek, German, Japanese, even an American family and one couple she thought might be Canadian—and made up stories for what they were saying or how they had wound up at the *De Roos* bar and restaurant in Brussels. When her enthusiasm for this waned, she had turned to count the large gray fieldstones that comprised the bar behind her. They were very similar to old pasture fences she'd seen in pictures. She'd counted to forty-seven when he finally arrived.

"You're late," she chided, glancing at her watch. "Hardly the way to say 'thank you for saving my life.'"

Major Richard Fitzwilliam shook his head at her and raised his hand to attract the attention of a waitress. When a buxom redhead in a tight red t-shirt and black trousers turned and spied him, he held up two fingers and she disappeared behind the bar. He tossed his sunglasses down on the table and slid into the seat. She noted his dark brown trousers and green polo shirt. *Everyone looks so different out of uniform,* she thought.

"A regular, I see," Bennet said. She was dressed in blue jeans and a dark red v-neck shirt. She stretched her toes out in her boots, feeling comfortable at last. She'd spent the day working on the embassy's computer network, including a physical inspection of some rather antiquated hard drives, which had included a good deal of crawling around on floors to check hardware integrity. Her specialty was actually tracking and identifying foreign encroachments buried in computer code—*a hacker of hackers* she liked to say—but the assignment was easy and it was in Europe, so she wasn't complaining.

Fitzwilliam had been in meetings all day at the Embassy, where he worked as a translator and an analyst, though Elizabeth suspected he hadn't always. He wasn't a handsome man, precisely, but his looks were pleasantly rugged. He was six feet tall, fit, and looked imposing in his uniform, but in his civilian clothes, he appeared more like a man she would have met at her father's country club once upon a time. Elizabeth had found him surprisingly good-natured for an officer in the month since she'd arrived in Brussels. They were both aware of the policy on fraternization, and though they did not work under the same commanders and there was little to no risk of compromising chain of command,

Major Fitzwilliam was too dedicated a Marine ever to cross the line with her. That being the case, Elizabeth felt safe enjoying his friendly banter as a colleague. It was a bit like having an older brother, something Elizabeth had always wanted.

"I am, but I'm not a lush if that's what you're implying," he said jokingly, running a hand through his sandy hair in a gesture that indicated a long day.

"Well, it would explain how you managed to purge thirty significant documents from your computer. . ."

"I'm still not sure how that happened," he breathed out a huge gust of air and tossed up his hands in frustration. "The entire program for the conference next month, including the papers. I could have gathered them all again, but it would have taken forever. I'm just grateful you could retrieve everything. You didn't save my life, but you sure saved my weekend."

"I'll let you in on a secret, but you have to swear not to name me," she grinned wickedly and raised one arched eyebrow.

He nearly laughed at her expression of glee. He could feel the corners of his mouth turning up. *Damn cheerful for all the menial labor she put in today.* "What is that?"

She raised both eyebrows before saying, "*You* didn't lose anything. The general logged onto your computer and tried to send the files to his own. He's the one who did the damage."

"Son of a bitch!" Fitzwilliam said, banging his fist on the table, feeling a rush of vindication. "I knew it! The old goat turned it on me immediately." He spoke through his nose in imitation of the general, "'It's *your* computer, Fitzwilliam,' he says."

Elizabeth grinned and prepared to goad the major a bit more about being hung out to dry by his boss, but was interrupted by the arrival of two large ceramic steins of beer. Fitzwilliam allowed his eyes to linger just a bit too long on the prominently displayed breasts of their server, and Elizabeth rolled her eyes before lifting one stein and sipping from it.

"What is this?" she asked, pleased. "It's really good."

"It's Trappist Westvleteren," he replied, taking a long draught of his own.

"Okay, I won't even try to pronounce that," she laughed, taking another sip. "Mmm."

Richard heard a happy "tap, tap" of her boots on the wooden floor and shook his head. Sometimes he forgot how young she was. *Twenty-three, maybe? Not so young for a Marine. I'm just getting old.* He assessed her, not for the first time, as a good-looking woman with an athletic figure, green eyes, dark hair, and a wide smile that lit up her face. He knew she was on the tall side, too, but wasn't boyish like many female Marines who, he suspected, were trying to fit in. *That's it,* he thought, *that's what makes her different.* A female Marine, a woman programmer. Professional soldier, not even an attempt at any makeup, but still feminine. *Bennet's comfortable in her own skin. She doesn't fit in, and she doesn't try to.*

It was always tough to say what a female Marine would look like in street clothes, but as he surveyed Bennet now, he could not help but approve. He tried to think of how she'd look in a formal dress at one of his cousin Darcy's charity events and shook his head. Even though Fitzwilliam was well known for his appreciation of the female form, his interest here was purely platonic, had been from the first. *I just can't think of Bennet that way. She's like a geeky, provoking little sister. She'd be fun to have around at one of those yawners, though.*

"So," he said, leaning back, relaxing. "Two months left?"

She nodded. "I'm hoping to get to see a bit more of Europe now that I've nearly completed the inspection here. They've had me everywhere but

Europe. I was in Japan for a while, and that was nice, but my Spanish wasn't much help."

"Yeah," he agreed amiably. "I was there years ago. My Japanese isn't great, though. My Dutch is good, French is better, and my Arabic isn't terrible."

Elizabeth nodded, impressed. She had struggled in Spanish class but had finally gained some fluency. She hadn't even tried another language.

"I think I mentioned I had a few tours in Afghanistan and Iraq," she said, "but I mainly stayed on base working out kinks in the systems and searching for hacks. Africa, too, but I couldn't tell you where—we were in a concrete bunker underground somewhere looking through code. It's been really nice to have normal off hours, even a weekend here and there, do some sightseeing." She took another sip of her beer. "And it's fun just checking hard drives." She grinned, but added, "I admit I'm hoping they don't find a reason to extend. I'm ready to go home." She took another sip, thinking maybe it wouldn't be as good. *Nope. Still excellent. Totally worth tracking the files down.*

Fitzwilliam nodded. "I'm getting pretty close to my ten."

"Are you staying in, then?" she asked curiously.

He shrugged. "Haven't decided," he replied.

As Elizabeth set her mug on the table and reached for a menu, four bearded men came through the front door almost in a straight line, temporarily flooding the bar with late afternoon sunshine. Elizabeth glanced at them out of habit, but something about the group made her look again. They appeared to be in their mid to late twenties, ranged in height from about 5'7" to 6', had dark skin and hair. They were dressed in layers though the day was warm, and one was wearing a brown canvas backpack. They did not look as though they had showered, and they stood awkwardly near the front entrance, blocking it while canvassing the room anxiously. Three stepped into the bar, one remained by the door. They did not spot the two Marines sitting in the high-backed booth ten feet behind them.

Elizabeth became very still, very serious.

"Major," she said, in a low, urgent whisper and gestured to the group with a slight movement of her head.

Richard turned his head, careful not to move too quickly, and spied the three men swaggering into the center of the room. He sized them up, immediately assuming there was another posted at the door. *Damn.*

Acknowledgments

Many people were instrumental in the writing of *Courage Requires*. I thank all my reviewers, readers, and supporters, those who pointed out errors or inconsistencies and who mused about potential storylines. Thanks to you, the story is better and stronger than it would have been without your assistance. In particular, I would like to thank my most diligent reviewers from fanfiction.net: Regency1914, phyloxena, Ayla, Deanna27, lizzybet, babykathy1961, Nellie86, IrishJessy, Motherof8, Englishlitlover, Shelby66, NancyBlakett, marinka, The Reader, wosedwew, and all of those who posted as Guest.

A special thank you to my parents—my father, who bought my book though his tastes run to spy novels, and my mother, who was pleasantly surprised by the first book and has been hounding me ever since to finish the sequel so she can read it. It helped me push on when I hit the wall in my writing.

Thanks must, as always, go out to my husband and daughter, who continue to put up with my many hours spent typing away on my computer when I might have been cooking, cleaning, or doing the million other things it takes to run a house. Thank you for your love, your support, including some great brainstorming sessions, and the invaluable gift of time.

About the Author

MELANIE RACHEL is a university professor and long-time Jane Austen fan. She was born in Southern California, but has lived in Pennsylvania, New Jersey, Washington, and Arizona, where she now resides with her family and their freakishly athletic Jack Russell terrier.

Website: melanierachel.weebly.com

Facebook: facebook.com/melanie.rachel.583

Made in the USA
Monee, IL
29 November 2019